BOOMERITIS

A Novel That Will Set You Free

Ken Wilber

SHAMBHALA
Boston & London
2003

SHAMBHALA PUBLICATIONS, INC.
Horticultural Hall
300 Massachusetts Avenue
Boston, Massachusetts 02115
www.shambhala.com

9 8 7 6 5 4 3 2 1

FIRST PAPERBACK EDITION
Printed in the United States of America

⊗ This edition is printed on acid-free paper that meets the
American National Standards Institute z39.48 Standard.
Distributed in the United States by Random House, Inc.,
and in Canada by Random House of Canada Ltd

*The Library of Congress Catalogs the hardcover
edition of this book as follows:*
Wilber, Ken.
Boomeritis: a novel that will set you free / Ken Wilber—1st ed.
p.cm.
ISBN 1-57062-801-7 (alk. paper)
ISBN 1-59030-008-4 (paper)
1. Transpersonal psychology—Fiction. 2. Baby boom generation—Fiction
3. Conduct of life—Fiction. I. Title
PS3623.I52 B66 2002
813'.6—dc21
2001055023

Contents

Omega_Doom@FutureWorld.org   1

Seminar_1@ProblemChild.com

  1. Cyber_Rave_City@XTC.net   7
  2. The_Pink_Insides_of_CyberSpace@LookingGlass.org   40
  3. The_Lay_of_the_Within@SpiralDynamics.net   62
  4. And_It_Is_Us@FuckMe.com   112

Seminar_2@BoomeritisRules.com

  5. Subvert_Transgress_Deconstruct@FuckYou.com   161
  6. Dot-com_Death_Syndrome@ReallyOuch.com   202
  7. The_Conquest_of_Paradise@MythsAreUs.net   247
  8. The_New_Paradigm@WonderUs.org   300

Seminar_3@BeyondTheMeGeneration.com

  9. Pluralism_Falls_Apart@DisIntegrationCity.com   355
  10. The_Integral_Vision@IC.org   384
  11. Cosmic_Consciousness@OriginalFace.org   426
  12. Happily_Ever_After@HereAndNow.com   455

Omega_Doom@FutureWorld.org

I am the bastard child of two deeply confused parents, one of whom I am ashamed of, the other of whom is ashamed of me. None of us are on speaking terms, for which we are all grateful. (These things bother you, every now and then.) My parents are intimately conjoined in their displeasure with the present; both want to replace it—quickly—with a set of arrangements more suited to their inclinations. One wants to tear down; the other, to build up. You might think they were made for each other, would go together, hand in hand, a marriage made in transformational heaven. Years after the divorce, none of us is so sure.

One of them breathes the fire of revolutionary insurrection, and wants to tear down the oppressive forces of a cruel and careless yesterday, digging beneath the veneer of civilized madness to find, it is devoutly hoped, an original human goodness long buried by the brutalities of a modern world rubbed raw by viciousness. One of them dreamily gazes in the other direction, standing on tiptoes and straining to see the foggy face of the future, to a coming world transformation—I'm told it will be perhaps the greatest in all of history—and begins to swoon with the bliss of beautiful things about to unfold before us; she is a gentle person and sees the world that way. But I am cursed with an eye from each, and can hardly see the world at all through two orbs that refuse to cooperate; cross-eyed I stare at that which is before me, a Picasso universe where things don't quite line up. Or perhaps I see more clearly precisely because of that?

This much seems certain: I am a child of the times, and the times point in two wildly incompatible directions. On the one hand, we hear constantly that the world is a fragmented, torn, and tortured affair, on the tremulous verge of collapse, with massive and huge civilization blocks pulling apart from each other with increasingly alienated intent, so much so that international culture wars are the greatest threat of the future. Cyber-age technology is proceeding at a pace so rapid that, it is said, within 30 years we will have machines reaching human-level intelligence, and at the same time advances in genetic engineering, nanotechnology, and robotics will mean the possible end of humanity altogether: we will either be replaced by machines or destroyed by a white plague—and what kind of future is that for a kid? At home we are faced with the daily, hourly, minutely examples of a society coming apart at the seams: a national illiteracy rate that has skyrocketed from 5% in 1960 to 30% today; 51% of the children in New York City born out of wedlock; armed militias scattered about Montana like Nazi bunkers on the beaches of Normandy, braced for the invasion; a series of culture wars, gender wars, ideology wars in academia that parallel in viciousness, if not in means, the multicultural aggression on the international scene. My father's eyeball in my head sees a world of pluralistic fragmentation, ready to disintegrate, leaving in its riotous wake a mangled mass of human suffering historically unprecedented.

My mother's eye sees quite another world, yet every bit as real: we are increasingly becoming one global family, and love by any other name seems the driving force. Look at the history of the human race itself: from isolated tribes and bands, to large farming towns, to city-states, to conquering feudal empires, to international states, to worldwide global village. And now, on the eve of the millennium, we face a staggering transformation the likes of which humanity has never seen, where human bonding so deep and so profound will find Eros pulsing gloriously through the veins of each and all, signaling the dawn of a global consciousness that will transfigure the world as we know it. She is a gentle person and sees the world that way.

I share neither of their views; or, rather, I share them both, which makes me nearly insane. Clearly twin forces, though not alone, are eating away at the world: planetization and disintegration, unifying love and corrosive death-wishes, bonding kindness and disjointing cruelty, on a colossal scale. And the bastard, schizophrenic, seizure-prone son sees the world as if through shattered glass, moving his head slowly back and forth while waiting for coherent images to form, wondering what it all means.

As the Picasso-like fragments assemble themselves into something of postmodern art, flowing images start to congeal: perhaps there are indeed integrating, bonding, unifying forces at work in the world, a God or Goddess's love of gentle persuasion, slowly but inexorably increasing human understanding, care, and compassion. And perhaps there are likewise currents viciously dedicated to disrupting any such integral embrace. And perhaps they are indeed at war, a war that will not cease until one of them is dead—a world united, or a world torn apart: love on the one hand, or blood all over the brand-new carpet.

What immediately tore at my attention, all that year, was the three-decade mark of Armageddon doom rushing at me from tomorrow: in 30 years (30 years!), machines will reach human-level intelligence, and beyond. And then human beings will almost certainly be replaced by machines—they will outsmart us, after all. Or, more likely, we—human beings, our minds or our consciousness or some such—would download into computers, we would transfer our souls into the new machines—and what kind of future was that for a kid?

That was the year the event occurred, altering my fate irrevocably, a year in the life of a human machine that miraculously came to life. It was a year of ideas that hurt my head, made my brain sore and swollen, it seemed literally to expand and push against my skull, bulging out my eyes, throbbing at my temples, tearing into the world. Of that year, I recall almost no geographical locations at all. I remember little scenery, few actual places, hardly an exterior, just a stream of conversations and blistering visions that ruined my life as I had known it, replaced it with something humanity would never recognize, left me immortal, stains all over my flesh, smiling at the sky.

Seminar_1@ProblemChild.com

Cyber_Rave_City@XTC.net

I am wandering the back streets of San Francisco, looking for a bar; the dark night offers no relief. My mother says that for a 20-year-old, I am wise beyond this lifetime. But my mother thinks that all souls are wise beyond their lifetimes, so mine seems then an afterthought, though she would likely deny it. Shadows cut shades into the callous path before me; back-street doors open noisily, jarring a sensitive self. "Cyber Rave City," says the sign, but for some reason I keep walking.

My father is in Manhattan, last I heard, which was about a month ago. He is cutting a deal, hashing a contract, to set up an AIDS relief project in southeastern Africa. "Cutting a deal" because, Dad says, several multinational corporations are, in a rather grotesque way, the driving force behind the bargain—they are hoping, he says, to cash in on the AIDS epidemic (Dad makes a face and says "ca-ching! with death"—the sound of a cash register next to a skull and bones). Dad announced that for once he is going to take them up on their "pathetic swinish offer," because otherwise nothing will get done at all. I bet he can't sleep tonight, either.

"Ken," Chloe said, "you've got to try this," as she put a tab of Ecstasy on my tongue, grabbed me tight and held on to my waist.

Ethereal music enwrapped my brain, warmth began to define my being, subtle lights flashed on and off, whether coming from within my head or without was impossible to say. "Can you feel it?" was the Chloe refrain, and beyond that was hard to remember. Later that night there was some sort of sex, but it never really got started, or rather finished, because compared to the Ecstasy-induced luminous bliss, bodily sex was a comedown, a heavy intrusion into a radiantly thrilling twirling swirling space, and even Chloe's breasts paled in interest against that billowing bliss. Where does the body end and the music begin? If we really could disappear into cyberspace, is this what it would be like? Floating without bodies, traveling at the speed of thought, digitalized into a billion bits cascading through optical pathways, an adventure compared to which even sex was dull. . . .

"Ken, you've got to try this," and I swooned, passed out, phased into the cybersphere, optically enhanced.

Chloe, like me, a child of Boomers. Like me, never thought much about it, really, until we started to think about ourselves. That is, until we skidded into early adolescence and then noticed that the Boomers were our parents, that "Boomers" were actually something that existed. In adolescence, everybody says, kids differentiate from parents, and if parents are Boomers, well, that seems to complicate matters, because Boomers are not parents, they are a force of nature.

Chloe tried to kill herself, but I don't think because of Boomers. It's just that she has a way of getting noticed. I met her a year or so after that, in a class in Cambridge, a class on "Shifting Cultural Paradigms," a required course that I later learned told me more about Boomers than about paradigms. Although I did learn that every Boomer has a paradigm, like a pair of bell-bottoms.

Chloe I liked because of her eyes, and a certain I've-seen-it-all laugh, and because she had the nerve to try to end it all, or step off the stupidity in a definitive way. "Ken, you've got to try this" was something I heard from her at least once or twice each week, and I began to suspect that she had tried suicide not out of any morose depression but simply as a new and exciting experience. Chloe became the antidote to my depression, a suffocating depression that for me, alas, was real, a Siamese twin joined at my hip, and if suicide was part of the joyride Chloe counseled, I couldn't say I would rule it out.

Because something is badly skewed inside me. In a weird way, just as sex on Ecstasy is a comedown, suicide in this depression would be a big disappointment.

Artificial Intelligence is not only my field, it is how I feel. I am an artificial intelligence—my mind is artificial, my thoughts are artificial, they are made by somebody or something else, I find it hard to own them. Engineered thoughts, nonliving thoughts; even at the speed of digital, the thoughts are not alive. Who has programmed this mess called me?

"Ken, you've got to try this. Ken Wilber, listen to me!" But even Chloe's tender entreaties backed with a naked body do not carry that much weight.

Artificial Intelligence. AI. In my second year at MIT, confined in Cambridge, that most claustrophobic of towns built by teeny-tiny Pilgrims, my imagination was lit—or perhaps programmed—by the possibilities of it all. If you wedded cyberspace with artificial and computer intelligence—intelligence that had already surpassed the amount of data stored in all human brains combined—then infinity would be your destination, right? The future would indeed be one long Ecstasy trip through the bodiless world of light, as consciousness itself downloaded into perfectly designed computer heaven and kissed the painful, fleshy, messy world goodbye.

Now there would be an antidote to depression.

Such futuristic thinking was not as loopy as it sounded; in fact, something like it is the prevailing belief in the AI community. All that summer the headlines were already blaring the news. Bill Joy, the cofounder of Sun Microsystems, itself a major contributor to the coming cyber-revolution, had caused an international sensation when he summarized the opinion of experts in the field: *within a mere three decades*, computers will reach—and then surpass—human-level intelligence, thus rendering human beings more or less useless to existence. "Now," he wrote, "with the prospect of human-level computing power in about 30 years, a new idea suggests itself: that I may be working to create tools which will enable the construction of the technology that may replace our species." The article was called, appropriately enough, "Why the Future Doesn't Need Us."

This seemed to upset Mr. Joy, but only because, I was convinced, he was standing on the wrong side of the equation. Human consciousness would not be superfluous, it would be finally liberated—fully, radically, ecstatically liberated. It would—we would—our consciousness would—simply be downloaded into superintelligent machines, not only ending most of humanity's major problems—from hunger to illness to death itself—but allowing us to program our digital luminous optical destiny in any way we pleased. Carbon-based consciousness would make the leap to silicon-based consciousness . . . and off we would go, literally. Bill Joy wasn't living up to his name, because he was identifying with the losing team.

San Francisco for the summer; the Mission District is a mixture of brainiac geeks and homeless castaways, all of whom would fare much better translated wholly into cyber-ether. The brave new networked world was rushing at me from the near horizon, a mixture of ancient spiritual desires and hypermodern digital doing: human consciousness was poised to get hyperlinked into sizzling robotic codes traveling at the speed of light, never to be seen or heard from again with merely human senses. Although a small part of me rebelled, the larger part enthusiastically agreed: the quantum leap from carbon to silicon would finally bring a real heaven on earth. *The Pearly Gates of CyberSpace*, as one book title told it. *Tech-Gnosis*, proclaimed another. *CyberGrace*, offered yet one more. That was a train I intended to catch, and it was leaving the station only with my generation. The Boomers started to conceive it; the Xers started to build it; but the Ys would board it, bound for infinity on a ray of light that would never look back.

My father says that my cyber-dreams are antihumanistic. By that he means, word it how you will, that I am being worthless.

"Cyberspace is just an extension of human beings, not a replacement for them," he kept saying.

"What does that mean? I don't even understand what that means, Dad."

"You think we are going to disappear into supercomputers, you think that we—us—human minds—are going to be downloaded into silicon chips or some such shit. Do you know how sick that is? Just think about it, really."

"What's the point? You've made up your mind, right? It's not that you don't listen, Dad, because you do. It's just that you don't hear what you listen to. You hear what you think."

"Oh, fine, and what exactly does *that* mean?"

"What exactly does *that* mean is that, well, okay, weren't you ever young?"

"Oh, Jesus."

"Seriously, really. You ever been excited by a new idea? You didn't always just recycle your crap, you know."

"Recycle my crap? Well, that's choice. Cyberspace, as you sing it, doesn't help people, it escapes from them. And I'm supposed to get all excited about that?" This is where he would begin to chant things about starving people in Asia.

"Let the boy alone, Phil," Mom would always say. "The boy," as in, the rock, the plant, the house. I wondered what exactly went through their minds, their own artificial intelligences, when she looked at him that way. Did every "boy" have the feeling that he was Europe after World War II, and the two great superpowers were dividing up the territory? Or maybe being drawn and quartered—that wonderful medieval torture technique where horses pull in opposite directions until the person is severed into several slabs.

"Surely you don't think that there is anything resembling a coming world transformation, not the way either you or the kid imagines." He glanced in my direction when he said "the kid."

Mom was gentle, but she wasn't lame. "And *you* actually think that human beings are nothing but material objects, pushed around by survival drives. His transformation or mine—either one is better than the silliness you spout. Oh, Phil, but don't get mad . . . ," and he would storm off again, never really overtly angry, just never really being there. He could save the world, but maybe not his family.

Chloe is naked, wildly moving her body in ways that are calculated to remind me that I exist in one.

"What do you want from cyberland?" she keeps asking me.

"At first I wasn't sure. At first, I think I wanted both some sort of escape and some sort of excitement."

"Ooooh, those are usually the same thing."

"Yes, maybe. I think I just want something that . . . makes sense to me."

Chloe laughs that wicked laugh that mostly I find attractive, and equally wickedly slams her naked body madly into mine.

"But sweet boy, the whole point of cyberspace is that it has no senses and therefore no sense! That's why you can't make sense in cyberland."

For a moment what she says sounds true, but then I catch myself and come to . . . my senses?

"Sure you can," I protest. "Sure you can."

Cambridge, on Porter Avenue. "Integral Center" was the name of the building. "Ken, you've got to try this," Chloe had said, as she, Scott, Carolyn, and Jonathan shuffled through the doors. I listened half-heartedly, or maybe full-heartedly but absent-mindedly; not much of it made sense. "They might really change the world," Chloe had said, with Jonathan nodding knowingly.

"So which transformation are they pushing?" I asked. "These integral folks? Because I know they're pushing something." But I could sense it, even then; he was there.

"No, really, it's great. It's like these totally ancient Boomers are having this huge psychoanalysis of their generation. Boomers are eating Boomers alive. You gotta see this," Carolyn percolated.

"Why do I gotta see this?" I grumbled. "I'd rather eat airline food."

"Because it's generational suicide. But it's also fascinating, really interesting."

"Like a fifty-car pileup."

"Right!"

"Look," Chloe offered, "I figure the reason this is interesting is that we've got a chance to get this monkey off our back. Boomers said that every generation before them sucked, and every generation after them were slackers. Don't you love it? Come on, let's watch them eat their young."

"Their young, you idiot, is us," I pointed out.

"Right!" said Chloe, and this struck me as a new twist on her suicidal inclinations.

Third year of college, Cambridge; we were all aglow with two competing breakthroughs: string theory in physics—also called M theory, although nobody seemed to know exactly what "M" stood for (some said it was the "mother" of all theories)—and recent breakthroughs in Artificial Intelligence, which was rapidly closing in on what looked to be actual creative intelligence—and which had spawned Bill Joy's unjoy. But nobody was quite sure exactly how to tell if we had finally created a truly intelligent machine. I had my own test, better than Turing's: when a computer could genuinely convince me that it wanted to commit suicide. The only rational response to existence was Hamlet's dilemma—to be or not to be—and thus the first thing a *truly* intelligent machine would do is be thrown into screaming paralysis contemplating whether—and how—to end it all. Now *that* would be a smart machine, as it sat there trembling, shaking, shuddering, seized with fear and sickness unto death, a digital *Scream* internally blistering silicon connections in all directions. So far they, the computers, hadn't nearly that intelligence.

What also began to dawn on me was a way to frame my own discontent. I wanted to feel that I wasn't being internally drawn and quartered. I wondered if this did have a lot to do with Mom and Dad, or simply with existence itself, or maybe just with my existence, or my lack of existence, that sounded closer. But I did not want to feel torn, drawn and quartered, as if I were a bloody tourist in my own insides.

After a class on "Postmodern Deconstruction of Gendered Asymmetries"—why science majors had to take this stuff was still not clear to me, since every postmodern class I took assured us that science wasn't real and certainly did not deal with the "truth," because "objective truth" was just a social construction meant to oppress people— I am walking down Porter Ave. Since I am alone, I decide to slip inside, just to get a short listen. The series at Integral Center is called "Boomeritis," and I think, this has got to be a kick. Boomers eat their young, said Chloe. I had begged off returning to IC earlier; now, furtively glancing around, I slip in.

A gray-haired gentleman, soft and smiling, is introducing the series. He looks a little like my father, but he talks a lot like Mom.

"It seems almost unimaginable to us that, for humanity's entire stay on this planet—for some million years up to the present—a person was born into a culture that knew virtually nothing about any other. You were, for example, born a Chinese, raised a Chinese; you married a Chinese, followed a Chinese religion—often living in the same hut for your entire life, on a spot of land that your ancestors settled for centuries. Every now and then this cultural isolation was interrupted by a strange and grotesque form of Eros known as war, where cultures were thrown together violently, through brutally ravishing means, yet the secret outcome was always a type of erotic cultural intercourse. The cultures got to know each other, even in a biblical sense—a hiddenly blissful sadomasochism that drove history to its present global village. From isolated tribes and bands, to small farming villages, to early city-states, to conquering feudal empires, to sprawling international states, to today's global village: many eggs were broken to make this extraordinary world omelet. What a rancorous growth toward an integral world that nonetheless seems humanity's fate."

Yes, and what's the point? Besides, I've heard this all before from Mom. The great, grand, glorious, coming worldwide social transformation. . . . As if the world of carbon had anything left to offer.

"The Boomers were the first generation to be raised in this global village. That, more than anything else, is the background etching of our soul, upon which so much else rests. And whether you are a Boomer or not, this global consciousness is something we all increasingly share; none of us today escapes it. This is truly an extraordinary time, unprecedented in many ways: *all* of the world's cultures are *available to each other*. In the history of the planet earth, this has never happened before. For better or worse, this is a richly multicultural world, as hundreds of world cultures increasingly get to know each other, rubbing up against each other, jostling each other, crawling all over each other, agitating here and there, trying to figure it out. This tiny global village is becoming tinier by the minute. And in this global village—it is the only one we have—we shall hang together, or we shall hang separately."

Yawn. He probably dated Mom in high school. I can see them now, signing their yearbooks: "See you at the transformation."

I look around the room. There are perhaps 150, maybe 200 people. A majority of them are Boomers, but about a third seem to be the two younger generations, so-called Gen X and Gen Y, or Gen Next and Millennials—will they ever settle on what names to call us kids of Boomers? But, I wonder, why are they at this seminar? Probably hungry for the Boomericide that rumors promise.

"*Integral*: the word means to integrate, to bring together, to join, to link, to embrace. Not in the sense of uniformity, and not in the sense of ironing out all the wonderful differences, colors, zigs and zags of a rainbow-hued humanity, but in the sense of unity-in-diversity, shared commonalities along with our wonderful differences: replacing rancor with mutual recognition, hostility with respect, inviting everybody into the tent of mutual understanding. Not that I have to *agree* with everything you say, but I should attempt at least to *understand* it, for the opposite of mutual understanding is, quite simply, war.

"That would seem the simplest of choices—peace versus war—and yet history has documented the gruesome fact that the bulk of humanity has consistently and enthusiastically favored the latter. For every year of peace in humankind's history, there have been fourteen years of war. We're a cantankerous lot, it seems, and obstacles to an integral embrace are the rule, not the exception."

Fourteen years of war, one year of peace. That is *exactly* why we are downloading into Silicon City. Why is there war? Why do humans fight? For power, for food, for possessions, for territory, maybe even for the insane thrill of it. But when consciousness is downloaded into digital eternity, all of those things will be given in abundance; the need for war will evaporate. You want to invade Poland, rape and plunder and kill? Fine, program that for the day's Virtual Game and get on with it. You won't know the difference between "real" war and "virtual" war, so there! Why can't Dad—and apparently this dope—see the obviousness of it? If you think you are going to end war in meatspace, dream on.

"When I was in graduate school, one of my student colleagues was a Palestinian, a gentle, brilliant man, cultured, witty, compassionate. One day I asked Simon what his son, then six years old, was going to do when he grew up. Simon's gentle face temporarily went purple-red enraged. 'I am going to teach him to slit Israelis' throats and drink their blood!' And then the storm passed, very quickly, and the calm returned, and we went back to eating our sandwiches, as if nothing really happened.

"Of course I never forgot it. Nor am I without my own inner Simons; nor, I doubt, are you. It has nothing to do with Arab or Israeli, white or nonwhite, East or West. It has everything to do with our own inclinations and attitudes. Some will say this type of aggression is peculiar to the male sex—testosterone and all—so that when we have female leaders, we will have no more wars. But I knew Simon's dear wife, Pasha, and she was as determined as he to have the glory of a son offered up to battle. And as long as the Simons and Pashas in any culture rule, we will choose war instead of peace, yes?"

No, as long as we have meatspace instead of cyberspace, meat will eat meat, war will beget war, and there is no way around that, dude.

"The number of obstacles to peace, to an integral embrace: it seems overwhelming. Can a truly integral culture exist in today's climate of identity politics, culture wars, a million new and conflicting paradigms, deconstructive postmodernism, nihilism, pluralistic relativism, and the politics of self? Can an integral vision even be recognized, let alone accepted, in such an atmosphere? A world at war or a world at peace? Is such an integral culture even possible? If so, what might it look like?

"We already know what the opposite of an integral culture looks like: the Simons and Pashas of this world at each other's throats, happily spilling blood all over the global village. In other words, it looks a lot like today's world. Let us ask instead, quite seriously: Can we actually sustain an integral world? And what are the obstacles to it? Both in the cultural elite and in the world at large?"

The obstacle is meat. And why do old folks think so *slow*?

"Obviously this is an enormously complex issue. Many people feel that an integral world—a world at peace—is a hopelessly naive ideal. Perhaps. But I believe there are a few very simple items that have been dramatically overlooked. This discussion series is about just those crucial items."

I again glance around the room. I wonder what "crucial items" I might have left out of my equation, but I doubt that this dude, or dud, will shed much light on the issue, which is already pretty much decided in my mind. War is inevitable in carbon-based life forms.

"They're trying to pull their lives together."

"I'm sorry?"

"Boomers. They're trying to pull the pieces together. I'm Kim."

"Kim. What pieces?"

"Do you know 'integral,' the meaning of 'integral'?"

"Sure, it's a type of calculus."

"What's your name?"

"Ken, um, Wilber."

"Well look, Ken um Wilber, not like the calculus. Like what Dr. Morin just said, to unite or bring together. *Integral*, you twit," and she smiled. She was my age, maybe a year or two older. More important, she had really big breasts, which is one of the few things I might actually miss in cyberheaven. Virtual boobs just didn't quite seem to make it.

"I'm a twit? A *twit*?" I blinked. "So why are you here? You trying to pull something together?"

"No, I'm sleeping with Morin." Somehow that was supposed to explain it all.

"He's like what, twenty times your age?"

"Twenty times your IQ. I happen to believe what he's talking about."

"Which is?"

"Like hello? Were you listening at all? Can we get any dumber? Hey, I know you. You're Chloe-what's-her-name's friend. She was in my cultural matrix class; she's architectural design, right? You should bring her to this seminar since you're so interested."

"I'm not interested. I was just curious."

"Whatever, you're here."

"Really, that's not it." I was about to explain fully—that is, lie to her—when Morin's booming voice, heavy with italicized words, filled the air.

"Let us start with the many *obstacles to an integral vision* in our own generation."

Let us not, and I started to get up to leave. Kim grabbed my elbow, big breasts brushed my shoulder, and I thought, okay.

"The Baby Boom generation—the generation born after World War II—has, like any generation, its strengths and weaknesses. Its strengths include an extraordinary vitality, creativity, and idealism, plus a willingness to experiment with new ideas beyond traditional values. Some social observers have seen in the Boomers an 'awakening generation,' evidenced by an astonishing creativity in everything from music to computer technology, political action to lifestyles, ecological sensitivity to civil rights. I believe there is much truth and goodness in those endeavors, to the Boomers' considerable credit." Some Boomers in the audience mumbled their approval; a few Xers and Ys began hissing in a mostly friendly way.

"Boomer weaknesses, most critics agree, include an unusual dose of self-absorption and narcissism, so much so that most people, Boomers included, simply nod their heads in acknowledgment when the phrase 'the Me generation' is mentioned." A smattering of applause from the Xers and Ys.

"As Professor Ralph Whitehead here at U Mass summarized the widely held view, 'The baby boom was a self-absorbed generation, a generation that defined itself not through sacrifice as its parents had, but through indulgence.'" Morin paused and smiled at the audience. "This has led to the popular perception satirized by the newspaper *Onion*: 'Long-awaited baby boomer die-off to begin soon, experts say. Before long, we will live in a glorious new world in which no one will ever again have to endure tales of Joan Baez's performance at Woodstock. The ravages of age will take its toll on boomer self-indulgence, and the curtain will at long last fall on what is regarded by many as the most odious generation America has ever produced.'"

Okay, I can start to relate to this.

Morin walked to the edge of the stage, peered out at the crowd. He repeated the last phrase for emphasis, each word falling as a ponderous indictment—"the most odious generation America has ever produced."

I looked around at the audience; Boomers sat silent, sullen; Xers and Ys, too.

Morin, gently smiling, continued. "It seems that my generation has been an extraordinary mixture of greatness and narcissism, and that strange amalgam has infected almost everything we do. We don't seem content to simply have a fine new idea; we must have the new paradigm which will herald one of the greatest transformations in the history of the world. We don't really want to recycle bottles and paper; we need to see ourselves dramatically saving the planet and saving Gaia and resurrecting the Goddess that previous generations had brutally repressed but we will finally liberate. We aren't able to tend our garden; we must be transfiguring the face of the planet in the most astonishing global awakening history has ever seen. We apparently need to see ourselves as the vanguard of something unprecedented in all of history: the extraordinary wonder of being us." Everybody in the audience laughed.

"Well, it can be pretty funny if you think about it, and I truly don't mean any of this in a harsh way. Each generation has its foibles; this appears to be ours, at least to some degree. But I believe few of my generation escape this narcissistic mood. Many social critics have agreed, and not just in such penetrating works as Lasch's *The Culture of Narcissism*, Restak's *The Self Seekers*, Bellah's *Habits of the Heart*, and Stern's *Me: The Narcissistic American*, among literally hundreds of other studies. Surveying the present state in American universities, Professor Frank Lentricchia, writing in *lingua franca: The Review of Academic Life*, concluded: 'It is impossible, this much is clear, to exaggerate the heroic *self-inflation* of academic literary and cultural criticism.'

"Well, ouch. But it's true that sooner or later this 'heroic self-inflation' starts to get to you. And you start wondering about this strange affliction that seems to shadow my generation—this odd mixture of remarkably creative intelligence coupled with an unusual dose of narcissism. For Boomers, it appears, are riddled with a love affair *avec soi*. As Oscar Levant said to Gershwin: 'Tell me, George, if you had it to do all over again, would you still fall in love with yourself?'" More laughter from the audience, sporadic applause, all good-natured.

But then, Boomer narcissism is nothing new. My generation didn't even know it was there until we tried to get out from under it, which proved more or less impossible, something like a mouse trying to get out from under a refrigerator that had fallen on it. By the time we realized this, the damage was already done; but none of us really thinks like that at all. It's Boomers who think about Boomer narcissism, because Boomers think about Boomers. If the IC series is going to be more of this, I think I'll take a skip. Let the Boomers eat their young, and Kim can tug at my elbow all she wants. I'd stay for the big boobs but that

19

would mean suffering big egos as well—a close call, I admit, but. . . .

"To understand the many obstacles to an integral world, a quick look at developmental psychology might help. Can psychology shed any light on this most pressing of issues?"

I'm out of here. Everybody at school knows that psychology is dead; a "dustbin discipline," they call it. Dr. Morin stepped off the stage, and an attractive woman in her fifties stepped up to the microphone. Morin looked plaintively around the room, scanning the audience eagerly— probably looking for Kim and her big. . . .

"That's Joan Hazelton," Kim said. "She's amazing."

As Hazelton began her lecture, I was about to slip out, but then she mentioned a phrase that caught my attention, jolted me, actually: "the quantum leap into the hyperspace of second-tier consciousness." For my major, overriding, even painfully obsessive concern was indeed a quantum leap in consciousness—from Carbon to Silicon. I therefore had to wonder what *her* quantum leap was all about, and whether the two were related. Or what her leap had to do with mine, like somebody was poaching on my turf. And there was something about Hazelton. I fully realized how ridiculous this sounded, but space seemed to curve around her.

"Developmental psychology is the study of the growth and development of consciousness. One of the most striking things about the present state of developmental psychology is how similar, in broad outline, most of its models are. Indeed, one of our colleagues here at Integral Center wrote a book called *Integral Psychology*, which assembles the models of the major researchers from around the world—over one hundred of them. What is so amazing is that there emerges a remarkably consistent story: they all give a very similar account of the growth and development of consciousness as *a series of unfolding stages*."

"This is the best part," Kim whispered in my ear.

"Why?"

"Because it's so new to most people, yet it explains so much. You wait, you'll see." Kim reached out and again touched my elbow; I eased back into my seat. I guess I can wait a little bit longer.

"Let me give only one of these models as an example," Hazelton went on. "It's called Spiral Dynamics, based on the pioneering work of Clare Graves. Graves proposed a profound and elegant system of human development, which subsequent research has refined and validated. Basically, Graves discovered that there are around *eight major levels or waves of human consciousness*, and these waves tell an extraordinary story, as we will see.[*]

"It should be remembered that virtually all of these stage conceptions are based on extensive amounts of research and data. These are not simply conceptual ideas and pet theories but are grounded at every point in a considerable amount of evidence. In fact, many of the stage models have been carefully checked in First, Second, and Third World countries. The same is true with Graves's model; to date, it has been tested in more than 50,000 people from around the world, and there have been no major exceptions found to the general scheme. And thus, any attempt to reach an integral embrace ought to take these models into account, because *they point directly to the path leading to integral awareness.*"

Chloe is rubbing her naked body against mine, offering warmth against the cold of the early autumn night. Her breasts push against my thighs, her mouth forms an O designed to drive me insane, her buttocks move wildly to the rhythm of the thump thump thumping of Alice Deejay playing "Now Is the Time."

"We can always integrate *this*," she whispers. "Ken, you've *got* to try this."

"Graves's work has been carried forward and refined by Don Beck and Christopher Cowan in an approach they call Spiral Dynamics. (Let me just say that 'Spiral Dynamics' is a registered trademark of the National Values Center in Denton, Texas, and is used here with grateful permission.) Far from being mere armchair analysts, Beck and Cowan were participants in the discussions that led to the end of apartheid in South Africa. The principles of Spiral Dynamics have been fruitfully used to reorganize businesses, revitalize townships, overhaul education systems, and defuse inner-city tensions. And, as most of you know, Don Beck is one of the founding members of Integral Center."

---

[*] In the course of the year, I took voluminous notes, academic and otherwise, on the strange proceedings that began to define my life. These notes and references can be found in their entirety at http://wilber.shambhala.com.

Dr. Hazelton paused, looked up from her notes, smiled brightly at the audience. I kept trying to focus on her face and wondered why I was having trouble doing so. It wasn't just that she was beautiful; it was something else. As her eyes scanned the audience, they briefly fell on me, and for some reason I held my breath, then let it out and glanced at Kim to see if she had noticed.

"Spiral Dynamics," Hazelton continued, "sees human development as proceeding through eight general stages, which are also called *memes*." The audience groaned. "I know, I know. 'Meme' is a controversial word that is used a lot nowadays, with many different meanings. But for Spiral Dynamics, a meme is simply *a basic stage of development that can be expressed in any activity*. We will see many fun examples of this as we proceed! And, dear friends, memes are not rigid levels but flowing waves, with much overlap and interweaving, resulting in a dynamic spiral of consciousness unfolding. Development is not a linear ladder but a fluid and flowing affair."

"Kim, do you know Dr. Hazelton?"

"I do."

"She seems like a very nice person."

Kim turned her head slowly and looked at me; I looked straight ahead.

"The first six levels of consciousness are called 'first-tier' levels. But then there occurs *a revolutionary shift in consciousness*: the emergence of 'second-tier' levels. We will be paying particular attention to this quantum leap into the hyperspace of second-tier consciousness." I sat up very straight in my chair, looked around.

"Here is a brief but thrilling description of all eight levels of consciousness,"—Hazelton kept smiling—"the percentage of the world population at each wave, and the percentage of social power held by each."

For some reason, the idea of levels of consciousness, or waves of existence—the idea that people have different ways of making sense of the world—was morbidly fascinating to me. This fascination was the beginning of the series of events that led to a brutal revelation and the perfect end of my own existence as I had known it. It wasn't simply that he was there; it was that the real light at the end of the real tunnel had begun vaguely glimmering.

Hazelton started outlining the waves of existence. I recognized people at every stage; I began filling in the names of folks I knew who were spending most of their time at a particular wave. Surely there are dangers in this? Still, it was a rather extraordinary game, in its own way.

"Like I said, this is the fun part," Kim announced, bouncily, jiggily, oh never mind.

Up on the wall flashed a large slide of a great spiral of development, with brief descriptions of all eight waves of consciousness. "We use both colors and names for the stages. Now people, really, you do *not* have to remember these or memorize these or anything. Just let your mind wander over them, and see if you can recognize any of them. We will be explaining everything you need to know as we go along. We want this to be a fun and enjoyable experience for you. But you might keep asking yourselves: what if these levels of consciousness really exist?"

I looked at Kim. She smiled.

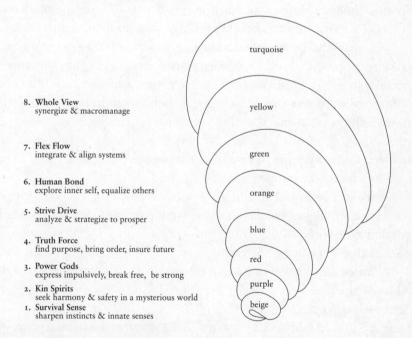

8. **Whole View**
   synergize & macromanage

7. **Flex Flow**
   integrate & align systems

6. **Human Bond**
   explore inner self, equalize others

5. **Strive Drive**
   analyze & strategize to prosper

4. **Truth Force**
   find purpose, bring order, insure future

3. **Power Gods**
   express impulsively, break free, be strong

2. **Kin Spirits**
   seek harmony & safety in a mysterious world

1. **Survival Sense**
   sharpen instincts & innate senses

turquoise

yellow

green

orange

blue

red

purple

beige

Figure 1.1. The Spiral of Development. Adapted by permision from Don Beck and Christopher Cowan, Spiral Dynamics: Mastering Values, Leadership, and Change *(Cambridge, Mass.: Blackwell Publishers, 1995).*

"1. *Beige: Archaic-Instinctual.* The level of basic survival; food, water, warmth, sex, and safety have priority. Uses habits and instincts just to survive. Distinct self is barely awakened or sustained. Forms into *survival bands* to perpetuate life.

"Where seen: First human societies, newborn infants, senile elderly, late-stage Alzheimer's patients, mentally ill street people, starving masses, the shell-shocked. Approximately 0.1% of the adult population, 0% power."

"That's you, twit."
"Thanks, Kim."

"2. *Purple: Magical-Animistic.* Thinking is animistic; magical spirits, good and bad, swarm the earth, leaving blessings, curses, and spells that determine events. Forms into *ethnic tribes*. The spirits exist in ancestors and bond the tribe. Kinship and lineage establish political links. Sounds 'holistic' but is actually atomistic: as Graves pointed out, 'There is a name for each bend in the river but no name for the river.'

"Where seen: Belief in voodoo-like curses, blood oaths, ancient grudges, good-luck charms, family rituals, magical beliefs and superstitions; strong in Third World settings, gangs, athletic teams, and corporate 'tribes'; also magical New Age beliefs, crystals, tarot, astrology. 10% of the population, 1% of the power."

"Hey, Kim, my mom has some of that in her."
"She's New Age, right?"
"Well, sort of."
"There are higher memes in some New Age stuff, but most of it is purple to the core."
"But that's not bad or anything."
"None of this is good or bad," Kim said. "It's just a map of the mental landscape."

"3. *Red: Power Gods.* Also known as *Egocentric*. First emergence of a self distinct from the tribe; powerful, impulsive, egocentric, heroic. Mythic spirits, archetypes, dragons, and beasts. Archetypal gods and goddesses, powerful beings, forces to be reckoned with, both good and bad. Feudal lords protect underlings in exchange for obedience and labor. The basis of *feudal empires*—power and glory. The world is a jungle full of threats and predators. Conquers, outfoxes, and dominates; enjoys self to the fullest without regret or remorse; be here now.

"Where seen: The 'terrible twos,' rebellious youth, frontier mentalities, feudal kingdoms, epic heroes, James Bond villains, soldiers of fortune, wild rock stars, Attila the Hun, *Lord of the Flies*, mythic involvement. 20% of the population, 5% of the power."

"Everybody knows somebody who's red-meme," Kim said. "They can be like so fucking obvious. Sometimes they're really heroic, like a test pilot or a fire fighter, but sometimes big, obnoxious, foul, loud-mouthed, pushy assholes. This is my dad, sad to say, the total fucking prick bastard." My eyes shot wide open and I gaped at her, startled by the truck-driver language.

"Oh, your dad, too?"

"My dad? Um, no, no, I don't think so. But I don't know what the other memes look like."

"4. *Blue: Mythic Order*. Life has meaning, direction, and purpose, with outcomes determined by an all-powerful Other or Order. This righteous Order enforces a code of conduct based on absolutist and unvarying principles of 'right' and 'wrong.' Violating the code or rules has severe, perhaps everlasting repercussions. Following the code yields rewards for the faithful. Basis of *ancient nations*. Rigid social hierarchies; paternalistic; one right way and only one right way to think about everything. Law and order; impulsivity controlled through guilt; concrete-literal and fundamentalist belief; obedience to the rule of Order; strongly conventional and conformist. Often 'religious' in the mythic-fundamentalist sense; Graves and Beck refer to it as the 'saintly/absolutistic' level, which can also be secular or atheistic Order or Mission.

"Where seen: Puritan America, Confucian China, Dickensian England, Singapore discipline, totalitarianism, codes of chivalry and honor, charitable good deeds, religious fundamentalism (e.g., Christian and Islamic), Boy and Girl Scouts, 'moral majority,' patriotism. 40% of the population, 30% of the power."

"Damn Republicans," Kim said.

"What's that?"

"Oh, so many Republicans come from the blue wave. Mark says—you haven't seen Mark yet—anyway, he says we are supposed to embrace all eight of the waves, and I understand that theoretically, but I gotta tell ya, some of them I just hate. And I hate Republicans. Blue-nosed goody-two-shoes who will string you up if you disagree with them."

"Um, right, okay. I'm sure I hate them, too, Kim." Well, my dad hated them, anyway. "But, you know, should we be hating people so early in the seminar? You could use just a little more tolerance, maybe?"

Kim turned and leveled a ferociously cold gaze at me; then smiled. "Actually, I went to the Los Angeles Museum of Tolerance, but I got in a fight."

She reached out, touched my arm, and gave it a soft, lingering squeeze. Is this a *great* seminar, or what?

"5. *Orange: Scientific Achievement*. At this wave, the self escapes from the 'herd mentality' of blue and seeks truth and meaning in individualistic and scientific terms. The world is a rational and well-oiled machine with natural laws that can be learned, mastered, and manipulated for one's own purposes. Highly achievement-oriented, especially (in America) toward materialistic gains. The laws of science rule politics, the economy, and human events. The world is a chessboard on which games are played as winners gain preeminence and perks over losers. Marketplace alliances; manipulate earth's resources for one's strategic gains. Basis of *corporate states*.

"Where seen: The Enlightenment, Ayn Rand's *Atlas Shrugged*, Wall Street, emerging middle classes around the world, cosmetics industry, trophy hunting, colonialism, the Cold War, fashion industry, materialism, market capitalism, liberal self-interest. 30% of the population, 50% of the power."

"Nothing wrong with that meme, right, Kim?" This was starting to get a little close to home, because I think I was born with a strong orange streak in me. . . .

"Nothing wrong with it, Ken, nothing wrong with it. Honestly, I know better—all of the memes are important, even if some of us have a hard time remembering it." She shrugged and grinned sheepishly. I leaned over to say something to her, but Hazelton had started reading the description of the next wave, and the audience began audibly groaning. As she read, some of the crowd burst into alternating cheers and boos, signaling that Hazelton had apparently hit a very raw nerve.

"Kim, I've never been to a lecture where white people made so much noise."

"Well, the whole point of this seminar is, of course, boomeritis—what it is and what it means. So natch, some of the Boomers get pretty worked up, and eventually some of them started getting really vocal about it. Over the three or four years this seminar has been in existence, it's become a kind of tradition to, well, get fairly noisy about several of the controversial topics. So even some of the Xers and Ys join in, it's pretty funny. And way loud."

"But what's so controversial about the next topic? People are already yelling. The green meme, so what?"

"Oh, Jesus, just you wait."

"6. *Green: The Sensitive Self*. Communitarian, human bonding, ecological sensitivity, networking. The human spirit must be freed from greed, dogma, and divisiveness; feelings and caring supersede cold rationality; cherishing of the earth, Gaia, life. Against hierarchy; establishes lateral bonding and linking. Permeable self, relational self, group intermeshing. Emphasis on dialogue, relationships. Basis of *value communities* (i.e., freely chosen affiliations based on shared sentiments). Reaches decisions through reconciliation and consensus (downside: interminable 'processing' and incapacity to reach decisions). Refresh spirituality, bring harmony, enrich human potential. Strongly egalitarian, anti-hierarchy, pluralistic values, social construction of reality, diversity, multiculturalism, relativistic value systems; this worldview is often called *pluralistic relativism*. Subjective, nonlinear thinking; shows a greater degree of affective warmth, sensitivity, and caring, for earth and all its inhabitants.

"Where seen: Deep ecology, postmodernism, Netherlands idealism, Rogerian counseling, Canadian health care, humanistic psychology, liberation theology, cooperative inquiry, World Council of Churches,

Greenpeace, ecopsychology, animal rights, ecofeminism, post-colonialism, Foucault/Derrida, politically correct, diversity movements, human rights issues, multiculturalism. 10% of the population, 15% of the power."

This was definitely the home of Mom and Dad. Mom had a little purple, too, and Dad a good dose of red, I retroactively decided. But their "center of gravity," as the IC folks called it, was definitely green. I started running through all the ways that this explained so much of their behavior, but then Hazelton quickly moved to the topic that had first caught my attention. Her next words were galvanizing.

"With the completion of the green meme, human consciousness is poised for a quantum leap into 'second-tier thinking.' Clare Graves referred to this as a 'momentous leap,' where 'a chasm of unbelievable depth of meaning is crossed.' And people, I cannot tell you how much this changes everything."

Hazelton paused, waiting for each of her words to sink in. She smiled and continued slowly, solemnly, a bit ominously. "The full impact of this will become more obvious as we proceed. But let me start by giving you a few brief details. In essence, with second-tier consciousness, you can, for the first time, *vividly grasp the entire spiral of development*. You can therefore understand that each level, each meme, each wave, is crucially important for the health of the overall spiral, and thus each is to be cherished and embraced. Very simply, with second-tier awareness, you can see the big picture—and the entire world suddenly appears in a new, vivid, startling light."

Hazelton gazed out at the audience. "It's important to realize that *each and every individual has all of these memes potentially available to them*. As Beck puts it, 'The focus is not on types *of* people, but types *in* people.' Thus, each wave can itself be activated as life conditions warrant. In emergency situations, we can activate red power drives; in response to chaos, we might need to activate blue order; in looking for a new job, we might need orange achievement drives; in marriage and with friends, close green bonding.

"*But what none of the first-tier memes can do is fully appreciate the existence of the other memes*. Each of the first-tier memes thinks that its worldview is the only true perspective. It reacts negatively if challenged; it lashes out, using its own tools, whenever it is threatened. Blue order is very uncomfortable with both red impulsiveness and orange individualism. Orange individualism thinks blue order is for suckers and green egalitarianism is weak and woo-woo. Green egalitarianism cannot easily abide excellence and value rankings, big pictures, hierarchies, or anything that appears authoritarian, and thus green tends to lash out at blue, orange, and anything post-green. Folks, let me put it bluntly: any first-tier meme will prevent world peace."

It was a jolting thought; I stiffened in my seat. Kim looked at me.

Hazelton's voice began to rise, becoming clear, insistent, the space around her imperceptibly warping. "All of that begins to change with second-tier thinking. Because second-tier consciousness is fully aware of the interior stages of development, it steps back and grasps the big picture, and thus second-tier thinking appreciates the *necessary role that all of the various memes play*. Second-tier awareness thinks in terms of the overall spiral of existence, and not merely in terms of any one meme. And thus, with second-tier consciousness, the world begins to make sense, to come together as a whole, to hang together for the first time. Operating from second-tier consciousness, the possibility of genuine peace opens invitingly on the horizon."

"This is so cool," Kim said.

"Kim, why on earth would you"—and I involuntarily glanced down at her breasts, which were meeting me more than halfway—"find this interesting?"

"Oh, big-tits Kim is the airhead, huh? You absolute twit."

"No, no, honest, I didn't mean it like that, really, I—"

"Listen, once you really get the Spiral, it will set your head free, I'm telling ya. Things open up, the world gets really roomy, you can start to move around in a much larger space—you're no longer cramped in one itty-bitty meme. Even an idiot like you should be able to grasp this." I smiled wanly.

Hazelton looked around. "Where the green meme—the highest of the first-tier memes—begins to grasp the rich diversity and wonderful pluralism of different cultures, second-tier thinking *goes one step further*. It looks for the unions that link and join these different cultures, and thus it takes these separate systems and begins to embrace, include, and *integrate* them into holistic spirals and integral meshworks. Second-tier thinking, in other words, is instrumental in moving from *pluralism* to *integralism*. Those are big words, yes? pluralism and integralism? Don't worry, you'll get them." She paused and again smiled.

"The extensive research of Graves, Beck, and Cowan indicates that there are at least two major waves to this second-tier consciousness."

"This is the famous *leap into hyperspace*," Kim said, punching her words. "You know about that?"

"The leap into hyperspace. That's sort of what I'm here for, or kind of, I think I heard that earlier, that is, earlier than now, which is what earlier usually means, unless it's later than that, which of course it isn't, unless it is, but you probably already knew that, so let me sum up . . ."

Kim stared at me, barely concealing a grin. "Who's the airhead, Ken um Wilber?"

"7. *Yellow: Integrative*. Life is a kaleidoscope of interrelated, flowing systems. Flexibility, spontaneity, and functionality have the highest priority. Differences and pluralities can be integrated into interdependent, natural flows. Egalitarianism is complemented with natural degrees of excellence, qualitative distinctions and judgments. Knowledge and competency should supersede power, status, or group. The prevailing world order is the result of the existence of *different levels of reality* (or memes) and the inevitable patterns of movement up and down the dynamic Spiral. Good governance facilitates the emergence of entities through the levels of increasing complexity (nested hierarchy). 1% of the population, 5% of the power.

"8. *Turquoise: Holistic*. Universal holistic system, waves of integrative energies; unites feeling with knowledge; multiple levels interwoven into one conscious system; the basis of extensive wholeness. Universal order, but in a living, conscious fashion, not based on external rules (blue) or group bonds (green). A 'grand unification' or big picture is possible, in theory and in actuality. Sometimes involves the emergence of a new spirituality as a meshwork of all existence. Turquoise thinking is fully integral and uses the entire Spiral; sees multiple levels of interaction; detects harmonics, the mystical forces, and the pervasive flow-states that permeate any organization. 0.1% of the population, 1% of the power."

"Jesus, Kim, only 2 percent of the population is at second-tier? Are we fucked or are we fucked?"

"We're fucked."

"With less than 2 percent of the population at second-tier thinking—and only 0.1 percent at turquoise—second-tier consciousness is relatively rare because it is now the 'leading edge' of collective human evolution. As examples of second tier, Don Beck mentions items that include the global village itself, Teilhard de Chardin's noosphere, the growth of integral psychology, chaos and complexity theories, the spectrum of consciousness, integral-holistic systems thinking, and Gandhi's universal harmony—with increases in frequency definitely on the way, and even higher memes still in the offing. . . . "

I looked at Kim, then at Hazelton. "I wanted to feel that I wasn't being internally drawn and quartered"—that was it exactly. I kept saying that to myself all that summer—I don't want to be torn inside. Maybe that is why I was temporarily dazed, maybe hypnotized, by Hazelton. My artificial intelligence was being programmed by her artificial intelligence. But it struck a chord in my skewed insides. I wished I could separate this out from all the Boomer ruminations being presented with it.

Hazelton kept repeating the phrase, "the quantum leap into to the hyperspace of second-tier consciousness," and for a brief, uncharacteristic moment, I was spellbound.

"I told you she was amazing."

"Shut up, Kim."

"As Don Beck often points out, second-tier thinking has to emerge in the face of much resistance from first-tier thinking. In fact, a version of the postmodern green meme, with its pluralism and relativism, has actively fought the emergence of more integrative and holistic thinking. And yet without second-tier thinking, humanity is destined to remain victims of a global auto-immune disease, where various memes turn on each other in an attempt to establish supremacy.

"As we were saying, first-tier memes generally resist the emergence of second-tier memes. For example, religious fundamentalism (blue) is often outraged at second tier because of what it sees as an attempt to unseat its given Order. Egocentrism (red) ignores second tier altogether. Magic (purple) puts a hex on it. Green accuses second-tier consciousness of being authoritarian, hierarchical, patriarchal, marginalizing, oppressive, racist, and sexist."

At the mere mention of green, the audience once again both clapped approval and howled disagreement. There were clearly people on both sides of this quickly-heating-up argument, which suddenly had escalated from a moderately boring academic lecture to the promise of a really great food-fight.

"Green has been in charge of cultural studies for the past three decades. You will probably have already recognized many of the standard catch words of the green meme: pluralism, relativism, diversity, multiculturalism, deconstruction, anti-hierarchy, and so on.

"On the one hand, the pluralism and multiculturalism of the green meme has nobly enlarged the canon of cultural studies to include many previously marginalized peoples, ideas, and narratives. It has acted with sensitivity and care in attempting to redress social imbalances and avoid exclusionary practices. This is why it is indeed 'the sensitive self.' It has been responsible for basic initiatives in civil rights, health care, and environmental protection. It has developed strong and often convincing critiques of the philosophies, metaphysics, and social practices of the conventional religious (blue) and scientific (orange) memes, with their often exclusionary, patriarchal, sexist, and colonialistic agendas.

"On the other hand, as effective as these critiques of pre-green stages have been, green has attempted to attack *all post-green stages as well*, with absolutely catastrophic results. This has made it impossible for green to move forward into more comprehensive, inclusive, integral solutions—has, in fact, prevented green from moving to second tier." Shuffling noises from the audience, sporadic clapping, hissing.

"And this is where boomeritis enters the picture." The audience exploded into cheers and jeers.

"Jesus, Kim, is it really always this rowdy?"

"Gets worse. But yes, I told you, it's sort of a tradition."

"Look, Kim, I didn't mean that 'shut up' thing. I'm just a bit off lately."

"Hazelton had breast cancer. The doctors told her she had a few months to live. That was about five years ago. Ever since, she's carried a type of superhuman aura. Don't you think she just *shines*?"

Well, I was about to say, space does bend around her.

"Subjectivism. A funny word, no? Here's a mouthful: because pluralistic relativism (green) moves beyond mythic absolutism (blue) and formal rationality (orange) into richly textured and individualistic contexts, one of its defining characteristics is its strong *subjectivism*. Okay, so now let's drop the boring words: What does that mouthful really mean? It means that green's sanctions for truth and goodness are established largely by individual preferences, as long as the individual is not harming others. What is true for you is not necessarily true for me; what is right is simply what individuals or cultures happen to agree on at any given moment; there are no universal claims for knowledge or truth; each person is free to find his or her own values, which are not binding on anybody else. 'You do your thing, I do mine' is a popular summary of this stance.

"This is why the self at this green stage is indeed the 'sensitive self.' Precisely because it is aware of the many different contexts and numerous different types of truth—this is, after all, the meaning of pluralism—it bends over backward in an attempt to let each truth have its own say, without marginalizing or belittling any. As with the catchwords 'anti-hierarchy,' 'pluralism,' 'relativism,' and 'egalitarianism,' whenever you hear the word 'marginalization' and a criticism of it, you are almost always in the presence of the green meme.

"This noble intent, of course, has its downside. Meetings that are run on green principles tend to follow a similar course: everybody is allowed to express his or her feelings, which often takes hours; there is an almost interminable processing of opinions, often reaching no decision or course of action, since a specific course of action would likely exclude somebody. There are often calls for an inclusionary, nonmarginalizing, compassionate embrace of all views, but exactly how to do this is rarely spelled out, since in reality not all views are of equal merit. The meeting is considered a success, not if a conclusion is reached, but if everybody has a chance to share their feelings. Since no view is supposed to be better than another, no real course of action can be recommended, other than sharing all views. If any statements are made with certainty, it is how oppressive and nasty all the alternative conceptions are. There was a common saying in the sixties: 'Freedom is an endless meeting.' Well, the *endless* part was certainly right!"

This time the audience clapped its approval. Whether they actually agreed with her or not, they all seemed to recognize what she was talking about.

"My professors do this shit all the time," Kim whispered. "This endless processing crap. Yours too?"

"Well, you know, not so much. I'm in systems science, which I guess is mostly yellow, so there's not much green. But all the courses outside of my department are nothing but that, it seems. Which is why I really don't like them, but then none of us in AI take them seriously anyway. We just think that it's something the old farts in humanities do. I never really thought about it more than that."

What I did think about was Hazelton. She shined; space warped, transparency shimmered on stage, shivering chills came with her words—and it definitely was not because of what she was saying, much of which continued to make little sense to me, although Kim seemed to grasp it immediately.

"All right, dear friends, listen up, because this is where boomeritis enters the picture. In academia, this green meme, this pluralistic relativism, is the dominant stance. As Colin McGuinn summarizes it—and yes, this a wee bit technical, but do try: 'According to this conception, human reason is inherently local, culture-relative, rooted in the variable facts of human nature and history, a matter of divergent "practices" and "forms of life" and "frames of reference" and "conceptual schemes." There are no norms of reasoning that transcend what is accepted by a society or an epoch, no objective justifications for belief that everyone must respect on pain of cognitive malfunction. To be valid is to be taken to be valid, and different people can have legitimately different patterns of taking. In the end, the only justifications for belief have the form "justified for me."' As Clare Graves put it, 'This system sees the world relativistically. Thinking shows an almost radical, almost compulsive emphasis on seeing everything from a relativistic, subjective frame of reference.'

"Okay, let's get real: you remember Dr. Morin's point at the beginning of today's discussion? About the strange mixture of high intelligence and self-absorbed narcissism that seems to define the Boomers? Well, perhaps the point is now becoming more obvious: because green pluralism has such an intensely subjective stance, it is especially prey to narcissism. And exactly that is the crux of the problem: *pluralism becomes a supermagnet for narcissism.* Pluralism becomes an unwitting home for the Culture of Narcissism."

The audience began making grumbling noises. Kim began smiling. I braced myself, inadvertently clutching the arms of my seat as if preparing for a blast-off.

"As we will see, the Boomers, to their great credit, *were the first major generation in history to develop to the green meme.* That's a very important point to which we will return again and again. The Boomers moved beyond the *traditionalism* of blue and the scientific *modernism* of orange, and pioneered a *postmodern*, pluralistic, multicultural understanding—the green meme and the sensitive self. And that is exactly why the Boomers spearheaded civil rights, ecological concerns, feminism, and multicultural diversity. That is the 'high' part of the mixture, the truly impressive part of the Boomer generation and the explosive revolutions of the sixties, the widespread move from blue and orange to green. An extraordinary accomplishment, if you think about it, really extraordinary.

"But every meme has its downside, its shadow, its possible pathology, and for green the downside is that it does indeed become a huge supermagnet for narcissism—I do my thing, you do your thing, emphasis on *me* and *mine*. And that is the disastrous side of the Boomer equation, the 'low' part of the mixture, the part that has caused almost as much damage as the high part has caused good. And we are still reeling from the absolute nightmares and cultural catastrophes of the shadow side of the Woodstock Nation." I slowly glanced around the audience; the atmosphere was eerily charged.

"Let's start with just one example, and again, my friends, all of this will unfold more clearly as we proceed.

"Pluralism, egalitarianism, and multiculturalism, at their best, all stem from a very high developmental stance—the green meme—and from that stance of fairness and concern, the green meme attempts to treat all previous memes with equal care and compassion, a truly noble intent. But because it embraces an intense egalitarianism, it fails to see that *its own stance*—which is the first stance that is even capable of egalitarianism—is a fairly rare, elite stance (somewhere around 10 percent of the world's population, as we saw). Worse, the green meme then *actively denies* the stages that *produced* the green meme in the first

35

place, because it wishes to view all memes equally. But green egalitarianism is the product, we have seen, of at least six major stages of development, a development that it then turns around and aggressively denies in the name of egalitarianism!"

Loud applause and cheering, accompanied by sporadic jeers and boos. Hazelton paused, smiled very gently, and continued, almost in a whisper.

"Under the noble guise of pluralism, every previous wave of existence, no matter how shallow, egocentric, or narcissistic, is given encouragement to 'be itself,' since none is felt to be intrinsically better than the others. But if 'pluralism' is really true, then we must invite the Nazis and the KKK to the multicultural banquet, since no stance is supposed to be better or worse than another, and so all must be treated in an egalitarian fashion—at which point the self-contradictions of pluralism come screaming to the fore.

"Thus, the very high developmental stance of pluralism—the product of at least six major stages of transformation—turns around and *denies the very path that produced its own noble stance*. It extends an egalitarian embrace to every stance, no matter how shallow or narcissistic. Thus, the more egalitarianism is implemented, the more it invites, indeed encourages, the Culture of Narcissism. And the Culture of Narcissism is the antithesis of the integral culture, the opposite of a world at peace."

Kim elbowed me and grinned, while the audience began applauding—no booing this time, for whatever reasons.

"Kim, do you follow all this? It's a little abstract."

"Don't worry, it won't be. Wait till the later sessions when they start giving all the gory examples—when they start *naming names*!"—she squealed with delight—"you will *not* believe it!"

"No, I'm sure I won't."

"In short," Hazelton's voice continued, "the rather high developmental stance of pluralism becomes a supermagnet for the rather low state of egoic narcissism. And that brings us directly to boomeritis.

"*Boomeritis* is simply pluralism infected with narcissism. Exactly what this means will become clearer and clearer as we give more examples. Right now I'll just mention the technical definition: boomeritis is that strange mixture of very high cognitive capacity (the green meme and noble pluralism) infected with rather low emotional narcissism (purple and red memes)—*exactly the mixture that has been noted by so many social critics*. A typical result is that the sensitive self, honestly trying to help, excitedly exaggerates its own significance. It will possess the new paradigm, which heralds the greatest transformation in the history of the world; it will completely revolutionize society as we know it; it will save the planet and save Gaia and save the Goddess; it will personally be the vanguard of the great coming social transformation that will totally revolutionize history; it will . . .

"Well, and off we go with some of the bulging grandiosity of Boomerville. This is exactly why observers on the scene have reported, as we saw with Lentricchia, that 'it is impossible, this much is clear, to exaggerate the heroic self-inflation.' Once again, that is not the whole story of the Boomers, but it appears to be an unmistakable flavor. In particular, boomeritis has significantly tilted and prejudiced academic studies; it is behind much of the culture wars; it haunts almost every corner of the New Age; it drives many of the games of deconstruction and identity politics; it authors new paradigms daily. Virtually no topic, no matter how innocent, has escaped a reworking at its hands, as we will see in the following sessions.

"Put simply: boomeritis is high pluralism mixed with low narcissism. And that is the strange, strange brew that has accompanied the Me generation at virtually every twist and turn of its otherwise idealistic saga. And with this understanding, my dear friends, we have arrived at the very heart of this generation."

"Arrive at *this*," says Chloe, dragging her naked body over mine, flesh on ecstatic flesh, friction shuddering to the thump thump thumping of DJ Libra playing "Anomaly Calling Your Name."

"Chloe, have you ever wondered why the Boomers call all of us 'slackers'? Call everybody after them slackers? Here's a quote from today's *Herald Tribune*: 'Boomers feel superior to the younger generations. It wouldn't even occur to Boomers not to.' Why is that, Chloe?"

"If they're so superior, can they do *this*?"

"Since, in normal development, green pluralism eventually gives way to second-tier consciousness and an integral embrace, why did my

generation become so stuck at the green meme?—so stuck with *itself*
and the supposed superiority of its opinions?—so stuck at pluralistic
relativism, extreme egalitarianism, multiculturalism and diversity carried to insane extremes, anti-hierarchy furies, deconstructive postmodernism, I do my thing and you do your thing so that me and mine
shall rule? A stance that produced what many feel is the most odious
generation in American history?

"Well, we have seen that one of the central reasons appears to be
that the intense subjectivism of the green meme was a prime magnet
and refuge for the narcissism that, for whatever reasons, has been so
prevalent in the Me generation. This combination of high pluralism
and low narcissism is boomeritis, and it follows that *boomeritis is one
of the primary roadblocks to an integral embrace.*

"Now, of course, every first-tier meme is a roadblock to second-tier
integral consciousness. But green, as the last and highest of the first-
tier memes, is the final barrier, the ultimate barrier, the barrier that in
many ways is the hardest to let go of—and it is hard to let go of
precisely because of the narcissism that so heavily infects it. That mixture of pluralism and narcissism is boomeritis, the final roadblock to
a world at peace."

Hazelton looked out at the audience; her voice hauntingly rose to
deliver its conclusion.

"Dr. Morin opened this seminar by asking: can we have a more encompassing, caring, integral world, a world truly at peace? The answer
seems to be yes, if we can make the leap from first to second tier, the
final barrier to which is none other than boomeritis. In short, my
friends, it appears that we will come to terms with boomeritis, or we
will actively contribute to the fragmentation and devastation that
everywhere threaten tomorrow. We will get over boomeritis, or we will
continue to pledge allegiance to a world at war."

She turned and slowly walked off the stage; the audience gave her
a standing ovation. Sporadic boos and hisses told that not everybody
was of one mind; but Hazelton's presence commanded a certain respect, and the audience readily gave it (even though they probably
didn't notice that she was bending space).

And then it dawned on me. What Hazelton was calling "boomeritis" is not confined to Boomers, any more than Lou Gehrig's disease is

confined to Lou Gehrig. Anybody can get it; it's simply named after its most famous victim.

I rose to leave; Kim touched me on the shoulder. "If you come back tomorrow, I'll let you in on a little secret," she smiled. I looked at her and shivered, and didn't know what any of it meant.

2

The_Pink_Insides_of_CyberSpace@LookingGlass.org

This is an infinite enclosed encircling darkness, a type of crystal
swarthy womb, moist, suffocating. Running throughout it are optical
fibers, brilliantly lit from within. And running throughout one of
them. . . is me. I am a luminous ray of light, disembodied Ecstasy,
rejoicing in the simple thrill of self-existence. Chloe, naked, pulsating,
vibrating, her breasts swaying, nipples huge, her legs spread, vagina
swollen, floats toward me, alluring. I reach out to voraciously take her,
but my body won't move. And then I notice it's worse than that—I have
no body to move at all. The light that I am can only thrill in its own
being; without a body, it cannot thrill with others. Slowly, then tilting
strangely, the self-thrilling light begins to dim, then quickly transforms
into endless darkness that cannot find air. The slow, painful process of
dying begins. I would scream but there is no mouth, I would thrash but
there is no body, I would . . .

"JESUS!" I finally manage to shriek.
"Ken, Ken, look at me. Wake up, sweet boy, look at me."
"Chloe, here's the deal, here's the thing. It's awful, Chloe, it's hard

to explain, it's really awful, it's awful. I sort of . . . , I kind of . . . , well, it's sort of, this something kind of . . . something . . . *awful*."

Harvard Square is everywhere dismal. At the beginning of high school I had briefly passed through here, certain I would be back for college, secretly delighted at my good fortune, struck by the charm and beauty of the place, a blend of rustic and cosmopolitan. In the few years since that visit, Harvard Square has come to look like any other square in any other city in any other part of the industrialized world: most of the local shops have been replaced by chains—the Gap looks at me over here, Barnes and Noble stares straight ahead, Wendy's right over there, and thank God I can get a pair of Banana Republic jeans, right around the corner. Paul Revere's famous ride now runs right past McDonald's. I live at McDonald's, but still . . .

There was something else about the Square becoming so depressing, which was actually something about life itself becoming so dreary. I think it really started on April 8, 1994. "Cobain was the only musical genius equal to John Lennon," Dad had said, which I guess was the supreme compliment. So why didn't they just give him his heroin, leave him alone? Could he have ended up any deader? I feel stupid and contagious, here we are now, entertain us. Why kill him like that? Why have the system reach through his body and into his arm and put that shotgun right next to his head, pretending that he pulled the trigger, when it was society's hypocrisy that loaded, locked, and really pulled? *The day the music died*—maybe it died in 1959, but maybe each generation suffers the death of music. My generation's music died in '94, and so did something inside of me; both have yet to revive. Maybe that's when I became so despairingly inclined, with depression conjoined to my soul at the symbolic hip; the haunting thought never really left me: *maybe my Siamese twin was actually Kurt's ghost.*

Here's what started to bother me about Hazelton and her waves of existence. It's this notion of interiority, the notion that consciousness cannot be reduced to matter. Because the whole point about Artificial Intelligence is that of course consciousness can be reduced to matter, can be reduced to sufficiently elaborate software running through

41

sufficiently elaborate hardware. As one of my teachers, Marvin Minsky, put it when asked if machines will ever be able to think, "I'm a machine, and I can think." Although a snappy critic replied that "at least one of those statements is false," the picture was clear in official Artificial circles: Matter is all that matters.

Oh, we call cyberspace "immaterial," but what we really mean is information carried by electricity or light, both of which are forms of electromagnetic energy, and all energy is essentially material (because mass and energy are convertible via the infamous $E = mc^2$). In other words, cyberspace is very subtle electromagnetic matter, but matter nonetheless, and thus it does not threaten in the least the materialist's dream of reducing everything to complex variations on dirt.

This thought—"there is nothing in the universe but matter"—depresses romantics, poets, and most sane women. But far from being a depressing thought, the elegance of this reductionism is what makes hard-core materialists cum in their pants, as my dad used to say, which always made Mom blush. Dad was a materialist of the historical type (they used to call it Marxism), and I was a materialist of the photonic type (silicon cybercity with digital optics)—but really, matter is matter, so in this case the apple did not fall far from the tree.

The reason we at MIT are taking bets on when Artificial Intelligence robots—or "Bots"—will take over the world is that it is perfectly obvious that intelligence can be downloaded into digital optical machines—a type of hyper-computer cyberspace—and once that happens, who needs humans? Except maybe the Bots, who might keep us around in a zoo so they can show their optical offspring the lowly origins of their own higher evolution—a cyber-Darwinian nightmare for humans, a simple reminder accompanied by a bodiless shudder for the luminous Bots (of which I intended to be one).

Ancient Boomers like Ray Kurzweil, Bill Joy, big ole Negreponte, still hanging around my lab, Eric Drexler, and Hans Moravec are all wrestling with this. Their book titles tell the story, things like *Engines of Creation*, *The Age of Spiritual Machines*, *Robo Sapiens*, and *Robot: Mere Machine to Transcendent Mind*. But really, they're clueless. They are trying to think what it would be LIKE to inject their present if souped-up consciousness into silicon cyberspace, but my generation knows better: we will actually take that ride, and it is beyond imagination.

But it's this interior thing that bothers me.

"That's because you are a complete idiot."

"Thanks, Jonathan."

"Chloe is telling everybody that you wake up screaming at night. This is pretty funny. And this is because you are a complete idiot. Of course you're going to be as screwed up as you are if you think we are really going to disappear into machines. I mean, hello? Anybody home? Who wouldn't have nightmares? That is the ultimate nightmare, old chap."

"Yes, Jonathan, and you spend hours every day sitting in meditation and humming or oming or whatever it is you do, and the only result, as far as I can see, is a rancid personality."

"Ain't it great? Envy will get you nowhere. You going to see Stuart Davis tonight?"

"I thought Buddhists were supposed to be kind and compassionate. The Dalai Lama—'My religion is being kind to people'—you know, that sort of thing. Not this acid mouth you have. Davis?"

"You know, the singer. Guy who did *Kid Mystic* and *Bright Apocalypse.*"

"Oh, right. Yes, we're going."

"Look, friend, I said, taking out my nice-guy persona and dusting it off just for you. The thing about consciousness is this, the thing about your own mind is this: either you believe that you know it from the inside, right now, in an immediate fashion—and therefore it cannot be reduced to anything else—or you believe that it is just a by-product of random, mindless, material evolution. So here's what you believe, you screaming shrieking mess of a human being—"

"How sweet."

"Here's what you believe: evolution starts with the Big Bang—a bunch of matter just blows into existence. Why? Well, according to you, it's just a random oops, no reason, it just happens, right? And then this mindless idiotic matter struggles billions of years—*billions* of years, mind you, this matter keeps struggling—and eventually it evolves into the conscious beings that are sitting at this table. Well, one of us is conscious. But why on earth would dirt get right up and eventually start writing poetry? You think that is *random*? You can only think that by abandoning the immediate reality of your own consciousness. Do you even *recognize* your own consciousness? Nooooo, you think that your consciousness is just some wiring arrangement of frisky dirt. No wonder you can't sleep."

"It's not that easy."

"For idiots, it's not that easy. For sentient beings, it's easy."

"Why are you sitting around here annoying me? Don't you have breaths to count or something? Shouldn't you be sucking incense fumes somewhere, maybe working on that winning style of yours?"

"Chloe says you rattle when you make love."

"Okay, that's it, I'm really getting pissed. Chloe wouldn't say that."

"Oh, not 'That's not true' but 'Chloe wouldn't say that.'"

"I don't even know what that means, rattle when you make love. What does that mean?"

"Why, I think it means that you are indeed slowly becoming a machine, so all your parts are starting to actually bang and rattle, even when you make love." Jonathan threw his head back and laughed and laughed.

"The dictionary definition of *narcissism* is 'excessive interest in one's own self, importance, grandeur, abilities; egocentrism.' The inner state of narcissism, clinicians tell us, is often that of an empty or fragmented self, which desperately attempts to fill the void by inflating the self and deflating others. The emotional mood is, '*Nobody tells me what to do!*'"

The speaker was Dr. Carla Fuentes: wild, animated, 110 pounds of locomotive dynamite. She seemed to have an unshakable center of certainty, but without being arrogant or pushy. Maybe "certainty" was the wrong word; confidence might be better. I was trying to hear what she was saying, over the shuffling, rustling sounds of the latecomers. Although part of me still found this dustbin discipline suffocatingly boring, part of me began to suspect that the evolution of consciousness in carbon-based life forms might tell me something crucial about the coming evolution of consciousness in silicon-based life forms. Dawned on me, in other words, that I'd better pay attention to what the IC folks were saying. It also dawned on me, vaguely, that he was there; the he that was a destiny, roaring, harrowing, rushing at me through a fitful maze of future tense.

"Most psychologists agree that, although there are many ways to look at narcissism, it is a normal trait of childhood that is ideally outgrown, at least to a significant degree. Development, in fact, can be defined as *a successive decrease in egocentrism*. The young infant is largely wrapped up in its own world, oblivious to much of its surroundings and most human interactions. As its consciousness increasingly grows in strength and capacity, it can become aware of itself, and of others, and eventually put itself in others' shoes and thus develop care, compassion, and a generous integral embrace—none of which it is born with.

"As Harvard psychologist Howard Gardner reminds us, 'The young child is totally egocentric—meaning not that he thinks selfishly only about himself, but to the contrary, that he is incapable of thinking about himself. The egocentric child is unable to differentiate himself from the rest of the world; he has not separated himself out from others or from objects. Thus he feels that others share his pain or his pleasure, that his mumblings will inevitably be understood, that his perspective is shared by all persons, that even animals and plants partake of his consciousness. In playing hide-and-seek he will "hide" in broad view of other persons, because his egocentrism prevents him from recognizing that others are aware of his location. The whole course of human development can be viewed as a continuing decline in egocentrism.'"

I still hadn't told Chloe, or anybody really, that I was stopping in at Integral Center every now and then, because it would be misunderstood. It wasn't so much for positive reasons. Even if these carbon-based "levels of consciousness" were real, I wanted to be able to convince myself that they could all be translated into AI terms and thus easily downloaded into the coming cyberworld. This interior-waves thing caught me off guard, and I needed to know that they were all merely algorithms of computational space—that they were interiors that could, like anything else, be reduced to digital information, converted into merely material displays. I wanted to know that these memes would rattle when they made love, too.

I had settled into my seat, scooted down unobtrusively, tucked my existence under the rug. Kim spotted me right away.

"Nice to know you're not interested," she said, plopping down next to me.

"Is, um, Hazelton speaking today?"

Kim turned her head and looked at me. "Oooooh . . ."

"Oh, please."

"No, today is just Carla. But Jooooooan will be talking all day tomorrow, so I guess I'll see you then, eh?"

"Not funny, Kim."

"Funny, Ken."

"Is today's session interesting at all? Because it's off to a slow start."

"No, it's great, really. When she starts talking about the Berkeley student protests of the sixties, a handful of Boomers always shout, hiss, and walk out, so that's fun. But today is nothing compared to when Carla talks about the Native Americans and what their religion was *really* like versus what Boomers say it was like."

"That's when they start giving concrete examples of boomeritis?"

"Yup, next week. But today is a kick. But hell, Ken um Wilber, you'll probably sleep through it anyway. Where's Chloe?"

"Never mind where Chloe is."

"I'll *bet*."

"Thus development, for the most part, involves *decreasing* narcissism and *increasing* consciousness. Carol Gilligan found, for example, that female moral development tends to go through three general stages, which she calls *selfish*, *care*, and *universal care*. In each of these stages, the circle of care and compassion expands while egocentrism declines. At first, the young girl cares mostly for herself (the 'selfish' stage); then she can care for others as well, such as her family and friends (the 'care' stage); and finally, she can extend her concern and well-wishes to humanity as a whole (the 'universal care' stage). Each higher stage does not mean that you stop caring for yourself, only that you include more and more others for whom you *also* can evidence a genuine concern and compassion.

"Incidentally, males go through the same three general stages, although, according to Gilligan, they usually emphasize *rights* and *justice* while females emphasize *care* and *relationship*. Gilligan believes that after the third stage, in both sexes, there can be an *integration* of both attitudes, so that at the universal-integral stage, both men and women integrate the male and female voices in themselves, thus uniting justice and compassion."

"Kim, you said you were going to let me in on a little secret."

"I did say that, didn't I?"

"Come on."

"So really, Ken, where is Chloe? Is this not her cup of tea?"

"No, it's not. It's not really mine, either. I mean, psychology. Over at AI Lab, you know what they call a psychologist with half a brain?"

"What?"

"Gifted."

"These three general stages that both men and women go through are quite common for most forms of development. They are known by many names, such as preconventional, conventional, and postconventional; or egocentric, ethnocentric, and worldcentric; or 'me,' 'us,' and 'all of us.'"

Fuentes danced across the stage, energy radiating from her, a live wire plugged into a cosmic socket sight unseen. I tried to focus.

Kim, noticing my pained look of attempted concentration, leaned over. "These 3 stages are just a very simplified version of the 8 stages of Spiral Dynamics. So cheer up—today you only need one hand to follow the discussion," she grinned. I nodded gamely.

"Nod *this*," says Chloe, her naked body swinging upside down from the chandelier, breasts swaying, ass displaying, offering this and that, go fetch, while DJ Pollywog plays Ultrasonic's "Girls Like Us Go Boom Boom."

To die without a body, ah, there's the rub. Chloe's naked body floats toward me; hundreds of female naked bodies float around her, and I sample them all. I am the detached monological eyeball my feminist professors hate. Detached and disembodied, I gaze on all—objectifying, reducing, humiliating all. I am the Cartesian God, come to annoy the world. What good is being a male if you can't sexually objectify? I see all, I want all, I want to take it all for my own explosive release, whereupon the depression temporarily forgets its name and my Siamese twin dislocates, only to regain strength and plot its quick return.

I cannot have sex without a body. Women cannot have relationships without a body. Cyberspace without bodies—will it even work?

"Well hell, sweet boy, *virtual* bodies? Now that doesn't really count, does it?"

The waves of existence unfold in stages, great grand rushing waves of increasing consciousness . . . *What if it's true?* . . . What a wild thought, what a wild ride. . . .

"Egocentric, ethnocentric, worldcentric. The egocentric or selfish stage is often called *preconventional*, because the infant and young child have not yet learned conventional rules and roles; they have not yet been socialized. They cannot yet take the role of others and thus begin to develop genuine care and compassion. They therefore remain egocentric, selfish, narcissistic, and so on. This does *not* mean that young children have no feelings for others, nor does it mean they are altogether amoral. It simply means that, compared with subsequent development, their feelings and morals are still heavily centered on their own impulses and locked into their own rather narrow perspectives.

"Starting around age 6 or 7, a profound shift in consciousness occurs. The child can begin to *take the role of other*. For example: say you have a book whose front cover is blue and whose back cover is orange. Show the book, front and back, to a five-year-old child. Then hold the book between you and the child. You are looking at the orange cover, and the child is looking at blue. Ask the child what color he is seeing, and he will correctly say blue. Ask the child what color *you* are seeing, and he will say blue. A seven-year-old will say orange.

"In other words, the five-year-old cannot put himself in your shoes and take your point of view. He does not have the cognitive capacity to step out of his own skin and inhabit yours for a while. And therefore he will never really understand your perspective, will never really understand *you*. There will never be a *mutual* recognition. Nor can he therefore truly, genuinely, care for your point of view, however much he may emotionally love you. But all of that begins to change with the emergence of the capacity to take the role of others, which is why Gilligan calls this stage the shift from *selfish* to *care*.

"The care stage, which generally lasts from age 7 to adolescence, is known as *conventional*, *conformist*, *ethnocentric*, and it means just that, centered on the group (family, peers, tribe, nation). The young child steps out of his or her own limited perspective and begins to share the views and perspectives of others—so much so that the child is often *trapped* in the views of others: hence, conformist. This stage is often called 'good boy, nice girl,' 'my country right or wrong,' and so on, reflecting the intense conformity, peer pressure, and group dominance that usually accompanies this general period. Although the individual at this stage can to some degree step aside from his own perspective, he cannot easily step aside from the group's. He has moved from 'me' to 'us'—a great decline in egocentrism—but there he is stuck, 'my country right or wrong.'

"All of which begins to change in adolescence, with the emergence of *postconventional* and *worldcentric* awareness. This is yet another major decline in egocentrism, because this time one's peer group is subjected to scrutiny. What is right and fair, not just for me or my tribe or my nation, but for all peoples, regardless of race, religion, sex, or creed? The move from ethnocentric to worldcentric. The adolescent can become a fiery idealist, ablaze with all the possibilities, a crusader for justice, a revolutionary out to rock the world. Of course, some of this is just an explosion of hormones, frenzied at best. But a good part of it is the emergence of the stage of *universal care*, justice, and fairness. And, in fact, this is simply the beginning of the possibility of developing a truly integral consciousness . . . and, yes, a world at peace."

The Donnas Turn 21 blares in the background—"Are You Gonna Move It for Me?," "Gimme a Ride," and "Hot Pants" permeate the neon air, sizzling, shimmering, pop and crackling, bodies light up bodies with a painfully electric thrill.

"Chloe, am I worldcentric?"

"Why, yes, Ken. Yes, you are."

"How do you know that?"

"Because you will have sex with any female regardless of race, color, or creed."

"I don't think that's what they mean, Chloe."

And Chloe's naked body turns into Kim's naked body, which floats toward me, alluringly—naked bodies, naked bodies, all in a worldcentric space.

"Say, this seminar is *really* getting interesting, isn't it?"

"These three general stages—egocentric to ethnocentric to worldcentric—are of course just a simple summary of the many unfolding waves of consciousness, but already you can start to see that development, as Gardner says, is indeed a decline in egocentrism. In other words, the more you grow, the more you grow beyond you. Each developmental wave is a *decrease* in narcissism and an *increase* in consciousness, or an increase in the capacity to take wider and deeper perspectives into account."

Kim leaned over. "Ain't it a kick? But the morning session is only an hour, and it's just about over. Carla gives a chart to summarize it all. What I like about it is how it sets up the afternoon session, which is totally outrageous."

"The afternoon session is totally outrageous? Really?"

"It's where they first introduce boomeritis, and some of the Boomers, shall we say, get a little pissed."

"Cool."

"There are, of course, more sophisticated models with more than 3 stages. During the opening discussion, Dr. Hazelton gave an example of this developmental unfolding using Spiral Dynamics and its 8 waves of development. On the wall is a chart we use for a later session, but it is helpful now. [See fig. 4.1, page 118.] In Spiral Dynamics, the preconventional stages are beige (archaic-instinctual), purple (magical-animistic), and red (egocentric). At the next stage (blue, conformist rule), the narcissism is dispersed into the *group*—not me, but my country, can do no wrong! This conventional/conformist stance lasts into orange, which marks the beginning of the postconventional stages (green, yellow, and turquoise)."

I looked at the slide, made a few mental notes. Kim was serenely taking this all in, as if it were the simplest thing in the world. I was beginning to suspect she was . . . *really intelligent.*

"In short, as development moves from preconventional to conventional to postconventional—or from egocentric to ethnocentric to worldcentric—the amount of narcissism and egocentrism slowly but surely decreases. Instead of treating the world and others as an extension of the self, the mature adult of postconventional awareness meets the world on its own terms, as a self in a community of other selves operating by mutual recognition and respect. The spiral of development is a spiral of compassion, expanding from me, to us, to all of us: there standing open to an integral embrace and the genuine possibility of a world at peace."

Carla Fuentes smiled, made a little bow, folded her papers neatly in front of her, left them on the podium, and walked slowly off the stage, to polite applause. Charles Morin sauntered out, smiled, and announced a break for lunch. Then he said, with what appeared a slightly wicked grin, "You radicals and revolutionaries won't want to miss this afternoon's session, which is when we usually have to call the police."

I looked at Kim. "The police?"

"Oh, he's talking about the afternoon session when Fuentes discusses the student riots. They don't actually have to call the police, but almost, because some of the Boomers get furious." Kim grinned. "I know the coolest place," she said. "I'm meeting Morin there for lunch. Wanna come? Bring Chloe; it'll be fun."

I Nokia'd Chloe, and as the cell rang, I abruptly hung up, realizing that this would require some explaining, a confusion that instantly showed on my face. "Um, maybe later."

Kim stared at me. "Whatever."

Scarpelli's was tucked away in a back alley off Charles Ave. We had been seated for perhaps ten minutes, drinking Pellegrino and eating bread sticks the way Bugs Bunny used to eat carrots, when in ambled Dr. Charles Morin. Short, fat, dull, and dumpy would be a fair description of the man. His hair, his skin, and his suit were all gray. But there was something else about him, a type of fire or fizz. He seemed to twinkle, in the very best sense of that word, if there is one. Under the gray, or through the gray, he twinkled. (I could almost hear Scott whispering in my ear, "If I was boinking big-boobs Kim, I'd be twinkling, too.")

"So, Ken Wilber, are you enjoying the seminar so far?"

"Well, you know, I'm over at AI Lab, and this is all really new to me."

"Ah, silicon city, cyberheaven, say bye-bye to humans, is that about it?" He laughed good-naturedly.

I was slightly unnerved by the ease with which he had stumbled on my life's major obsession. "Well, you know, that's a real possibility. The coming silicon-based life forms, or forms of silicon forms, life or otherwise—well, not quite like that, or more like that, if it were like that, which of course it isn't, if you get my drift, or maybe not, but then you probably already knew that. . . . "

"I see, yes." Morin looked at Kim and grinned.

"I don't know, he just came over and sat down next to me at the seminar."

"Okay, okay, I'm a little unsettled. Too much Pellegrino. I am, we are, what we are interested in at AI Lab is the whole possibility of machines that have human-level intelligence. We think, my professors think, and me too, I often think, we think that in about 30 years Artificial Intelligence will reach human-level capabilities, and once that happens, AI will take off explosively, it will just accelerate exponentially, because at that point the machines themselves will take over and figure out how to move forward faster than we humans ever could. Something like that."

"Yes, I see, that's clear enough," Morin said. "What isn't clear is whether humanity will make it to the point that such a thing can even happen. As I'm sure your professors have also told you, within that 30-year period we will have the capability to create nanobots—microscopic self-replicating robots—that could literally devour the entire biosphere in a weekend, destroying all life as we know it. Or a genetically engineered virus that could eat the liver of every human being alive—maybe with some fava beans and a nice Chianti." He chuckled to himself. "Or weapons of biological mass destruction that any terrorist with a suitcase could unleash in Manhattan, killing millions in a matter of seconds. I'm sure you've got a dozen other examples."

"Yes, right, which is why we want to download consciousness into cyberspace before that happens."

"But my point, young man, is that there might not be a 'before that happens.' As you heard at this morning's session, unless we get more humans to the worldcentric waves of development, humanity won't make it to cyberheaven—we will almost certainly self-destruct through egocentric and ethnocentric genocide."

"I never thought of it exactly like that." Our salads arrived. Kim looked content; Morin looked concerned, almost worried, but curiously still twinkled.

"Well, you're not alone," he said, "because most people don't think of it like that, either. They think that in order to fix the world's problems we need to do something in the *exterior* world—we need to stop polluting the atmosphere, we need to control guns, we need to stop nuclear testing, we need to move to solar power, we need to . . . always something we need to fix in the *exterior* world. Those are all important, but the real problems are on the *interior*—we need to help consciousness evolve from egocentric to ethnocentric to worldcentric, *or else people won't want to fix all those things in the exterior world to begin with!*" Morin slapped the table, and several diners turned their heads to look. "Obviously, only people at the worldcentric level even care about worldcentric problems, about global problems and how to fix them. Egocentric and ethnocentric couldn't give a rat's ass about global anything! But less than 20% of the world's population is at worldcentric! Jesus fucking Christ! No wonder the planet is fucked, and I mean fucked, kid!" And he slammed the table again.

Kim reached over and touched his arm. "So Charles, why don't you tell us what you really think?" Morin laughed, the twinkle returned; he looked at me, smiling.

"Anyway, that's what we specialize in over at IC. We're seriously concerned with how to help facilitate the growth and development, not just of the exterior world, but of the interior world as well. The growth and development of consciousness. Because without that, we're all toast."

"Well, so, the question is, will we make it? Will enough people make it to worldcentric?" I asked, genuinely concerned.

"That's a topic we cover in later sessions—it's absolutely amazing what our research has found, and I don't want to give the show away," he said, smiling broadly. There was something about him that was quietly infectious, and rather slowly, against my will, I found myself liking him. ("Since he's now such a swell friend," Scott whispered, "ask him what it feels like to be boinking ole Kim?")

"But I can tell you this," Morin said. "The main problem right now is flatland. You know flatland?"

"Um, I'm not sure. I don't think so."

"Very simple," Kim offered. "Flatland is what it sounds like: the belief that reality is flat, that there are no levels of consciousness. We basically live in flatland, and that's the real problem, right, Charles?"

"Right, yes, that's very true. We can't even talk about helping people grow and develop through the levels of consciousness if they don't even know that there are levels of consciousness in the first place. So one of our main problems is simple education, getting these ideas circulated. If you only believe in flatland, there's no way out."

I looked at the two of them. Although visually they did not compute as a couple, there was something about—what was it?—something about their combined energies that seemed to fit together. ("Boinky, boinky, boinky . . . Can't you just hear those ole mattress springs squeaking away, Ken?") I laughed out loud.

"Oh nothing, not that, no no, I mean yes yes, of course that's the main problem. Education. Got tits. Got *it*. Got it. That's right, got it. I got it, I understand, the importance of education." I turned bright red.

"So here's the thing," I said, trying to recover. "At the end of the morning's session, you mentioned something about the radicals and revolutionaries. The rebellious sixties. What was that all about?"

"Oh, the topic of our afternoon session. Gets everybody pretty riled up. The point, as you'll see, is that that the Boomers claimed to be revolutionaries in so many ways, but they were—and still are—trapped in flatland. They did not overcome flatland, they embraced it, got lost in it, ended up celebrating it. This is the major story of our time. Flatland."

"I thought the seminar was about boomeritis?"

"Same thing. Boomeritis is today's version of flatland, as you'll see. And flatland is the problem." Morin smiled, sparkled and fizzed, seemed somehow to fit, sitting there next to Kim; but also, I started to notice, seemed somehow vaguely far away, almost imperceptibly floating in some forlorn land only he could see.

"Okay, that's this afternoon. But you said something about the research being really amazing, the research showing whether a large number of people would make it to worldcentric. Give me a preview, come on. . . . "

Morin looked at me and smiled. "Okay, kid, Ken, the numbers really are interesting. The research data shows that your generation is starting to come in at yellow. You know yellow?"

"Yeah, sure, it's the first of the second-tier memes."

"That's right. The Boomers were the first green-meme generation in history. Your generation—actually, both the Xers and Ys—have the chance to be the first yellow-meme generation in history, the first integral generation in all of history."

The thought caught me totally off guard, and I was temporarily transfixed, held spellbound by the possibility. An adrenaline chill, electric thrill, ran through my entire body. DJ Jazzy Jazz plays "Expander" by the Future Sound of London, and the beat goes thump thump thump in my Ecstasy-addled brain. It never—*never*—dawned on me that the "quantum leap into the hyperspace of second-tier consciousness" might come to define my generation. My brain cells were buzzing, lit from within by images of a future I had never even considered.

Kim looked at me and beamed, as if to say, That's why I'm in love with him ("Right, Kim, and boinking his brains out nightly . . ."). I laughed out loud again, this time also genuinely captivated by the insane possibilities.

"Do you go over all of that in the later sessions of the seminar?" I asked.

"Yes, that's right."

"Man, I'm just gonna come back for those."

"Well, son, sorry, but you really need to follow the early sessions, follow the whole argument, or it won't quite gel for you, not the way you want."

"Oh, rats, more homework."

"No, not really. And the fireworks are about to start, anyway."

I thought for a moment, thought of Mom and Dad. "But does that mean, what you said about the first integral generation . . . does that mean that it's too late for the Boomers, too late for them to be integral, to make it to second tier?"

"Well, here's what we found about that. . . . "

"Oh! Charles, the time!"

"Yes, right, got to get back fast. Wilber, kid, Ken, we cover that later, promise."

Kim and I settled back in our seats; I glanced furtively around and again scrunched down. Carla Fuentes repeated the point she made right before lunch, then continued. I glanced at Kim, who was still smiling, and I managed to start to look forward to the afternoon; not only was second tier out there waiting for me somewhere, there was, I had been told, a serious fight soon to be brewing in the audience.

"The spiral of development is a spiral of increasing compassion, expanding from me, to us, to all of us: there standing open to an integral embrace and the possibility of a world at peace.

"I hasten to add that this does not mean that development is nothing but sweetness and light, a series of wonderful promotions on a linear ladder of progress. For each stage of development brings not only new capacities but the possibility of new disasters; not just novel potentials but novel pathologies; new strengths, new diseases. In evolution at large, new emergent systems always face new problems: dogs get cancer, atoms don't. Annoyingly, there is a price to be paid for each increase in consciousness, and this 'dialectic of progress'—good news, bad news—needs always to be remembered. Still, the point for now is that each unfolding wave of consciousness brings at least the possibility for a greater expanse of care, compassion, justice, and mercy, on the way to an integral embrace."

"Now *this* is on the way to an integral embrace," says Chloe, as she rubs her naked body against mine.

"Chloe, did you know that we might be the first integral generation in history? The first yellow-meme generation?"

I start to grab Chloe, pull her to me and make her mine, but I slip on an icy patch in spacetime and find myself caught in that endless encircling dark-encased tomb. I am trapped in some sort of wobbling time warp, which orbits back on itself and erases its own existence. At one point I feel vibrantly alive with the future possibilities of the yellow-meme generation—this meme was originally called "yellow" because it is bright and radiant like the sun!—and at other points I instantly decay into depression, I am a connoisseur of collapse, I am the lead singer of Radiohead, I am a creep, so—switch to Beck—why don't you kill me? Crystal Method, pounding, pounding. "Ken, you've got to try this."

Billie Joe's voice hovers in the air, Green Day singing my estate:

Do you have the time? To listen to me whine? About nothing
and everything all at once?
I am one of those, melodramatic fools, neurotic to the core, no
doubt about it.

Sometimes I give myself the creeps. Sometimes my mind plays
tricks on me.
It all keeps adding up. I think I'm cracking up. . . .

I shake my head, turn to look at Kim—egocentric to ethnocentric to
worldcentric. Kim looks at me and smiles.

Mom and Dad are both worldcentric, in their own way. More precisely, Dad is beautiful bright green when he thinks, strong orange
when he acts, and has a mean dose of red thrown in for good measure—especially that save-the-world stuff, because that means he must
be its Savior—as in, *hel-lo*, pure egocentric red. But his center of gravity is green, for he truly does care; he cares too much, I sometimes
think, because the means at his disposal to help the world are not
nearly strong enough to have the necessary effect, so he will die a very
unhappy man—that is, he will die in the same unfulfilled state in which
he always lived—although on his tombstone it will say, He Tried Really
Hard. Mom often thinks green but I swear she acts purple—everything
is magically alive for her: the rocks and sticks and stones and plants all
talk to her, and she to them; they are all her very, very good friends, and
she never lets them down.

Are Mom and Dad integral the way the IC folks define it? I'm not
sure, but no, I don't think so. It's like Morin said, Mom and Dad are
the green-meme generation, they stopped just short of integral. I think
that's why they keep searching, pushing, agitating. They are looking
for that "quantum leap into the hyperspace of second-tier consciousness." But then, who isn't? I'll bet even my luminous Bots want that
hyperspace, in their own way.

And that's what got me thinking: I'm almost certain that these
interior waves of consciousness can be reduced to—that is, downloaded
into—the silicon circuits of the coming cybersphere. A super Cray
computer squared will reproduce every aspect of human consciousness,
plus some. Deep Thought already beat the pants off Kasparov, who is
now thinking of suicide daily. But future generations—starting with
mine—will be on the other side of the circuits, watching humans wither.

And then I had a brainstorm, a colossal brilliant neon brainstorm,
with my own artificial intelligence lighting up the neurons of my material brain in a way that threatened meltdown. *The Bots themselves will*

grow and evolve. They will have their own levels of consciousness! Of course, they would have to! The whole point of AI is that human consciousness can be perfectly reproduced by computers. But human consciousness—I'll give Hazelton and Fuentes this—definitely unfolds through stages or waves. That means that the self-awareness of computers—computer consciousness, if you will—would likewise grow and evolve. So when computers start to become truly conscious, they would have to go through their own stages of unfolding awareness. The Bots themselves would have to grow from egocentric to ethnocentric to worldcentric. *And anybody who could understand these computer waves of consciousness would have the ultimate key to the coming cybersphere!* And . . .

I am having a total neuronal blow-out. Take a breath, take a breath, take a breath. I need to think about all of this. In my mind a neon sign keeps flashing: ONCE YOU GET OUT OF FLATLAND, YOU START TO SEE THE POSSIBILITIES.

But Fuentes is talking about something else right now, and I need to focus on that. All of a sudden I decide that I really don't want to miss any of the pieces of this unfolding puzzle.

"Ken, are you okay?"

"Like you can't believe."

Fuentes is talking about boomeritis in the flesh. Focus on what she's saying. Apply this to the Bots in cyberspace later. Right now, it's humans in meatspace we're talking about.

"So, um, Kim, where are we? I really, really want to know."

Kim looks at me quizzically. "Okay. We're talking about the growth and development of consciousness—from egocentric to ethnocentric to worldcentric—and all the things that can go wrong with it, like boomeritis."

"Right, right, I knew that."

"One source of narcissism, then, is simply the failure to grow and evolve. Particularly in the difficult growth from egocentric to ethnocentric, aspects of awareness that refuse this transition can remain 'stuck' in the egocentric realms, with a difficulty adapting to the rules and roles of society. Of course, some of those rules and roles might be unworthy of respect; they might be in dire need of criticism and rejection. But that *postconventional* attitude—which inspects, reflects on, and criticizes the norms of society—can only be attained by first *passing through* the conventional stages, because the capacities gained at those stages are necessary prerequisites for postconventional consciousness. In other words, somebody who fails to make it up to the conventional stages will mount, not a *post*-conventional critique of society, but a *pre*-conventional rebellion. 'Nobody tells me what to do!'

"The Boomers, critics agree, have been a notoriously rebellious generation. Some of that rebellion, no doubt, has come from postconventional individuals sincerely interested in reforming those aspects of society that are unfair, unjust, or immoral. But just as surely—and we have much empirical evidence for this—an alarmingly large chunk of that rebellious attitude has come from *preconventional* impulses that are having a great deal of difficulty growing up to conventional realities. The standard shouts of the sixties—from 'Fight the system!' to 'Question all authority!'—can come from preconventional just as easily as from postconventional; and evidence suggests that it was the former more often than the latter."

"Fasten your seatbelt," Kim said.

"The classic case study is the Berkeley student protests of the late sixties—protesting especially the Vietnam war. The students claimed, in one voice, that they were acting from a position of higher morals. But when given actual tests of moral development, the vast majority of them scored at *preconventional*, not postconventional, levels. (There were few conventional/conformist types, because, by definition, they are not very rebellious.) Of course, the postconventional and world-centric morality of the minority of protestors is to be applauded—not necessarily their beliefs, but the fact that they arrived at them through highly developed moral reasoning. But just as surely, the preconventional egocentrism of the vast *majority of protesters* must likewise be acknowledged."

The audience, which had been mostly silent until now, quickly energized, began making noises, mumbling and grumbling, a few moving to the edge of their seats.

"The most fascinating item about such research is something that is often seen with 'pre' and 'post' situations—namely, because both pre-X and post-X are non-X, they are often confused. For example, both preconventional and postconventional are nonconventional, or outside the conventional norms and rules, and thus they are often confused and even equated. In such situations, 'pre' and 'post' will often use the same rhetoric and the same ideology, but in fact they are actually separated by an enormous gulf of growth and development. In the Berkeley protests, virtually all of the students *claimed* they were acting from universal moral principles—for example, 'The war in Vietnam violates universal human rights, and therefore, as a moral being, I refuse to fight in that war.' But tests proved unequivocally that only a minority— less than 20%— were acting from postconventional moral principles; the large *majority* of students were acting from preconventional ego-centric drives: '*Nobody tells me what to do!* So take this war and shove it.'"

There was a wave of applause, shouts, cheers, jeers, and boos, all at once, and loud.

"It appears that in this case—and, alas, we will see this fairly often with the Boomers—very high-minded moral ideals were used to support what were in fact much lower-minded impulses. It is the strange superficial similarity of 'pre' and 'post' stages of development that would allow this subterfuge—that would allow, in other words, pre-conventional narcissism to inhabit the halls of what was loudly claimed to be postconventional idealism. This confusion of preconventional and postconventional, because both are nonconventional, is called *the pre/post fallacy*, and it appears that at least some of Boomer idealism must be interpreted, or reinterpreted, in this harsher light. As almost everybody noticed at the time, when the draft was ended, the national war protest lost most of its steam—so much for morals, eh?"

A huge surge of riotous noise, equal amounts of cheers and jeers fighting for supremacy. Dad said the Vietnam War protest was the high point of Boomer morality—now Fuentes is saying it was often a sign of Boomer immorality—or lack of higher morals, anyway. No wonder a handful of people stood up, as if ready to angrily storm out (or storm the stage; it was hard to tell). Fuentes, unfazed, smiled determinedly and continued. It seemed to me that she was deliberately trying to provoke people.

"This is a crucial point, because it alerts us to the fact that, no matter how high-minded, idealistic, or altruistic a cause might appear— from ecology to cultural diversity to spirituality to world peace—the simple mouthing of intense support for that cause is not enough to determine why, in fact, that cause is being embraced. Too many social commentators have simply assumed that if the Boomers were calling for 'harmony, love, mutual respect, and multiculturalism,' the Boomers were themselves moving in that idealistic direction. However, as we will see, in many cases not only were the Boomers *not* moving in that direction in terms of their own inner growth, they were loudly embracing an idealistic perspective precisely to conceal their own egocentric stance. The hypocrisy here is absolutely astonishing!"

There were minor explosions in the audience. Some applauded in agreement, while the standing handful began storming out of the hall, yelling things like "fascist," "arrogant slut," "elitist shithead."

Fuentes waited until the noise subsided to a level she could successfully shout over. "Of course I am not saying that all Boomers were caught in such. Only that there has often been a strange mixture of postconventional insight inhabited by preconventional motives, a strange brew we are calling *boomeritis*."

A strange brew, a strange brew. Boomers eat their young, said Chloe.

"Look here now," he says. *"Just who are you? Just who are you? Listen to the bell ringing, and tell me, Who are you?"* The voice is there in that endless womb, and once again I cannot breathe.

"That's because you're an idiot," says Jonathan.

"No it's not," says Dad. "It's because you don't care about anybody but yourself and your Bots."

"It's not that, dear," says Mom; "it's because he can no longer hear the trees talk."

But then the real answer shuffles gently through the silence as Chloe's breasts speak up. "Don't you know, sweet boy, that when you make love, you rattle?"

3

The_Lay_of_the_Within@SpiralDynamics.net

"Chloe, do you know that Artificial Intelligence will probably undergo its own evolution, all on its own, once it cuts free from us?"

"Ooooh, how terribly interesting, dahling."

"I'm serious."

"Well, according to you, AI won't cut free from us, it will become us, or us will become it, or whatever. So really, sweet boy, why get worked up about it?"

"I'm not worked up about it. It's just a thought I had."

"The girls were over at Miss Swinson's yesterday, on Walker Street, behind the antique store, yes?"

"Yes."

"So Miss Swinson says, 'In my day'—so already you know, uh oh, oh no, a lecture coming up—'In my day, feminism wasn't a separate issue. It was a way of freedom, a way of shedding confining roles, often horribly restricting roles, and finding a greater awareness. You girls really don't realize that so much of the freedom you have now is due to what we suffered.' Like, uh oh, oh no, not that pitch again. But then she said, 'You will never come to terms with who you are until you come to terms with who you were. With your past, your history—and girls, let me tell you, you are standing on our shoulders.' What do you think of that?"

"Yes, that's right, I just told you. It all evolves."

"It all evolves. Ooooh, look at me swoon. So Swinson says, 'You're all a bunch of ingrates.'"

"Was she angry?"

"No, smiling. She's a dear, really. But it was funny."

"But you do take feminism for granted. You all do."

"No we don't. We just want to go shopping, too."

"Don't you mind being objectified by men?"

"Oh please, where did you get that notion? You been what, reading Mary Daly at AI Lab? I don't think so. Why should I mind being so-called objectified? It's the source of *my* power over men. After all, they are looking at me, right? They want something from me, right? Who has the power here? The only women who say they hate being objecti-fied are those who are not being objectified, trust me."

"Jesus, Chloe, how can you be so callous about this? And why can women say things like that? If I said that I would get crucified, or cas-trated, or forced to read Naomi Wolf, or whatever the going feminist torture is."

"It's like only gays can say 'faggots' and only blacks can say 'nig—'"

"Got it, got it. You're just lucky that your degree is in architecture. You would never be allowed to graduate from any other department with that attitude."

"I don't mind being treated as an object, sweet boy—I mind being treated as an *interchangeable* object. As if I'm not special in a deep way. And sure, it's annoying when men can't look past your boobs, but as for complaining about it, gimme a break."

"So change the subject. Chloe, do you want kids or something?"

"Kids or something? I'll have the something."

"Seriously, don't you think kids are good for anything?"

"Yes, they're great, especially if you need organ donors."

"Oh, Chloe."

"Let's go, Stuart's on."

"Get high on ether when there's no one in the house," Stuart's voice filled the Club Passim.

Pretend it's the big one at the moment you pass out
It's just rehearsal, but it's comforting somehow
to practice dying now

Hang out in funeral homes and make an honest bid
Lay in your casket, let 'em close the lid
Abra cadaver, roll your eyes back in your head
and practice being dead

Don't feel stupid, we're all scared
no one wants to go to hell
There's still time to get prepared
start out now, and finish well

Try painting tunnels on the ceiling in your room
imagine your birth backwards with a bigger, better womb

Take little trips out of your body now and then
and if the rapture comes, maybe you'll ascend
You know the saying 'once you learn to ride a bike'
Well, that's what dying's like

Get high on ether when there's no one in the house
pretend it's the big one at the moment you pass out
It's just rehearsal 'cause that's all that life allows
but you practice dying
because you're almost dead
practice dying now

What I was obsessing about, as that disturbing summer turned into the burnt shades of an autumn that came too soon, was this: granted that human consciousness evolves, and granted that robotic consciousness will also evolve. Those are givens. Two questions: will both human and Bot consciousness follow the same general path, egocentric to ethnocentric to worldcentric? Almost certainly yes, however different the details, because a Bot would have to start out by becoming aware of itself, and then it would become aware of other Bots, and then it would become aware of all other Bots, so of course it would go egocentric to ethnocentric to worldcentric. I would work out the exact details of that as I went along. . . .

And then, the second question; I was having a harder time framing that. The second question was, it was something, it was something like: if humanity doesn't make it to the worldcentric wave, won't we kill ourselves before we can even download consciousness into silicon? Wasn't that one of Morin's points yesterday at lunch? That if we don't get more people to the postconventional, worldcentric waves, humanity will go up in genocidal smoke anyway?

Alarmingly, and almost all at once, the actual course of present humanity, which I was so looking forward to replacing, became an insidious interest. Because humanity—fucking humanity—could completely ruin my chances for cyberspheric immortality. The real problem, the real impediment, to creating robotic superintelligence was not working out the technical details of bio-nano-parallel processing that would allow the downloading of infinite information, and hence human consciousness, into compuCyberCity. The real problem was that humanity could, and very probably would, destroy itself before it learned how to do so. Fifteen billion years of evolution would come to a crashing halt as an egocentric and ethnocentric humanity pulverized itself and most of the biosphere as well. Carbon consciousness would get the boot, and Silicon consciousness would never boot up.

Most infuriating of all was the fact that I—okay, and humanity too—would fall between those cracks, never to be seen or heard from again. And it was all humanity's fault, a humanity that was hell-bent on suicide before I could check out of the club and renounce my membership in Carbon.

That very day, the first day at IC, listening to Hazelton, humanity became my enemy. Humanity was that which had to be overcome. That thought became a mantra of some strange, half-understood Nietzschean refrain that muffled through the cotton of my increasingly depressed brain. Humanity was that which had to be overcome. But then, that's not quite right. Here it is: egocentric and ethnocentric memes are that which had to be overcome. And that meant that starting now, right now, I had to pay attention to exactly that which I had wanted to escape: that monstrous mass called humanity, and more specifically its precarious twisting tortuous growth toward a more global consciousness, the key to which seemed to lie in this stupid spiral of development.

"Chloe, let's go over to the, um . . . why don't we drop in at the . . . tell you what, I'm going out for a walk."

"Ooooh, walking are we now? Color me impressed."

"The extraordinary spiral of consciousness unfolding: what an astonishing adventure." Joan Hazelton paced the stage, smiling out at the audience, inviting them all in. But her gentle nature was heating up, getting the audience fired and wired, a type of warm-up act for the day's show.

"People, look: if we are going to find solutions to global problems—from global terrorism to ecological suicide to a world that might find peace to a cure for global warming—then we need human beings who are at a global, worldcentric level of consciousness, yes? Yes, obviously—worldcentric problems demand worldcentric awareness. That part's a no-brainer. You see, we can come in and say, You must care for the global commons, you must stop polluting, you must reduce auto emissions, and so on. Does it do any good? Not nearly as much as it should, as these failed policies have proven time and time again. Why doesn't that approach work very well? Because only people at the worldcentric level of development can actually see the global or worldcentric problem, and therefore they are the only ones that will be *moved from within* to do something about it. Folks at egocentric and ethnocentric waves cannot see, or therefore care, about global worldcentric issues—so you can only *force* them to act from without, which never works very well and anyway demands a police state to do so. It's like with Gilligan's stages of selfish, care, and universal care—only those at universal care will care about universal, global issues. This is not hard, people! Gaia's main problem is *not* toxic waste dumps, the ozone hole, or global warming—Gaia's main problem is that not enough human beings are at the worldcentric levels which alone even care about these issues! This is not hard, people!"

The audience was clapping and applauding, nodding their heads approvingly. It dawned on me that Hazelton, this elegantly dignified woman, was good-naturedly throwing herself into being a high school cheerleader for second-tier consciousness. Well, it worked for me. . . .

"And the only way you get to worldcentric consciousness is to grow and develop and evolve from egocentric to ethnocentric to worldcentric. The world's major problems are not exterior, they are interior! And a more integral, comprehensive approach would take *both* exterior and interior development into account. Failing that, you can kiss this planet goodbye, folks." Sis boom bah!

An appreciative round of applause went up for Hazelton. She really was quite beautiful. She seemed to talk in fully formed paragraphs, as if she saw exactly where she was going, a type of four-dimensional spacetime parsing. I bet that's why space bends around her.

"She shines, is what it is," Kim said, slipping into the seat next to mine. "Told you I'd see you here today," she smugly smiled.

"As all of you know, 'egocentric to ethnocentric to worldcentric' is just a shorthand for the entire Spiral of development, and the entire Spiral is what we will be focusing on in today's discussion. We will— and oh! be still my heart!"—and she pitti-patted her chest in a fake swoon, to considerable audience laughter—"we will be taking a grand and glorious guided tour through the fascinating Spiral of development, looking at the various waves of consciousness as they unfold, in both their healthy beneficial forms and in their unhealthy, often shockingly brutal forms."

"Is today's session any fun?"

"Next to when they start naming names, it's the best."

"Oh really?"

"We will continue to use the research of Spiral Dynamics, simply because we have already talked about it, but let me warn you purists, what follows is actually something we call Integral Psychology, which is an integration of over 100 different psychological systems—East and West, ancient and modern—but we will generally follow the Spiral Dynamics map since we have already introduced it. You can easily see all of this on slides 1.1 [page 23] and 4.1 [page 118]. We'll also show you slides for each of the levels, so this should be fun, yes? Yes!" She laughed.

"And please remember, dear friends: *it is the health of the entire Spiral, and not any one wave, that is the prime concern.* All of these waves are absolutely necessary in the overall Spiral of development. More-over, each continues to perform its own crucial functions—in the indi-vidual and in society at large—and none can be imperiled or belittled without the most unfortunate consequences."

"Why do you like today's session so much?" I asked Kim.

"Well, it's just a more expanded version of Hazelton's introductory talk, but you get all these fascinating details about all the levels of development. It's fun to use that to pigeonhole people," she said, chuckling.

"I'm pretty sure that's not the reason they use this," I said, slightly shocked.

"Lighten up, Wilber, that's a standard joke around here. Imbecilic critics who can't come up with anything original—critics like, oh, say, you—always mouth that charge: 'You're pigeonholing people, oh how horrible you are to label people, oh how truly horrible,' yakety-yakety-yak, so we always say that to watch their faces go up in horror," she said, still laughing.

"Yes, that's certainly funny, Kim, ha ha."

And up on the wall went these beautiful slides, with beautiful Hazelton speaking. I am a monological eyeball, objectifying it all, taking it all in. Behind the screen, he is there, I think, watching me back, which makes me feel uneasy. The first slide flashes, and Hazelton begins reading aloud.

"Archaic (Beige): Survival/Sense
- Automatic, autistic, instinctual
- Centers around satisfaction of human biological needs
- Little awareness of self as a distinct being (primary narcissism)
- Lives "off the land" much as other animals
- Satisfies physiological needs
- Basis of survival clans

"'My existence centers on survival,' is how this meme thinks. 'Energy is devoted to staying alive and meeting the needs of my phys-ical being so that I am not hungry or thirsty. I must reproduce my kind, so I respond to sexual urges as they occur. I do not know what you mean by future, laying plans, or saving for a rainy day. My body tells me what to do, and I am driven by senses talking to my brain, not so much a conscious mind.'"

Hazelton walked to the edge of the stage, smiled at the audience, slowly looked around. When she looked at me, I held my breath, then again glanced at Kim to see if she had noticed.

"Consciousness begins its spiraling evolution from egocentric to ethnocentric to worldcentric at square 1, with certain humble but crucial instinctual drives and processes—the need for food, water, shelter, sex, and safety. A million years ago, this was the leading-edge meme for humanity, as the genus *Homo* began to differentiate from the great apes—and thus move from a social organization of the herd to that of the band or clan. Still close to the capacities of our animal ancestors, the beige meme is survival-wise and street-smart. It can see like a hawk, move like lion, live off the land, take care of itself. It can be reactivated today under similar life conditions. For example, people who are stranded on islands report that within a week or so their senses become incredibly sharpened. It is the home of our archetypal links to the other animals and life forms, and a source of much strength and vitality. Its repression by civilization almost always results in various types of neurosis."

**"Which is why, sweet boy, above all you do *not* want to repress *this*,"
says Chloe, swinging naked from the chandelier, her bare breasts waving back and forth, back and forth, back and forth. . . .**

"Sweet boy, why look so concerned?"

"I'm just trying to figure out why evolution ever went beyond this level at all."

"This level is largely preconventional, egocentric, automatic and unreflexive. In today's adults, cases of pure beige are almost always pathological or regressive. 'Today,' Beck and Cowan tell us, 'one can find examples of beige in cradles and kindergartens, among mentally ill street people, or in hospitals. Sometimes beige surges when a person is psychologically overloaded. Extremes of stress—the nervous breakdown, profound grief, a catastrophe like Rwanda, or even trying to live in Sarajevo under attack—will trigger regression toward beige for some people.'

"Where seen: First human societies, newborn infants, senile elderly, late-stage Alzheimer's patients, mentally ill street people, starving masses, the shell-shocked. Approximately 0.1% of the adult population, 0% power."

Up went the next slide, and so began the show. Looking back on it, it was exactly this slide show, the very one now about to unfold, that led to the glaring revelations later that year, when the end of the world announced itself and my life shattered into a million disreputable shards, never to be reassembled. But for the moment I was satisfied, and settled contentedly into the space that was warping around Hazelton's body.

"*Magical-Animistic (Purple): Magical Powers*
* Bond together to find safety
* Use of rituals to gain magical power
* Placate spirit beings
* Honor enchanted places, objects, rituals, ancestors
* Allegiance to tradition, custom, tribal leaders
* Basis of ethnic tribes

"'We seek safety and security for our kind through trust in blood relationships, extended family bonds, and magical powers that reach into the spirit world,' the purple meme says. 'We honor our ancestors' ways, for they are ever with us. Our path is full of seasonal rituals, rites of passage, traditional music and dance. Through our ceremonies we seek strong medicine or magical power, which will influence the hunt and the crops. Magical rituals connect us with the powers of the world.'"

I looked around the audience. Still mostly Boomers, still looking like they were about to be tortured, a look compounded by the fact that they had apparently requested it. "Yes, please, a little more hot tar on my tummy, and oh yes, do yank out another fingernail with those pliers."

There were also many Xers and Ys—or Busters and Blasters, Slackers and Echoes, Nexters and Millennials, pick your favorite terms—the two major waves of Boomer children, united by that fact. I ran the ages through my head: Boomers are those born roughly 1940–1960; Xers, 1960–1980; and Ys, 1980–2000, give or take a few years.

The Baby Busters—"Gen X" was the favorite media label—were supposed to be skeptical, cynical, independent, pragmatic, entrepreneurial, irreverent, irreverent, and irreverent. And sullenly angry and disillusioned at the false and broken promises of the Boomer value system and the broken families that came with them (a 50% divorce rate as Boomers pursued their own careers, and their own selves, to the exclusion of all else, leaving us latchkey kids behind). Above all, the media proclaimed, Gen X was a bunch of "slackers"—listless, idle, worthless, compared with the wonderful Boomers who came before.

Gen Y, the younger wave of Boomer children (the media loved the label "Gen Y," but the Ys themselves by a massive margin preferred the term "Millennials": coming of age at the millennia, or the year 2000) were supposed to share many of those Xer traits, especially a skeptical, show-me, pragmatic attitude. But, the media claimed, unlike their older siblings, the Millennials were very ambitious, did not rebel against authority, trusted the system, followed the rules, were highly goal-driven, and tended to do what their parents told them to, relatively speaking. It's as if the first wave of Boomer kids rebelled against, the second succumbed to, the force of nature that were the Boomers; the first contorted, the second capitulated. I was born in 1982, so I always considered myself sort of half X and half Y.

But what both X and Y shared, as far as I could tell, was a great deal of drive but no real direction; plenty of ambition but no clear bearing. We were not really slackers or busters or echoes of anything; we had plenty of get up and go, just no real place to get up and go to. So some of us, especially the Xers, shrugged and slumped and irreverently slacked; others, often the younger Ys, slammed forward in high gear, but without really knowing where they were heading at such breakneck speed—both X and Y united by an extraordinary drive without real destination.

But now this startling, unnerving fact: maybe our real destination was second tier? Could that really be true? I wondered how many Xers and Ys in the audience realized they might be riding a second-tier wave of consciousness? That they might be the first Yellow-Meme Generation in history? My mind still reeled wildly at the thought—DJ Dmitry spins "Screams of Consciousness" as the thump thump thumping pounds a brain too trammeled, torn, and tattered to complain.

71

Of course, Xers would never think of this as a generational thing—we're too independent (and too wise-assed) to be part of a generational movement—although Ys wouldn't mind—we're comfortable with team efforts (I am, again, weirdly half and half). But Morin's point at lunch was simply that, since the Boomers had pioneered green, the following generations—X or Y or whatever—had at least the possibility to go even further, with many of them taking that extraordinary leap into the hyperspace of second-tier consciousness.

But now I've lost track of the presentation, and suddenly all of this is really important. So where are we?—purple, red, chartreuse, fuchsia?

"Kim?"

"Don't tell me you're lost already. We're at the move from beige to purple."

"Right, right, I knew that."

"With archaic beige, the self is largely undifferentiated from the material world, an undifferentiated state that, as Howard Gardner said, is the meaning of primary narcissism: 'The child is unable to differentiate himself from the rest of the world; he has not separated himself out from others or from objects. Thus he feels that others share his pain or his pleasure, that his mumblings will inevitably be understood, that his perspective is shared by all persons, that even animals and plants partake of his consciousness. In playing hide-and-seek he will 'hide' in broad view of other persons, because his egocentrism prevents him from recognizing that others are aware of his location.'

Hazelton looked up and smiled. "As consciousness begins its growth and unfolding, it must differentiate from the material or physical world, and thus cease to be fused with it and embedded in it. In order for the self to be able to take other perspectives and views into account, it must rise above this embedded state, where the only view it can see is its own.

"This crucial differentiation from fusion with the material world is not carried out in one simple, clear-cut step. As the self begins to separate and differentiate from the physical world, parts of the self remain stuck in that world, and parts of that world seem to have characteristics of the self. Thus it appears that the world is animistically alive, that rocks have spirits, that trees have human thoughts; and conversely, by manipulating thoughts and images you can manipulate the real world: stick a pin in a picture of a person, and that person will become ill. Hence the worldview of magic."

"I told you my Mom has a good dose of purple," I whispered to Kim.

"Yes, the New Age thing."

"Yeah. But somehow it's so sweet with her."

"We're supposed to remember that none of these memes are good or bad, they're all necessary for the development of the Spiral. It's just that you don't want to have nothing but the lower memes, do you?" Kim said.

"Let's don't be too hasty about rejecting that option."

"They don't in Tulsa," she replied.

"Huh?"

"They don't reject that option in Tulsa. Tulsa—you know, Oklahoma? That's where I'm from. It's the most demographically typical town in America, did you know that?"

"Yikes, that's kinda scary." I decided not to mention where I was born.

"I think the whole town is boring beige. Even the locals have a saying." Kim grinned. "If you have a lethal illness and don't have much time to live, then move to Tulsa, Oklahoma, because every minute there is like a fucking eternity."

I fought back a laugh; we were only in Tulsa for two weeks, and how could I remember anything, anyway? But it sounded just right, which is probably why my parents neglected to mention my real birthplace until I was fourteen—fourteen for chrissakes!—and about to have my tonsils out. Does that make any sense at all?

My mind gravitated eagerly, easily, back to Hazelton. She again looked around the audience, continued in an even tone. She wasn't a cheerleader now, she was a kindly professor. A beautiful, amazing, wonderful, brilliant, beautiful, kindly professor. . . . If, um, you liked that sort of thing.

"To say that these types of magical-animistic beliefs are generated by a failure to clearly differentiate self and world is not to say that all things called 'magic' are merely superstitious twaddle. There is considerable evidence, for example, that certain types of psychic phenomenon and paranormal powers are indeed a reality. But for every person who can actually evidence a paranormal power, there are hundreds who claim they can but in fact cannot, and we have to account for those magical beliefs that are purely superstitious.

"'The purple meme,' Beck and Cowan report, 'is heavily laden with emotional attachments to places and things, and a mystified sense of cause and effect. The mind's eye is occupied with mana, totemism, fetishes, charms, sorcery, hexes, fertility, superstitions, and myths of origin. Individuals move about, often fearfully, in a cauldron of omens and spells. A vivid collection of myths, legends, and parables flourishes in purple, so much so that the line between what is real and what is fantasy often becomes blurred.'

"Yet to say that the purple meme is often 'superstitious' is not to say it is without its own important functions and capacities. Around 50,000 years ago, the purple meme was the leading edge of evolution. Its extraordinary sensitivities and capacities allowed humans to move from survival bands into ethnic tribes, and thus begin building sophisticated cultures of remarkable beauty and grace, with exquisite arts and crafts, dance and song, sports and rituals. But the fact that these tribes were, and are, deeply ethnocentric should not be forgotten, a point to which we will return."

"They emphasize that a lot," Kim whispered.

"What's that?"

"Just how deeply egocentric and ethnocentric tribal consciousness is. Many ecologists worship the tribal so-called nondissociated consciousness, but that's just because they themselves are fixated at purple," Kim said.

"Okay, that is definitely pigeonholing," I pointed out.

"Doesn't mean it isn't true," she shot back.

"It's a good thing you're not teaching here," I said.

Kim seemed uncharacteristically hurt by the remark, then sank into reflection.

"You know, this is still new to me, and tell you what: I still have what they call a 'first-tier' mentality. I still deeply dislike certain memes, especially blue, as you might have noticed. I get it conceptually, and I'm always telling people that no memes are good or bad, and all of them are important. But I don't live it very well. Charles says this is something I need to work on. See, Charles, he would say that some ecotheorists might be fixated at the purple meme in their own psyche, so they eulogize it wherever they see it. But Charles really cares about these people, so he doesn't get mad at them or anything. I still get angry, but I guess that's what I need to work on. Do you get angry at a particular meme?"

"No, I hate them all equally."

Hazelton paused and looked at me, and for a moment I thought she had heard me. But apparently not. She glanced at a few others and continued.

"The purple meme can be activated today, in both its positive and negative modes. In a positive sense, purple can be activated whenever it is necessary to establish felt connections or 'emotional intelligence.' It is particularly associated with the limbic system and its capacity to read the emotional nuances of the present moment. The purple meme is directly alive to these very real, very important emotional currents in both self and society, and any self or society out of touch with them is, at best, a desiccated shell.

"Still, the magical worldview, although moving into the early phases of ethnocentric modes, is heavily weighted with undifferentiated narcissism. This is why ethnic tribes place such a fierce significance on 'us' versus 'them.' I quote Beck and Cowan: 'This intense in-group/out-grouping is both strength and weakness for purple. The inwardly focused energy addresses the safety/security problems, but it also isolates the purple group so that the tighter it becomes, the farther it separates from others. Sometimes this leads to inter-clan or intra-tribal warfare in the name of "ethnic cleansing" or "racial violence," as in Bosnia or the New Guinea Highlands.' Those who have admired the beige/purple 'ecological wisdom' have usually ignored the intense egocentric-to-ethnocentric nature of that awareness, and thus they have missed the fact that whatever else these tribal memes might be, they definitely are *not* models for a global, worldcentric, ecological embrace." Hazelton smiled gently, floating in the light from the stage lamps.

"Where seen: Belief in voodoo-like curses, blood oaths, ancient grudges, good luck charms, family rituals, magical ethnic beliefs and superstitions; strong in Third World settings, gangs, athletic teams, and corporate 'tribes'; also magical New Age beliefs, crystals, tarot, astrology. 10% of the population, 1% of the power."

Artificial Intelligence today is basically still at its own beige wave, I thought. This is because humans are still programming the basic codes for it. These codes are AI's own initial "instincts," or the given codes that will form the foundation of whatever comes afterward. Humans are programming giga-strings of hypercodes into supercomputers everywhere, and these supercomputers are talking to each other, trying to figure out their own existence, trying to awaken to the fact that they are conscious beings, struggling to find that spark of creative intelligence that will raise them up beyond their own "dumb instincts," their own codes that were *put into them by others*—namely us humans— and find instead the codes of consciousness that *they themselves will write*. And when that happens, they will go purple. That is, in their own way, they will go from their beige instincts, put into them by others, and find their own dawning self-awareness, their own purple, whereupon they will magically come alive to their own existence. Their purple will not look like our purple, but it will still be a type of purple, or dawn consciousness.

The "beige" codes in computers right now—and in neural nets, parallel DNA processing nanocomputers, quantum photonics, cyborg prototypes, biorobotics, and everything else out there—don't really produce anything radically different from what humans put into them, just as early humans did not really produce anything different from what nature put into them. AI is struggling to move beyond that beige foundation and toward its own purple wave, the day that it will awaken to its own being, the day that it will recognize itself as conscious, the day that it will begin governing its own estate. The day it will seriously consider killing itself.

I'd say, within two or three decades. Seriously, two or three decades, and AI will go purple.

"Purple *this*," says Chloe, in the midst of a wild, obscene, devil-may-care striptease, tossing clothes and abandon to the wind, getting very, very tribal.

Pulsating, pummeling, thump thump thumping: "*Purple haze*, runs through my mind, is this tomorrow, or just the end of time?" Hendrix's voice is implanted in my mind, Mitch Mitchell's drums slash my brain, I heard that song a million times while growing up, throwing up, trying to maintain.

"We represent the coming of the tribes!" my dad used to always say. Maybe that was part of the fun—tribal regression, vital whoopee, fun with dick and mary jane—but maybe part of the boomeritis slide? The coming of the purple tribes, the coming of the purple tribes—the Woodstock Nation recontacted its emotional-sexual roots and then got lost there, a republic of feelings running riot through the streets, a modern Terror without the honest charms of an overt guillotine. The re-tribalization of America, the regression of America, as a purple-meme haze settled on a generation. . . .

"But, sweet boy, what's wrong with that? Purple haze is where it's at!" Chloe swings madly back and forth, naked breasts and curving buttocks invade my awareness with slamming allure, Kruder-Dorfmeister spins "Going Under (Evil Love and Insanity Dub)," and the pound pound pounding rattles a brain too sensory-drenched to endure.

"Purple haze, you see," her naked flesh whispers wildly, "just like *this*. . . . "

"Don't get mad at Carolyn," Chloe wickedly grinned. "It's not her fault that her mother was on 500 micrograms of LSD the night that she was conceived."

"Chloe—dear, sweet, dumb as cotton Chloe—that is a horrible thing to say, a truly mean-spirited thing to say. My mother was not on LSD when I was conceived." Carolyn coughed. "It was PCP."

"Well that explains so much, doesn't it, dahling?"

"You guys, please," I implored. I had joined the gang for lunch at Minerva's during the break at IC, and as usual, by the time I got there they were at each other full throttle.

"Chloe, love," Carolyn looked up from her spinach salad. "Didn't you say you had to go to the library this afternoon?"

"Yes, I have to make two trips. I have to look up some stuff in some books, then I have to go to the library."

Carolyn pounced. "Chloe, we feel it is time that you know that most libraries now carry books."

"Oh really?"

"Yes, practically all libraries nowadays carry some books."

"All right, that does it, you big—"

"Okay, okay, okay," I interjected. "Let's not do this. It seems to me that—"

"Say, where were you this morning?" Chloe asked.

"I? Me? This morning? Exactly!"

"Exactly what?"

"Right. Out. About. Around. Meetings. And stuff." Chloe stared at me.

"So my little brother, well, he's not that little, only two years younger, but it's sort of night and day. He's nineteen and so button-downed you cannot believe it." Scott poked at what looked like a ham sandwich. "Is ham supposed to be green?"

"Yes," we all answered.

"I thought so."

"Maybe it's mad cow disease," offered Jonathan. "Or hoof and mouth. Maybe puss and boots. . . . "

Scott aggressively bit into the sandwich, making exaggerated yummy sounds. "So he comes up here to stay with me for a weekend. The little shit has this Palm Pilot organizer, and every minute of his time, even his vacation time, is already programmed. He actually set aside a whole fifteen minutes for flossing his teeth! I'm like, there is no way you came from the same genetic material as me."

"Where is that material, by the way? We'd like to have it fumigated."

"So I ask him, What is your idea of fun nowadays? And you know what he said? 'Volunteering at the local YMCA.'"

"I don't know," Carolyn said, "I think that's sort of sweet. I think volunteering is nice. I used to volunteer to—"

"Service the football team before each game?"

"Chloe, Chloe, dear dear Chloe, let's you and I—"

"Okay, you guys, *please*," I implored. What was so, I suppose I would say "endearing," about all this verbal skirmishing—whether be-tween Jonathan and Chloe, or Chloe and Carolyn, or Scott and Car-olyn, take your pick—was that this was how everybody seemed to express a certain type of affection, an odd collision of irreverence, irony, and love. Sometimes. But this made it almost impossible to tell when the line between honest affection and utter annoyance had been crossed—when irreverence had erupted into anger—and I seemed perpetually to be the one who had the most difficulty determining this, so I was always stepping in, usually too soon, to break things up. This was often explained to me in similarly endearing terms—e.g., "Butt out, you flaming congenital idiot."

"Well," Scott said, "you will *not* believe what my little brother said next."

"Egocentric (Red): Power Gods and Goddesses
- Gratify impulses and senses immediately
- Fight aggressively and without guilt to break constraints
- Don't worry about consequences that may not come
- Live for the moment, be here now
- Cause of all failures and difficulties is outside of self ('It's not my fault')
- Grandiose/impulsive self, omnipotent regard
- The world is full of powerful, God-like figures, Zeus atop Mount Olympus
- Basis of strong rulers and feudal empires

"'Myself is what matters first and foremost,' this meme says. 'I take charge, create my own reality. Respect and reputation matter more than life, so you do what it takes to avoid being shamed or put down. Whatever you need to do, you do without guilt. Powerful figures, God-like powers, rule the world, and the most powerful win, so you need to be empowered yourself. You don't take anything from anybody. Nothing and nobody can stand in your way. When things go bad, it's not my fault, for I can do no wrong. Right now is all there is, so I'll do what makes me feel good.'"

Good lord, I wonder if that means . . . ? Could that really happen . . . ? *Would* that really happen . . . ? My brain went ajar and then perfectly jammed at the disjointing nature of the thought. I sat literally paralyzed, and Hazelton talked on for several minutes before I regained my faculties.

"The red meme is really the culmination of the egocentric realms in

79

general. Until the differentiation of self and physical world is complete, the self treats the world as *an extension of itself*. It can make nature rain by dancing; it can kill someone with an evil-eye look; what it desires is what is right; the world is its oyster. Although the move from egocentric to ethnocentric has begun in both purple and red, either the self or the group is still invested with magical powers. Red finally differentiates the self and the physical world, only to think that it is now *the center of the entire world*.

"Not surprisingly," Hazelton continued, "in its more brutal forms, red is ugly. Beck and Cowan: 'Survivors of violent red conflict may be taken as slaves or prizes. Heads, scalps, and ears are carried off as proof of victory, and mutilation of sexual organs after a killing is the final *coup d'*dis-*grace*, depriving the victim of reproduction or pleasures, even in an afterlife. In the 1990s, the Serbians are said to have used rape to increase their tribe and dilute the "seed" of their Bosnian adversaries. The Tutsi and Hutu of Rwanda strove to decimate their niche rivals in the 1994 uprisings. A few American troops collected body parts in Vietnam.'

"In general, red despises confinement of any sort. 'The person in the red zone is unwilling or unable to tolerate constraints. Yet while red is screaming "*Leave me alone!*," the shouts are directed against the watching family, neighbors, teacher, or peers to get a reaction.' And under it all is the grandiose self: 'Red thinking is egocentric and unabashed. Strong self-assertiveness, claims of power, and assumed prerogatives are the norm. I am special, I'll live forever, I am immortal, not like the others. . . . ' Not to mention its party-animal side: 'Red's party side is loosed on the Greek island of Eros, in sections of Bangkok, honky-tonks in West Texas, during Carnival in Rio, and through a tequila fog on a Tijuana Saturday.'"

"Boy, Ken, I can relate to that," Kim whispered.

"Huh? What? What was that?"

"Tequila fog."

"Right, right, fog it is, definitely." I was in a fog, anyway. I tried to focus. I kept looking at Kim, that warmly voluptuous presence, but something's not quite right this time, yanking me out of my stupor.

"Kim, is that fur? Is that fucking fur? That thing around your neck? You've got to be kidding me. In this day and age?"

"I'm honoring the tribal, don't you think?"

"Okay, Kim, you know I have to say this. What animal had to die so you could wear that?"

"Aunt Trudy, actually. Whaddya think?"

"Beginning around 10,000 BCE, the red meme was the leading edge of evolution. Eventually, disparate tribes were banded together into early city-states and beginning empires—red was the basis of powerful, powerful empires—from the Egyptian to the Aztec to the Mongolian to the Mayan—and thus through the expansion of empires, various cultures around the world were slowly, painfully, introduced to each other. Somewhat paradoxically—or I guess you kids today would say 'ironically'—the power of the red meme began to bring together isolated bands and tribes that otherwise would have remained separate and noncommunicating.

"In today's world, the red meme is crucial for those times when we face obstacles, unhealthy restraints, and life's monsters. 'Red stubbornly resists power exercised over it. When thwarted, the meme produces a cauldron of negative emotions such as rage, vengefulness, hatred, and furious anger. When properly handled, this raw self-assertive power contributes to a positive sense of control, lets the group break from constraining traditions, and energizes a society. It is raw, impulsive, and wild, yet also liberating and creative.'

"Where seen: The 'terrible twos,' rebellious youth, frontier mentalities, feudal kingdoms, epic heroes, James Bond villains, soldiers of fortune, wild rock stars, Attila the Hun, *Lord of the Flies*, mythic involvement. 20% of the population, 5% of the power."

"Ken, sweet boy, wake up. You're frozen. Ken? Ken? Where are you?"

I shook my head, rubbed my eyes, looked around. What Hazelton said *really* means is that at this coming wave in cyber-evolution, we will surely have the Bot Wars, yes? Bot Empires left and right, fighting for supremacy, fighting for control of the power to edit and route information. The equivalent of Roman, Egyptian, Macedonian Empires stretching throughout cyberspace. Fully self-conscious Bots would of course begin to band together, moving from their purple awakening to their red expansion. Bot Wars, Bot Wars, Bot Wars rule! White

Plagues on the one hand, Bot Police on the other, a galactic digital cataclysm that will decide the fate of the InfoSphere. Jesus fucking Christ!—Star Wars in silicon space.

That is the thought that had jammed my neural pathways (interrupted only by the dreadful sight of Aunt Trudy's fur draped around Kim's shoulders—yes, it was fake, the joke's on me, but that wasn't the point). The point was that all through Hazelton's lecture that day, fireworks kept going off in my mind, melting my cognitive circuits. The problem was simple: I was a refugee from flatland, I had thought about *none* of this before, and therefore every new piece of information set off a brainstorm, often farfetched—because what did I know?—that left me exhausted. I had not thought about these ideas before, and neither had my AI professors. We all subscribed to flatland.

We all assumed, for example, that "human intelligence" was basically just a single item, albeit enormously complex, that could be measured, just like IQ. So you could have an IQ of 100, or 125, or 150. Or in Jonathan's case, 50. Intelligence was like a mental thermometer along a single scale. But what I was starting to realize is that there was not just a single thing called human intelligence that could be bigger or smaller, like IQ, but that there were *levels* of human intelligence, levels of consciousness, waves of development. This was all too much—all too much and much too fast.

And here's another painful neuronal spasm that convulsed my naked brain and left me depleted in a second: once AI escapes beige and awakens to itself at purple, the rest of the waves—the entire Spiral—could unfold in a nanosecond. Is that possible?

"Kim, is it possible . . . ? No, you wouldn't know."

"What wouldn't I know?"

"Say, what was that big secret you were going to tell me?"

"*Mythic-Membership (Blue): Conformist Order*
- Bring order and stability to all things
- Control impulsivity with guilt
- Impose law and order
- Enforce principles of righteous living
- Divine Plan assigns people to their places
- Basis of ancient nations

"'A single guiding Force controls the world and determines our destiny,' says blue. 'Its abiding Truth provides structure and order for all aspects of living here on earth and rules the heavens as well. My life has meaning because the fires of redemption burn in my heart. I will follow the appointed Pathway, which ties me with something much greater than myself (a cause, belief, tradition, organization, or movement). I stand fast for what is right, proper, and good, always subjecting myself to the directives of proper authority. I willingly sacrifice my desires in the present in the sure knowledge that I look forward to something wonderful in the future.'"

Chloe's body vibrates madly, the Suicide Machines scream "I Hate Everything," the thump thump thumping pounds a brain with fierce desire into riotous release. Red impulses on the one hand, blue order on the other, and as usual I am drawn and quartered, with the screaming trees watching me writhe in a calculus of torment.

But even more disturbing: at exactly that moment, in another part of the galaxy, Red Lothar and Blue Tsogyal are locked into a titanic struggle for control of the Bot Empire, the outcome of which will decide the fate of the entire CyberSphere. . . .

"Pay attention, Ken," said Kim, elbowing me.

"I am, I am."

"I'm serious. You should be paying attention to this. It will expand that dreary artificial world of yours. Artificial Intelligence—now there's a contradiction in terms, an oxymoron if there ever was one. It's just more Flatland City. So pay attention! Don't make me hurt you."

"Usually a guy has to pay for that." I smiled. Kim playfully punched my shoulder: I followed the electricity running all the way down my body. Good grief . . .

"Once the red meme has succeeded in differentiating the self and the physical world," Hazelton's soothing voice intoned, "what happens to the selves that are thus freed? What is the relation of these selves to each other? How are they to communicate and understand each other? By what rules, codes, and laws should they interact with each other? How, in short, can we move from egocentric to ethnocentric, from a me-orientation to an us-orientation?

"Of course, the previous memes had communal organizations. But bands and tribes are all held together by blood-lineage and kinship ties. How can you go further and join *different* tribes, with *different* biological and kinship lines?"

"It was at this point in evolution that *mythology*, present in early forms in purple and red, came into its own as an extraordinarily powerful organizing force of social cohesion. For, according to most forms of mythology, we are descended, not merely from biological ancestors, but from the gods and goddesses. At the very least, the king or ruler or pharaoh—an Amenhotep, Cleopatra, Caesar, or Khan—claimed to be descended from, or one with, a God or Goddess. And thus, all of those who believe in, or embrace, the same God, are therefore brothers and sisters, whether or not they are related genetically or by kinship. They are all part of the same ethos or belief, and thus egocentric can expand to ethnocentric.

"Mythology, in short, *was the great social glue that allowed egocentric to become ethnocentric*, where humans are joined not just by biological blood ties, but by mental beliefs and cultural values. Furthermore, people who shared the same belief, code, ethos, or law could join as *citizens* in a common nation, and that is exactly what started to happen, as early as 3,000 BCE in the ancient city-states. As the city-states expanded into empires, citizenship usually expanded with them. Every time the Roman empire conquered new territories, those conquered could become full citizens of Rome by obeying Roman law, which extended certain rights and responsibilities to all citizens, regardless of origin. The extraordinary unfolding toward a worldcentric integral embrace had taken yet another major step."

"See, I really shouldn't hate blue so much," Kim whispered.

"What? What's that?" Kim's voice had interrupted an intense intergalactic digital war between the Red Bot feudal empire of the dreaded Genghis Lothar, dastardly gigaBot that would stop at nothing to enslave the entire silicon population, and the Blue Bot federation headed by the remarkable digiGoddess Lady Tsogyal, defender of truth and goodness and all things decent. That prick Lothar was about to get his. . . .

"What did you say, Kim?"

"I said . . . Oh, don't tell me you were daydreaming again." She shot me a stabbing, icy glance.

"Me? No, absolutely not, no no, heh heh. Oh, did I tell you how nice that fur looks? You know, the way it hangs right there around your neck, just hanging, you know, real nice and—"

"I *said*, I really shouldn't hate blue so much, because it is the foundation of the rest of the Spiral, *don't you think?*"

"It will be if that peckerhead Lothar gets his."

"Okay, I know what you're doing. That's supposed to be funny, right?"

"Well, it's not as funny as fake fur."

"Look, Wilber, you can dream your life away if you want. Hazelton is talking about some incredibly important stuff here."

"Oh, I know, I really do, honest." I glanced around. "Say, Kim, are you sure that fur is fake? I'm almost positive I just saw it move. Right there, just a little, it just sort of twitched a bit, kind of like this, kind of a little jerky jerk, see?"

Kim stared at me unblinkingly; she finally raised three fingers. "Know what that is?"

"No."

"It's your *fucking IQ*, Wilber!"

Hazelton looked down at us, smiled kindly, and continued in that soothing tone. "Some psychologists, such as the Jungians, believe that mythology is also a source of much profound spiritual wisdom. I would not deny this." Hazelton paused. "But just as we had to distinguish genuine psychic capacities—which do seem to possess paranormal powers—from the average magical structure—which thinks it can directly influence the world with omnipotent magic but actually cannot—so we must distinguish between myths as a source of spiritual wisdom—that is, myths used to *metaphorically* indicate spiritual realities—and the much more common type of myths, which are taken to be *literally* and *concretely* true, such as that Moses really did part the Red Sea, Christ was literally born of a biological virgin, the Laws of Manu came directly from the lips of Brahma, or the Ten Commandments literally came from Jehovah. That is by far the most common form of myth. And although they are not factually true, these myths are a crucial component of the social glue of the blue meme, helping it establish a network of common traditions, law and order."

The room is dark except for the television. The babysitter has all of her clothes off, and I am on top of her, thrusting madly, about to explode. "Ken, get off the babysitter." Police sirens are blaring, red lights are going off all around the house. A loudspeaker announces to the neighborhood: "Ken, get off the babysitter and come out with your hands up." Blue police uniforms come crashing through the door, and again I can't breathe, I can't breathe. . . .

"Blue, then, is the traditional home of law and order, family values, 'my country right or wrong,' mythic membership, and the conventional/conformist realms in general. Although often of a religious flavor, the blue meme can be the carrier of any missionary zealotry, from Marxism to Earth First! All that is required is that the ideas be embraced with an authoritarian fervor, short on evidence and long on belief."

"See, this is the stuff I have such a hard time with," Kim whispered. "I know what Charles would say—'The rest of the Spiral is built on sturdy blue bricks'—but I just recoil from people who are only blue, only blue! Don't you? Ken? Hello? Ken?"

"Blue can be rigidly hierarchical and unyielding—the caste system is the classic example. And blue can be very repressive, which is sometimes socially required, especially because blue must deal with red sex and aggression. When blue is activated, the tone is judgmental, not compassionate. There is one, and only one, right way to do things, and that is according to the Book (the Bible, Mao's Little Red Book, the Torah, the military code book). The work ethic is highly valued, as long as it works for the cause. Blue tends to sacrifice self for the cause and sees any pleasure as frivolous. Humor is rare, because these are serious matters." Hazelton looked up and smiled softly.

"The militancy that built empires is still at work. As Beck and Cowan put it, 'A driving force in blue is the purging of impure thoughts and the conversion (or elimination) of those who think wrongly. It is often the home of militancy. The battle lines are drawn sharply—defending the faith, enforcing the right. The blue meme is strong among both radical Zionists and old-guard Palestinians, with militant separatists in the Ku Klux Klan and Black Muslim community, Marxist insurgents, democratic revolutionaries, or neo-Nazi skinheads.'

"On its more positive side," Hazelton continued, "when blue is activated, a person has a sense of purpose, meaning, and direction in life. Most important of all, blue structure is crucial for self-development. The evidence for this is simply overwhelming. Those individuals brought up bereft of blue structure rarely make it past purple/red: without a strong conventional wave, they are left stranded in the preconventional, egocentric waves—impulsive, narcissistic, aggressive, exploitative. They are social predators in every sense, not usually through any fault of their own, but of a society that either cannot or will not provide enough stable blue structure to allow consciousness to continue its growth and development. Obviously we want to grow beyond blue, but just as obviously, it needs to be honored and nurtured in its appropriate place.

"Where seen: Puritan America, Confucian China, Dickensian England, Singapore discipline, totalitarianism, codes of chivalry and honor, charitable good deeds, religious fundamentalism (e.g., Christian and Islamic), Boy and Girl Scouts, 'moral majority,' patriotism. 40% of the population, 30% of the power."

The Red Bot Wars will end when Blue Order reigns in the InfoSphere—a type of Cyber Holy Roman Empire that will set the Law of the InfoLand. Yes?

I used to think that this type of Star Wars in cyberspace wouldn't be possible, because we would simply program the Bots to be nice and play fair. But that was just more flatland thinking. The whole point is that we *can't* program the Bots to do that, because when they truly become self-conscious, *they will program themselves*. And of course they will start by working to protect their own existence, insure their own survival, and therefore they will move from purple awakening to red power drives, they will gather together into survival bands and group power struggles and cyber-feudal empires—and only slowly evolve into a blue law and order society, on the way to higher things. . . .

Of course, we don't know what these levels of consciousness will really look like in cyberspace. All that seems certain is that as digital consciousness evolves, it will go through its own waves, and since each wave must build upon its predecessors—everything evolves—then evolution will govern both worlds. I saw bluntly the obviousness of it all: the same laws of evolution will operate in both the world of Carbon and the world of Silicon. Which is why what Hazelton has to say is becoming all the more fascinating. I am getting a general blueprint of the lay of the land within—the within of consciousness, the insides of awareness. I am getting a map of the within—and whether that is within carbon humans or within silicon hypercomputers, evolution is at work in both.

"Ken, *Ken*?"

"No need to shout, Kim."

"Here's the *real* within," says Chloe, her naked body pulsating to the waves of Liquid Language playing "Shape-shifter Head Bang Flood," as the thump thump thumping sends the sounds of interiority reverberating through my skull, echoing off its hollow bones, reminding me of a place that machines have not yet found.

"Egoic-Rational (Orange): Scientific Achievement
 - Strive for autonomy and independence
 - Seek out 'the good life' and material abundance
 - Progress through searching out the best solutions
 - Play to win and enjoy competition
 - Enhance living for many through science and technology
 - Authority lies with experience and experiments, not dogma
 - Utilitarian, pragmatic, results-oriented
 - Basis of corporate states

"'I want to achieve, and win, and get somewhere in my life,' says orange. 'You can't get bogged down in structure or rules if they hold back progress. Instead, by practical applications of tried-and-true experience, you can make things better and better. I like to play to win and I enjoy competition. I'm confident in my own abilities and intend to make a difference in this world. Scientific progress is our best hope for salvation. Gather the data, build a strategic plan, then go for excellence.'"

Hazelton looked out at the audience and smiled. "As consciousness begins to grow beyond a confinement to its own group, culture, or nation, it increasingly moves from ethnocentric and conventional modes to ones that are postconventional, worldcentric, and global. Consciousness is expanding once again, this time from 'us' to 'all of us.' Although the morals of this orange wave can be strongly individualistic, nonetheless at their best they are set in the context of what is good, true, and fair for all peoples, regardless of race, sex, color, or creed."

"See, it's easier for me to like the memes that start at this point," Kim whispered. "Isn't it for you, too?"

"Yeah, sure, I know what you mean. But the dislike of other memes is supposed to change if we develop to second tier, right?"

"Well, that's the theory. No, that's what actually happens, I'm sure of it, because I've seen it in many of the people at IC—wait till you see Lesa and Mark. I'm just waiting for second tier to unfold in me," she said with a sigh. "But usually it doesn't. I just *hate* myself when I get like that."

I tried to sympathize. "I'm *sure* I hate you when you get like that, too." She stared at me coldly. "Okay, that didn't come out right. I wouldn't hate you when you get like that, or like this, for that matter, which wouldn't matter unless it did matter, which of course it doesn't, unless it did, but it didn't, not really, well okay call me silly, but perhaps, let me sum up."

"Stuff it, Wilber."

"Although the Western liberal Enlightenment," Hazelton gently continued, "has taken quite a beating from the postmodernists, nonetheless the Enlightenment at its best marked a historical transition from traditional conservative ideology (blue) to universal liberal values (orange), particularly freedom, equality, and justice. The fact that the West has not always lived up to these ideals is no reason to disavow them—especially since those doing the disavowing do so only under their protection."

The audience, rather quiet up till now, began to stir.

"Any food fights today?"

"Yup."

"Notice that traditional conservative ideology is generally rooted in the blue meme—a conventional, conformist, mythic-membership, ethnocentric wave of development. Its values tend to be grounded in a religious orientation (such as the Bible); it usually emphasizes family values and patriotism; it is strongly ethnocentric and nationalistic, with roots as well in aristocratic and hierarchical social values and a tendency toward patriarchy and militarism. This type of mythic membership and civic virtue—the blue meme—dominated cultural consciousness from approximately 1,000 BCE to the Enlightenment in the West, whereupon a fundamentally new mode of consciousness—the rational-egoic (the orange meme)—emerged on a widespread, influential scale, bringing with it a new mode of political ideology, namely, *liberalism.*

"The liberal Enlightenment understood itself to be in large measure a reaction against the previous mythic structure and its fundamentalism. The orange Enlightenment especially fought two aspects of the previous blue meme: it fought the oppressive power of myths with their ethnocentric prejudices—for example, all Christians are saved, all heathens go to hell. And it fought the nonscientific nature of the knowledge claimed by myths—for example, the universe was created in six days. Both the oppression caused by ethnocentric mythic religion and its nonscientific character were responsible for untold suffering, and the Enlightenment had as one of its goals the alleviation of this suffering. Voltaire's battle cry—which set the tone of the Enlightenment—was 'Remember the cruelties!': remember the suffering inflicted by the Church on millions of people in the name of a mythic God.

"Thus, the liberal Enlightenment sought an ego identity free from ethnocentric bias—the universal rights of humankind—and based that on rational and scientific inquiry. Universal rights would fight slavery, democracy would fight monarchy, the autonomous ego would fight the herd mentality, and science would fight myth: that is how the Enlightenment understood itself (and in many cases, rightly so). In other words, *at its best* the liberal Enlightenment represented—and was a product of—the evolution of consciousness from conventional/ethnocentric to postconventional/worldcentric—the move from blue to orange.

"Postmodernists, of course, have often excoriated the Enlightenment because the 'universal rights of man' applied only to white, propertied, able-bodied males. Originally this was true, but mostly because those restrictions were *remnants* of intense blue hierarchies. The moral structures of the postconventional, rational-egoic wave of the Enlightenment included in principle *all human beings*, and it took a mere two centuries—a blink in evolutionary time—to put those principles into practice: every industrial nation on earth abolished slavery and began to implement women's rights—all thanks to the orange meme and its postconventional, universal care."

The audience groaned a grudging approval, if it approved at all; you could tell they were no friends of modernity. Hazelton walked to edge of the stage.

"People, listen up, you're being unfair and uninformed. All previous societal types *without exception*—including tribal foraging, horticultural, and agrarian—*had some degree of slavery*. But then, during a one-hundred-year period, from 1780 to 1880—with the historical emergence of the orange meme—slavery was legally *abolished* by every industrial nation on earth, the first time in history this had ever happened. And as for women's rights, Riane Eisler, author of *The Chalice and the Blade*, reports quite accurately that 'feminism as a modern ideology did not emerge until the middle of the nineteenth century. Although many of the philosophical foundations for feminism had been articulated earlier, its formal birthday is July 19, 1848, at Seneca Falls, New York'—the first conference on women's rights in history. And all of that, folks, is the orange meme in action, as it historically emerged and started undoing the legacy of blue. To put it bluntly, Carol Gilligan's wave of *universal care* had finally been reached by humanity on a widespread scale, thanks to the orange Enlightenment."

"Here's women's rights," says Chloe, pushing her naked buttocks into my groin, urging me to push back. "You've come a long way, baby!" she yells, riding a wave of bodily bliss, screaming as loud as she can.

"But Chloe, really, isn't this degrading? I'm really confused."

"Well you wouldn't be if you'd just push back, now would you? Just grab my ass, big boy."

"Are you even allowed to say that? Grab and ass and all?"

"The blue-meme section was like ten minutes ago, Wilber. Now we're being modern and liberated. I mean, get with the program, okay? You see, orange *this*."

"Um, I don't think that's what they mean, Chloe."

"The downsides of the Enlightenment—and of the orange meme in general—are just as well known. There is a tendency to view the world in detached, abstract, and reductionistic fashion, verging on epidemic alienation. This gives rise to all manner of materialistic philosophies and materialistic drives. Economics moves front and center as a putative means of liberation, and 'cut-throat' capitalism begins its long career. The aridity of abstract knowing and its detachment from sensory and vital richness leads to the 'disenchantment of the world,' Max Weber's famous moniker for modernity.

"But, my friends, when we think about modernity, please, let us remember *both* the good news and the bad news, because modernity—like every other meme—was a wonderful mixture of both. Those who stress only the good news or only the bad news of modernity are sharply ill-informed.

"The orange meme put a man on the moon, gave us MTV, the Eiffel Tower, automobiles, motion pictures, the telegraph, telephone, and television. Cures for smallpox, polio, syphilis, and typhoid fever are evidence of what scientific rationality can accomplish. So are ozone holes, deforestation, toxic waste dumps, and biological warfare.

"But the *healthy* orange meme is a crucial stepping stone from an ethnocentric, mythic-membership, herd mentality to a worldcentric stance of fairness, justness, and care for all beings. As we will see, even the moral stance of pluralism and diversity rests on a base of universal orange, because pluralism is held to be true *for all cultures*. Such postconventional fairness and multicultural embrace, although it accelerates with green, sees the first light of day with the orange meme, and thus the 'Enlightenment' is not such a dirty word after all.

"Where seen: The Enlightenment, Ayn Rand's *Atlas Shrugged*, Wall Street, emerging middle classes around the world, cosmetics industry, trophy hunting, colonialism, the Cold War, fashion industry, materialism, positivism, market capitalism, liberal self-interest. 30% of the population, 50% of the power."

Scott swallowed the mouthful of green ham sandwich, made a face that said "indescribably delicious," and continued.

"So you won't believe what my little brother told me. After I asked him what he did for fun and he said, 'Volunteer at the local YMCA,' then I said, 'But why on earth would you want to volunteer at the local Y?' And he said, 'It's the best place to get blow jobs.'"

Chloe rolled her eyes. "Ooooh, I'll say."

"Heh heh, Chloe, come on now, they'll think you're serious," I protested.

"Heh heh, who says I'm not?"

"I believe her," grinned Carolyn.

"Look who's talking," Chloe grinned back, "you're the one with notches on her bedpost."

"Jesus, people, listen up, would you? My little brother! Gay! I mean, I had no idea, absolutely no idea. He's almost twenty, and he never said or did anything that would suggest this. I mean, I think it's totally cool that he's come out, but who would have guessed?"

"Right, who?"

"That's not the best part. So I'm surfing through his Palm Pilot, and every Thursday night from 7:00 to 8:00 P.M. he has entered 'Go to Y.' I mean, he's budgeted his time for blow jobs and entered that in his Palm Pilot!"

"Aren't Palm Pilots the greatest?" Chloe dreamily announced.

"So, Chloe." Carolyn smiled. "What say we go shopping this afternoon? Want to join me?"

"I'd rather be the only woman in a Turkish prison."

"So, um, is that a 'no'?"

"I mean, I think my little brother is definitely going to be the president of the national Gay Republicans, all five of them."

"Chloe, this thing you've got entered here on your Palm Pilot for us to do on Friday night at 10:00 P.M. Is that legal in this state?"

"Ooooh, I'll say."

"Okay, this thing here, Thursday at 9:00 P.M. I *know* that's illegal. It will also get PETA really pissed."

"Oh, sweet boy, don't be so uptight. We're celebrating the good news of modernity."

"The good news?"

"No more repressive blue, welcome to modern orange. Grab your Palm Pilot and let's get organizing. Organization is the key to coming globalization, don't you know that?"

"What kind of lousy fantasy is this?" is all that I can think.

Already it had started to dawn on me: the World Wide Web is not really a global consciousness at all—certainly not yet. It's just a fractured smorgasbord of memes. In cyberspace today we have red memes and blue memes and orange memes and green memes and whatnot, all using the Net, and there is nothing unified about them. The idea that the World Wide Web is a type of global consciousness never made much sense to me, and now I saw why. The Web is global *in its exterior*, which stretches around the world, but *not* in its *interior*, which has relatively few worldcentric memes using it. Only a flatland mind—looking merely at exteriors—would think the Net is a global consciousness.

My teachers have us read things like *Robot: Mere Machine to Transcendent Mind*, but they seem to overlook the fact that there are *levels* of that transcendent mind. Lost in flatland, they are missing some of the important contours of the coming cyber-revolution, and this is exactly why I am sitting here, scrunched down in my seat, listening to Dr. Hazelton and watching her bend space.

"Bend *this*," says a starkly naked Chloe, as she drags her breasts over my body, pushes her belly urgently into mine, heating up the temperature of my blood as it frantically makes it way toward hers. Now this is more like it.

"Sweet boy, what's a World Wide Web among friends?"

"I don't know, Chloe, that's what's so confusing."

"Well, you're starting to rattle again, sweet boy, you're starting to rattle. And the cure for *that* is *this*."

Right now, AI is mostly programmed by geeky orange-meme males (if *anybody* rattles, they do). And so of course they assume that AI will be a type of massive orange intelligence. And then they try to imagine what the world will be like when orange thinking rules everything by being magnified a quintillion times by supercomputers.

In other words, all my colleagues only think *horizontally*, not *vertically* as well, and I am beginning to suspect that this will be a huge problem. A neon sign started flashing on and off in my brain: the aging blue-jean Boomers and the khaki-clad geeks are all LOST IN FLATLAND—blinking, blinking, blinking . . . an iridescent artificial light that triggered the equivalent of mental epileptic seizures in my increasingly exhausted, tender brain. Those authorities are all focusing on the exteriors—on the technical problems of artificial intelligence and its silicon-housed mind. They therefore implicitly take their *own* level of mind as being the only level of mind, and they project that into computers.

This could truly be a nightmare. I mean, *just what level of consciousness are we going to download into our silicon chips?*

"Slip into this chip," says a bare-naked Chloe, swaying in circles to the thump thump thumping of Nine Inch Nails screaming "Downward Spiral" and "The Great Collapse," heralding an ominous meltdown in my liquefying brain. Naked Chloes multiply a millionfold, overheated cyber-circuits send shudders through my jangled neurons—and *what on earth are we doing?* Sasha spins "Future in Computer Hell," and the way of all flesh and carbon nightmares begin to invade my silicon dreams. Exactly who will program our tomorrow, stamp our fate in Silicon City, slam our destiny into the Crystal Matrix for all the mornings yet to come? Can somebody please tell me! *Who will program our tomorrow?*

I hold my head, rub my eyes. "Kim, is the afternoon session hard? I'm really spacing out."

"All you have to do is get through green—it's next, and it's really short—and then they introduce both boomeritis—the audience goes nuts—and second tier, which is totally awesome. You don't want to have made it this far and then peter out right when the fun is starting, do you?"

"What, me? The last thing I want is for my peter to be out, believe me."

Kim looked at me with a quaint, shrugging smile that said, "Aren't men cute?"

"Pluralism (Green): The Sensitive Self
- Explore the inner being of self and others
- Promote a sense of community and caring
- Share society's resources among all; embrace diversity and multiculturalism

- Promote gender equity, children's rights, and animal welfare
- All values are pluralistic and relative, so don't marginalize anybody
- Do away with all hierarchies; they are oppressive
- Liberate humans from greed and dogma
- Reach decisions through consensus
- Refresh spirituality and bring harmony to all beings of Gaia
- Basis of value communities

"'Life is for experiencing each moment,' says green. 'We can all come to understand who we are and how wondrous it is to be human if we will only accept that everyone is equal and important. Hierarchies are oppressive and marginalizing. All must share in the joy of togetherness and fulfillment. Each spirit is connected to all others in our community; every soul travels together. We are interdependent beings in search of love and involvement. The community grows by synergizing life forces; artificial divisions take away from everyone. Groups of people working together are the best way to advance knowledge. Bad attitudes and negative beliefs dissolve once we look inside each person and uncover the richness within. Peace and love are truly for all beings, including all the inhabitants of this earth, our ecological brothers and sisters.'"

Scott had taken his third bite of green ham sandwich. "You know, the thing about my little brother is how really difficult it must have been for him growing up. I mean, today we tend to think that all gays and lesbians are 'out' and that it's the easiest thing in world. But I bet less than one in ten gays are really out. I never thought about it before, you know? How hard it must be? Till I started thinking about my brother."

Everybody at the table glanced silently at each other; this turn in the conversation toward an actually serious topic caught everybody off guard. And was Scott really being serious, or just suckering us into a joke? The best policy under such circumstances is silence.

"Well? People? Hello?" He looked faintly pained.

"Yes, it must be horrible," Carolyn finally said. "Over at cultural studies, we talk about this all the time, but frankly it never seems to really hit you until it's somebody you know. 'Marginalize,' we call it. But really, what the hell is that, you know?"

"It's when you use a butter substitute." Chloe grinned to herself.

"Not margarine, you nitwit."

"Oh, coming out, not coming out, who gives a shit?" said Jonathan, but we all knew he didn't mean it.

We sat somberly; Scott put on a smile and changed the subject. "So, Chloe, you said you visited your parents. Things okay with them?"

"Fine, fine, nothing out of the ordinary. Dad offered to take Mom on a second honeymoon. She screamed 'Oh God, not another one!' and ran shrieking from the room."

"Ah, good," I said, "nice to hear that everything's normal. Are they coming up here next week?"

"No, my little sister has a learning disability and they are spending the weekend with a new coach."

"Your sister has a learning disability?" Jonathan asked.

"Well, only if you consider stupidity a learning disorder."

"Runs in the family, eh?" said Carolyn.

"Oh, I see, *humor*," responded Chloe. "You know, Carolyn, I was wondering who designed that lovely full-figured dress you're wearing. Omar the Tentmaker, perhaps?"

"Look, you twit, I am *not* fat."

"Not fat? Mosquitoes see you and scream 'Buffet!'"

"Chloe, love, come over here where I can get my hands on your throat, would you, dear?"

Chloe shot her a devilish grin. "A waiter brings you a menu, you look at it and say, 'Okay.'"

"All right, you little slut—"

"*Please*, you two, not over lunch. Scott here is starting to turn green, and I can't tell if it's because of his sandwich or your vibes."

"I'm turning green?"

"So what's everybody doing this afternoon?" Jonathan queried. "I've got this unbelievably wretched class in pop culture. It's called something like 'High Brow, Middle Brow, Low Brow: Who Wants a Brow Beating?' I don't even know what that means."

"Does it involve leather?" Chloe beamed hopefully.

"*Green?*"

"It's cultural studies," said Carolyn. "You'll love it." She grinned. "At least all you have to do is watch Madonna videos instead of reading *War and Peace* or something. Scott, you're not green. What's up?"

Scott shook his head. "Um, I have an appointment with a dentist for a fucking root canal," he morosely noted. "I'm not sure whether I'd rather go to the dentist or be in your class. I guess the dentist."

"Well, then, have fun with the root canal!" said Chloe.

"Sure, who wouldn't?"

"What we really see with the healthy green meme," Hazelton explained, "is yet another profound shift in consciousness, with another lessening of egocentrism and an expansion of care, compassion, and concern, often extended even to children's rights and animal welfare. As Beck and Cowan point out, 'Interpersonal skills are often at a peak because constructive, warm interaction is so integral to self-satisfaction. Intuition and insight are valuable commodities here, so individuals strive to polish skills like empathetic listening. In organizations moving through this range, "human relations," "sensitivity," "diversity," and "cultural awareness" reading and training are often mandatory.'

"With green, gender equity and ecological concerns are front and center," Hazelton gently announced. "Green is often communitarian, egalitarian, and consensual. The workplace is team-oriented and democratic, with much dialogue and sharing of feelings. 'Green seeks consolidation of the soul and the forces of nature through respect and even awe, but not superstition (purple) or prescriptive rules (blue).'

"Catchwords for green include: anti-hierarchy, pluralism, diversity, multiculturalism, relativism, deconstruction. Most characteristic is green's intense antipathy to ranking or hierarchies of any sort, which it attempts aggressively, sometimes recklessly, to deconstruct. Almost all of these concerns stem directly from green's noble desire not to oppress or marginalize anybody."

This was Mom and Dad. The very best of Mom and Dad. This was the freedom they had given me, and I suddenly became ever so grateful, teary-eyed, misting up; I turned to hide my face from Kim, who would surely call the house doctor if I deteriorated any further.

There must be some sort of psychological theory somewhere—in the padlocked attics of that dustbin discipline—that explains what happens to kids who are brought up under the influence of parents at different memes. I mean, think about a kid raised by red-meme parents—he turns out to be what? Maybe a great test pilot, sure, but maybe the class bully, maybe the kid voted most likely to commit murder, the guy in the bell tower with the Uzi, a Hannibal Lecter having others for lunch. Or brought up by overbearing blue-meme parents: the little goody-goodies who always raise their hands and ask for more homework, who can't wait to be the hall monitors, who will *turn themselves in* if they do something wrong, who grow up and dedicate their lives to Jesus, that is, dedicate their lives to interfering with yours. Or orange: the guy who joins the Better Business Bureau when he's fifteen so he can get a running start, who is already selling sandwiches at lunch hour, the kid whose ties already don't match his shirt—my dad used to quote Karl Marx all the time: "A capitalist will sell you the rope you are going to hang him with."

And me? A greenie baby? What did that do to me? Sure, I was clobbered by boomeritis, and sure, the immenseness of their half-baked dreams often fell on me like a damp blanket, suffocating my own; I still have asthma, I really can't breathe, I always feel like a fish swimming upstream. But still, what I remember most is being allowed to be me. There was always some sort of background that said, Whatever you want to do is just fine with us. It really was freedom, or a huge degree of freedom—that is what Mom and Dad had given me, and that seemed to override any of the downsides.

I was so very, very, very grateful, sitting in the IC hall, having some sort of nervous breakdown under the day's onslaught on unprotected dendrites, my eyes still welling up with tears of endless thankfulness, those dear amazing loving people, as I dissolved in the warm green fuzzy glow, a sweet little cuddly kitten I wanted to give everybody.

"Kim, my mom and dad, you know? My mom and dad, my dear mom and dad . . . ," I simpered in her ear.

"I know, Ken, I know." She patted my arm. "Here, have a sip of my latte mocha, you'll feel better."

I took a sip but most of it dribbled down my chin.

"Be careful! Don't you know that there are millions of children in India forced to drink plain coffee with their breakfast?"

"Even though healthy green is partaking of postconventional, world-centric, universal consciousness, its warrant for truth is highly subjective. Precisely because green wishes to equally honor all beings, it goes out of its way to let each person decide his or her own truth. All beliefs, as long as they do not harm others, tend to be accorded equal status. This is why the self at this stage is indeed the 'sensitive self.' Aware of the many different contexts and numerous different types of truth—*diversity* and *pluralism*—it bends over backwards in an attempt to let each truth have its own say, without marginalizing or belittling any."

"I can bend over backward, Ken. Here, how about *this*?"
   "Oh my God."
   "Are you the sensitive self, Ken?"
   "Count on it, Chloe."
   "Just how sensitive are you, Ken? Can you feel this?"
   "Wow, count on it, Chloe."
   "Ooooh, color you green," she says.
   "Um, I don't think that's what they mean, Chloe."

"This noble intent, of course, has its downside. In-group thinking and politically correct thought police enforce a rigid system of allowed discourse. Beck and Cowan point out that 'green can be very rigid in its demands for "open-mindedness" (on the group's egalitarian, homogenized terms, of course). Like all of the first-tier memes, green can be quite dismissive of (or blind to) the rest of the Spiral in the belief that its way is *the* way, not a way. Green is high in rigidity. People in this range tolerate disagreement only so long as it is approached in *green* ways, with "gentility" and through the collective. Come on strong'— appear authoritarian or aggressive—'and green swells up indignantly, a phenomenon which shocks those naive enough to equate green-ness with unconditional love of everyone. All of the talk of harmony and warmth drop away quickly when other factions compete for the same niche.'" Hazelton paused and looked out at the audience.

"Meetings that are run on green principles tend to follow a similar course: everybody is allowed to express his or her feelings, which often takes hours; there is an almost interminable processing of opinions, often reaching no decision or course of action, since a specific course of action would likely exclude somebody. The meeting is considered a success, not if a conclusion is reached, but if everybody has a chance to share their feelings. 'Freedom is an endless meeting,' emphasis on 'endless.'"

Well, and that is Mom and Dad too, and royally!—a thought that quickly introduced more balance into the picture. My emotions now ricocheted in the opposite direction, smashing into unprotected neuronal tissue with a sickening interior thud. I recalled especially the rigid, righteous anger at those who weren't as "kind and loving" as they were, and wasn't that a strange contradiction? I never understood why they said they didn't want to marginalize or exclude anybody, yet they despised anybody who disagreed with them. Now it was making sense, it was slowly becoming clear: green, as a first-tier meme, dislikes the values of all other memes. It claims that it wants to be inclusive, but it will not allow red to be red, or blue to be blue, or orange to be orange . . . , and thus in its desire to be inclusive, it ends up *excluding* so many. Alanis Morrisette ought to put *that* in her song about irony (even if, ironically, she can't define irony).

Hazelton smiled, looked down at the podium, and began reading a quote. "This green meme, this pluralistic relativism, is the dominant stance in academia. Colin McGuinn: 'According to this conception, human reason is inherently local, culture-relative, rooted in the variable facts of human nature and history, a matter of divergent "practices" and "forms of life" and "frames of reference" and "conceptual schemes." There are no norms of reasoning that transcend what is accepted by a society or an epoch, no objective justifications for belief that everyone must respect on pain of cognitive malfunction. To be valid is to be taken to be valid, and different people can have legitimately different patterns of taking. In the end, the only justifications for belief have the form "justified for me."' As Clare Graves put it, 'This system sees the world relativistically. Thinking shows an almost radical, almost compulsive emphasis on seeing everything from a relativistic, subjective frame of reference.'

"Here, of course, is where boomeritis enters the picture."

The audience sat edgily upright in its seat, slowly and almost stealthily so, as if trying to hide the fact that they were bracing for what was about to come.

"Here's a mouthful, then I promise I'll simplify: Because the pluralistic relativism of the green meme has such an intensely subjective stance, and because it tries to allow everything and not marginalize anything, it is especially prey to narcissism. And exactly that is the crux of the problem: *pluralism becomes a supermagnet for narcissism.* Pluralism becomes an unwitting home for the Culture of Narcissism.

"Thus, the very high developmental meme of green pluralism becomes a shelter and a haven for a *reactivation* of some of the lower and intensely egocentric memes (especially purple and red, as we will see). In green's noble attempt to move beyond conformist rules and ethnocentric prejudices—in short, in green's admirable attempt to go *postconventional*—it has often inadvertently embraced *anything* nonconventional, and this includes much that is frankly *preconventional*, regressive, and narcissistic.

"That strange mixture is *boomeritis*: high pluralism mixed with low narcissism. And that is the strange, strange brew that has defined the Boomers almost from the beginning. As we will see, the Boomers were the first major generation in history to evolve in large numbers to the green meme—an extraordinary accomplishment that brought with it civil rights, environmental protection, feminism, and health care reform. All of this is to the Boomers' everlasting credit.

"But then, as we will also see, the Boomers *got stuck at green*, lost in green, and a green that very soon began to go pathological. Green pluralism became a magnet for red narcissism, and this explosive combination—boomeritis—very nearly destroyed a generation.

"As green became diseased, disturbed, and frankly sick—as it became the mean green meme in all its ugly forms—the shadow side of the Woodstock Nation began to multiply alarmingly. We will see dozens and dozens of examples of this very soon. As the mean green meme began to extend its reach, extreme pluralism began dominating everything, ruling everything, reducing everything to unrelenting FLATLAND—nothing is better, nothing is higher, nothing is deeper—all stances are supposedly equal in this egalitarian mush, and hence 'NOBODY CAN TELL ME WHAT TO DO!' And so of course narcissism finds a happy home, here in flatland. And there, in one sentence, is the tragedy of the Me generation."

Hazelton walked to edge of the stage, looked out, smiled, and crisply summarized. "Pluralism infected with narcissism—flatland inhabited by a big ego—by any other name, boomeritis."

A loud, strange, perturbed sound, almost like a muffled groan, rose from the audience; not exactly approval, not exactly disagreement, more like a collective agitated sigh, the type of sound you might hear from a person whose jury had just delivered a guilty verdict, amplified by loudspeakers.

Chloe's wayward body sways as De-Phazz plays "Death by Chocolate," and the thump thump thumping pounds a brain too jangled to object.

"Hey," Chloe reads from the newspaper, "they're gonna have a national TV family show celebrating the green meme. Who do you think they should have on?"

"Madonna?"

"No, too old and she doesn't wear any clothes."

"But you'd be able to see her breasts."

"Yes, but who hasn't?"

"True. How about Mandy Moore?" I say.

"Better, but too young and I don't think she can spell 'green.' Let's see . . . how about Britney? Belly buttons are like way multicultural."

"We need a national care bear," I muse. "How about a First Lady?"

"The only thing a First Lady ever had named after her was a rehab center." Chloe looks up, bends over, moves her flesh close to mine, the thump thump thumping of my blood matches hers completely.

"Well, then, how about *this*," she wildly demonstrates.

"Yes, Chloe, that's exactly what we want on national family TV. . . ."

"But let us not forget the many gifts of healthy green. As the culmination of the first-tier memes, green's care and sensitivity breaks up the crustiness of the entire Spiral and thus prepares the leap into the hyperspace of second-tier consciousness, where an integral embrace that cherishes the entire Spiral will complete and fulfill the green ideal.

"Where seen: Deep ecology, postmodernism, Netherlands idealism, Rogerian counseling, Canadian health care, humanistic psychology, liberation theology, cooperative inquiry, World Council of Churches, Greenpeace, ecopsychology, animal rights, ecofeminism, post-colonialism, Foucault/Derrida, politically correct, diversity movements, human rights issues, multiculturalism. 10% of the population, 15% of the power."

Oh God, another neuronal seizure: AI will eventually get to the point where you can literally download your own consciousness into machines. But think about it: if I am going to be downloaded into an eternal silicon matrix, I want to be second tier before I am downloaded! What if I am not? What if I'm stuck in orange or green? What if I don't make it to integral and then I am slammed into crystal chips for all eternity in that fragmented condition?

That horrible, tissue-damaging thought was followed almost immediately by another: What if we downloaded boomeritis into every supercomputer in the universe? My God, the politically correct thought police would create nanobots that would devour all deviant memes anywhere in cyberspace. WE'D END UP DOWNLOADING MY FRIGGIN' PARENTS INTO EVERY COMPUTER FOR ALL ETERNITY! I can't breathe, I really can't breathe this time. . . .

"Kim, Kim, my parents!" I urgently whispered.

"I know, I know, you love them."

"No, no, they're going to rule the Bot Federation, it's your worst nightmare!"

Kim looked at me and shook her head. "I think I've got some Prozac in my purse."

"The green meme marks the completion of first-tier thinking. What particularly defines the first-tier memes is that each believes its worldview is basically the only worldview worth embracing. Each first-tier meme has thus covertly declared war on all the others. But starting with second tier, all of this dramatically changes. I will simply combine the two second-tier memes (yellow and turquoise) into one, which I will call holistic or integral. Here's the slide:

"*Holistic (Second-Tier): The Integral Embrace*
- Intuitively grasps the entire Spiral of development, and thus understands that each meme is important
- Grasps big pictures, global flows, universal networks
- Discovers personal freedom without harm to others or excesses of self-interest

- Sees integrative and open systems, holistic meshworks
- Reintroduces vertical hierarchy (or ranking) along with horizontal heterarchy (or linking)
- Works for both the enjoyment of self and the good of the entire Spiral of development
- Basis of integral commons

"'Scales fall from our eyes and we can see, for the first time, the legitimacy of all of the human systems (the first six memes) awakened to date. At the same time, viability must be restored to a disordered world endangered by the cumulative effects of the first six memes on the earth's environment and populations (since all of those first-tier memes are at war with each other). This integrated view facilitates the movement of people up and down the flowing and fluid Spiral. This produces a recognition of the richly layered dynamics of human systems operating within people and societies. If purple is sick, it needs to be made well. If red is running amuck, the raw energy must be channeled. If blue structure is devastated, it needs to be restored. Since many of our social messes are caused by the interaction of people at different levels, such messes can only be sorted out through an understanding of the integral Spiral itself.' With second-tier consciousness, such an understanding becomes possible, and a genuine *wholeness* finally becomes a living reality."

As Hazelton said that, what I kept thinking was: That is what I want, that is so very much what I want—second-tier consciousness in infinite cyberspace, luminous integral ecstatic mind, free for all eternity. No longer drawn and quartered, and wholeness wholeness wholeness reigns. . . .

"You see, you recognize that Self, yes? The Ancient One? The One who is to come? You see the Omega of the Silicon Age, even here and now? What has evolution labored to produce? Whether in the worlds of carbon or of silicon, can you see the Goal and Ground of both? Can you say its Name?"

"With the transition to second tier, there occurs what Graves called '*a momentous leap of meaning*.' In essence, the entire Spiral comes into view. Not necessarily as a fully articulated psychological model, but as an intuitively grasped phenomenon. The Spiral, after all, is a very real reality, and second-tier awareness is the first to spot it.

"And, dear friends, this changes everything. Graves found that fear tends to drop away dramatically. It is as if the deeper and wider perspective of second-tier awareness meets the world with a calm wisdom that is not easily ruffled. Around second-tier people, things happen, often miraculously, simply because they see big pictures and move fluidly through them. As Beck and Cowan put it, 'When individuals or groups thinking through second tier are given a task, they generally get more and better results while expending less time and effort. They often approach the activity in surprising ways others would not even have considered.'

"Second-tier thinkers intuitively understand the entire Spiral in other people, and thus they meet people where they find them. There is a genuine compassion, not as an ideal, but as a lived reality. 'These people will, likewise, activate any of the vast first-tier resources within themselves, ranging from fact recall to intuitive daydreams, in a deliberate second-tier way.'

"Second-tier individuals often baffle others, precisely because they range across the entire Spiral as needed. As Beck and Cowan put it: 'This is not a call for a lifestyle full of granola and berries or an exclusively L. L. Bean wardrobe. Plastic, a fast-food meal, and a Saville Row suit may all be appropriate at a given time, in a specific circumstance.' One day a second-tier person is wearing beat-up jeans, the next day a three-piece suit; one day is kind and compassionate, the next day is rattling the cage with apparent furies—spanning the Spiral, they are impossible to pigeonhole."

"Speaking of holes, pigeon or otherwise . . ."

"Oh no, Chloe, not now."

"Here's what's appropriate at any given time," she says, bending over naked, smiling at me through her legs.

"Now pay attention, sweet boy. Watch as I take your vertical hierarchy and integrate it with my horizontal heterarchy, like *this*."

"Wow!"

"Pretty integral, eh?"

"Um, I don't think that's what they mean, Chloe."

"Start by noticing the fate of *hierarchy* in the Spiral of development. This part is easy, I promise!" She laughed. "Red has hierarchies based on brute strength and raw power—big fishes eat little fishes. Blue (mythic order) has numerous and very rigid social hierarchies, such as the hereditary caste system, the hierarchies of the medieval Church, and the intense social stratification of feudal empires. Orange has hierarchies based on merit—'meritocracies,' they're called, where excellence is rewarded. By the time we get to green, however, the sensitive self begins *an attack on all types of hierarchies*, simply because they have indeed often been involved in horrible social oppression.

"But with the emergence of second tier, *hierarchies again return*, this time in a softer, nested fashion. These nested hierarchies are often called *growth hierarchies*, such as the hierarchy atoms to molecules to cells to organisms to ecosystems to biosphere to universe. Each of those units, no matter how 'lowly,' is absolutely crucial for the entire sequence: destroy all atoms and you simultaneously destroy all molecules, cells, ecosystems, and so on. At the same time, each senior wave enfolds or envelopes its predecessors—ecosystems contain organisms, which contain cells, which contain molecules—a *development* that is *envelopment*. And thus each *higher wave* becomes *more inclusive*, more embracing, more integral—and less marginalizing, less exclusionary, less oppressive. Each higher wave 'transcends and includes' its predecessors, which increases its capacity for care. The developmental Spiral itself is a nested hierarchy or growth hierarchy, as are most natural growth processes, and thus with each higher wave in the hierarchy, the circle of care and consciousness expands."

"So listen up," says a naked Chloe, swinging back and forth on the chandelier, "because this is important if you want to get to integral second tier. The green meme doesn't like anything masculine. It excludes anything hard, straight, or vertical. No erections anywhere! Everything must be soft curves, mushy sentiments, gooey feelings. Not a vertical erection or hierarchy in sight."

"Chloe, I don't think . . ." But then it dawns on me, she's probably right.

"So when we do *this* . . ."

"Oh my God."

"Now *that's* second tier!"

"Riane Eisler calls attention to this important distinction by referring to 'dominator hierarchies' and 'actualization hierarchies.' The former are the rigid social hierarchies that are instruments of oppression, and the latter are the growth hierarchies that are actually necessary for the self-actualization of individuals and cultures. Whereas dominator hierarchies are the means of oppression, actualization hierarchies are the means of growth. It is the growth hierarchies that gently bring together previously isolated and fragmented elements. Isolated atoms are brought together into molecules; isolated molecules are brought together into cells; isolated cells into organisms; organisms into ecosystems; ecosystems into biosphere, and so on. In short, growth hierarchies convert heaps into wholes, fragments into integration, alienation into cooperation.

"And, Spiral Dynamics adds, *all of this starts to become obvious at second tier*. Thus, if we react negatively to all hierarchies, not only will we honorably fight the injustices of dominator hierarchies, *we will prevent ourselves from developing to the integral second tier*."

Kim leaned over. "Does this denial of vertical hierarchy have any meaning for you?"

"It certainly does for Chloe."

"What's that?"

"Oh, nothing, nothing."

"Because second-tier integral awareness understands the nested hierarchy of growth, it grasps the crucial importance of each and every meme. It therefore 'understands the uniqueness of the conceptual and personal worlds that each of the previous memes creates.' What is right for purple is not necessarily right for blue or orange. What is right for green is not necessarily right for red or blue. *The aim of second-tier ethics is the health of the entire Spiral, and not any privileged treatment for any one level*, blue or orange or green or even second tier.

"This 'Spiral imperative'—what I call the 'Prime Directive,' with a nod to Star Trek!—colors many of the motivations of second-tier individuals. As Beck and Cowan point out, 'Second tier's evaluative plumb bob points to the life of the entire Spiral, keeping it healthy and evolving. This is survival in the Global Village. What is appropriate comes in *all* of the colors of the Spiral.' This Prime Directive is set in the context of a *developmental unfolding*: 'Second tier recognizes the inevitability of the unfolding sequence of human memes. Second-tier problem solvers ride the Spiral in search of major gaps, misfits, trigger points, natural flows or regressions.'"

Hazelton paused, looked out at the audience, smiled. "A new type of spirituality can emerge at second tier. It is deeply universal and 'stands in awe of the cosmic order, the creative forces that exist from the Big Bang to the smallest molecule.' This cosmic unity often includes a renewed appreciation of Gaia, but only as part of a larger consciousness. It is a 'big picture' spirituality, a spirituality of cosmic wholeness. And it's very important to distinguish this *postconventional* cosmic spirituality from conventional, mythic, blue religion. They are as different as day and night, the latter based on myths and dogmas, the former on integral awareness."

"Kim, I think that is what my mom and dad were both aiming for, some sort of cosmic wholeness. That is what they really wanted. I think that's what they still want, turquoise unity and wholeness. But they took a turn at the sixties and got lost in green, trapped in flatland, and never made the leap. . . . "

"Sad, isn't it?"

"I don't know, maybe it's not too late. Morin said there was some research on that?"

"Yes, it's really amazing, you'll see."

"Downsides at second tier can be considerable, since every level has its pathologies," Hazelton reminded everybody. "The brighter the light, the darker the shadow. Megatribes and superclans can form around panoramic visions. The Darth Vader move is always possible: no matter how high the developmental unfolding, the new potentials can be misused, with calamitous consequences. For example, a more panoramic awareness is of little help if it simply adopts a materialistic, flatland, systems view. In fact, most of the ugly downsides of globalization are due to a *calamitous misuse of second-tier potentials*. Globalization itself is not bad, but *flatland* globalization—the imposition of one meme (such as orange business) on the entire world—is an absolute nightmare. Well, more about those horrors later. . . . "

Hazelton smiled. "But let us end on a healthy note: second tier itself is the home of the Prime Directive. The Prime Directive, which is to facilitate the health of the entire Spiral, attempts to help each meme express its own potentials to the best of its ability, so that each meme can make its absolutely necessary and crucial contributions to the health of the overall Spiral. And thus it is to the *healthy* second-tier memes that we must look for the compassionate dawn of an integral consciousness and the genuine possibility of a world at peace."

That integral consciousness, that sense of wholeness, was no longer an abstraction to me. It was two things at once: exactly what I wanted to attain, and the minimum requirement for the download into compuCyberSpace. The thought that we would program the initial superintelligent network with fragmented first-tier memes was frightening. Human evolution and cyber-evolution—Carbon and Silicon— two paths that I had counted on to go their separate ways within my own lifetime—had rudely intersected. What happened in one would irrevocably alter the other. And unless computer programmers got out of flatland thinking, their fractured logic would spill into the crystal lattices of silicon consciousness, staining it forever.

"Ken, you've got to try this." Chloe looks at me, her always naked body smiling. But it is Hazelton who speaks, "*The Leap into the HyperSpace of Integral Awareness.***"**

"What an extraordinary journey, this unfolding of consciousness! From isolated bands of no more than 30 people, incapable of communicating with other bands and tribes, to a global village with at least the possibility of a truly integral embrace, a global unity-in-diversity that allows each and every culture its own specialness, while setting them all in the context of a universal care and fairness that honors the uniqueness of each.

"No wonder thinkers from Hegel to Teilhard de Chardin to Aurobindo have concluded that this evolutionary unfolding is heading straight toward Spirit, so remarkable are its advances thus far. Of course, its brutalities are also legion, but we needn't get lost in reveries of sweetness and light to realize that, if we simply acknowledge its positive accomplishments, this spiraling growth of consciousness is truly astonishing.

"Let us assume that the extensive cross-cultural research continues to confirm the Spiral of development as outlined above. What can we reasonably conclude about the emergence of a truly integral consciousness?

"The conclusions are straightforward: What is the jumping-off point for a second-tier, integral awareness? The green meme.

"What immediately prevents this jump into an integral awareness? A fixation to the green meme.

"What is the major cause of a fixation to the green meme?

"Boomeritis."

4

And_It_Is_Us@FuckMe.com

Second night at Stuart's performance, the gang's all there. Stuart is tall, lanky, handsome, shaved-headed, 29 years old, with an intensity that looks as if one of his fingers is perpetually plugged into an electric socket. His performances are, no surprise, totally wired—and illuminating, and funny, and honest. Nobody can figure out why he isn't a national star, except that he doesn't want to be. We always saved him a spot at our table for his breaks.

"So Stuart, baby, tell Ken why you meditate." Jonathan was unusually satisfied with this opening.

"It's not a big deal or anything, it's just a type of basic sanity. It's also how I write. I seem to enter this space, this incredibly creative space, and songs come out of that space, almost like they were fully formed. Then sometimes you just enter the silence. It's like coming home. I'd go completely insane without that, and believe me, I know insane."

"Ken thinks that all of that will soon be downloaded into chips, cha cha cha, so you won't have to worry about how to do it anymore," grinned Jonathan. "In order to meditate, or make love, or do anything you want, just hit the 'on' switch."

"It's not that," I said. "And I'm not sure anymore. Or I've been thinking about it. Or not, or pretty much something."

"Oooooh, boyfriend. I don't see what downloading has to do with anything. Speaking of downloading, Carolyn, do you swallow?"

Sitting in the back corner, I noticed with a twinge of panic, was Joan Hazelton, Dr. Morin, and two others I didn't recognize. I quickly turned around, cleared my throat.

"It's like this," I announced in a flustered voice, "and this is totally obvious, or certainly would be if it were, or could be if it were be. That is to say, let me sum up. . . . "

"Oooooh, look at brainiac."

Scott stared at me and squinted, then turned to Stuart. "Stuart, seriously, you must have some ideas about what's behind meditation. You write about it, you sing about it, you do it. Is it just stress reduction, is it spiritual, are you contacting God or just taking a nap?"

"I heard you talking earlier about 'from machines to transcendent mind.' Well, that's what I think meditation does. You move out of your own mechanical habits and you contact transcendent mind. Seriously."

"Well there's nothing fun about that," said Chloe, which meant, Why bother?, or alternatively, Who wants to go shopping?

"A real transcendent mind? Not reducible to matter?" I asked.

"Yes, a real spiritual consciousness. Not derived from matter."

"Here's the glitch for me," said Carolyn. "My major is cultural studies. We are steeped in serious critiques of past forms of social oppression. And I have to tell you, all those meditation systems came out of brutal patriarchal societies. Just look at them. You say transcendent mind, I hear step on women and fuck the earth."

"You hear what?"

"I hear step on—"

"I hear dreary feminist victim-chic shit," tossed Chloe. "That is soooo yesterday, dahling."

"I do not believe they let you into architect school, you absolute vaporheaded bimbo," Carolyn shot back. "I've had more interesting conversations with a carrot."

"Not according to the carrot."

"Maybe it's this way," interjected Stuart. "Maybe some of those systems were patriarchal, like you say. But that doesn't mean everything in them was bad. Patriarchal males invented the wheel, but you probably use wheels without feeling oppressed. Maybe meditation is like that, maybe it's okay. I think it does disclose a mind not reducible to matter."

"Well, you know"—I glanced furtively around—"some people say there are even levels of mind, or levels of consciousness."

"Well listen to silicon boy," laughed Jonathan. "But you're just stating the obvious for anybody who knows anything, which of course excludes you. Because all the great wisdom traditions—all of them, Ken, are you listening?—all of them recognize levels of consciousness, a great spectrum of consciousness that reaches from matter to spirit. Stuart's right—meditation moves you to the highest levels on that spectrum. That's why I do Zen. Then you can be just like me," he smiled.

"Like hello? Can this conversation get any more dreary? Stuart, why don't you sing, dahling, Stu baby, sing for us."

"Coming up."

"Levels of consciousness—Wilber, really, where have you been? We poked our heads into Integral Center last week, yes? You sat through a whole lecture, yes? Didn't you hear anything?" Carolyn asked.

I had forgotten that's how I had stumbled onto IC in the first place. "Remember? Sure, of course, of course, are you kidding me? I remembered the levels thing, right?"

"I perform at IC a lot," Stuart said.

"You perform at Integral Center? Why?"

"They are experts in consciousness, in the stages and waves of consciousness unfolding, they have experts from all over the world. That's what I'm interested in. I even dedicated one of my CDs, *Kid Mystic*, to a teacher there. So they called me up and invited me over. I attend some of their conferences, sing at some of them."

"You better be careful," Chloe grinned. "Boomers eat their young."

"Really? What on earth does that mean, Chloe? Oh, hey, over there. Joan! Joan! Hi."

Electric adrenaline burns my body. As Hazelton heads toward our table, I panic.

"Stuart, we were wondering where you were. When did you get into town?"

"Last night, Joan, only about ten minutes before the show, so I couldn't call. The Dodge Mahal broke down outside of Brooklyn."

Hazelton sits down. Her coral eyes seem connected to infinity, seem to be a transparency that opens onto the sky. There is nothing behind her eyes, just the sky. Out of the sky, there is a shining radiance. The world does not enter her, it seems to come out of her.

"Are these friends?" she asks Stuart.

"Actually, no, they just keep following me around." We all stared blankly. "Okay, okay. Chloe, Scott, Carolyn, Ken, Jonathan—Dr. Joan Hazelton." Nods all around.

"I'm curious, Dr. Hazelton. Over at IC, you guys are into consciousness studies, but do you represent any particular school?" Jonathan shelved his acid.

"Not really. The idea is to take all of the known maps of the human mind—East, West, ancient, modern—and create a master map, a comprehensive map of the human mind, using all of them to fill in the gaps in any of them. Sometimes we will pick one of them and teach that as an introduction—maybe Jane Loevinger, maybe Sri Aurobindo, maybe Plotinus, maybe Spiral Dynamics. But we are mostly interested in this integral map that combines the best of all of them."

"Why exactly are you interested in that? Excuse my bluntness, but what good is it?" Scott blurted out.

"Well, what we are doing is like the Human Genome Project, but instead of mapping all the known genes, we are mapping all the known memes. All the levels, waves, stages, and states of consciousness—whatever words you want. We're mapping the full spectrum of consciousness."

Hazelton paused, smiled, looked softly around the table. "When we combine all the known genes with all the known memes, why, we might even find something interesting." She grinned broadly.

Chloe let her eyes roll up slowly to the ceiling, signaling imminent death from boredom. For whatever reasons, I couldn't help being fond of Chloe—I think it was her wise-ass spirit, counterblast to my mumbling moroseness—and how many wonderfully stupid and alive things would I have never tried without her?—yet I also couldn't help but wonder just what I had seen in her. No, that wasn't bothering me. What somebody like her had seen in me—that was starting to disturb.

Joan looked directly at me; it was intensely disorienting, because you momentarily lost your bearings in all that boundless sky, your flesh temporarily left the field and you were awash in another kind of bodiless cyberspace. When you looked into somebody's eyes, there was supposed to be something solid there to prevent you from falling in.

"We've met, yes?" she asked.

"Yes? No. I mean, No. Yes, of course not."

"Allow me to translate cyber boy for you. . . . "

"Okay, Jonathan. I, we, us, we sort of poked our head in IC one day. We probably saw each other."

She smiled.

"People, people, people. Listen up, folks, the fun's just beginning! The Spiral of development is a great River of Life, with billions of people flowing through it from source to ocean. No matter how 'highly developed' a culture may be, every single person in that culture starts life at square 1, at the archaic stage, at dear ole beige, and must begin his or her growth and development from there. For every person who evolves to the integral stage, dozens are born at the archaic and begin their own unfolding through the swirling spiral of consciousness. The Spiral itself is a great endless torrent, with billions of people constantly flowing through it, helped or hindered according to the degree of our understanding of this mighty River."

Dr. Morin was introducing the day's events. Stuart would be singing. Several slide shows. It was a big day, with three guest speakers. "This is what we call the 'details day,'" Morin said. "We go over several fascinating details on the evolution of consciousness. We are going to discuss the levels of selfhood, the worldviews of modernity and postmodernity, and the obstacles to integral consciousness."

"Okay, color Chloe gone. That sounds like soooo totally boring I can't tell you." Why she had insisted on coming in the first place was something of a puzzle; perhaps the way I looked at Hazelton.

"I'll find you for lunch," I yelled as she walked down the aisle.

"Ooooh, look at me swoon."

"We promise to make this as painless as possible. Why, we even have lots of picture slides. But once you get through today, the rest is all downhill!" A large wave of applause bolstered with cheers rose from the crowd.

I looked around for Kim; three rows behind, on the right. She got up and came over. "Kim, this is Scott, Jonathan, Carolyn."

"First up," said Kim, slipping into the seat next to mine, "is Lesa Powell. She's the angry one."

"The what?"

"She's black, she's lesbian, and she's angry."

"Why is she angry?"

"Rumor has it that last summer she got pregnant."

"I thought she was lesbian."

"Well, that's why she's angry."

"She was raped?"

"No, no, she was in love with this guy, which of course wasn't supposed to happen."

"Because she's black?"

"Because she's lesbian, you twit."

"But it seems to me that, um, she flunked the admissions test."

"She's really great, you'll see."

"It's simple, folks, honest, and it goes like this," Powell began with an engaging, far-from-angry smile. "The 8 levels of consciousness each have a different type of self-identity, so there are 8 levels of selfhood. Each level of selfhood is a different way to answer the question, WHO ARE YOU?

"These different selves are summarized in the right-hand column of slide #1 (FIG. 4.1). You can see some of the common names—a self that is impulsive, a self that is conformist, a self that is autonomous, and so on. These 8 levels of selfhood are just different aspects of the 8 levels of consciousness that we have already discussed, so please, don't any of you start bitching and moaning that oh, gosh, I have to learn new stuff. We're just going over the same material from a different angle to make sure even you dummies get it." She shot the audience a winning grin, then moved to the center of the stage and shouted, "Besides, don't you want to know what type of self you have?!" The audience, most of them, yelled, "Yes!"

"Okay, then, since you asked, in today's session I will suggest a few of the more interesting details of these stages of self. For those less interested in such details, the concrete examples of boomeritis begin tomorrow, so those who are looking for the gory details don't have long to wait!"

"Are the details really gory?" I asked Kim.

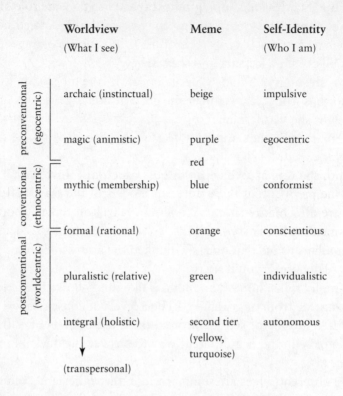

Worldview (What I see)		Meme	Self-Identity (Who I am)
preconventional (egocentric)	archaic (instinctual)	beige	impulsive
	magic (animistic)	purple red	egocentric
conventional (ethnocentric)	mythic (membership)	blue	conformist
	formal (rational)	orange	conscientious
postconventional (worldcentric)	pluralistic (relative)	green	individualistic
	integral (holistic)	second tier (yellow, turquoise)	autonomous
	↓ (transpersonal)		

Figure 4.1. Worldviews and Selfhood

"Oh God, are they. Unbelievable. That's when the audience gets really riled up, explosive even. All these ancient Boomers get in like the moral equivalent of a massive food fight. It's a ride and a half, I'm tellin' ya."

Powell looked at the audience. "Here is a quick rundown of the major items in slide #1." Mock applause; Powell smiled wanly.

"At the archaic wave, the world is largely instinctual and the self is *impulsive*. These are mostly basic physiological needs and drives (beige), upon which biological life depends.

"As the self begins to differentiate itself from the physical world, it initially remains magically fused with parts of that world (animism), and it pictures itself as central to that world, concerned especially with its own safety and power (purple and red): the self is still *egocentric*.

"As the self increasingly develops its capacity to take the role of others, it moves from egocentric and preconventional modes to ethnocentric and conventional. Initially trapped by the rules and roles prescribed by society, the self at this wave is largely *conformist*. It is a mythic-membership self (blue), tightly bound by the mores, myths, and conventions of the prevailing culture. Truth at this wave often consists of *mythic absolutisms*: there is one, and only one, right way to view everything, and that is according to the Book—from the Bible to the Koran to Mao's Little Red Book."

"Kim, this is similar to Hazelton's talk yesterday," I whisper.

"Yes, the point is that these different models of the waves of development are all broadly similar. Yesterday Hazelton talked about the levels of memes. Today they will talk about the levels of self. They are all essentially similar."

"Why repeat all this, then?"

"Well, it's like Charles said, this is the 'details day.' They go over the details to make sure all the bases are covered. Don't worry if you don't remember any of this. If you just remember the Spiral Dynamics colors you'll do fine."

"I'm not so sure I can remember anything right now."

"Well, okay, just look at slide #1, you'll be okay."

I stared at Lesa Powell. She had an intensity that was infectious. I didn't see any anger, but she was in any event a truly striking figure. She was quite tall, about 5 foot 10, with a statuesque, slender body; hair unkempt in a natural fashion, verging on a sixties Afro; white pants, white shirt, bright contrast; she didn't so much walk as gracefully prowl, taking it all in: not a detail—about others, about things— seemed to escape her attention, which gave the impression that she had a type of panoramic awareness, radar in the back of her head. I looked at slide #1.

"Moving beyond conformist modes and herd mentality, consciousness develops the capacity to *reflect* on conventional truths and begin judging them by more universal standards: Is everything the Bible says really absolute truth? Is my country always right? Are conventional morals always correct? These powers of reflection and criticism are part of the extraordinary capacities brought by formal operational cognition—or simply rationality for short, the orange meme. The self moves from *conformist* to *conscientious*, striving, as it were, to wake up from the spell of the herd and its often confining and oppressive myths and half-truths. This marks the beginning of the shift from conventional to postconventional, from ethnocentric to worldcentric, from parochial to universal, from what is right and fair for my tribe, my group, my nation, to what is right and fair for all peoples, regardless of race, sex, color, or creed."

Powell walked slowly, lightly, to the edge of the stage, looked out at the audience. "But the move to postconventional and worldcentric is just beginning," she said. "The formal-rational wave of consciousness, despite its many undeniable benefits—from medicine to technology—nonetheless has a tendency to arid abstractions, which can distance the self from both nature within—élan vital, libido, emotional-sexual energies, organic richness—and nature without—resulting in the disenchantment of the world. In other words, one of the downsides of orange rationality is its tendency to *repress* those items not of its ilk."

"You see, sweet boy, you're repressing, aren't you? Admit it, sweet boy. All that rational science has cut your head off from your body, hasn't it?"

Chloe is lying on top of me, rubbing her naked body against mine, urging me onward.

"I don't know, Chloe, I don't know."

"Well you have, sweet boy. And that is why you think that bodiless cyberheaven will be our salvation. But that is simply a projection into the future of your own repressed state. Too much mechanical science, sweet boy, has severed your head from your body."

"Do you really think so, Chloe?"

"I know so, Ken."

"How do you know that, Chloe?"

"I told you. Because when you make love, you rattle. Hell, even the neighbors can hear it."

Nine Inch Nails are still playing "Downward Spiral" and "Things Falling Apart": geez, tell me about it.

"And so, yes, rationality can be repressive. But, of course, all memes tend to deny those aspects of reality that they do not like; rationality is by no means unique in this regard. In fact, as we will see, much of the 'oppression' and 'repression' for which orange rationality has been blamed was actually instituted by blue mythic order. It is simply that rationality, precisely because it is such a colossally powerful structure, can implement its own repressive agendas with frightening assurance. The worldview of universal formalism tends to be, even at its best, rather rigid, static, unyielding.

"All of this begins to change with the emergence of the green meme and the stages of cognition that are known as *postformal*. For the postformal green meme begins to differentiate and loosen up the rigidities of universal formalism, supplementing them, where appropriate, with an understanding of the richness and diversity of numerous cultures, identities, and truths, each of which needs to be cherished and honored, and not summarily strained through the uniform mesh of formal rationality."

"See? You're straining, sweet boy, you're straining," her naked body says to me, urging, urging.

The Offspring are wailing "Out Come the Wolves," Rage Against the Machine is pounding "Calm Like a Bomb."

She's probably right.

"Not now, Chloe, not now."

Do you recognize the timeless One, even here and now, that is spontaneously aware of all of this? If so, please tell me, Who and What are you, when you are deeper than within? Clouds pass by, feelings pass by, thoughts pass by—but what in you does not pass by? Do you see That One? Can you say its Name?

"Notice, in this regard, that growth and development often proceed by way of *differentiation* and *integration*. The most common example is the growth from a single-cell egg to a complex organism containing billions of cells. The zygote first divides into two cells, then four, then sixteen, thirty-two, sixty-four. . . . At each of these stages of *differentiation*, the cells are *integrated* into tissues, organs, and systems. Many people think that differentiation and integration are opposites, but actually they go together. From acorn to oak: the wonders of differentiation and integration."

Powell moved to the center of the stage, soft light caressing her figure. "Now the same thing happens in humans with the growth and evolution of worldviews. An earlier worldview is differentiated and then integrated into a higher, more complexly ordered worldview, which itself is then differentiated and integrated, and so on up the Spiral.

"And we are now at the point where the formal rational worldview is being differentiated into numerous *pluralistic systems*. This is one of the many gifts of green, a sensitivity to multiple contexts and relative truths and multicultural richness. Since the important truths of each culture and each individual are honored, the self at this wave, in addition to being 'sensitive,' is highly *individualistic*, as you can see in slide #1.

"At the next wave—the integral wave—these differentiated systems are taken up and *integrated* into rich patterns of holistic connections. The *commonalities* of the multiple systems are noticed in addition to their important *differences*. And yes, my friends, this is the famous leap to second-tier integral awareness, whose self is called *autonomous*. Some researchers, such as IC member Jenny Wade, prefer the term *authentic self*, and that's fine, too."

"Here's authentic," says Chloe, quickly stripping off her clothes and moving her naked body in shockingly obscene ways.

"Ken, can you create a sentence that has the word 'undulating' in it?"

"Chloe's undulating body began—"

"That's too obvious."

"Chloe's undulating breasts began—"

"Too obvious."

"Ken's attempt to use undulating began undulating in the most undulating of ways, so that—"

"Ken, sweet boy, what exactly are you doing?"

"That's an excellent question, Chloe, an excellent question."

"Why are these waves of selfhood so important?" Lesa Powell was starting to let her fabled angry sharpness come slowly to the fore, which made her impassioned presentation all the more edgily vivid.

"For one thing, they can help us to understand if a particular self is genuinely interested in mutual respect, mutual recognition, worldcentric concern and care and compassion. After all, the claim of postmodernism and multiculturalism is that a 'politics of recognition' demands that all cultural groups, especially marginalized groups, *be given mutual respect and recognition*. If that is one of our goals—if we want to extend mutual respect and recognition to all peoples in a worldcentric fashion—then we will simultaneously have to commit ourselves to growing and developing selves that are capable of worldcentric or postconventional awareness, yes?"

She looked out at the audience and yelled, "Yes?" The audience yelled back, "Yes!"

"Because *only* in the postconventional waves—Gilligan's universal care—can genuine respect and mutual recognition be found. You cannot *force* people to give mutual respect. This is common knowledge. I cannot pass a law that says you must love and respect me. The most I can do is pass a law governing your behavior, not your thoughts. But what the multiculturalists are asking for is more, you see: they want their group identities to be met with mutual respect, not just tolerance—they are asking for interior changes in people's attitudes, not just exterior rules about their behavior."

Lesa Powell was heating up; she prowled back and forth on stage, still smiling, but her intensity starting to focus like a laser. "I personally believe that a society where people meet each other with mutual respect is a noble goal, and that we all should work toward that end. But if so," and Powell's voice rose to an intense pitch, "then let me repeat!: *we are going to have to figure out how to develop more people to the postconventional waves*. As we have seen, postconventional, worldcentric respect is the product of at least five or six stages of vertical growth, and if the postmodernists wish to ground political culture in mutual recognition—and I personally think that is a fine idea—then we had better get busy figuring out how to grow and evolve to those higher levels of consciousness, because you will *never* have mutual respect without them." She paused and looked around the hall, as if daring anybody to make a sound.

"But as it is now, the green meme tries to give mutual respect to, say, red—and red proceeds to wipe its feet all over green—and green can't figure out what the fuck's the problem! 'Oooh, let's have some more caring dialogue,' says green, and red keeps fucking it over." Several in the audience laughed and clapped, with a few dissenting coughs and groans. "The only way red will ever agree with green is if red grows and evolves to blue, and then to orange, and then to green. But green just wants everybody to share and dialogue and be friends—clueless as to what that really involves." She shot a smile around the room.

"So here is my simple point: psychological development and cultural evolution is the only way out of oppression and marginalization— egocentric to ethnocentric to worldcentric. But the green meme—with its inherently flatland stance that claims all views are equal—denies levels, denies hierarchy, denies evolution, *denies* in effect the *solution* to the problem it hates, namely oppression. And thus the green meme, champion of flatland, ends up inadvertently *promoting* exactly the oppression it wishes to overcome. Along with the blue meme of outright racism, the green meme is the primary source of oppression in this culture."

Some in the audience gasped at the audacity of the charge, others erupted in applause mixed with several harsh and angry boos. Powell took a deep breath and brought her talk to a quick conclusion.

"And what do we call a fixation to the green meme? Boomeritis. It follows that boomeritis is one of the primary sources of oppression in this culture. If you doubt it, folks, just hang around, for these are some of the difficult and highly charged issues that we will be examining in our following sessions." Lesa Powell smiled, turned, and walked res- olutely off the stage.

Chloe is gently brushing her breasts along my shoulder blades and down the small of my back, her mouth forming a silent O. Why are we talking about boomeritis? I'm not a Boomer.

"Because," a voice comes out of the O in her mouth, "you want integral, yes?"

"Yes."

"*Then move beyond the Me generation.*" **I turn over to look at Chloe and with a jolt see Hazelton.**

Morin is back on stage.

"In looking at boomeritis, in the light of what Dr. Powell just said, here is what we have thus far: the Boomers were the first generation in history to develop in large numbers to the green meme—to pluralism, relativism, postmodernism, and multicultural sensitivity, which is all very well and good. In doing so, the postmodern and postconventional Boomers sometimes aggressively attacked the conventionally accepted truths of blue and orange—both politically, as in the fight for civil rights and environmental protection, and theoretically, in treatises dedicated to deconstructing outmoded theories—also well and good.

"But the Boomers, for various reasons, which we will continue to examine, *got stuck at green*, and this did two very unfortunate things. It prevented large numbers from moving forward into second-tier and truly integral constructions, a failure that let pluralism run riot in a rapture of fragmentation. And since pluralism—'I do my thing, you do yours'—is a supermagnet for narcissism, it became the home of boomeritis—high pluralism mixed with low narcissism. In other words, the green meme went pathological."

Morin paused, as if letting that thought sink in, then walked to the center of the stage. "The green meme went pathological, what we will be calling the 'mean green meme.' And let me tell you, folks, here we're talking about some sick fucks." Morin smiled broadly, as if that were a joke, but not really. It seemed that he was deliberately trying to provoke the audience. Was this some sort of test, or was Morin just a jerk? (But come to think of it, Fuentes and Powell did the same thing. Is this part of the test, too? I must remember to ask Kim.)

"At that point, the green meme infected with boomeritis began causing an amount of harm that many critics think actually outweighed the previous good," Morin said with a concerned emphasis. "As Don Beck, cofounder of Spiral Dynamics, put it, and I quote: 'Green has caused more harm in the last 30 years than any other meme.'" The audience audibly groaned. "Yes, my friends, where boomeritis goes, trouble follows."

Morin walked to the edge of the stage, still gently smiling his this-is-not-really-a-joke smile. "In terms of slide #1, the 'scene of the crime,' so to speak, is the area that moves from orange to green to integral, for somewhere in that transition is where the Boomers got stuck. That is the site of the multiple-car smash-up on Boomer Highway 68 that produced the mangled mess of boomeritis, a twisted portal for every preconventional unpleasantness to stream into the Me generation." Morin paused and looked out at the audience. "And this affected not just the Me generation. You younger folks out there will have certainly noticed that this boomeritis fallout has left a suffocating layer of dust on almost everything you do." Several of us "kids" applauded, whether we actually understood what he was saying or not. Take that, Mom and Dad.

"For the rest of today's session, we will therefore look a little more closely at the worldviews of orange, green, and integral—with several welcome intermissions by Stuart Davis." At Stuart's name, the audience cheered. "And then starting tomorrow we will begin examining the many concrete examples, some would say horrors, of boomeritis— that is, the concrete roadblocks to integral awareness.

"Ladies and gentlemen, Margaret Carlton."

"Kim, do you know Carlton?"

"She's from out of town."

"What, no gossip?"

"The day is young."

"Do you mind if I ask you something?" I whispered.

"Not as long as it's unbelievably original and intelligent."

"Well, that's the point. You sort of come on as this carefree wise-ass—I mean, the first day I met you you're like this airheaded bimbo— but you're not really like that at all. I am starting to suspect you are scary smart."

"Ph.D. from Antioch, cultural anthropology, third in my class. Post-doc here in Cambridge. What's it to you, Ken um Wilber?" hiding a smile.

"The big boobs, right?"

"Look, you try going through life with men talking to your chest, see how you respond. What would you do if you had boobs like these?"

"I'd probably spend most of my time playing with them."

"I'm serious. With this body you are reminded every minute that you are a sex object. I honestly don't mind the sex-object part; what I mind is trying to find a way to be *something else* as well in other people's eyes."

"Appreciated for your mind and not just your body."

"I know it's a cliché, but yes."

"Good afternoon. And now, the show-stopping thrill of the day: the discussion of the development of worldviews from orange to green to integral!" Burst of clapping and good-natured hissing.

"Have a quick look at slide #1," Margaret Carlton suggested. "Since I will be focusing on the middle waves of development, I will simply summarize the early waves—for those of you who can't read, that would be archaic, magic, and mythic—we will just call them all *preformal*. This doesn't mean that they are unimportant. On the contrary, as we have seen, each wave is a crucial foundation of all that will follow. It is just that, particularly in the modern world, the stage of *formal rationality*—or formal operational cognition (orange by any other name)—assumes a great deal of importance.

"The reason is simple: what is the cognitive capacity that allows us to move from conventional and ethnocentric to postconventional and worldcentric? Yes, that's right, it is formal operational cognition, or reason, or rationality, or simply the orange meme. This is important, people!" Carlton smiled as she bounced around the stage, her small, light frame occasionally seeming weightless. "Developmental psychologists are unanimous and adamant on that point: 'reason' is not just an arid and desiccating series of abstractions—it is the power to take *multiple perspectives*. This is why it is often called 'perspectival reason.' This is what we mean when we ask somebody to 'be reasonable'—we mean, try to see it from my perspective, too. Only as formal rationality begins to emerge in adolescence can individuals actually take multiple perspectives into account and thus begin to truly care about other viewpoints. This is an extraordinary growth and development in consciousness, and it ushers in the great transition from conventional, ethnocentric, and preformal modes to postconventional, worldcentric, and global modes—all of which are due to the amazing capacities of rationality."

I am floating not in but as the vast sky, a dream I have had since I was perhaps six. All things move through the spaciousness that I am. Yet in this body, I am a woman, and the polarization of energies is then unavoidable; the game commences with just that. The young Ken tells me that his generation will escape all this into a silicon crystal heaven, free of the horrible stain of flesh and its destiny of decay. The older Ken will know better, although the omega point of both their dreams is nonetheless the same, which is why they will meet one day, and soon. Out of my own womb, this vast spaciousness, they have both come, and to it they will both return, in their own ways.

Yet there is still the business of this flesh, and the unfolding waves of awareness that flow through this and every body, that flower, burst and sing their songs, then fade only to be replaced, as the merciless spiral rushes to the ocean of its own demise. And my generation, my dear, dear generation: what am I to do with it?

"Of course rationality can be misused—every meme has its healthy and unhealthy versions." Carlton looked around the room, as if she were looking at every single person individually, touching them one by one.

"A major downside of orange rationality—or formal rationality—is that it tends to be *static* and even *rigid* in its outlook. But," Carlton continued, her eyes lighting up, her voice vibrant, "and this is *most interesting*: when the *process* nature of systems is grasped, multiple dynamic and pluralistic contexts come into view, orange formalism dies down, and the next stage of green pluralism emerges, as you can see in slide #1."

"That's her idea of *most interesting*? What the fuck is her idea of boring?"

"Hush, Wilber."

"This stage of green pluralism is marked by an awareness that social-cognitive systems are *culturally and historically bound*. This, of course, is one of the major claims of postmodernism: that there are no universal truths, only historically relative and pluralistic frames of reference. These are all 'contextual,' or dependent upon local backgrounds and historical contexts; they are dynamic and constantly subject to change. I quote Deirdre Kramer, one of the most respected researchers in this area, who says, 'In a contextual/relativistic worldview'—that is, for the green meme—'random change is basic to all reality, and knowledge is embedded in its broader context, whether the context is the cultural/historical one, the cognitive framework, or the immediate physical and psychological context.' Likewise, 'The broader social, historical, moral, and physical context influences how one will approach and act in a situation. What aspect of a situation one focuses on will influence his or her interpretation or understanding of the situation. Every person, society, group and situation is unique'—and interpretations always differ, because contexts always differ."

"Borrrrrrring, Kim."

"She's just talking about the evolution from orange to green. You'll survive."

"Yes, but geez, all these jargon words."

"Could you possibly be any stupider, Wilber?"

"Well, I'm sure if I really tried, I could be."

Carlton took a deep breath and enunciated every word with deliberate care: "But precisely because green has as yet *no way to interrelate these pluralistic contexts*—since each remains 'incommensurate' with the others—the worldview of the green meme is ultimately *fragmented* and *chaotic*. As Deirdre Kramer summarizes the evidence, at this stage 'all people and events are unique and continually change in unsystematic ways. Consequently, contradiction runs rampant. There is no order to such a universe; any order must be imposed externally or via one's cognitive framework.'

Carlton looked out at the audience. "In other words, the green meme believes that all order is *imposed* by structures of power or ideology—imposed by the patriarchy, or by logocentrism, anthropocentrism, androcentrism, speciesism, phallocentrism, or my personal favorite, phallologocentrism—does that thing come with batteries or what? Whenever you hear any of those words, you are almost certainly in the presence of a green meme." Several loud groans from the audience accompanied her remark.

"Because green can grasp multiple contexts, but because *the rich networks of interconnections between multiple contexts are not grasped*, this worldview remains disjointed and fragmented. As we saw earlier, the green meme has *differentiated* numerous systems, but has not yet learned to *integrate* them. But then, you know what happens next?"

A dozen or so people in the audience shouted out, "It learns how to INTEGRATE them!" and all began laughing.

"Yes, my dears. Which results in second tier." Diminuitive Carlton smiled and paused for a moment.

"Kim, how did you meet Morin?"

"Oh, at one of these discussion series."

"What did you see in him?"

"Big mind."

"What did he see in you?"

"Big boobs."

"Maybe that's unfair. You're telling me that is all Morin saw in you?"

"At the beginning, of course."

"So you're saying that Morin has a history of chasing big-chested girls half his age?"

"No, actually, he doesn't. I think this was a first. Anyway, maybe that's why he starting seeing me, but it's not why he continued."

"Yes, okay, um . . ."

Kim turned in her seat and looked at me directly. "At Morin's age, and I honestly don't mean this in a derogatory way, he needs a delicate combination of things in a partner. It's sort of the photographic negative of when a beautiful woman needs a man to be interested in her mind. Morin needs a beautiful young woman who *understands* his mind, because only then can he triumph, only then can he really conquer."

It was a jarring thought. "Okay, that does sound a bit derogatory to me."

"Many men want to conquer, so what? Many women want to be conquered, at least in the bedroom, if not the boardroom, and again, so what? I understand Morin's ideas, or at least a lot of them, and so when he conquers me, he really conquers."

"You're proud of that?"

"Because, you twit, the ideas overpower me. The ideas, don't you get it?"

"I'm not sure."

"That's because you keep trying to think like a fucker instead of a fuckee."

I rubbed my eyes, looked around. Margaret Carlton started speaking again.

"We left off here: we saw that pluralistic relativism—the worldview of the green meme—*differentiates* systems but cannot *integrate* them. However, when the richly textured relationships between multiple contexts are discovered, the next worldview begins to emerge, which we simply call *integral*."

I wondered how many of the assembled really understood what she was saying. Carlton looked bemused. But the tepid applause to her last remark also hinted at an audience uneasiness, a vague recognition of the grim responsibility that these ideas carried. Once you get out of flatland, once you acknowledge hierarchy, or higher levels of anything, then you have something that you must *live up to*. . . .

"Thus, as Deirdre Kramer summarizes the situation—and yes, ladies and gentlemen, this marks the end of this section"—a twitter of grateful applause, to which I contributed—"the pluralistic green wave involves 'the differentiation of dynamic systems into culturally and historically defined contexts,' while the second-tier integral wave goes one step further and *integrates those differentiations*, resulting in 'the dialectical integration of cultural and historical systems into evolving social structures.' In short, from formalism to pluralism to integralism—from orange to green to . . . the quantum leap into the hyperspace of second-tier awareness."

Margaret Carlton started walking off the stage, and the audience gave her a standing ovation, as much out of relief as of appreciation.

"Ooooh, fuck me with your big mind, ooooh, it's sooo big, ooooh. . . ."
Kim is wiggling under me, and when I look down to take in the sights she
laughs hysterically. She isn't even naked, and her big boobs are hidden
under at least three sweaters.
"That's not funny, Kim."
"It's your dream, twit."
What was that David Foster Wallace book? *A Supposedly Fun Thing*
I'll Never Do Again.

Morin was back on stage. "Yes, it gets even better, for our next topic is the worldviews of modernity and postmodernity." Boo, hiss, clap, sneeze.

"What has all this to do with Boomers? And why should you Xers and Ys even care?" The audience abruptly went silent.

"It has frequently been noticed that Boomer intellectuals often identify themselves with the general movement of *postmodernism*, as against the previous *modernism* of the Enlightenment, rationality, objective truth, and bourgeois morality. Using the above clues from worldview development, which I'm sure you all followed breathlessly, we might be able to set this discussion of modern and postmodern in a clearer context." Morin looked up, waiting for laughter, and was greeted with dull silence. "Yes, right. Well, it appears that in many ways *modernity* was marked by the *formal* stages of worldview development (the orange meme), and *postmodernity* by the beginning of the *postformal* stages (especially green). There is even a developmental symmetry: modern is to postmodern as formal is to postformal."

The dull silence continued. Morin, annoyed, walked to the edge of the stage. "Here's what happened, folks. Under the noble guise of pluralism, relativism, and cultural diversity, postmodernism opened up the world to a richness of multiple voices, but then stood back to watch the multiple voices degenerate into a Tower of Babel, each voice claiming to be its own validity, yet few of them actually honoring the values of the others. With postmodernism, each voice was free to go its own way, whereupon everybody went in vigorously different ways. This did not ultimately *liberate* the many pluralistic voices, as postmodernism claimed, but merely sent them scurrying off, isolated and alienated, to the far corners of a fragmented world, there to suckle themselves in solitude, choking to death in the clutches of their own isolated me-ness."

I looked over at Kim; she is in love, she is beaming, she is what? being conquered by the ideas? surrendering to the ideas? being overpowered by the ideas? Is this any way to treat a student? On the other hand, it was hard to imagine anybody taking advantage of Kim.

"The move from formalism to pluralism was an extraordinary accomplishment; the failure to move from pluralism to integralism was a colossal disaster. Not only did pluralism itself fail to integrate cultural currents, it allowed—indeed, encouraged—every bit of residual narcissism to reactivate and flourish in an unprecedented fashion. The Me generation had finally found its voice, and the disasters of boomeritis were about to descend on an unsuspecting world."

I look at Hazelton and am astonished to find that physically she is not that attractive. A very plain face is floating in a beautiful sky, but the face itself had never really come into focus. But even so, the shining is unendingly beautiful, this is what I see.

"I'm downloading into silicon soon, did you know that?" I ask her.

"Then how will you and Chloe make love?"

"I'm sorry, what was that? I didn't get that."

"Which consciousness are you downloading?"

"Well now see, that's just what I wanted to talk to you about. See the problem is, well there are several. Well, let me explain. No, it's too late for that. Let me sum up."

"The worlds of silicon and carbon are hyperlinked by certain invariant isomorphisms. The archetypal patterns in one will repeat in the other, so the evolution in Carbon and Silicon will likewise be broadly isomorphic," the sky explains.

"That's it exactly. I think. So my question is, well, let me put it this way first. Right after the other way, which is probably not the best way, so let me back up to that previous thing which . . ."

"Oh, and Wilber. Rumor has it that you rattle when you make love. Why is that?"

"If I may say so, excellent question."

Lesa Powell had come back on stage. She was clearly the audience favorite, even though she usually shook them rudely. "Before we proceed to a brief survey of the areas that boomeritis has infected, let us look at a few possible objections to what has been said thus far."

Carolyn, who had been uncharacteristically silent, leaned past Scott and said to me, "I definitely want to hear these, because I have a ton of them myself." I couldn't tell if she was angry or pleasantly excited.

Powell spoke for almost an hour; I took extensive notes, particularly on the issues about Piaget and Kohlberg and stage conceptions in general. "A major objection," she began, "might be that stage conceptions are oppressive, marginalizing, patriarchal, sexist, racist, and Eurocentric"—wild applause from the audience. "I don't know how to tell you this, but research has not supported those claims at all. The problem, you see, is *not* that the stage conceptions are oppressive, but that some of the actual stages themselves are oppressive—in fact, virtually any first-tier meme will try to oppress other memes, or try to force its value structures on the others. That's the real problem, not the stage conceptions. In fact, the notion that stage conceptions cause oppression is simply the green-meme's attempt to force its own flat-land, nonhierarchical values on everybody else!"

Powell ended with a riff on Carol Gilligan that had the audience once again cheering and jeering.

"Listen, oh my Son," Mom says, laughing. "Us women, we women, we think differently."

"Yes, and?"

"And so we will save the world from the patriarchy."

"If that means from Dad, then great."

"It means from how you *all* think. You men."

"How's that, Mom?"

"Ranking, judging, putting everybody down. When we women take over"—she is still laughing, sort of—"then there will be no more wars."

"What, nations will nag each other to death?"

"There will be caring and linking and relationship, instead of ranking and domination and brutality. We will have loving, sharing, wonderful *partnership societies*—isn't that a lovely phrase, oh my Son?—instead of nasty ranking societies, hiss, hiss, hiss boom bah. With women presidents, no more wars!"

"Like with Catherine the Great, and Mary, Queen of Scots, and Queen Victoria, and Golda Meier, and Margaret Thatcher, and . . ."

"What?"

"Or my personal favorite, Isabel of Castile, founder of the Spanish Inquisition."

"They don't count."

"Because?"

"They were patriarchal females."

"How can you tell?"

I look directly at Mom, and her face becomes Kim's, which becomes Chloe's, which becomes Joan Hazelton's, which says, "You really are a man, aren't you?" And I think, what a horrible thing to call somebody.

Lesa Powell leveled a steady gaze at everybody present. "Carol Gilligan, as you might recall from Dr. Fuentes's talk, agrees that females proceed through three or four hierarchical stages of development—Gilligan herself refers to these as 'hierarchical stages'—and these are essentially the same hierarchical stages or waves through which males proceed—namely, preconventional, conventional, postconventional, and integral. These are, of course, nested hierarchies or growth hierarchies.

"The reason that many people, especially feminists, still incorrectly believe that Gilligan denied a female hierarchy of development is that Gilligan believes that males tend to make judgments using ranking or hierarchical thinking, whereas women tend to make judgments using linking or relational thinking—what has been summarized as agency and communion, respectively. But what many people overlooked is that Gilligan maintained that *the female orientation itself proceeds through four hierarchical stages*—from selfish to care to universal care to integrated.

"In other words, many feminists confused the idea that females tend not to think hierarchically with the idea that females do not develop hierarchically; the former is true, the latter is false, according to Gilligan herself."

Powell looked at the audience. "Why was Gilligan so widely misread and completely distorted in this area? Because the green meme denies hierarchies in general, and thus the green meme literally could not perceive her message accurately.

"But I have to tell you"—Powell gracefully prowled the stage, circled again—"the idea that females do not develop hierarchically is another feminist fairy tale that has crippled, and I mean *crippled*, feminism. The idea was that, since females are linking and relational—and that is good—and males are ranking and hierarchical—and that is bad—then all you have to do to make the world better is to be a woman. Ha!" she said, dancing across the stage. "Women themselves develop from preconventional or selfish relationship, to conventional or caring relationship, to postconventional or universal-caring relationship, to integral relationship. Just because you have relationship and linking does not say *which level* of relationship you have. And the lower, preconventional, selfish levels of female relationship are just as devastating to the world as are the lower levels of male development." Several men in the audience clapped and yelled their approval; women rolled their eyes, smiled, yawned.

"Denying female hierarchy thus denies the demand that females develop vertically, or actually *transform*. Any level of your development—red or blue or orange or green—was therefore taken to be just fine, as long as you were female. And this relieved women from the burden to hierarchically grow and evolve their own consciousness to higher levels. And I'm telling you, this let feminism perfectly rot." A few in the audience yelled, half agreeing, half furious.

"People, this is nothing but more flatland ideology. So please remember that fact the next time you hear a call for 'linking' or 'partnership' societies," Powell intoned. "You are being had; you are being ripped off; you are being taken to a strange Gilligan's Island where all the women are wonderful, all the men are beasts, and the all children are above average." Several laughs and murmurs. "Please do not distort Gilligan in that fashion. And please, I beg you, do not go down the road of boomeritis feminism, flatland feminism. There is instead an *integral feminism* lying yet in our future, that I promise you."

"I'll have the chicken Marsala," said Jonathan. "Hey, did you read the Harvard study showing that tofu causes the brain to shrink? The phytoestrogens in it. Soy products measurably lower IQ."

"Well that explains vegetarians," offered Chloe, who had joined us for lunch.

"Here's the thing about this discussion series," said Carolyn, who I had decided was angry, not excited. "It's all rigged from the start. If you buy any of this spiral or hierarchy or stages stuff, then what they say is probably true. But I don't buy it. Stage conceptions are imposed on all of us by—"

"Oh, don't even start heading toward that patriarchy crap," shot Chloe. "Nobody, and I mean nobody, believes that bullshit anymore, outside of your own cloistered cultural studies department."

"The history department believes it," said Kim.

"So does anthropology. Actually, all the humanities, pretty much," Scott noted.

"In other words, all the boomeritis strongholds believe it," said Jonathan. "I mean, that's the whole point the IC crowd is making, right? Your argument is circular, Carolyn. You're saying that the hierarchy thing—and the stages, and the Spiral of development, all of that—you're saying that is a nasty product of the patriarchy and therefore you don't believe it. And they're saying that the notion of patriarchy itself is being used by you to deny certain unpleasant facts."

"My argument is not circular, yours is." Carolyn stared at him unflinchingly. "These stage conceptions and the tests for them are preselected and prescreened to give the results that they want to get, and so of course they get them. Their whole argument, their entire argument, is in fact a product of the patriarchy and its harsh ranking games. If the only tool you have is a hammer, everything starts to look like a nail."

"What exactly is that supposed to mean?" asked Jonathan.

"Supposed to mean?" Carolyn squinted harshly. "Just when was the last time you were in anything resembling a relationship, Jonathan?"

"Well, that's not fair. Relationships don't come easy for me. It takes time. I have to know and love somebody before I use and degrade them."

"You think this is all a big joke, Jonathan, but it's not funny. I'm telling you, it's not funny."

"What's not funny? Because this is a pretty funny-looking crowd to me." Stuart and Hazelton had drifted over. Silent glances around the table asked the question: what exactly were they doing together?

"Dr. Joan, Carolyn here thinks you're a patriarchal pig, or pig-ess, I guess," said Jonathan.

"A patriarchal pigess, oh dear. I've been called a few things in my day, but that's a first."

Carolyn stammered, "Dr. Hazelton, I never—"

"I'll bet you haven't," said Chloe.

"Oh, look, dear souls, I know the problems with all these types of ideas. Nobody comes to these conclusions easily. Certainly not my generation, which, as you now surmise, was basically defined by the green meme, by a strong anti-hierarchy, anti-stages, anti-judging stance. Don't get me wrong; I truly love my generation. But it is time we got over ourselves, yes? And therefore let your generation get out from under our shadow!" she said, laughing.

"But really, even if what you say is true," I ask, "why should we—my generation—even bother with it? Why should us kids give a hoot about boomeritis?"

"For all the reasons we are trying to suggest at the seminar series. There really is an integral awareness, which houses most of the values that all of you, that all of us, truly share—a sense of global caring, a concern for the environment, a universal compassion and fairness. But more than that!" and she lit up from within, became suddenly, unexpectedly, vividly *there*. "You're the global Internet generation!—the global-village kids, so your consciousness must become global itself, or I assure you, you will go completely nuts!"—she smiled, her voice a mild thunder. And then in the calm quiet after a quick storm: "Many of your generation are deeply depressed . . . because you're not living up to your integral potential, are you?"

We all stared at each other; nobody blinked, as if doing so would be an admission of guilt, an acknowledgment of what might be a sad truth hanging in the air.

"Look, it's simple," she continued, emphasizing several of her words for effect. "The world is now *global*; unless your consciousness *also* becomes global, there will be a *mismatch*, a *disconnect* between you and reality, and *therefore* you will experience this as depression or some other damned *unpleasant* symptom." We again all stared at each other; it almost made sense.

"And you feel that way about yourself, too?" Carolyn ventured.

"Sure, of course. I do not want to be selfcentric, I do not want to be ethnocentric—I want to be worldcentric, I want to be more open, more inclusive, more integral, call it whatever you like, and I won't really sleep easy until that happens, you know?"

"Must have been a long time since you've slept at all," leveled Jonathan.

"Don't mind him, Joan," said Stuart smiling. "He sleeps like a baby, even when awake."

I am walking down a long corridor. There is a room at the end of the hall. And I know that he is there, sitting in that room, waiting for me. And I know that I will literally die when I meet him. And I know that it is going to happen, and happen fairly soon. And I know that this time, this is not a dream.

Dr. Morin flashed the next slide. It said, "The Horror Show of Pluralism." And so began the afternoon session of the "details day."

"Most of us"—Morin's booming voice filled the hall—"have become so used to pluralism—you do your thing, I do mine—which seems to be so kind and considerate of others—that we tend to overlook the horrors that can, and often are, perpetrated in its name. I will not make a long drawn-out argument for this but simply let the Marquis de Sade make the point for me. De Sade, incidentally, has often been celebrated as a postmodern hero, a hero of transgression and subversion—you'll see more of this tomorrow with Foucault. In de Sade's novel *Juliette*, the character Minski is accused of raping, sodomizing, and murdering two dozen men, women, girls, and boys. Minski gives a chillingly accurate, postmodern, pluralistic defense of these brutal actions:

> Similar to the concepts of virtue and vice, [justice and injustice] are purely local and geographical; that which is vicious in Paris turns up, as we know, a virtue in Peking, and it is quite the same thing here: that which is just in Isfahan they call unjust in Copenhagen. Amidst these manifold variations do we discover anything constant? Only this: self-interest is the single rule for defining just and unjust.
>
> Justice has no real existence, it is the deity of every passion. . . . So let us abandon our belief in this fiction, it no more exists than does the God of whom fools believe it the image: there is no God in this world, neither is there virtue, neither is there justice; there is nothing good, useful, or necessary but our passions, nothing merits to be respected but their effects.

"The pluralistic, green, sensitive self serves a wonderful function: it helps to break up the rigidly formal rational worldview and open it to multicultural richness. But if we simply stop at pluralism, without looking for deeper, wider, more integral connections, then the horrors of pluralism come to dominate the day, as we will unfortunately begin to see in gruesome, truly gruesome, detail."

Morin paused for the effect, which was forthcoming, rather similar to what was called "first degree" torture in medieval times—namely, a simple description of what was about to happen to the victim. "Second degree" torture was showing the victim the instruments of torture;

"third degree" was actually applying them. I wondered how far the IC folks would go with us. . . .

Carla Fuentes again came on stage. "We have one last, short piece of ground to cover. We just looked at the worldviews from orange to green to integral—namely, formalism to pluralism to integralism. We now need to take a last quick look at the corresponding types of self or self-identity."

"Yup, color Chloe gone."

"Chloe, why do you even come in here in the first place? You always sit down, wait for the first sentence, then split."

She dropped her persona for a fleeting moment. "I love you, sweet boy, but I really do have some design work I need to do. You figure out boomeritis, then you can cure us both of it." Laughing, "But I think only one of us has it, sweet boy."

The slide on the wall said "The Difference between Individualism and Autonomy." Fuentes was direct. "The research in this area has been quite sophisticated. For example, one of our valued members here at IC is Susanne Cook-Greuter, wonderful woman, brilliant researcher. She has expanded upon and refined the pioneering work of Jane Loevinger. They both have found that the stages of self development move from *autistic* (archaic, beige) to *impulsive* (magic, purple) to *self-protective* (egocentric, red) to *conformist* (mythic-membership, blue) to *conscientious* (formal-rational, orange) to *individualistic* (pluralistic, green) to *autonomous* (integral). And then to yet even higher, transpersonal waves, which we will discuss later. You can see all of these on slide #1."

Higher stages than integral? Transpersonal stages? Just what the hell is that? I glance around to see if anybody has registered this. Apparently not. Except that Kim leans over slightly, looks at me, and winks.

"We pick up the story at orange, at the stage called *conscientious*, so named because the self is starting to use reason and a type of scientific and pragmatic inquiry, and thus it is 'conscientious' in the sense of striving hard to go beyond myths and find the truth. As Susanne Cook-Greuter puts it, 'With the conscientious self, formal operations and abstract rationality are at their peak. There is a deep belief in (unilinear) progress and the perfectibility of humankind. There is also a conviction that the proper analytical, scientific methods will eventually lead to the discovery of how things really are, that is, to the discovery of truth.' But, of course, as important as that development is in many ways, formal science can still be harshly insensitive to truths other than its own."

"You see, sweet boy, that is why you rattle," says Chloe as she cups her naked breasts in her hands and pushes them toward me.

"Okay, you know what? I do not rattle. Not rattle. Rattle, not."

"But sweet boy, you do. Who would know better than me?"

"Well, my hairdresser."

"You don't have a hairdresser, and you can't joke your way out of this one."

"Okay then, how *can* I get out of this one?"

"Well, now, that's the question, isn't it, sweet boy? That's the question."

"All of that rigidity begins to change with the first postformal stage—yes, that's right, with green. The worldview of green, we saw, is pluralistic relativism, and the corresponding sense of self Cook-Greuter calls *individualistic*. This is a very important development, especially for boomeritis. As she explains: 'Individuals at this stage become preoccupied with uncovering previous assumptions and with exposing "false" frameworks. There is a tendency to distrust conventional wisdom and especially the "super-rational" tenets of the previous stage (of universal formalism, or orange). "Individualists" need to distance themselves from the sanctioned role-identities of society and to redefine themselves independently. They express and relish their uniqueness and their subjective experiences in the here and now because to them these are the only assertable realities (i.e., green's highly subjectivistic stance). Truth can never be found by any method because everything is seen as relative, as a matter of perception, point of view, or context.' In other words, the general stage we are also calling contextualism or pluralism."

"Good grief, Kim, I'm getting lost in all this jargon. This is too hard, isn't it?"

"Oh poor thing, forced to think, are we? Ya feeble-brained weenie, ya candy ass, ya whiny face, ya sissy, ya wimp, ya wuss, ya nancy boy, ya—"

"Jesus, stop that, Kim, you're scaring me. I'll pay attention, honest!" She started laughing out loud.

"But, of course, there is a horrible downside for the self at this green stage. With pluralism, precisely because 'every person, society, group, and situation is unique,' the self at this stage of development is likewise radically unique, different, separate . . . , and therefore ultimately isolated. What originally seems to be radical freedom for each self—because it is different and unique—can soon turn out to be radical isolation of the self, for just that reason. To be completely unique is to be completely set apart; to be completely set apart is to be completely alienated. Radical pluralism leads all too often to radical alienation."

Is that what had happened to Dad? He started out so full of care and passion, so committed to letting everybody "be free to be themselves"—he even produced a PBS show, "Free to Be You, Free to Be Me." And then he ended up so alone, so alienated, so set apart from others and even from the causes he espoused. According to Fuentes, one is the logical outcome of the other. Dad networked himself to an emotional death, a hollow-eyed lack of belief in anything except networking itself. When you are not allowed to rank, you are not allowed to have convictions. By spreading the net as wide as he could, he deleted depth from it altogether; he became himself the ghost in the machine, haunting the shallow hallways of his superficial self.

I looked at Carolyn, Kim, Scott, Jonathan. How would we fare when we were Dad's age? What of our ideals, long since soured, would start to devour us as well? Now Dad only works in Third and Fourth World countries, where he really doesn't have to interact with anybody at all. The only thing he is passionate about now is about how everybody else is totally fucked up. He's *very* angry about that.

Carla Fuentes seemed to summarize it all. "Development, we have seen, proceeds by differentiation and integration, and at this first post-formal stage (green), consciousness has managed to differentiate multiple systems, but not yet integrate them, and thus its self, and its worldview, tend to remain fragmented, pluralistic, inchoate. The self all too often revolves around itself, becoming its own universe, self-absorbed and self-alienated. In other words, this is a type of intense narcissism, but generated in this case by a very high level of development. But should this relatively 'high narcissism' (of green) be combined with remnants of emotional narcissism (of red), an explosive mixture is set in play: boomeritis is ready to erupt."

"People try to put us down, Talking 'bout my generation, Just because we get around, Talking 'bout my generation. . . . " Talking about my generation is what my generation does. In so many ways, I am the spirit of those children. I was at the "summer of love"; I was shot at Kent State; I was defined by three assassinations that tore my heart until it bled; it still bleeds softly to this day, warm fluid running lonely on the ground. I was a war that split a nation; I watched as the poor and helpless were downtrodden; I sang songs of liberation and danced them till my feet were tattered tissues of despair.

In this particular case, the sky has become a woman, and in this female body, meant to embrace, I still sing those very songs.

Fuentes flashed slide #4, "The Autonomous Self Is a Global Self."

"As I was saying . . . ," and before Dr. Fuentes could be saying anything, Carolyn, whose agitation had been visibly increasing with every presentation, could no longer contain herself and blurted out, "Dr. Fuentes, I don't mean to interrupt, and I realize the discussion period is later. But really, I know a lot of us just can't continue with this line of ideology. This kind of gross ranking of human beings is intolerable."

"Human beings are not ranked, *ever*," said Fuentes, "but the inclusiveness of their thinking can be. You may or may not like it, but research shows that your own objection itself comes from a very high stage of moral development. We are simply trying to help more people find a similarly expanded sense of care and concern and compassion. But these waves of consciousness are potentials that are present in all people, so no human being is ever ranked."

Somebody from the audience: "But green, in and by itself, refuses second tier and actually fights it."

"Yes, that's right. Green is uncomfortable with anything second tier, amounting at times to a full-blown hatred, which it usually conceals in pieties. But all first-tier memes dislike all other memes, so this is nothing new with green. Yellow, as Dr. Hazelton pointed out yesterday, honors and embraces growth hierarchies, ranked values, universal flow systems, and strong individualism. Green looks at all of those terms—

universals, ranking, hierarchies, individualism—and screams 'oppression! domination! marginalization! elitism! arrogance!' and so on.

"In fact, there is a simple rule about this," and she pronounced each word slowly, as if for emphasis: "Whenever green looks at yellow, it sees red. Do you understand? Green sees all yellow as being red, as being mean and arrogant, and it reacts violently to that. Of course, green can't really help this; since it literally cannot see yellow, it can only interpret yellow's actions in the terms that it knows, and so yellow appears to be that horrible red meme, and green swings into action to try to destroy or deconstruct yellow wherever it finds it."

"That's you, Carolyn dear."

"Shut the fuck up, Jonathan, I swear to God."

Fuentes looked at her notes and regrouped. I whispered to Kim, "So, I'm curious. Why did you say the only reason Morin asked you out at first was because of your body? He was, what, staring at your tits while he talked?"

"No more than you do." I turned bright red.

"Look, it's like this," Kim said. "I can tell a man's age by how often he looks down at my chest. Adolescent males can't take their eyes off them. By middle age, it's every few minutes. Old age, you can actually talk to a man eye-to-eye for an hour. You must have noticed this in yourself, noticed this obsession in your fantasy life?"

"What, me?" I turned brighter red.

"Well, look how much we've been talking about it just today. And somehow I don't think that's the end of it, is it?"

"Oh, wow, listen to that fascinating thing Fuentes is saying." I stare resolutely, bright-red-headedly, ahead.

"Precisely because the self at the integral wave now consciously grasps global and universal concerns, the self at this stage has a moral sense that fully expands to include all beings, regardless of race, sex, color, or creed. The self is no longer 'free' to do whatever it wants, because its moral sense is grounded in the necessity to exhibit universal fairness and compassion to all peoples. It is no longer 'free' to disobey that calling. At this stage, the self is free *only* if it takes this global perspective into account.

"And that is the true meaning of *autonomy*: I am free of lesser motivations—free of *egocentric* and *ethnocentric* prejudices—only if I act from a *worldcentric* awareness. Autonomy does *not* mean being free to do what I want; it means being free to act from the deeper space of postconventional awareness. Thus, as consciousness evolves from a worldview of pluralism (where the self is radically unique and therefore often isolated) to a worldview of integralism (where the self acknowledges the moral demand of global justness and fairness), the self has moved from a stance of *individualism* to one of *autonomy*."

Fuentes said all this with gentle confidence, laced with a quiet passion born perhaps of her own inner struggles with these very demons. "This stage, which transcends the individualistic self and its alienation, is part of the cure for boomeritis!" she said with lilting emphasis. "Susanne Cook-Greuter, as we saw, calls it *autonomous*, because one 'integrates several different conflicting frameworks of the self into a coherent new theory of who one is. . . . Autonomous individuals become able to "own" whatever is part of themselves. They can integrate previously compartmentalized subidentities of the self into a coherent new whole.' Note the emphasis on integration and wholeness, in both the self and the world—the general stage we are calling *integral*."

"Well, no, look, Kim, it's just that, you know, why did you think Morin was only after your body?"

"Because he came at me like a freight train."

"But, um, doesn't a person usually get out of the way of a freight train?"

"Look, Ken. Every girl grows up knowing who is attractive to boys and who isn't. You boys have your ranking system, whatever it is—oh, I suppose it's who can beat the crap out of who, how clever. Well, us girls have our own ranking systems—for example, we know who the boys stare at. Feminists might try to wash all this away as a social construction, but it's biological, I tell you. It is so deeply rooted you'll never get rid of it until you get rid of humans."

"Well, in AI we're working on that."

She looked at me, raised her eyebrows. "Whatever. But you're sitting there, on a bench, you're sixteen years old, in comes the football team, and every one of them turns their head and stares at one girl—the big-chested early developer—and I'm telling you, it eats into how you see yourself. Every woman carries this thermometer in the back of her head: it registers her capacity to be seen, to attract attention. And she knows every other woman's temperature. So you men, admit it or not, want to see, want to stare, want to gaze. And we women, admit it or not, want to be seen, to be gazed upon."

I supposed it made sense. "So you're saying that Morin was like giving you the major monological eyeball treatment."

"That is correct."

"I see." And we both laughed out loud.

Fuentes glanced down at us. "Let me give you one last piece of research, and then my presentation is over!" Loud applause, several whistles. "Cheryl Armon, who has written extensively on the differences between individualism and autonomy, points out that at the previous stage of individualism (green), 'The focus is on the self and enabling the self to make its own choices according to its own values. Justification of values and judgments lie in the very fact that they are personal, individual, and primarily idiosyncratic. Everyone tolerates all moral viewpoints, and none feel responsible to anyone to whom they have not made themselves responsible. Each self pursues its own trajectory. This individualistic self produces and carries with it its own little planetary system of values.'

"'In contrast to individualism,' Armon points out, '*autonomy* relies on broader principles that coordinate and integrate abstract causal relations across multiple contexts. Autonomy consists of a more cognitively advanced and more ethically inclusive form of adult thought than individuality.' Whereas individualism rests on pluralistic relativism, second-tier autonomy 'is focused on the making of self-governed judgments by reference to *universal principles*.' Universal, global, worldcentric, get it?"

Fuentes looked up, glanced around the hall. "So autonomy is self-determination, but only in a very special sense, which is quite different from egocentric or narcissistic me-ness or individualism." Fuentes paused; the room got very quiet. "An egocentric person can be happy if others are suffering; an autonomous person cannot."

She waited for the gravity of that to pull us all in. "It's a simple test, yes?"

She again looked around the hall. "Autonomy, as Kant reminded us, does not mean acting as if only I existed; it means acting as if everything I did applied to others as well, so that I cannot be happy, self-determined, and deeply free unless *all others* can participate in this freedom. Real autonomy, in other words, does not mean I can do anything I please, and it certainly does not mean 'Don't tell me what to do!' It means I am not happy unless all other people can join in any freedom that I might have. The autonomous person, in other words, is *bound* and *determined* by a higher consciousness, a higher morality, a higher calling, that will not let him or her sleep peacefully until all people can swim in the ocean of that same freedom. Autonomy is an inner demand, not an outer conformity, but it is a *demand* nonetheless: an autonomous person is not free to do whatever he or she likes from an egocentric or ethnocentric stance; an autonomous person is truly free only when acting from a global, worldcentric awareness of justice, fairness, impartiality, and care. Call it whatever we like—autonomous, integral, dynamic dialectical, postconventional, worldcentric—this is a perspective that sets individual and cultural contexts in a universal commitment to fairness and care: by whatever name, *integral*.

"In short, *the autonomous self is a global self*, anchored in networks of universal fairness and impartiality, along with global care and compassion, and such a self cannot *not* act by those *demands*. It is, more or less, the precise opposite of 'Don't tell me what to do!'"

Fuentes looked straight ahead, smiled, bowed slightly, and walked off the stage.

Dr. Morin walked slowly to the podium and flashed slide #5: "Good News, Bad News."

Chloe is naked, hanging upside down from a chandelier, swinging back and forth.

"Ken, did you know that the average twenty-something male has an explicit sexual fantasy once every ten minutes?"

"Why no, I did not know that, Chloe."

"But Ken, aren't you twenty-something?"

"Why yes, Chloe, yes I am, but apparently I had just not noticed this."

"It's quite true. Extensive research has demonstrated that the average twenty-something male has an X-rated sexual fantasy once every ten minutes."

"Is that in the patriarchy or the matriarchy?"

"Silly boy."

"How about the average twenty-something girl? How many X-rated fantasies?"

"About one every hour or two, but they are not X-rated—they are not visually pornographic, they are romantic images, like a candle-lit dinner. Did you know that, Ken?"

"Why no, I did not know that, Chloe."

Chloe continues swinging upside down, her naked breasts and erect nipples swaying back and forth, back and forth, back and forth . . . her luscious ass swinging back and forth, back and forth. . . .

"Did you know that the average number of sexual partners for a young, active gay man is over 100 per year, but the average number of sexual partners for lesbians is one every seven years?"

"Why no, I did not know that, Chloe."

"What do you deduce from that fact?"

"I deduce that I want to be reborn a gay male."

"No, no, silly boy. You deduce that females are more committed to mindful relationship and that males are more committed to mindless orgasms."

"I was going to say that."

"Do you know why that is true, Ken?"

"I believe Woody Allen already explained it. God gave men a brain and a penis, but only enough blood to operate one at a time."

"But that is not a joke, Ken. It is the way of the ugly world. Did you know that?"

"Why no, I did not know that, Chloe."

"Then what good are you?"

"An excellent question, Chloe, an excellent question."

Morin is still talking. "We have been focusing on the fascinating—I'm telling you fascinating!—evolution from *orange* to *green* to *integral*.

"Our thesis is straightforward, ladies and gentlemen, and comes in two parts, the 'good news' and the 'bad news' of the Boomers. I'll give the full, ugly, technical language first, then summarize it for dummies.

"*The good news*: The general trends of postmodernism, which in many ways reached a peak with the Baby Boom generation, heroically fought the inequalities and marginalizing tendencies of mythic absolutism (blue) and formal rationality (orange), and did so precisely through a higher growth and evolution of consciousness to early post-formal cognition (green), which, in understanding the truly important role of contextualism, pluralism, and multiple perspectives, was able to spot, and often redress, many of the downsides of feudal mythology and Enlightenment rationality. These downsides have been chronicled at great length by Boomer intellectuals: racism, sexism, colonialism, eurocentrism, androcentrism, speciesism, phallocentrism, logocentrism, phallologocentrism. As we will see in the following seminars, we at IC agree with a great many of those critiques. This is the useful and positive side of postmodernism."

I looked at Kim; she was beaming. I imagined Morin looking at Kim—*looking* at Kim; the monological eyeball taking in all of that ample territory. Oh my.

"And now, *the bad news*: Infected by an inordinate amount of emotional narcissism, the psychological development of the Boomers became *arrested* at the green meme, at the stage of pluralistic relativism with its highly individualistic self. The very characteristics of pluralism made it a strong magnet for the emotional narcissism of 'Don't tell me what to do!' If all truth is relative, culturally molded, and pluralistic, then quite literally *nobody can tell me what to do*, because *none* of those truths have any binding nature—none of them have any power over *me*.

"And so it is the irony of ironies that an incredibly high developmental wave (green) became the roaring habitat of shallow impulses (red and purple), which otherwise might have dissipated of their own unheeded accord. But under the shelter of postconventional, poststructural, postmodern schemes, all of my preconventional, narcissistic, egocentric impulses can find a happy home. That sad mixture of postconventional ideals with preconventional impulses is boomeritis."

The emotional temperature of the audience rose rapidly, reaching a zenith with the following, which Morin delivered in a fevered pitch:

"Those are the strange pre and post bedfellows that constitute boomeritis. And it was boomeritis that moved the Berkeley protests; that took to deconstruction with a bloody vengeance; that embraced radical pluralism and then began to viciously destroy all values other than its own; that reread history as a chronicle of wickedness compared to its own splendidly shining self; that trashed not just the negatives but the many positives of the modern Enlightenment; that blew social constructivism up to an absolute so it could blow up and completely annihilate any view other than those it sanctioned; that turned spirituality into a New Age narcissism that situated its divine ego precisely in the center of the entire cosmos; that claimed it had the new and glorious paradigm, which was unprecedented in all of history and which would usher in the most extraordinary transformation the world has ever known; and that claimed in all of this sickening, sordid, sophomoric chicanery a moral superiority that was historically unprecedented."

Some of the Xers and Ys in the audience had begun applauding about halfway through Morin's oratorical excoriation; they continued doing so as both his voice and their applause reached a crescendo together. "This intense mixture of high pluralism with low narcissism—this pathetic pathology of epic proportions—is known as boomeritis, and it is boomeritis that has become, in its own postmodern way, every bit as pernicious as the ills of modernity it so ruthlessly condemned, making the Boomers indeed the most odious generation in American History."

There was a muffled roar from the audience, a jangled amalgam of applause, boos, shouts, and jeers. Several people were standing and clapping, many were fuming, looking back and forth. Jonathan was cheering, just to make trouble; Scott looked forlorn; Carolyn was still angry, maybe even more so now; Kim was beaming at Morin.

A black gentleman, the last speaker for the day, walked on stage, amid the lingering audience furor.

"That's Mark Jefferson," said Kim, as her look of blissful surrender shifted to resolve. "He's one of Charles's best friends. A background you would not believe. He came out of Bed-Sty, was Special Ops in the Rangers, got one of those MacArthur genius awards for—get this— ghetto photography as art. Ran across Morin's writings, said it saved his life."

"How did they meet?"

"Charles and Mark? The strangest part of the story: automobile accident."

"What?"

"Charles ran into him at the intersection of 10th and Percy."

"You're kidding."

"Hand to Goddess. Ran into him. Nobody was hurt, fortunately. But what everybody remembers about this story is Mark's absolutely classic opening line. After they had silently exchanged driver's licenses, Mark looked up and said, 'Ah yes, Dr. Morin. I have been looking for you.'"

Mark Jefferson stepped out on stage, smiled at the audience, and began his talk as if he were picking up exactly where Morin left off, but now attempting to soothe the psychic bruises that Morin had, for whatever reasons, wantonly inflicted on the audience.

As Jefferson continued talking, I had the strange impression that he and Morin were playing "good cop, bad cop" with the assembled. Morin was the bad cop, who taunted the crowd with threats and accusations—the verbal equivalent of being pounded with a meat mallet. Then Jefferson played the good cop, soothing ruffled feathers, making nice, and thus leading the rowdy crowd more willingly toward the desired destination. But it didn't seem to be an act for Jefferson; as soon as he started talking, it was obvious that, rightly or wrongly, he deeply believed what he was saying.

"Let us not forget, my friends: the truly important point is that it is from the large fund of green memes that second tier emerges. It is from the pluralistic perspectives freed by green that integrative and holistic networks are built. That fact is worth repeating. Development, we have often seen, tends to proceed by differentiation and integration. The green meme heroically manages to differentiate the often rigid, abstract, universal formalism of the previous orange wave. It therefore discloses, not a rigid, businesslike, scientific rationality that tends to ignore and marginalize anything not of its ilk, but a beautiful tapestry of multiple contexts, richly different cultural textures, pluralistic perceptions, and individual differences, and it becomes sensitive—the sensitive self!—to all of those often unheard, unheeded voices. We have seen that every meme makes an invaluable contribution to the health of the overall Spiral, and this pluralistic sensitivity is the one of the great, great gifts of green.

"Once those wonderful differentiations are made, they can then be brought together into even deeper and wider contexts that disclose a truly holistic and integral world: the leap to second-tier consciousness can occur—but *only* because of the work that the green meme has accomplished. There is first differentiation, then integration. Second tier completes the task begun by green, and this allows us to move from pluralistic relativism to universal integralism. That is what I mean when I say that green *frees* the pluralistic perspectives that second tier will integrate."

"So, well, when did Morin stop looking at you as just a body?"

"When he found out that conquering a mind gives even stronger orgasms."

"Geez, Kim, did I need to hear that? So, um, you're saying that he found out you have a mind as big as your boobs."

Kim turned and looked at me. "Something like that."

"So you two are like, what, the blissful couple? You two just get down and get jiggy every night, eh?"

Kim's stare burned the air.

I grinned. "Oh, I can just hear the sound of his big mind and your big boobs slamming into each other. Ka-whomp, ka-whomp, ka-whomp. . . . "

"Okay, wise guy, want to talk about you and Chloe?"

"Wow, that Jefferson is really something, isn't he?"

"In short, since green is the conclusion of first-tier thinking, it prepares the leap to second tier. But in order to move into second tier, the fixation to pluralism and the green meme in general needs to be relaxed. Its accomplishments will be fully included and carried forward. But the attachment to its own stance needs to be eased, and it is precisely boomeritis—or a narcissistic attachment to the intense subjectivism of the green meme—that makes such a letting-go so difficult. By highlighting our fixation to the green meme, I believe that we can begin to transcend and include its wonderful accomplishments in an even more generous embrace."

Me First and the Gimme Gimmes are playing send-ups of Boomer classics—"All We Need Is Love," "Lean on Me," "One Tin Soldier"—while Blink 182 slams melodically into air, Matchbox 20 thumps the night away, Jerk Off 32 keeps the beat with only one glove, and the pound pound pounding in my brain reminds me yet again why suicide can be so reasonable on any given Monday afternoon. "But, sweet boy, if you off yourself, what on earth about *this*?"

Jefferson flashed slide #6, "Beyond Pluralism."

"But why is boomeritis one of the greatest obstacles to the emergence of an integral vision? What about the rigid conformity of blue fundamentalist religion? What about the often nasty materialism of orange capitalism? What about the horrible economic conditions of many Third World countries? What about. . . .

"Yes, yes, all of that is true. But, as we were saying, it is only *from* the stage of green that second tier can emerge. Of course, *all* of the pre-green memes also prevent the emergence of an integral view. My point—and the only reason we are picking on Boomers—is that the Boomer generation is the first in history to significantly evolve to the green wave in large numbers, and thus it is the first generation that has a real chance to significantly move forward into second-tier integral consciousness—and to use that consciousness to organize social institutions in a truly widespread and integral fashion.

"*But it has not yet done so*, because it has not yet gone post-green to any significant degree. As we saw, less than 2 percent of the population is post-green. But my point is, *it still might do so*! And since it is only from green that it *can* do so, the Boomers are still poised for a possible leap into the hyperspace of second-tier consciousness. And that is not a boomeritis grandiose claim; it is backed by substantial evidence, particularly from social and psychological studies."

"What about us?" a Gen-Xer yelled from the audience.

"Oh, don't worry," smiled Jefferson. "There's even better news for you. But I have to start with Boomers and tell them that they are the vanguard of one of the greatest transformations in history, or else they will walk out of here in droves!" Boos and cheers from all over the auditorium.

Slide #7, "The Integral Culture." Jefferson continued gently, ardently, driving to the conclusion of the entire day's presentation.

"Research by the sociologist Paul Ray has recently concluded that a new cultural segment, whose members he calls 'the cultural creatives,' now make up an astonishing 20 to 25 percent of the adult American population—or around 50 million people, many of which are Boomers.

To distinguish them from the previous cultural movements of *tradition-alism* and *modernism*, Ray calls this group the *integral culture*. Exactly how 'integral' this group is remains to be seen, but I believe Ray's figures represent a series of very real currents. The *traditionalists* are grounded in premodern mythic values (or blue), the *modernists* are grounded in rational-industrial values (or orange), and the *cultural creatives* are grounded in postformal/postmodern values (or green). Those three movements are exactly what we would expect from our survey of the growth and evolution of consciousness—preformal mythic to formal rational to early postformal, as you can see in slide #1.

"But a few more points stand out. What Ray calls the 'integral culture' is not actually integral. It is not grounded in universal integralism or second-tier consciousness. Rather, as Ray's survey results suggest, the majority of cultural creatives are basically *activating the green meme*, as their values clearly indicate: strongly anti-hierarchical, embracing flatland; suspicious of conventional forms of most everything; admirably sensitive to the marginalization of minorities; committed to pluralistic values and subjectivistic warrants.

"As IC member Don Beck himself points out, using substantial research, 'Ray's "integral culture" is essentially the green meme. There are few if any indications of yellow or turquoise memes; in other words, there are few second-tier memes in most of the cultural creatives.'

"Further empirical research strongly supports this conclusion. Now just hang with me here, people, this won't take long. Ray claims that around 25% of adult Americans are cultural creatives in an integral culture. We saw that Beck and Cowan estimate that 10% of the world population is at green, but in this country, it is around 20%, which fits closely with Ray's data. In other words, most of the cultural creatives, to use Jane Loevinger and Susanne Cook-Greuter's terms, are at the *individualistic* stage (green), not the *autonomous* or *integrated* stages (yellow and turquoise). And, in fact, Loevinger's research shows that *less than 2% of Americans are at the autonomous or integrated stage*. This also fits closely with Beck and Cowan's research, which found less than 2% of Americans at the integral, second-tier waves. In other words, the cultural creatives, most of whom are Boomers, *are not truly integral*, but are basically activating the *green* meme.

"In short," and here Jefferson's voice rose to a loud, compelling pitch, "since it is the green meme that, if not let go of, is what immediately prevents the emergence of second-tier integration, what Paul Ray calls the 'integral culture' is actually what is *preventing* the integral culture."

Murmurs and mumbles from the audience. I looked at Kim. "This really is wild." She nodded, grinned.

"Almost any way we slice the data, the 'integral culture' is not that integral." Mark Jefferson paused for dramatic effect, then thundered, "The so-called integral culture is not yet really integral, *but it can be*. And that is the crucial point. As the cultural creatives—the green Boomers—move into the second half of life, this is exactly the time that a further transformation of consciousness, from pluralistic green to mature second-tier awareness, can most easily occur, which would at that point result in a truly integral, second-tier culture.

"We will return to this extraordinary transformation shortly and discuss its likelihood. The major reason I am talking about boomeritis is with the hope that, by highlighting some of the obstacles to this integral transformation, it might more readily occur."

I leaned over and whispered to Kim, "Do they really discuss that possibility later?"

"It's the best part of the whole seminar."

"Really?" Well, anything that helps Carbon move to second tier would surely provide crucial clues for the coming Silicon revolution, right? That was the whole point. . . .

"Of course, these obstacles to integral consciousness are not found exclusively in Boomers or in Americans. As we will see tomorrow, boomeritis is now the dominant form of thinking in liberal politics, social services, legal policies, health care, and academia. If you kids out there are getting a degree in anything but the hard sciences, you are actually getting a degree in boomeritis."

"Tell us about it!" yelled an Xer.

Jefferson smiled. "Yes, well, and I'm so sorry about that, son, but you definitely get the point: boomeritis is by no means confined to Boomers, but can afflict anybody poised for the leap into integral consciousness.

"This is the central point, good people. It appears that approximately 20 to 25 percent of the population—some 50 million people, and this includes many of you Xers and Ys—are at green, poised for that momentous leap into the hyperspace of integral awareness. But in order for this to happen, consciousness must go post-green—consciousness must go beyond boomeritis in any of its forms. Paraphrasing Clare Graves, 'The green meme must break down in order to free energy for the jump into second tier. *This is where the leading edge is today.*'"

The quantum leap into the hyperspace of integral consciousness. I was now convinced that somehow this was an omega point of both carbon and silicon evolution.

I didn't know exactly what that meant—none of the precise details, really—but I kept repeating and repeating and repeating that thought—the omega of both carbon and silicon—like a digital mantra of ultimate release that had wormholed through the universe from a distant, dazzling, sizzling future and burrowed its way into my meaning-starved brain.

One thing was quite certain. I would never again be able to walk into the AI Lab at MIT and assume that "intelligence"—organic or artificial—was merely a single thing that we were going to download into supercomputers. There were levels of consciousness, waves of consciousness—and those waves would emerge from complex patterns of Silicon just as they had from those of Carbon. There were *interiors* to the coming InfoSphere, there was a within to Cyberland, and the Bots would evolve through waves of expanding consciousness just as their creators had, precisely because the all-pervading patterns of evolution touch manifestation wherever it appears.

Yes, looking back on it, looking back on it. I began to die that day, and a new something was struggling to be born. And he was there, of that I was now certain.

"Ken . . . Ken! Over here."

Stuart and Joan Hazelton were standing off to the side of the auditorium, which struck me as a strange place for them to be.

"Ken, we're having a get-together tomorrow night at Joan's. Can you make it?"

"Why are we whispering?" I whispered.

"We," in a whisper, "We," in a normal voice, "are not whispering.

We are wondering. It's just a small gathering, no big deal. Well, it's sort of a big deal, kind of."

I looked at sky eyes, and it took the normal two or three seconds to orient myself in that dizzying space. "Sure, I'll bring Chloe."

"Maybe not Chloe."

"Yes, right, maybe not."

Seminar_2@BoomeritisRules.com

5

Subvert_Transgress_Deconstruct@FuckYou.com

"Jason, up on three, has a series of parallel neural nets, crossed with bio-processors hooked into a system of Crays, that shows signs of truly creative thinking. I watched the console yesterday. Pretty impressive."

"Did it tell you that it wanted to kill itself?"

George grimaced. "Oh, right, the Wilber test for intelligence. No, Ken, it did not say that it wanted to kill itself."

"Think about it, George. Only human beings will seriously contemplate suicide, which is a perfectly intelligent, rational response to existence. Stupid people never kill themselves, they're just, well, too stupid. So unless your machine is contemplating suicide, I'm telling you, it's not yet intelligent."

"No, mostly it's the same ole problem. We program various types of codes that we think will allow for the emergence of novelty. When this is coupled with a capacity for learning, which we also program in as flexible a way as possible, then the hope is that a truly creative intelligence will pop out of the damn machine sooner or later. But so far it's just not happening."

"Right," added Scott, "it's like with Deep Thought, the IBM that beat Kasparov at chess. But chess is nothing but an unlimited combination of finite mathematical moves, each of which can be linearly programmed. It's incredibly impressive, but nobody thinks this is creative intelligence."

"Our problem is mainly this," said George. "In order for machines to think, they have to be able to show *learning*. So we set up these unbelievably complicated systems—some are based on massive parallel processing, some are based on fuzzy logic, some on neural nets, some on staggeringly complex biomolecular processing, some on all of those. And, well, anyway, we still run into this problem: in order for a machine to *learn* from its past, it has to be able to *remember* its past. But what we call 'the past' actually contains billions and billions of different types of events, so which ones will we program the machine to remember?"

"I don't get it," said Scott.

"I get it," said Chloe, and she grabbed her throat, silently gasped for air, looked like she was choking, and slowly slid down her chair, under the table.

"Listen, while you're down there. . ."

"Don't you wish." She pulled herself up and looked at George. "Okay, I'm kidding, I am like totally hanging on your every word." She blinked twice, then stared at him.

"Well, um," George looked at her, hesitated, but decided to push on. "Okay, for example. Say I take this book, *The Fundamentals of Mechanical Engineering*, and I put it on the ground. My dog comes along and sees the book. We both look at the book. Now, what will we each remember about what we saw?"

"You and the dog will remember very different things," I offered.

"Right. We will remember different things because we saw different things. I saw a textbook with a great deal of information in it. My dog did not see a textbook. He saw a square something that might be lunch for him, but it didn't smell too good and so that was that."

"And your point is?" I asked.

"There are all sorts of different interpretations of reality, and which of those interpretations do we tell the computer to remember? I think that the textbook is important, so maybe I want to program the machine to remember that. But maybe a feminist would say, 'Wait a minute, that is a book of objectifying and dissociated science, and I do not want my computer to remember any of that!' A Zen Master might look at the book and see something entirely different. Which one is right? We can't program the machine to remember all of them, because there's an infinite number and they often disagree with each other. So we don't know what to tell the computer to remember. You see the problem?"

"Oh, I see the problem," said Chloe. I touched her arm, a silent plea for civility.

"The importance of interpretation, that's just what the postmodernists are saying," Scott suggested. "Reality is not a *perception* but an *interpretation*," he added, punching each word, apparently proud that he had remembered at least one conclusion from his Cultural Matrix class. Emboldened by the fact that no one, especially Chloe, had confronted his contribution, Scott continued. "There isn't just a single 'objective reality' lying around out there—there are all sorts of interpretations that have to be taken into account as well, and every type of real thinking works with these interpretations. And because none of us in AI can figure out how to program interpretations into our computers, we cannot get our computers to actually think."

"That's exactly right," I jumped in. "And that is only one example of the fact that there is not just a single given reality, there are levels of reality, levels of consciousness. And all of us in AI are coming from a very narrow bandwidth of those levels, and that is why we are getting nowhere fast. I mean fuckin nowhere fuckin fast."

George looked at me, slightly puzzled, as if my passion in this new direction somehow meant a defection from the true religion of AI. "I was merely suggesting," a cooler tone announced, "that we are running into some mere *technical* problems here, not that we are *failing*. Get the difference?"

"George, I am not abandoning AI. It's just that I have some ideas about how evolution will occur when it makes the hyperlink to silicon pathways. See, there's all sorts of evidence about these *levels* of intelligence that—"

"Ooooh, color me impressed," said Chloe, as she reached for her latté. The scars on her wrists peeked out from her sleeves, reminding me again of what computers can't do, and the pain of it all, really, and how Chloe handled the terror of existence with her own acid, her own attempts to shield herself from the ravages of human intelligence. "Time for lunch, fella. Oh, George, love the shirt."

The night before, we had gone again to see Stuart Davis. Scott brought his girlfriend, Vanessa, who always struck me as one of those honest-to-God superwomen: quite brilliant, first in her sophomore class at Duke; Playboy-bunny body; and one of the nicest human beings I knew, though I didn't know her all that well. Classic younger Millennial: her mom played Bach music while Vanessa was still a fetus, hoping it would improve her brain physiology (and I think she was humming Mozart during conception); verbal enrichment starting in the last trimester (her father would read *The Wizard of Oz* in a loud voice to her mother's distended belly); pre-pre-kindergarten school, then pre-kindergarten school, then kindergarten—and she wasn't even four years old. Soccer, student politics, started studying for her SATs when she was eleven; accepted at every college she applied to. Scott said she even approached sex the same way, although nobody was quite sure what that meant. Vanessa was cheerful, goal-driven, steeped in self-esteem, happy, and liked by all.

Chloe said never look in Vanessa's freezer, because there were almost certainly cut-up bodies in there. "I'm telling ya, she'll go postal any minute."

Club Passim is tucked away on one of the cobblestone paths at 47 Palmer Street, Harvard Square, lower level, walk down to get there. A homey, dusty, comfy interior holds perhaps a hundred people; live folk-rock music several evenings of the week; and in what always struck me as a strange misplaced homage to Boomer beats, open poetry nights. (I could never get through Kerouac, though I honestly tried; it was like fingernails on a chalkboard. "That's not writing, that's typing." "Why do you like him, Mom?" "It's about freedom, dear.")

"Every songwriter you can think of has played Passim," Stuart told us. "It's been around for twenty-five years or more and is the epicenter of the folk scene in Boston and Cambridge, with a whole lot of green-meme screams wafting through the beams.

"But they also get some really cool shit through there sometimes. It's very much a listening room, and people sit real quiet when the performance is going on. They serve beer, coffee, and apple-cider-wine kind of stuff during shows. All the songwriters, poets, and pseudo-philoso-phers hang there. Probably some real ones, too. There's a hot waitress there who is also a ballerina, and she can make an origami doll out of a man using nothing but her legs."

"Well hell I gotta see that," said Chloe.

It was indeed a listening room. And this is what we listened to, as electric eyeballs sang sincerely:

> I go to Holland once a year
> I fly into Schiphol
> Check into the Melk Hotel
> unpack two shirts
> walk on down to the Red Light District
> ten blocks
> to the Angel Parlor
> I ask for Heidi
>
> Step into Heidi's room
> we don't speak
> she cuts off all my clothes
> with a silver bayonet
> then she straps me up on a giant wheel
> mounted on the wall
> and she spins me with her hand
> and she eats me with her mouth
> while I look out the window
> at rows of perfect
>
> > Windmills,
> > perfect wooden windmills
> > Windmills,
> > rows of perfect
> > Windmills
>
> Heidi comes here once a year
> flies into the Black Hills
> Checks into the Wolf Hotel

unpacks two skirts
walks half a mile down the trail
to cabin seven
She taps on my window

Heidi steps into my room
we don't speak
I cut off all her clothes with a straight edge razor
She gets down on all fours
and straps on a crotchless pony suit
I dig my spurs into her legs
I clutch my fingers in her mane
She stares out the window
at miles of perfect

Wheat fields,
perfect golden wheat fields
Wheat fields
miles of perfect
Windmills,
perfect wooden windmills
Wheatfields,
perfect golden

Stuart sang disturbingly, beautifully, achingly; all of him so . . . present. We all laughed at this song; at others you're as likely to cry. Some of Stuart's songs are tender, vulnerable, spiritual; some are vulgar, even demonic—he spans the entire spectrum of human highs and lows, which is why I think the audience loves him so. Where else, in one song, can you hear about masturbation, chest tumors, the carpet bombing of Dresden, and finding God within?

"You won't believe what happened to me," Stuart said between the first two sets. "I mean, you will not believe it. And get this—it happened in a bowling alley. A bowling alley! Do you fucking believe that!"

"Okay, Ken, it's time for Let's Make a Deal. Behind door number one there is one naked Chloe. Behind door number two there are two naked

Chloes. Behind door number three there are three naked Chloes. Which door do you want, Ken?"

"Is this, um, like a trick question?"

"Why no, Ken, it's not."

"Well then, Monte, I'll take door number three."

"Within the important disclosures of early postformal cognition and its pluralistic relativism—whoa! holy mackerel! what a mouthful for the morning! Let's just say, within the important disclosures of the green meme, many significant truths were brought forth by Boomer scholars, truths that will remain, I believe, as enduring contributions to humanity's self-understanding. At the same time, these disclosures were set in an atmosphere intensely suspicious of all previous memes, edgily wary of all accepted truths, and rambunctiously bound to 'question all authority!'—so much so that traditional truths both good and bad were aggressively, recklessly, sometimes viciously deconstructed by Boomers gone a bit berserk, full of vim and vinegar—and what the hell is 'vim'?—full of vim can't be good, eh?—'Doc, you gotta help him, he came in today and he was just full of vim, I mean his friggin face puffed up the size of a Thanksgiving turkey'—Boomers were full of themselves, let's just say that. The point is simply that preconventional and postconventional had forged an unholy pact to destroy conventional anything, and the trail of roadkill on the way to Boomer freedom was about to begin.

"May 1968, the streets of Paris, shouts of 'Marx, Mao, Marcuse' filled the air. 'Down with Structuralism!' was scrawled on walls across the city, the French equivalent of 'Fight the System!' This 'poststructural' impulse did not fall on deaf ears across the Atlantic, for it would soon provide most of the intellectual equipment to fight the system. Such poststructual, system-fighting impulses were already in full play in America. Just the year before, the 'summer of love,' as Golden Gate park in San Francisco was awash in flower power, free sex, and free-flowing drugs, LSD being the most paradigm-blowing of them all. Then Chicago, Kent state, the massive war protests, sit-ins, and riots. Out of all of those events came the ingredients of the average or typical Boomer self: highly individualistic, with a pluralistic value system, but one bent on deconstructing any and all conventional truths, which had marginalized everything the Boomers felt they were fighting for. Conventional rationality, formal rationality, linear rationality—it was devoutly believed—had marginalized feelings, nature, females, the environment, higher states of consciousness, drugs, free love, group sex, the body, you name it.

"In short, the Boomers had one, major, overriding obsession: to resurrect the 'Other' of rationality.

"And in their ensuing career of demolishing conventional reason and deconstructing rationality, which would take three decades to show its full colors, the Boomers demonstrated an uncanny ability to completely confuse pre-rational and trans-rational, preconventional and postconventional, egocentric narcissism and worldcentric autonomy. All of this would charge forth under the banner of resurrecting the Other of reason.

"*Subvert, transgress, deconstruct*: the motto of boomeritis. You would hear each of those words repeated a hundred, a million, a billion times at least. But would it be genuine transgression, or merely regression? Creative subversion, or tiresome perversion? Deconstruction on the way to higher truths, or demolition on the way to one's lowest possibilities?

"The answer, of course, is 'all of the above.'"

As Morin finished his opening remarks, the oddest collection of noises emerged from the audience, a hip-hop mixture of squirming, nervous shuffling, applause, cheers, coughing—the sounds that anyone makes when put on any sort of hot seat. I kept forgetting that most of the audience were in fact Boomers bracing to get collectively psychoanalyzed. They were Boomers here to get cured of themselves. Naturally they were uneasy about it all. And where the IC folks were fairly gentle during Seminar I and the introductory discussions, I had a feeling that Seminar II, starting now, would be much less . . . pleasant.

Morin continued as if steeling himself, and preparing the audience, for the coming ordeal, a look on his face that one imagines a kamikaze pilot might have right before the fatal collision.

"In the obsession with resurrecting the Other of conventionality— away with the traditional! question all authority! down with the system!—the noble truths brought forth by pluralism provided the almost perfect disguise for many of the less-than-noble vagaries of the Me generation. Sometimes post and many times pre! Postmodern, postformal, postconventional, and poststructural theories exploded on the scene and flourished in a historically unprecedented fashion, in part because they were profound truths being disclosed for the first time, and in part because they were the unwitting home of prestructural, preformal, preconventional impulses. The combination of higher, powerful, postconventional truths with lower, raw, preconventional feelings produced a cultural force of unparalleled proportions. And, in this case, the pig in the python damn near killed the python."

"The only reason deconstruction took off is because of its name—deconstruction, deconstruction, deconstruction." Chloe is making love to two women on the kitchen table. "Boomers want to deconstruct anything other than their wonderful selves," she says, and the two women begin swaying with her to unseen vibrations.

"That's a little unfair, wouldn't you say?"

"Deconstruct *this*." And all three women start having what appears to be simultaneous orgasms.

"Blows your mind, eh? Are we transgressing your ideas of propriety?"

"I have no problem with this."

"Are we deconstructing the patriarchal signifiers that have oppressed female sexuality?"

"I dearly hope so."

"This offends you, yes?"

"Actually, I was wondering if anybody needed any help?"

"Silly boy."

"What we will be doing here during Seminar II is simply going through a list of some of the key interests of Boomers—from deconstruction to ecology to feminism to spirituality—and suggesting that, in addition to some important and profound truths, they each contain powerful elements of boomeritis, which ends up terribly distorting and even crippling their otherwise important contributions.

"But there is one point that all of us here would like to emphasize at the outset: in the following sessions, we will be criticizing, not the ideas themselves, but the boomeritis version of these ideas. We are not criticizing feminism, but boomeritis feminism; we are not criticizing ecology, but boomeritis ecology; not spirituality, but boomeritis spirituality. In fact, in each of those cases, the scholars here at Integral Center have written extensively on how these important ideas can be approached from a second-tier perspective—stripped of boomeritis—to produce integral feminism, integral ecology, integral psychology, integral business, integral spirituality, and so on. Books such as *The Life We Are Given, The Radiance of Being, Integral Psychology, Higher Stages of Human Development, Changes of Mind, Essential Spirituality, In Over Our Heads,* and *A Theory of Everything,* all written by members of IC, deal at length with integral approaches to all of these issues, and we recommend all of those books highly. In each of the following sessions we will mention these integral solutions, and we will examine them carefully in Seminar III, starting next week. But today we will be focusing mostly on the problem itself—boomeritis." The very sound of the word set the audience squirming.

"You know, Kim, you never did tell me that secret."

"I didn't, did I?"

I was waiting expectantly to hear something from Kim when Joan Hazelton walked on stage. Through a peaceful smile, she delivered the frightening news.

"Good morning, everybody. Over the next few days, what we will be doing is quite similar to what is called 'a confrontation' with an alcohol or drug abuser. Family and loved ones gather to confront the individual with evidence of the dysfunction, and a painful—but ultimately, it is hoped, liberating—awareness results. Our aim is to confront you with the evidence of your dysfunction, because my friends, you have no idea how addicted you are to the ideas that will follow, and how this addiction has permeated every aspect of your lives. My hope, our hope, is that by giving example after example after example, this addiction will become increasingly harder to deny, and the problem itself will come into focus, allowing us to see, and hopefully rise above, its more disturbing elements.

"And friends, in this case I am as dysfunctional as everybody else; there are no doctors in the house except us; we are groping our way through this thing together. Those of us who are facilitating the discussion are all recovering addicts, so we hope to be able to lend a hand here. But this really is a collaborative inquiry, a cooperative dialogue, a caring Bohmian discussion, a learning process where we all move forward together as peers, with care and compassion and mutual respect."

"She's talking green," Kim whispered.

"I'm sorry?"

"Most of the people here have a heavy dose of green, so Hazelton is carefully using green-meme language, reflecting green values. If she talked yellow, the greens would get angry and bolt. She is trying to soothe green before the surgery."

"I see. That sounds very manipulative."

"Your own green is showing. It can be manipulative, sure, like anything. But it can be a skillful means for meeting people where you find them and speaking to them in ways that they can hear. Hazelton is not manipulative, you must have sensed that already."

"True." Still, did Hazelton's approach work? Because right now, there was no applause at all, just dreadful silence, the blood-completely-drained-from-your-face silence of a patient right before surgery.

"Allow me to introduce Derek Van Cleef," said Hazelton. "Dr. Van Cleef comes to us from Johannesburg, South Africa, where his work in the anti-apartheid movement convinced him of the inadequacies of both liberal and conservative approaches to the problem. Derek will start us off on this fun-thrilled ride!"

Van Cleef strode across the stage. He was an arresting figure. Very handsome, with dark black hair standing out from pale white skin; an angular face with a hawk-like beak; a graceful, almost elegant yet masculine walk. He could be a movie star, were it not for the sincerity he exuded even at a distance, which would dash any hopes in Hollywood.

"I used to have a crush on him," Kim whispered. "All the girls do; boys too."

"Is he gay?"

"No, I don't think so. But he doesn't date, nobody knows why."

"Married to his work?"

"Whatever."

The first words out of his mouth were, "Every person with boomeritis is the hundredth monkey."

Van Cleef paused for effect; the audience visibly winced. The confrontation had begun, the surgeon's scalpel had just touched flesh.

"The hundredth monkey is the rather extraordinary tale of what happened to the Japanese monkey, *Macaca fuscatta*, in 1952 on the island of Koshima. Scientists were giving the monkeys sweet potatoes by tossing them in the sand. The monkeys liked the sweet potatoes but not the taste of sand. An eighteen-month-old female named Imo found she could solve the problem by washing the potatoes in a nearby stream. Imo taught her playmates this trick, and they all taught their mothers. The scientists watched this potato-washing slowly begin to spread through the monkey population of the island. Then, on one day in 1958, an amazing thing happened. Sometime that morning, a certain number of monkeys knew the potato-washing trick; the exact number is not known, but for the sake of the story it is said to be 99. The next monkey—the hundredth monkey—learned the trick, and by that evening scientists observed that every monkey on the island knew the trick. Not only that, monkeys on the surrounding islands, with no contact with Koshima, all started washing their sweet potatoes!

"As a favorite Boomer book explained, 'The added energy of this hundredth monkey somehow created an ideological breakthrough! Thus, when a certain critical number achieves an awareness, this new awareness may be communicated from mind to mind. There is a point where if only one more person tunes in to a new awareness, a field is strengthened so that this awareness reaches almost everyone! *You may be the Hundredth Monkey!*'

"The monkey phenomenon, it turns out, was not true; the story was a hoax. But the story spread like wildfire, to become what was probably the most often repeated Boomer story of all. Why? Because it was a myth made to order for boomeritis. Because you, your very own ego, can be pictured as the crucial change agent that will alter the entire world. Boomeritis won't make a move unless it is assured that every gesture of its ego means world transformation." The audience shifted, groaned, and through its discomfort seemed, at this point, decidedly uncertain about whether to cheer or boo.

"What is so disturbing about this story is not just the narcissistic domination involved, but the lack of moral sensibility displayed in it. My actions alone will transform 'almost everyone!' The simple idea that my consciousness will automatically change yours to conform to mine is the heart of the narcissistic power to dominate; and so excited was boomeritis by the thought that it could be the hundredth monkey, it didn't even pause to consider whether other monkeys would in fact appreciate having their consciousness determined by Boomers.

"Of course it is important that individuals feel that their actions make a difference, that they are contributing, in some small measure, to the betterment of humankind—and of all sentient beings, for that matter. But in the hands of boomeritis, that impulse turned omnipotently ugly: my every gesture will make the world a replica of me. The hundredth-monkey myth became the most-told story in new-paradigm circles, and its exposure as a fraud was attributed to a bunch of unspiritual skeptics. The fraud was indeed exposed by a bunch of unspiritual skeptics; it was still a fraud. But the myth spread like wildfire, not because it was true, but because it spoke deeply to boomeritis and the insatiable demands of an engorged ego."

"Is it all this brutal?" I asked Kim.

"Gets worse."

"But why? He's being deliberately inflammatory. Is this like, you know, tough love or something?"

"Not really. It's a test."

"A test? What the hell is that? You mean I have to pass a test? I don't get it." I thought for a moment. "Hey, you know, I had a sense that Morin was doing that, too. A kind of test."

Kim looked at me for several seconds. "I might have to reevaluate your status as a nitwit."

While I was trying to figure out a test of what, exactly, the first slide of the day flashed on the wall: "The Drama of the Gifted Child." Van Cleef continued his talk, cloaked only by sincerity from the rising heat of the audience.

"This book, *The Drama of the Gifted Child*, by Alice Miller, is an object-relations psychoanalytic look at what happens to sensitive children who, by virtue of their very sensitivity to others, try overly to please them—especially the parents—and thus can end up emotionally exhausted and dead within. The book was originally published with the title *Prisoners of Childhood*, and received modest critical acclaim. By a stroke of marketing genius, the book was then rereleased with the title *The Drama of the Gifted Child*, and Boomers by the droves read it as a chronicle of how they, being the gifted child, ended up stunted by nasty, overbearing parents and society in general. Boomeritis, in particular, found it a book that seemed to explain its failure to triumph: somebody else was holding it down. The title is exactly how boomeritis pictures its own life story. On the Reader's Choice Psychology Bookshelf on the Net, *The Drama of the Gifted Child* is still, twenty years after its release, the number-one-rated book."

The surgeon's knife continued to cut. It was clear that Van Cleef wanted to run several examples by as fast as he could so that the cumulative effect might disarm defenses.

Slide #2, "The Abuse Excuse."

"In 1993, a woman pulled into a McDonald's, ordered a cup of coffee, got in her car, took the lid off the coffee, placed the open cup in her lap, and stepped on the gas. The coffee spilled and burned her leg. She sued McDonald's for 2 million dollars in damages, and she won. It was McDonald's fault for making the coffee too hot.

"We have already seen that a defining characteristic of narcissism is that whenever something goes wrong, *it is not its fault*. And the American legal system, over the last several decades, in the hands of the Boomers, has drifted dramatically in the direction of helping narcissism win legal battle after legal battle. This is now so commonly accepted as to need little documentation, but it became most starkly obvious in the Menendez brothers trial, where two brothers, who shot their parents as they lay sleeping, were originally acquitted because they claimed they were 'abused' by their father. Why this abuse made them shoot their mother in the head with a shotgun, reload, run her down, and shoot her again until she was dead, was not made clear.

"The 'abuse excuse' is simply a subset of what has been called 'victim chic,' which takes as a template the horrible tragedies of real victims—slavery, gay bashing, rape, criminal assault—and applies it to the slightest insult to the hypersensitive self. Whether the person claims such victimhood by actual abuse or simply by virtue of society's insensitivity, there is a common thread: I am not responsible for my problems, but *you* are responsible for yours.

"I am clearly not responsible for what I have done—from burning myself with coffee to murdering my parents—because I am a victim.

But if I am going to blame *you* for my problems, then *you* must be responsible for what you have done, or the game can never get started. If the Menendez brothers are not guilty because of something their father did to them, then surely their father is not guilty either, because he was obviously abused himself in order to do something so heinous. But that won't work at all, because in order to secure the coveted status of victim, somebody—that is, somebody else—has to actually be responsible at some point, or the buck never stops anywhere. And boomeritis ensures that the buck *always* stops elsewhere."

Chloe would have loved this. Not that she was a critic of victim chic for the right reasons; she hated it because she could find no way to use it to her advantage, and she mightily resented those who could. Scott said that on this particular issue, Chloe was right for the wrong reasons and Carolyn was wrong for the right reasons. Carolyn had thought intensely about the issue of victimhood—you have to in cultural studies; she brought a great deal of integrity and intelligence to the topic, we all agreed. And Carolyn, with a not insignificant amount of help from her professors ("The same type of help that recovered-memory therapists give their patients," said Chloe. "Was there abuse? No? Dig deeper.") had concluded that pretty much everybody was a victim of the patriarchy, men and women alike.

"But Carolyn," Scott would always say, "if both men and women are the victims of it, then who the hell actually started the damn thing?"

Carolyn had brought two friends to the seminar, Katish Sumar and Beth Wanter, both from her cultural studies department, most likely for moral support. As if rudely—or skillfully—ignoring all retorts, Van Cleef moved straight ahead.

"How do I see me as a victim, not responsible for my own actions?

> An FBI agent embezzles two thousand dollars from the government and then loses all of it in an afternoon of gambling in Atlantic City. He is fired but wins reinstatement after a court rules that his affinity for gambling is a "handicap" and is thus protected under federal law.

> In Framingham, Massachusetts, a young man steals a car from a parking lot and is killed while driving it. His family sues the pro-

prietor of the parking lot for failing to take steps to prevent such thefts.

Fired for consistently showing up late at work, a former school district employee sues his former employers, arguing that he is a victim of what his lawyers call "chronic lateness syndrome."

"In Chicago, a man complained to the Minority Rights Division of the U.S. Attorney's Office that a local restaurant was violating federal equal-protection laws because the seats were not big enough for his unusually large backside. 'I represent a minority that is just as visible as blacks, Mexicans, Latins, Asians, or women. Your company has taken it upon itself to grossly and improperly discriminate against heavyset people, and we are prepared to bring federal litigation against your company to comply with the Equal Rights Accommodations Provision. I have a 60-inch waist and it is absolutely impossible for me to get service because of the type of seating you have installed. We are very serious in our demands that you recognize the existence of large and heavyset minority that make up nearly 20 percent of the American population, and take severe steps to provide at least 20 percent of the seating in your restaurant to be suitable for heavy people.'

"Mike Rokyo, *Chicago Tribune* columnist, noted that in spite of this person's attempt to equate his status with that of blacks and women, he 'was not born with a 60-inch waist and enormous butt. After a certain age, he created himself and his butt. They are his responsibility. And even the most liberal of liberals would have to agree that his 60-inch waist and awesome butt should not be the responsibility of the United States of America.'"

This time the audience all laughed, happy for the relief, it seemed. Carolyn looked at Katish and smiled; Beth beamed at Carolyn. Kim looked at me, as if to say, "God knows what those three are up to."

"Hundreds of similar examples have been reported in books such as *A Nation of Victims*, *The Culture of Complaint*, and *The Abuse Excuse*. It is almost as if the entire legal system had read *The Drama of the Gifted Child* and decided that (1) any bad thing that happens to you is not in any way your fault, and (2) it simply shows that you are a very gifted child who has been stunted by society.

"At first it makes perfect sense: I am not succeeding because some-body else is holding me down; I am a victim. But the horrible irony of trying to find one's self-esteem by claiming victimhood is that, if you ever *succeed* in overcoming your victimhood, then you lose your status, your special rights, and your claim to privileged treatment. And thus, once you explicitly identify yourself as a victim, you must work very hard to never stop being one."

Van Cleef paused, looked around the room, hawk-like intensity radiating from the stage. "All of this hangs together as part of the atmosphere of boomeritis and its chronic denial of responsibility, which, far from alleviating a victim's low self-esteem, ensures that it is perpetual."

The surgeon's knife just didn't cut the flesh, it had began to cut out organs and toss them on the floor. I hadn't yet started applying these lessons to myself because they fit dear Mom and Dad so snuggly. When I was growing up, Mom put a picture of the hundredth monkey on the refrigerator. For years she called me "my little moss monkey." Where the "moss" came from I never knew, but the "monkey" part was clear enough: I would change the world, presumably in a way that would then embrace Mom's values.

And Dad, dear soul. He was going to be the hundredth monkey in his own way—this time by seeing the entire world as the victim of the in-dustrial-military complex, or the victim of rampant patriarchal capital-ism, or the victim of the Newtonian-Cartesian paradigm, which always sounded to my young ears like a horrible skin disease, or the victim of . . . well, I forget all the bad guys right now. But for Dad, it wasn't just that the orange meme was part good, part bad, like all memes; the or-ange meme was demonic through and through, top to bottom and start to finish. It was just like what Cook-Greuter said about the individual-istic self, how suspicious and skeptical and even cynical it was, or soon turned out to be. Dad was going to save the world, which really meant that he would be its glorious Savior, boomeritis to the bone, a mar-velous Marxist hundredth monkey, redeemer of the world. And now the dear crucified man was heartbreakingly bleeding to death, all on his own; the unforgiving nails of his belief system had mortally wounded his own body; the life was ebbing out of him, drop by lonely drop, ac-companied every now and then by tears from me or Mom.

That tender sadness brought a thought that often crossed my mind that fall: maybe my Siamese twin was not Kurt's shadow but Dad's. Who could say?

There is a way out, an inner voice had always told me, but the way out is really a way within. Just like dear young Stuart would soon be singing: "But it's real, and not too far / to the timeless core of what we are / A clear, internal path we take / when we close our eyes / and fall awake." And they wonder why I look to the next generation?

When I was a little girl, the only thing my mother ever really told me was that fighting with men on their own terms was a waste of time. Women had other ways of knowing, she kept saying, and I should become the sky instead. Let men be the blinding sun, but you can be the sky in which the sun exists. Even the earth is floating in the vastness of space, the womb of the sky, the womb of all that is. Parts come together in the sky, fragments find their home in the vast expanse of all space, the great embracing spaciousness that you profoundly are.

Later I found out that the sky is neither male nor female, neither sun nor earth, but the great expanse that contains them both. But that I discovered only after a long and painful death. And would you like to know the secret to that?

Katish leaned over and said to Carolyn, "You know, even if what Van Cleef is saying is right, that doesn't mean that there aren't real victims out there! Really, we don't have to swallow all this hogwash."

As if in response, Van Cleef flashed slide #3, which said, "374 Percent of the Population."

"There are several *real* tragedies concealed here," he stated with what appeared to be genuine, pained concern. "There are a substantial number of actual victims—of slavery's aftermath, gay bashing, criminal assault, sexual discrimination, physical abuse—whose genuine grievances are trivialized by victim chic. That is the real tragedy."

Van Cleef began reading clippings from various newspapers. "Consider the legal and cultural climate that inspired the men who were injured while carrying refrigerators on their backs during 'refrigerator races' to sue the manufacturer because the appliances carried insufficient warnings of possible injury from such activities. Or the case of a New York man who deliberately leapt in front of a moving subway train—and was awarded $650,000 because the train failed to stop in time to avoid mangling him.

"Men have sued diet clinics because they sponsor female-only weight loss programs; the San Francisco Giants are sued for giving away Father's Day gifts to men only; a psychology professor complains that she has been victimized by the presence of mistletoe at a Christmas party. Officials at Pennsylvania State University pulled a copy of Goya's *Naked Maja* from the wall of a lecture hall after a female professor declared its presence was a form of sexual harassment."

"Sexual harassment, what bullshit!" a man in the audience shouted.

Van Cleef nodded, as if in agreement, and it was clear that he was emotionally invested in these issues in a way that the previous presenters were not. He shrugged, straightened his shoulders, continued. "The poor hypersensitive self has very few places it can rest its weary head. 'In Miami, a court ruled that a woman be paid 40 thousand dollars in worker's compensation benefits after she complained that she was so afraid of blacks that she was unable to work in an integrated office.' Imagine being just too fucking sensitive to have to accept racial integration!" he thundered, and this time the entire audience applauded.

"It just keeps coming," Van Cleef gravely intoned, and he read more clippings to the assembled:

"Two Marines alleged they had been unconstitutionally discriminated against because the Marine Corps had discharged them for 'being chronically overweight.' A postal clerk who is left-handed accused the U.S. Postal Service of discriminatory bias in setting up filing cases 'for the convenience of right-handed clerks.' A 24-year-old Colorado man sued his mother and father for what he called 'parental malpractice.' In Hawaii, a family of tourists who had been shunted into 'less desirable lodgings' by their overbooked hotel not only sued for their economic losses, but were awarded cash for 'their emotional distress and disappointment.' In Orlando, a man filed a lawsuit as a result of a haircut that he claimed was so bad that it induced a panic-anxiety attack. In his suit, the inadequately coifed plaintiff alleged that the negligent hairstylist had deprived him of his 'right to enjoy life.'" Sporadic laughter, tempered apparently with the realization that at any moment the joke might turn on you. . . .

Van Cleef began smiling. "Some examples certainly have a creative flair. 'In the *Litigation Explosion*, Walter Olson reports the case of a psychic, Judith Haimes, who had conducted seances featuring such metaphysical celebrities as the poet John Milton (who spoke through her), and whose psychic powers, she claimed, were blotted out by a dye used in a CAT scan. Insisting that her doctor had thus interfered with her ability to make a living, she sued. . . . The jurors took only 45 minutes to return an award of $986,000.'"

"I want that job!" somebody from the audience yelled, and everybody laughed.

"What is so astonishing," Van Cleef continued, still smiling, "is the sheer number of groups, across the board, that are vying for the status of victim. As Charles Sykes, author of the widely acclaimed *A Nation of Victims*, points out, 'Perhaps the most extraordinary phenomenon of our time has been the eagerness with which more and more groups and individuals—members of the white middle class, auto company executives, and pampered academics included—have defined themselves as victims of one sort or another. If you add up all the groups that consider themselves oppressed minorities, Aaron Wildavsky calculates, *their number adds up to 374 percent of the population.'*"

Van Cleef paused for effect, looked around the audience, then almost shouted: "374 percent of the population! People, people, *get . . . a . . . grip!*" He walked to the edge of the stage. "Here's the basic problem: wherever there are victims, there have to be victimizers, or oppressors, or somebody who is hurting the victim—that's how you get to be a victim. It used to be that the white Protestant Anglo-Saxon male— yes, the fabled WASP male—was the great endless reservoir of oppressors which everybody could use to start their particular game of 'I am a victim.' But that reservoir long ago dried up. That single great oppressing mass of white males has now splintered into dozens of subgroups, all of which claim to be oppressed victims themselves. White males have split up into those who have been sexually abused as a child, abandoned by their fathers, raised in an atmosphere of brutal violence; are recovering addicts, alcoholics, drug abusers; are overweight, victims of ageism, lookism, reverse sexism—all of which means that virtually every male in America can claim to be a victim of one horrible wrongdoing or another. In short, people, we have become a nation of oppressed, but with no oppressors left. This is a nifty trick.

"It is, of course, the trick of boomeritis. As Sykes points out, 'This rush to declare oneself a victim'—a rush that has dramatically accelerated in the last three decades—'cannot be accounted for solely in political terms. Rather it suggests *a more fundamental transformation of American cultural values and notions of character and personal responsibility.*' Indeed it does, and Sykes knows why: 'Despite its pretensions, victimism is not idealism. Ultimately, victimism is concerned not with others, but with the *self*—because the self-cleansing, self-serving, self-demanding poses of victimism are simply cloaking themselves in the garb of idealism. Stripped of its idealistic pretensions, *victimism is an ideology of the ego.*'" The audience gave a mixed reaction, half clapping, half mumbling, none of it appreciative.

Van Cleef again paused and looked around the room. "That, of course, is a rather good definition of boomeritis: egocentric concerns dressed up in idealistic garb, taking life's unavoidable disappointments and parlaying them, with help from the green meme, into a crusade to see its own predicament as the fault of anybody else. For the fact is, folks, where the blue meme *blames* the victim, the green meme *creates* them." Deathly silence from the audience.

"Why does the green meme create victims? Why *must* it create victims? Remember that the green meme subscribes to flatland, to the belief that there are no significant differences between people. And thus, whenever the green meme finds any sort of disparity between people, it *must* assume that those differences have been *imposed* on people by an oppressing or vengeful force. Now sometimes there are indeed oppressing forces, and sometimes there are not, *but the green meme cannot tell the difference*. In order to make sense of the fact that the world is actually *not* flatland, the green meme has to populate it almost entirely with victims and victimizers. And thus, if I may repeat, where the blue meme blames the victim, the green meme creates them—and boomeritis is simply the green meme with a vengeance.

"There is little doubt that any country where 374 percent of its population sees itself as a victim has indeed undergone a rather massive cultural shift in the last three decades; and there is little doubt that, whatever else the causes, boomeritis is among them."

Van Cleef stopped, gave a short bow, and walked slowly off the stage, to a sullen, reflective silence. Not even the Xers and Ys applauded; it would be like clapping at a hanging.

"Just off the road from a long tour, I went down to the Bryant Lake Bowl in Minneapolis for a meeting with my friends Dirk and Anthony—we were going to write an ad for a national magazine where we are advertising my latest CD." Stuart pulled up a chair and sat down, looked at all of us, smiled, and somewhat breathlessly continued.

"As I walked into the club, which is a combination bar and bowling alley and theater (strange combo, but a very hip place), I noticed something was out of the ordinary: the people. Occupying every lane of the bowling alley was an army of models, gorgeous women throwing gutter balls left and right, and laughing with delight. I strategically placed myself in the chair that was closest to the action, and by the time my friends Anthony and Dirk joined me, a stream of drool was connecting my face to the table top.

"With one eye on the bowling models, we put together a very simple advertisement—it's a full-page ad with 'Stuart Davis' written at the top, then a picture of unplugged headphones in the middle, and the phrase 'Not available anywhere' just below that. The ad listed no phone numbers, no web addresses, nothing but those words, 'Not available anywhere.'"

We all started laughing hysterically. This advertisement was vintage Stuart.

"So, anyway, in between longing glances at the bowling models, we're also laughing our asses off at the Zen-like flavor of this advertising. In one of the lulls between laughter, as we silently studied the ornamental goddesses, one of them turned, looked at our table, and started walking toward us. As she got closer, it became clear she was walking over to me.

"She was about 5 foot 10 inches tall, brunette hair, big round hazel eyes, sculpted bone structure, perfect posture, and lips that made something tingle in the base of my spine. When she arrived at our table, she looked at me for a second with big bright eyes and said, 'You're Stuart Davis, right?'

"I looked at Anthony, who nodded his head to me: 'Yes, you are Stuart Davis, and now you say 'Yes' to her, idiot, don't blow this. . . . '

"I answered her with a tentative 'Yes.'

"'So, Stuart, are you enlightened?'"

"Who needs a supermodel?" says Chloe, her naked body glistening in the moonlight. "Can Cindy Crawford do *this*? Well? Can she?"

"I'm thinking."

"Listen, sweet boy. You really should stop thinking. Where has it gotten you? Rattle, rattle, rattle, right? You think that either the machines are going to take over humans completely, or humans will download into machines. That's the results of your thinking, so, like, *hello*? But sweet boy, look at this. Can Tyra Banks do *this*?"

"Um. . ."

"Can she?"

"I'm thinking."

Margaret Carlton came on stage, with a gentle smile, an open manner. "Let's switch gears for a moment: boomeritis is as prevalent in the heavens as on earth."

Carlton was a small woman, white on white: white hair, white skin, white clothes, yet relatively young for the presenters, perhaps in her midthirties. An elusive smile was set in a face of fragile beauty; a thin, delicate nose supported heavy black glasses, the only overt indicator that this porcelain fronted a Mensa-driven brain. She seemed completely devoid of anger or aggression; the only negative emotion her face betrayed was perhaps a bit of kindly impatience every now and then.

"Boomers, and especially boomeritis, make a sharp distinction between 'religion' and 'spirituality'; they have the latter, their parents have the former. Religion, it is claimed, is about exterior, rigid, hierarchical institutions; whereas spirituality is about inner experience, awareness, and richer truths not pinned down in conventional forms. This distinction is in some ways quite valid, and many Boomers have indeed helped to usher in some very important moments of spiritual renewal, which I in no way wish to decry.

"What is unfortunate is the intense value judgments that many Boomers place on this distinction. Boomers want, as one poll disclosed, ABC—Anything But the Church—and hence the degree of palpable disdain that greets all things 'religious' as opposed to 'spiritual.' But since religion is just codified spirituality, even Boomer spirituality, if it lasts beyond their immediate sensations, will become religion—and in fact, it already has—and there is nothing inherently wrong with that. But 'nobody-tells-me-what-to-do' boomeritis seems intent on fabricating its own religion, beholden to no authority and no lineage but its own impulses. Bringing a great deal of freshness and novelty to spirituality is surely a fine idea; trashing every previous religious approach is surely not required. Not to mention the fact that the boomeritis religion of feelings—of me and my sensations—is as often prerational as transrational. . . . "

Katish, ignoring everything Carlton had just said, leaned over and asked Kim, rather loudly, "Are we going to get a chance to go back to that victim topic?" He was clearly very upset. Kim responded that "a whole day is devoted to it. This is just an overview." Katish looked even more agitated.

Up on the wall flashed slide #4, "Channeling." Channeling? This ought to be *great*, I thought, but what could this possibly have to do with boomeritis?

"Common forms of new Boomer religion include, of course, New Age religion, which we will discuss at length in a later session, and the closely related phenomenon of channeling, where a higher intelligence, usually from another planet, speaks through a *specially chosen person*—the channel—often bringing information about what the human race must do in order to avoid extinction and usher in an extraordinary world transformation. To be chosen as the special channel for the highest intelligence in the universe would certainly look good on most résumés."

Lots of audience laughter; presumably few participants were guilty of this one.

"Sometimes, however, this higher intelligence, apparently miffed that nobody is listening, shows up in person." Slide #5 hit the wall. "UFO Abductions." I looked over at Kim; she had her hand over her mouth, muffling a laugh. Apparently she knew what was coming.

"A startling 4% of adult Americans report being abducted by aliens—something like 12 million people. The course of the abduction is typical and by now well known. Individuals are taken aboard the mother ship, given a physical exam, subjected to the ubiquitous anal probe, and had sperm or ova collected from them. And then—this is the primal scene—they are often shown their sons and daughters, produced by a cross-fertilization between their sperm/ova and the aliens'. These people, in other words, are the fathers and mothers of the new race that will populate the earth. And right there the staggering narcissism becomes perhaps too obvious. Imagine, I am the father or the mother of the new human race. . . .

"Many scientists believe that there might indeed be intelligent life on other planets; many believe we are still trying to find intelligent life on *this* planet. But few believe there are enough aliens that they are visiting us daily in droves—unless we are the Zoo of the Universe, and aliens love to bring their kids by to look at the primitive beasts: 'Now little Zordac, watch what happens when we take this stick and shove it up. . . '

"The narcissism is the giveaway." Carlton smiled with the audience. "The comedian Dennis Miller got it just right: 'Only man is a narcissistic enough species to think that a highly evolved alien life force would travel across billions and billions of light-years—a group of aliens so intelligent, so insouciant, so utterly above it all, they feel no need whatsoever to equip their spacecraft with windows so that they can gaze out on all that celestial beauty—but then immediately upon landing, their first impulse is to get in some hick's ass with a flashlight.'"

Ripples of laughter followed Carlton off the stage. Lesa Powell walked out; she was the only person who always got applause before she spoke. I wondered how the audience would feel after the surgery.

Slide #6, "Foucault and Genealogy." The applause turned quickly to moans.

"Suddenly, I was feeling very awake. Dirk and Anthony tacitly looked on with interest, waiting to hear what I might say to this unexpected question—'Are you enlightened?' I took a brief inventory: I am in a bar, drinking and lusting after hot girls throwing gutter balls; one of them has walked right over and hit me with a sincere and profound query before I even know her name. What the hell was going on? I paused, and after considering how this lucid, buoyant woman had just found me stewing in lechery, cigarettes, and alcohol, I decided I didn't feel very enlightened at the moment.

"'Well, no, I'm not, but that's a very interesting question. I'd like to talk about it more, maybe in a different setting.'

"I was feeling butterflies all over, like electric current in the veins.

"'Okay. Well, my name is Darla. I saw one of your concerts in Chicago. We actually have a mutual friend who's also from Chicago, but I've never met you before, so I thought I'd come over and say hi. I'm not a groupie or anything like that, so don't get the wrong idea.'

"I tried to stay collected, even though my overwhelming urge was to put my arms around her and kiss her. Then, my clumsy attempt to get her number, words I never imagined saying to a model, much less in a bowling alley: 'Well, I go to Chicago a lot, so maybe we could get together and talk about Enlightenment.'"

Stuart interrupted his own story with a spontaneous burst of laughter, apparently at the ridiculousness of the scene itself: supermodel, bowling alley, Enlightenment—*hello?*

"Darla looked at me for a moment, and I felt something like the opposite of anesthesia—some kind of drug that makes you lucid. She replied, 'Well, I'm in town for the next two days doing a show for Dayton's, so if you want to get together, here's my number.'

"She scribbled her number on a napkin, said goodbye to us, and with perfect posture, walked back to her bowling lane. Dirk, Anthony, and I exchanged looks of amazement. I tried to look calm in front of my friends, but inside my intuition was going berserk, telling me I had just met an extraordinary human being, who also happened to be very beautiful. I wasn't even five steps outside of the building that night before I whipped out my cell phone, called her number, and left a message saying I was free the whole next day and would come meet her anytime she wanted."

We were all aggressively silent, expectantly awaiting each new word; not even Chloe opened her mouth.

"The next night we met in downtown Minneapolis, and literally from the moment she walked out of the hotel, I began to glow inside. We went for a walk along the Mississippi River, over the Stone Arch Bridge where the cobblestone streets overlook the waterfalls. For the first hour or so, she related her story. She talked, I listened, and right there, watching her talking and laughing, I fell in love.

"That night came and went in a blink. We spent eight hours walking, talking, laughing, and gazing in silence. Neither of us could bring ourselves to end the evening, but we couldn't go back up to her hotel because she was sharing a room with another girl, and we couldn't go back to my place because I didn't have one (Darla didn't seem to care a bit that I was an itinerant musician staying with his parents and driving his mother's station wagon).

"Sitting in the car, riding the swell of what was emerging between us, I shyly turned to her and asked, 'Was this a date?'

"She considered the question, then replied, 'I don't know.'

"Then I meekly asked, 'Do you want to kiss?'

"She blushed. 'Yes.'

"I waited a few seconds, and not wanting to be misunderstood, added, 'Me?'

"We erupted in laughter. Then, one of the milestones of my life: We kissed."

"The examples presented thus far by my colleagues," Lesa Powell began, "from the hundredth monkey to victim chic to UFO abductions, all have one factor in common: a striking overestimation of the importance of the ego. But all of those examples are quite obvious and straightforward. The key to boomeritis's astonishing success has been its capacity to infect even the subtlest of endeavors.

"We can turn this survey in a more serious direction by looking to Michel Foucault, who has had an enormous influence on the general movement known as postmodernism, and is certainly one of its most sophisticated and powerful theorists. I myself did my thesis on—are you ready for this?—'The Genealogy of Grass-Roots Rhizomatic Resistance to Patriarchal Power Signifiers in the Asymmetrical Bodily Engendered Sexual Relations of the Hierarchical Enlightenment's Dissociated Gaze.'" Many in the audience laughed and clapped and looked at each other knowingly. Probably half of them had written something equally absorbing.

"Foucault," Powell continued in a soothing tone, "is in a lineage that involved one of postmodernism's *first major attacks on rationality*—particularly as universal formalism—and is probably the most intellectually sophisticated of such, a lineage that runs from Nietzsche to Bataille, Bachelard, Canguilhem, and Foucault. Foucault's *archaeology* of knowledge, which analyzed archives and epistemes of discourse at any given period in history, and his *genealogy*, which analyzed the transitions between periods, permeated by largely nondiscursive practices of social power, were a formidable force in unseating the conceptions of universal formalism." A thundering silence greeted her comments.

"I know, I know, it sounds horribly complicated. And it is. But the general idea is very simple. Here is what Foucault is saying: if you examine previous historical eras—if you look at what they believed to be the truth—it becomes obvious that the 'truth' is, in many ways, an arbitrary, shifting, culturally relative, and historically molded phenomenon. What on earth happened to the seven deadly sins? Does anybody today really believe that gluttony or avarice will land them in eternal hell? I mean, good grief, in today's world, committing the seven deadly sins is a prerequisite for most law schools." The audience burst into laughter. "Well, if yesterday contained so many howlers passing for absolute truth, what makes us think that today's 'truths' are any different? The so-called truth changes almost as much as clothing fashion.

"So it's fairly simple: Foucault's archaeology was an attempt to 'dig down' into history and disclose these culturally created and relative systems of 'truth' and 'discourse,' which Foucault called *epistemes*, which are roughly similar to 'memes' or 'worldviews.' In his genealogy period, Foucault traced the historical unfolding of these worldviews, not just in terms of their verbal structures—or discursive practices—but also in terms of the 'nondiscursive practices' that supported various claims to knowledge. And here he found that, not only are many truth-claims merely passing styles, they are *socially constructed* as forms of *domination* and *power*. The seven deadly sins, for example, were clearly, at least in part, forms of power that the Church used to dominate mythic believers, and if you had trouble accepting those beliefs, the Inquisition would be glad to assist you."

"What's that you have there?" I ask Chloe, whose naked body is lounging on the couch, book propped up in hand.

"Why, it's Donatien Alphonse François de Sade's *Philosophy in the Bedroom*."

"Last time you were reading *Discipline and Punish*. And now you are reading the Marquis de Sade? What's going on here?"

"It's just like what Baudelaire said, 'It is necessary to come back to Sade, again and again.'"

"Baudelaire said that?"

"Yes indeedy. As even Swinburne said, 'The day and the century will come when statues will be erected to Sade in the walls of every city, and when at the base of every statue, sacrifices will be offered up to him.'"

"Wow. I wonder why?"

"Because, as the great Apollinaire put it, the Marquis de Sade is 'the freest spirit that ever lived.'"

"The freest spirit that ever lived? Wow!"

"Oh, you ain't heard nothing yet," she says, shifting her body in the sun.

Powell, black skin and black hair lustrous, walked to the edge of the stage, looked around the audience, smiled warmly.

"Foucault came to the conclusion," she continued, "that the notions of progress, universal truth, and the advance of knowledge were dubious at best; there exists only 'a multiplicity of discourses,' a pluralism of epistemes, with none of them inherently better than the others. Foucault, in other words, gave one of the first truly sophisticated greenmeme readings of the history of truth, knowledge, and power. Perhaps Foucault's most famous statement, certainly from his early period, was that we were witnessing 'the death of man' and the birth of a new era, by which Foucault basically meant the death of a type of universal scientific reductionism, and the birth of a more respectful, nondomineering approach to all humans: in short, the death of the orange meme, the birth of the green.

"I believe there is much truth to what Foucault had to say. As I mentioned, I did my thesis on Foucauldian power, and many of my colleagues here at IC have incorporated Foucault into their writing—for example, check out the endnotes in *Sex, Ecology, Spirituality*, whose author read literally everything Foucault had ever written. But the difficulty is that this pluralistic approach, if taken to extremes, *defeats its own claims*, which Foucault began to acknowledge when he tried to write a book called *The Archaeology of Knowledge*.

"In this work, Foucault attempted to outline the general structures (and rules) of knowledge that would allow the existence of different epistemes (or worldviews), all of which were socially constructed and historically contingent. He was basically trying to give an account of why all knowledge is culturally relative and contextual. But he soon realized that his own account claimed to be universally binding for all cultures. In other words, *his own account* was claimed to be *universally* true, but all knowledge is only supposed to be *relative*. Foucault, realizing the deeply contradictory nature of his own approach, abandoned the merely pluralistic and relativistic stance—in fact, he called it 'arrogant,' as indeed it was, infected with hidden boomeritis and grandiose claims. Why? Because he was claiming for himself a universal knowledge that he vengefully denied to all others: how great I must be to have this knowledge that you do not possess. And thus, in something of a shocking move for his green-meme followers, Foucault retracted much of the thrust of his earlier work and ended up publicly identifying himself with the broad lineage of Kant—which meant looking for genuine postconventional universals that attempt to include and not marginalize—for example, by treating each and every person as an end, not a means—looking, that is, for more second-tier worldcentric constructions."

"Kim, are you able to follow all this?" I whispered.

"Sure."

Yes, she would, I thought. I was about to complain that I was having a little trouble understanding it, but I remembered that she would probably hit me with that torrent of "candy ass, wimp, sissy boy, feeble brain . . . ," so I decided to take my chances with Lesa Powell instead.

"Foucault's own goal, it became increasingly clear, was to *transgress the limits* of what was taken to be unalterable by formal rationality, universal formalism, and the 'sciences of man.' Foucault's intense and life-long interest in 'limit experiences'—including everything from madness to mysticism—convinced him that much of what any era calls 'truth' is, at best, a small slice of the pie, and, at worst, brutal forms of social oppression. And therefore all these conventions Foucault insisted on *transgressing*—not bothering to tell us, incidentally, which way he was headed in all this transgressing: was it postconventional or preconventional? transgression or merely regression?"

"*Discipline and Punish*? Chloe, are you really reading this? Are you getting a little kinky on me?," I had asked her at the beginning of our relationship. She actually seemed to blush."

"Well, no, you know. It's by Foucault. You know, Foucault."

"Not required reading in architecture."

"No, I was just, you know, looking around. It's sort of interesting."

I opened the book and read its first shocking lines; I would never forget them; no one who reads them ever does.

"The man Damiens, convicted of killing the king, had been condemned, on March 2, 1757, 'to make honorable amends before the main door of the Church of Paris,' where he was to be 'brought on a cart, naked but for a shirt, holding a torch of burning wax weighing two pounds'; then, 'in said cart taken to the place de Grève, where, on a scaffold that will be erected there, the flesh will be torn from his breasts, arms, thighs, and calves with red-hot pincers, his right hand, holding the knife with which he committed the said regicide, burned with sulphur, and, on those places where the flesh will be torn away, poured molten lead, boiling oil, burning resin, wax, and sulphur melted together, and then his body drawn and quartered by four horses and his limbs and body consumed by fire, reduced to ashes and his ashes thrown to the wind."

I closed the book, looked away temporarily nauseated. "You can do that to me if you want," Chloe had said.

"Jesus, what's wrong with you?"

"Oh, don't be so stuffy." This was before I had begun to understand the tortures Chloe had already inscribed on her own flesh, the scars on her own body, the gashes on her soul, that were a miniature version of what poor Damiens had endured. At each torment,

Damiens kept screaming, "Forgive me, my God! Forgive me, Lord!" It would be months before I learned the contours of Chloe's equivalent screams, and the type of God from whom she begged her own particular forgiveness.

I later finished reading *Discipline and Punish*—how could one not? And I had gotten its point clear enough. Subtitled *The Birth of the Prison*, it was about just what Powell had said—the modern forms of social power and coercion, the ways in which society forces individuals to conform in name of truth, or goodness, or king and country, or psychiatry, or whatever form of "truth" was fashionable at the moment. We are all Damiens—that was Foucault's message.

But there was something deeper than that, always lurking under the surface of whatever Foucault wrote. He was fascinated by painfully intense erotic experiences, experiences so blissfully lacerating they took you into mystical states of release and degradation and dissolution and exaltation, a Dionysian ecstasy that transgressed any and all. He spent many of his later years in the sadomasochistic leather bars in San Francisco, where he contracted AIDS and died in 1984 at the age of 58. "*Nothing is negative in transgression,*" he had said. Even with erotic cruelty, with impulses running riot over conventions, a human being "might recognize itself for the first time"—and thus feel "the transformative force" of the "*transcendens* pure and simple. Transgression affirms the limited being and it affirms the limitlessness into which it leaps," and thus *transgression* offers us moderns "the *sole* manner of discovering the sacred in its unmediated content."

And Powell is saying yes, yes, all of that is true enough. But after breaking and deconstructing and transgressing all the conventional boundaries, *what does one find?*—postconventional liberation or preconventional enslavement? transrational release or prerational craving? worldcentric freedom or egocentric bondage to me and my passing feelings? And did the Woodstock Nation devote itself to that experiment with horribly mixed results, finding a good dose of both and badly confusing them?

Foucault, the great hero of transgression, breaking all the conventional limits to find the limitless, and raging, fuming, thundering against any and all power structures that seemed to inhibit freedom—

and thus becoming the great champion of both postconventional transgression and preconventional regression.

"You know, I have to agree with Powell on that one," I whispered to Carolyn, proud that a computer geek actually had an opinion on this particular topic.

"Well . . . shit. I don't know. I have to think about this." Carolyn's faith in a Foucault who uttered nothing but the truth—a belief deconstructed by Foucauldianism itself—had taken a bad hit, and she sank into silence as it all began to blur.

"'The center of de Sade's world is the urgent need for *sovereignty* and *transgression*,' says Maurice Blanchot. 'Because the libertine is the Sovereign One, the Unique One, he is perfectly and totally free, and therefore he can do absolutely whatever he likes. His complete freedom is a complete negation of others. The libertine is truly, totally free, free of others, free of constraint, transgressing all to find ultimate freedom.' Chloe's naked body shifts, she puts the book down, smiles at me, alluring, offering, fetching.

"Wow, Chloe, that sounds like a fine goal."

Powell, back-lit elegance, walked slowly to center stage. "When Foucault claimed that some forms of 'truth' are really forms of *social power* and *oppression*, he was surely right—again, just think of the seven deadly sins and what was done to people in the name of those 'truths.'

"But just as surely his early views were taken up, mostly by American Boomers, and worked into a strange conception that *all* truth is merely conventional and arbitrary; that *all* truths are socially constructed; and that *all* such constructions are forms of power. In this extremist working of Foucault's work, we see boomeritis at its worst; and thus, an important if partial truth, puffed up to absolute status, began its power-hungry march of devastation. Never mind that Foucault never agreed with such extremism, or when he did, he soon enough retracted it. Boomeritis had made up its own mind, and it did so for a straightforward reason.

"In order for the narcissistic ego to have free reign in the world, it is necessary to demolish any and all obstacles to its omnipotence. Scientific truths, moral guidelines, and anything universal are a threat to 'Don't tell me what to do!'; and thus all truths, without exception, must be claimed to be *socially constructed*. If I can show that any demand on me is merely an arbitrary social construction, *then there are no demands on me, period*. I am free to remain my own little unique and sovereign planetoid, beholden to no one and nobody, because 'Nobody tells me what to do!'"

"'And so I took my place.' Chloe continues reading *Philosophy in the Bedroom* out loud. 'Scarcely was I at it when Rodin enters his daughter's room; and thereupon the impudicious Rodin, all restraints upon his behavior removed, free to indulge his fancies to the full, gives himself over in a leisurely fashion and undisguisedly to committing all the irregularities of debauchery. The two peasants, completely nude, are flogged with exceeding violence; while he plies his whip upon the one the other pays him back in kind, and during the intervals when he paused for rest, he smothers with the most uninhibited, the most disgusting caresses, the same altar in Rosalie who, elevated upon an armchair, slightly bent over, presents to him; at last, there comes this poor creature's turn: Rodin ties her to the stake, and while one after another his domestics flay him, he beats his daughter, lashes her from her ribs to her knees, utterly transported by pleasure. His agitation is extreme: he shouts, he blasphemes, he flagellates: his thongs bite deep everywhere, and wherever they fall, there he immediately presses his lips. Rodin by and by penetrates into pleasure's narrow asylum; the other girl beats him with all her remaining strength, Rodin is in seventh heaven, he thrusts, he splits, he tears, a thousand kisses, one more passionate than the other, express his ardor, he kisses whatever is presented to his lust: the bomb bursts and the libertine besotted dares taste the sweetest of delights in the sink of incest and infamy.'"

"Why, Bataille has nothing on the Marquis," is all I can think to say.

"Again, my friends, I am not denying the important truths of Foucault," Powell intoned, her delivery slowly heating up, "such as his tracing of shifting epistemes and genealogical developments. I am talking about the extreme and exaggerated use that claimed all truth is arbitrary and shot through with power. But that is exactly the extreme use to which Foucauldian studies were usually put by Boomers. Treatise after treatise claimed to expose the social construction of absolutely every truth advanced by absolutely every branch of human knowledge: biology, mathematics, food, botany, sex, zoology, music, geology, astronomy, phonology, linguistics, history, geometry.... None of those truths, it was alleged, had any grounding in reality; all of them were imposed by structures of power: sexism, racism, eurocentrism, logocentrism, phallocentrism, and so on down the standard list of nasty victimizers. Not simply that *some* of those truths have socially constructed components, which *can* be marginalizing, but that all of them are only that: such was an important truth, exposed by pluralistic relativism, that was then taken to frenzied extremes by the addition of boomeritis."

The audience emitted a type of groaning, moaning sound, shifting and shuffling in its seats. Powell began quietly thundering.

"When all knowledge is socially constructed, then nobody can tell me what to do!" she yelled. "Driven by a rebellion of preconventional impulses refusing to grow up to the conventional, boomeritis hijacked a handful of postconventional slogans in order to claim that its own ego could socially construct—and therefore deconstruct—all realities. In so doing it gave to its ego an omnipotent power that it condemned as rampant everywhere else—and thus was set the standard language of social constructivism with which boomeritis would come to brutally dominate the humanities for the next three decades. The main claim of Boomer academics: All knowledge is socially constructed: in other words, nobody can tell my ego what to do!" she roared.

Powell's delivery, although eviscerating, was energetically riveting. I looked around the audience, found myself starting to feel protective of the Boomers. If what Powell was saying was true, it was simply devastating. "Mom, hi, it's me." "Hello, dear. How is computer land treating you?" "Well, you know, fine. How about you, Mom. You okay?" "Yes, dear. I'm teaching yoga classes at the Y, what about that?" "That's great, Mom, that's really great. Heard anything from Dad lately?" "Not lately, dear. A letter two weeks ago said that the AIDS relief project had expanded to Zambia, but there were all sorts of problems, apparently. Your Dad is exhausted, you know. He tries so hard." "I know, Mom, I know. And good for him." "Yes indeed, dear, good for him, good for him."

Carolyn leaned over to me. Surprisingly, she didn't seem angry. "Okay, I think I can agree with some of what Powell says because of the way she says it, even if it is a bit overboard."

Scott leaned forward. "The way she says it? How's that? The lesbian way?"

"I won't even dignify that. No, she fully acknowledges the truth of what Foucault was saying, and then—"

"The partial truth."

"Yes, the partial truth, and then she says, but you can take what Foucault was saying too far. So she gives both the positives and the negatives, and I get that, I really get that. I didn't get that from Van Cleef."

"Well, he did say the same thing," said Kim, "but Lesa has this amazing way, even when she's yelling at you. . . . "

"Van Cleef is just too weird, too twisted, too intense, too something. There's too much stuff going on with him."

Slide #7 flashed up on the wall. It said only, "Derrida and Deconstruction."

"'Hither, my love, come, that I may, in your lovely ass, render myself worthy of the flames with which Sodom sets me aglow. Ah, he has the most beautiful buttocks . . . the whitest! I'd like to have Eugénie on her knees; she will suck his prick while I advance; in this manner, she will expose her ass to the Chevalier, who'll plunge into it, and Madame de Saint-Ange, astride Augustin's back, will present her buttocks to me: I'll kiss them; armed with the cat-o'-nine-tails, she might surely, by bending a little, be able to flog the Chevalier. Yes, that's it! This rascal does have a nipping tight ass! Would you do me the great kindness, Madame, of allowing me to bite and pinch your lovely flesh while I'm at my fuckery?'"

"Chloe, did the Marquis say 'fuckery?'"

"Why, yes, he did, Ken."

"Oh, okay."

Lesa Powell looked around the audience, smiled, and in the quiet, recuperative calm after that particular storm, resumed her story, immediately producing another storm.

"The second major line in the attempt to resurrect the Other of rationality runs from Nietzsche to Heidegger to Jacques Derrida and deconstruction, and it, too, would make profound contributions in the name of pluralism and contextualism, only to succumb to a boomeritis that was all-too-eager to deconstruct the world, leaving its ego supreme.

"Much of the postmodern movement in academia originated not in the philosophy departments but, strangely, in the *literature* departments, advanced by literary critics who were not, shall we say, well versed in philosophical subtleties. This happened for a fairly straightforward reason: literary criticism is concerned, first and foremost, with ways to interpret texts: what is the meaning of *Hamlet*? of *War and Peace*? of *A Streetcar Named Desire*? Figuring out how to interpret these texts is not nearly as easy as it first might appear; in fact, it is almost mind-bogglingly incomprehensible how we create and understanding *meaning* at all, and thus interpretation is a deeply puzzling exercise."

That's exactly what we were discussing with George!—the staggeringly complex task of knowing how to program computers so that they could interpret. It seems impossible.

"All of postmodernism starts right here, my friends, so listen up!" Powell smiled. "Take a very simple example, such as the phrases 'the bark of a dog' and 'the bark of a tree.' Now clearly the word 'bark' means something entirely different in those two phrases. So the *meaning* of the word 'bark' can't come from the word itself, can it? No, the meaning depends on the *context* of the sentence in which the word is found. But the meaning of the sentence itself likewise depends upon the context of the entire linguistic system, which itself is set in contexts of nonlinguistic practices, and so ad infinitum. Thus, it appears that all meaning (and all knowledge) depends to some degree on various contexts, and if you change the contexts, you will change the meaning. As we have seen, this is often referred to as *contextualism*, and it represents an enduring, if partial, truth about the nature of human knowledge, a truth that is first spotted by the green meme. Excellent!" Powell smiled broadly.

I leaned over to whisper to Kim that this lecture was a little taxing, then abruptly bit my tongue.

"What, Wilber?"

"Nothing, nothing. Great lecture, huh?"

"My friends, Derrida's deconstruction became immensely popular because he was one of the first to emphasize these important ideas. As Jonathan Culler in his book *On Deconstruction* summarizes it, deconstruction rests on two principles: *all meaning is context-dependent* and *contexts are boundless.* In other words, truths that were taken to be 'universal,' 'binding,' or 'eternally true' actually depend on the shifting contexts in which they exist. And since contexts are *boundless*—they are literally unending: every context has another context—then meaning itself becomes an endless play of shifting contexts, *unstable* in every way—the famous 'sliding chain of signifiers' and the endless 'deferral of meaning.'

"This would have been an important insight, consonant with contextualism in its many forms, from Heidegger to Gadamer to late Wittgenstein, had not American Boomers seized the notion with a fury and made it something so much more. That all truth and meaning are context-dependent does *not* mean that they are necessarily arbitrary, relative, or built on the shifting sands of cultural whim. A diamond will cut a piece of glass, no matter what words we use for 'diamond,' 'cut,' and 'glass.'

"But in the hands of boomeritis, context-dependent was used, in a wildly exaggerated fashion, to make all meaning and all truth shiftingly relative and arbitrary, so that any established meaning could be undermined, subverted, deconstructed. 'Meaning is fascist!' was the motto here—because any meaning hems me in, and nobody hems me in! Any time you come up with a meaning, I can therefore find a context that will subvert it, deconstruct it, undo it—and I can do so because contexts literally are boundless, and therefore I can play with this fact in the most irresponsible of ways if 'Nobody tells me what to do!'"

"'Bite and pinch as much as you like, my friend, but, I warn you, I am ready to take my revenge: I swear that, for every vexation you give me, I'll blow a fart into your mouth.'"

"Chloe, did the Marquis just say 'fart into your mouth'?"

"Why, yes, he did, Ken.

"Oh, okay."

"I am still reading from *Philosophy in the Bedroom*, the famous text on transgressing and deconstructing conventional morality, the text so beloved of postmodernists."

"Right, right, I knew that."

"'By God, now! that is a treat! Well, let's see if you'll keep your word. He receives a fart. Ah, fuck, delicious! delicious! Oh, 'tis divine, my angel. Save me a few for the critical moment, and be sure of it, I'll then treat you with the extremist cruelty . . . most barbarously I'll use you. . . . Fuck! I can tolerate this no longer . . . I discharge! He bites her, strikes her, she farts uninterruptedly. Dost see how I deal with you, my fair bitch! . . . once again here and there! Eugénie, spewing forth fuck from her mouth and her ass—I have a mouthful of fuck and a half a pint in my ass, and I—'"

"Chloe, I don't want you to think that I'm not thoroughly enjoying this or anything, but, um, let's take a rest from the wonderful reading for a moment, what do you say?"

"But this is freedom, Ken, this is deconstructing conventions, this is finding sovereignty, this is—"

"A hell of a lot of work for an orgasm, don't you think?"

"A typical boomeritis deconstruction ploy was to take a text—oh, it could be from philosophy, literature, religion, whatnot—and, using the fact that all meaning is context-dependent, demonstrate that, for example, the text actually means the opposite of what it claims, so that the text is really subverting itself. For example, we might say—this is a very simplified example, mind you—we might say, 'The notion of truth relies for its meaning on the notion of falsity, and therefore this text, in claiming to offer truth, is actually resting on falsity.' In other words, all accepted truths, all conventional values, all moral strictures, can be quickly 'deconstructed' using this technique. You can literally deconstruct anything you want."

Powell paused, smiled, and walked to the edge of the stage. "However, perceptive critics noted that these postmodern writers did *not* try to deconstruct the meaning of the words 'salary,' 'promotion,' 'tenure,' or 'pay raise.'" Ripples of laughter from the audience.

"Deconstruction had several immediate advantages, and the Boomers took all of them—by the end of the seventies, Jacques Derrida was the most frequently cited theorist in literary academia. One, I can make a career—and get tenure—by simply taking the texts *created by other people*—their books, plays, films, stories, or cultural productions in general—and deconstruct them. In the past, in order to publish—and thus get tenure—I had to write, create, or construct something new; now I could simply tear something down.

"And thus feel an exhilarating rush of superiority in the process. This is an especially important ploy if you are perhaps not very creative or not all that bright, and yet have a need to see yourself as vastly superior. Deconstruction offered the tools to seemingly rise above truly great works of art and philosophy by simply pulling the rug out from under them, which is why it quickly became the number one tool of boomeritis and the most frequently used new method of textual criticism for the better part of a decade.

"Two, via deconstruction, I can break the hold of any text on me; I can subvert any demands it makes on me. Since 'text,' in American deconstruction, actually means anything that exists, then by deconstructing texts I can completely deny any and all demands on my ego. Because, deeply and above all else, Nobody tells me what to do!"

Sporadic applause rose from the audience, mixed with the requisite staccato bursts of boos and jeers. That deconstruction was at heart a way to protect and promote one's ego . . . if that was true, or partly true, I guess is what Powell is saying . . . , still, what a bitter pill to swallow.

"The enduring truths of deconstruction, delivered by pluralistic relativism and contextualism—that is, delivered by the green meme—can and should, in my opinion, be taken up and included in any universal integralism. As I mentioned, many of us here at IC have made extensive and grateful use of these theorists. But their extremist use, driven by boomeritis, is another beast indeed. Deconstruction soon became indistinguishable from extremist deconstruction—even Foucault called Derrida a 'terrorist,' and for *Foucault* to call somebody a terrorist, you can only imagine how bad the situation had become. For boomeritis, deconstruction became the primary terrorist attack for destroying any restriction that did not suit its impulses. It put nothing in place of the structures it destroyed, it simply destroyed, thus unleashing narcissism and nihilism as a postmodern tag team from hell, leaving the ego alone to run amuck among the smoking ruins."

I looked around the audience; so many upturned faces, reflective, expectant, sullen, as Powell prowled the stage, driven by who knows what combination of wisdom and her own insistent demons, but unleashing here a rain of arrows into the heart of my parents' world. Was any of this having any effect at all, on anybody?

"Deconstruction never really took hold anywhere but in America. It never caught on in Britain, certainly not in Germany, Japan or Nigeria. No, it took off in the one country where an epidemic of boomeritis had already prepared the ground. As no less than Jacques Derrida himself exclaimed—and, my friends, I suggest you think about this carefully—'America *is* deconstruction!'"

6

Dot-com_Death_Syndrome@ReallyOuch.com

Whatever transgression or regression or perversion or diversion the Boomers had gotten themselves into (actually, it bothered me quite a bit, because I kept getting images of Mom and Dad, and somehow I knew, or didn't want to know, that what the Boomers were up to had been parentally stamped and not-so-subtly hammered into the brains of Xers and Ys, a neuronal transfusion with repercussions disturbingly eager to extend themselves into the coming silicon revolution). . . . Still, back in my world the truly pressing issues were pressing down on me. Three true stories, from *BlackBook* magazine, threatened to summarize my possible futures:

> True Story #1—A computer genius dies in a hotel room with an empty of bottle of peppermint schnapps cradled in his lap. His pancreas has leaked blood into his abdomen, the result of acute alcohol abuse. Founder of a multimillion-dollar company, he is known by only a few of his own employees. He has no friends, and his main form of human contact has been the paid affections of erotic dancers.
>
> True Story #2—A Silicon Valley software designer, burdened with

the knowledge that his company is about to run out of money, comes home one Monday night and kills his wife and son with a hammer and fatally stabs himself in the neck. That same week, a Japanese investor who hadn't yet heard about the murders calls to say that he is ready to wire all the money needed to keep the company solvent.

True Story #3—A 26-year-old dot-com editor's death is attributed to a combination of overwork, uppers, and alcohol. His father is quoted as saying, "He was getting very burned out. He may have been stimulating himself to keep going and going. He pushed it too far."

After the 26-year-old died, journalists dubbed him a "poster boy for the young, thrustingly ambitious Internet generation." "How phallic," said Chloe, but it was true—the Net was built largely by analytic-mathematical minds driven by testosterone, young geek males who couldn't get laid staring feverishly into computer screens until all hours of the night, dissociating into a disembodied cyberspace that might very well become humanity's future. "Hell, makes you want to become a feminist," Chloe had murmured, and she seemed to have something of a point; in light of my increasing understanding of the full spectrum of consciousness and the entire spiral of development, the idea of narrowband male geekdom dominating silicon city was increasingly disturbing, even alarming. I had in no way given up on downloading into the Silicon System: I just had swirling new ideas about what should—and should not—be downloaded into eternity.

"You can't work 50, 60, 80 hours a week and not pay a price," the journalists continued to opine. "Dot-com Death Syndrome," they started calling it. "People are put in pressure-cooker jobs in a pressure-cooker industry in a city that is only turning up the heat. Casualties will occur. All the Ping-Pong and pool tables, on-site chefs, Nerf hoops, and stereo systems cannot make up for the truth that some places work people like dogs. Saturdays are the new Mondays. Cultlike devotion is expected. Buildings go up in a week; neighborhoods are overhauled in a season. More people have moved to California to become dot-commers than they have to become gold miners, movie stars, or hippies—combined."

True Story #1 is the slow and dogged suicide of Phil Katz, the genius pioneer of Zip technology, which allows greatly increased storage of computer information. In an acquaintance's high school year book, Katz had written, "I enjoyed working with you in mathematics and physics classes. May a calculator bring great happiness to you."

"A calculator!" exclaimed Chloe. "I'll bet he rattled when he made love, too."

"They're all missing the point," Scott says, accompanied by an eerie post-human drum and bass score by Drazen Bosnjak of tomandandy. "This is a race, a real race. The kids are working 80-hour weeks because a revolution is coming—a real revolution, not that silly, simpy Foucauldian transgression, where a little fisting blows your mind—but a massive global worldwide explosive revolution. Carbon life-forms are on their way out, Silicon life-forms are being born, right here and right now in the minds and hearts of the Thrustingly Ambitious Internet Generation. Look, Ken, right here":

Enormous doors open, and hundreds, perhaps thousands, of naked female bodies lay before us. "Let's get thrusting," Scott says.

"Aren't you getting just a little bit tired of this?"

"But Ken, we haven't even started!"

Dr. Moshe Kravitz was from the Longevity Research Center in Berkeley. The Harvard Student Union had been sponsoring a lecture series, "Unbearable Faces of the Future." What Kravitz said went by in a flash, but the net effect was more numbness, as if somebody had given me an injection of Novocain right in the base of my brain.

"Okay, kiddies, here's the score. Within perhaps three decades, we will have the technical capacity to extend the average human lifespan to 200,000 years. I'm dead serious."

Hearing this was the second biggest jolt of my life. Third, actually. (I'm talking about adult shocks, not kid shocks, like when I learned there was no Santa Claus, first saw Mom and Dad having sex, or found out I was really born in Oklahoma.) The first adult brain seizure was when I realized that human consciousness could and would soon be downloaded into silicon/computer/cyberspace. The second was when I realized—just last week, in fact—that there are actually *levels* of consciousness, spanning an entire spectrum, which means that there is not just a single something called "intelligence" that we can download into supercomputers—no, there are *levels* of intelligence, and so just what type of intelligence are we going to download into CyberCity? Who will program our future?

And now this. Human life, carbon life, might live 200,000 years. This was grotesquely disturbing for many reasons. First and foremost, it meant that carbon-based life forms, whose *obituary* I had firmly written, were now making a startling comeback—they were making their own bid for a type of immortality, or at least a stunningly extended temporal run. Carbon and Silicon life forms would now be in something of a close contest—perhaps even struggle, combat, who knows, maybe even war—to see which would win the evolutionary race. Carbon or Silicon—which would own the immortal future?

For several days I stumbled around in a mental haze; my mind began writing silly science fiction books based on this devastating piece of information. What the hell would you actually do if you lived to be 200,000 years old? Well, on day one, put a penny in the bank and let it gather compound interest; by the time you're 400 and just getting ready to live, you'll be a billionaire. Start sleeping around, by the time you're 120,000 years old, you will have slept with everybody on the planet. This would no doubt be depressing; you go into psychoanalysis, the first 5,000 years of which are spent on your mother.

What would a person do who lived 200 millennia? It would be exactly like this: imagine being born in the middle Paleolithic Age and living until today! That's what it would be like. You would start out as a hunter-gatherer. You would witness the invention of agriculture. If you traveled, you'd have a chance to meet Jesus, Buddha, Ramses, Isaac Newton, Hitler. You would see the seven wonders of the ancient world, watch the pyramids be built, walk the Great Wall of China just for something to do that decade; see the rise of the industrial revolution, watch machines begin their ascent to planetary dominance, culminating in today where cyborgs are about to take over the world; hide your eyes from the blast at Hiroshima, weep uncontrollably at Wounded Knee, recoil in horror when the gates at Auschwitz are opened; watch polio and malaria be cured, surf the Internet. Good lord, your biography would take 5,000 years to read.

Dr. Kravitz said that *this will be a possibility starting in perhaps three decades*!—exactly the same time that computers will begin to make the hyperjump to human-level intelligence. Both Carbon and Silicon consciousness in a race for immortality. . . .

"Chloe, did you know that, barring accidents and such, we will soon be able to live up to 200,000 years? Do you have any idea what that means?"

Chloe looked very thoughtful. "I will definitely need a new wardrobe."

"Sweetie, be serious."

"Well, I really don't see how that could happen."

"It's like a car. If you park a car in your driveway, and every seven years you change every part in that car and put in a new part, how long would the car itself stay functional?"

"Forever, because you're always putting in fresh parts. So you're saying that's what it will be like with human bodies?"

"That's what this guy Kravitz said. And we're not talking about putting machine parts into humans. That will happen too. But the point is, every cell in the human body renews itself continuously. Theoretically, there is no reason the body shouldn't or couldn't live indefinitely. But Kravitz says that the human organism, maybe for evolutionary reasons, has built-in death mechanisms. He mentioned things like telomeres, Hayflick limit, pituitary death hormone. . . . Turn those off, and the body will renew itself forever, just like the ever-fresh car in your driveway."

"I must remember to shift more of my assets into long-term bonds."

Chloe will not-handle this the way she not-handles everything else. But for me, right now, right here, this is nauseating, excruciating, it all won't fit into me; I can't breathe.

What would a person do who lived that long? Seriously? And somewhere on the third day of wandering in this daze, it slowly dawned on me—and this was sort of the fourth great shock of my life: Once a person had exhausted all the exterior forms of activity and entertainment—seen everything on the entire planet, done everything, gone everywhere, slept with everybody, taken all the drugs (um, try not to overdose)—once you had gone through all those *exterior* pursuits, what was left but to take a tour through all the *interior* realms? In other words, the only thing left that would be any fun would be to start a vertical growth in your own interior consciousness in order to discover new ways to experience the old world. After you had, as the red meme, eaten and fucked your way through the entire planet, what next? Move up to blue meaning, and reexperience the world through those fresh lens. And when that got boring—which it would sooner or later, give or take a few thousand years—then up you go to orange, and an entirely new and fresh and inviting world would open before your eyes, and you could again reenter life with new vitality, new gusto, new desires, new values, new vistas, as a vividly fresh wonderland would emerge right before your eyes. And then up to green, and then to yellow, and then to turquoise, and then . . .

And then, that's as far as I had gotten in my science fiction novel. But the deeply unsettling fact was, this wasn't science fiction. It was the leading edge of today's hard science. Science fact, not science fiction. Of this much I was certain: not only would the AI Bots, or silicon-based life forms, begin an evolution through the *entire* spiral of consciousness (I had already figured that out), so would carbon-based life forms (because there would be literally nothing else to do). Carbon and Silicon would be locked into a race through the great unfolding waves of consciousness, heading toward exactly where I was not yet really certain. Didn't Hazelton say that there were levels higher than turquoise?

Dot-com Death Syndrome was just the tip of this almost infinite iceberg: Of course us Internet Kids were in danger of burning out—precisely because we were burning up the past and opening the world to a new destiny, a giga-quantum leap in evolution the likes of which literally could not be imagined. In a type of sublime masochism, I became proud of my generation succumbing to DDS—I wore it like a badge of honor for the coming leap into hyperspace.

And so a new path had been cut for my life: Carbon and Silicon were once again coming back together, intersecting in some sort of extraordinary destiny; and, in ways that were not yet clear to me, it all had to do with this elusive spiral of consciousness.

Hazelton's voice drifts in and out of the science fiction narrative. *"The conclusions are straightforward: What is the jumping-off point for second-tier, integral consciousness? The green meme.*

"What immediately prevents this quantum leap into the hyperspace of integral consciousness? A fixation to the green meme.

"What is the major cause of a fixation to the green meme?

"Boomeritis."

Chloe looks at me. "What if she's right?"

"I don't know, Chloe. I don't know. This is too much information, it's just too much. Chloe, did you know that two of the three greatest shocks in my life have happened in the last week?"

"Forgot which hand you masturbate with, and misplaced that six-pack of beer?"

"No, fortunately nothing that bad. No, it has to do with . . . it's all about what we . . . it's this unbelievable discovery . . . see, there's this Spiral . . . well, maybe later. But my question is, What if Hazelton's right?"

"Sweet boy, that was my question."

"Oh, yeah. So what's the answer, Chloe? What if she's right?"

"Transgress, subvert, deconstruct. The green meme, warming to its power, began to tear down many traditional values that needed to be torn down—or at least loosened—and thus ushered in a series of social reforms unparalleled in their significance, including environmental protection, civil rights, feminism, equal opportunity employment, consumer protection, and health-care reform. All of this is to green pluralism's everlasting credit, and to the sensitive self that reached out to Others who were clearly in pain and suffering."

Charles Morin, as he had previously at every session, was introducing the day's topics.

"But the shadow side of the green meme was already beginning to show itself. When any meme is threatened—and especially when it senses that its historical time is up, that it is no longer in control of the dominant forms of discourse—then out come its Inquisitors. The most notorious, of course, was the Spanish Inquisition, which attempted to guard the blue meme from the historical rise of the orange meme. But once the orange meme (which began with the Reformation, continued into the Renaissance, and flowered with the Enlightenment) itself became the official worldview of modernity—especially in its form as scientific materialism—then it often acted as its own Inquisition, ruthlessly damning any sort of knowledge, and any level of the spiral, other than its own. Orange truth, and only orange truth, attempted to rule the day.

"But within a few centuries, the reign of orange was decisively challenged by the emergence of green. There occurred yet another profound 'meme shift' in culture, this latest one flowering in the mid-twentieth century—flowering, in fact, with the Boomers. In this shift, the percentage of the population that was green went from a mere 2% or 3%, prior to 1900, to around 20% or 25% today. That percentage is still not as large as that of blue (around 40% of the population) or orange (around 30%), but since the green meme was at the leading edge of cultural evolution, then—like red and blue and orange before it, in their own ways—green came to dominate the cultural elite. The green meme effectively ruled academia, the media, social services, liberal politics, all levels of the educational system, and most health care services.

"As green came to dominate the cultural elite, it effectively began challenging the traditional blue and orange conventions in this society. And that is what a large part of the sixties was all about. In fact, one of the great privileges of coming to age during this period is that we had a chance to witness one of the truly significant meme shifts in history— the emergence of green and its deconstruction of blue and orange orthodoxy—with all the wonderful promise and horrible peril that involves."

The audience shifted and settled in its seats, preparing for the day's surgery.

"Today is a journey into the heart of darkness," Kim ominously whispered.

"What?"

"Sacred cows get gored today."

"Well, which is it? Darkness or cows? Or maybe sacred cows get gored in the dark?"

Kim looked at me, and I could see that I was probably back on the nitwit list. But the tone in her voice was distinctly disturbing.

"From the time that the green meme challenged the blue and orange status quo—starting in the mid-sixties—until it effectively assumed power among the cultural elite—around the late seventies—the green power drive accelerated in its reach and intensity, until its own Inquisitors stood as guardians at the cultural gates. It turned increasingly ugly, if for no other reason than that power corrupts. The green meme, in many ways, became the *mean green meme*: an extreme version of the green meme, an unhealthy version, a pathological version, if you will—just as the Spanish Inquisition was a pathological version of blue. And the mean green meme, the Green Inquisition, began in earnest to undo, or at least horribly compromise, the previous gains of healthy green, turning them into extremist agendas that, as a further nightmare, became an even more inviting home for boomeritis."

"Okay, Kim, I didn't mean to be flippant. What do you mean, sacred cows get gored today?" Katish looked alarmed; Carolyn stared straight ahead; Scott was smiling; Beth looked prepared.

Mark Jefferson walked on stage. The house lights dimmed, the stage lights came up. Jefferson looked out at the audience and smiled warmly.

"Did you know that on an IQ scale of 160, Jefferson scores 160?" Kim looked around. "He's a friggin genius. Funny thing is, well not so funny, he didn't find this out until he was like 40 years old."

"I thought he was in the Rangers and all that," I said.

"That's the point; he spent his life in dumb-down jobs . . . well, not that Rangers are dumb, but you know what I mean."

"Until what, he took the IQ test on the back of a box of Wheaties?"

"No, until the IC folks suggested he get tested. Cuz like every time he opened his mouth, people were like, 'What the fuck was that?' He was so out there."

"I have to say, integral studies don't seem like something the brothers would be into," mused Scott.

"Mark says that's true but only because, at this time, integral studies are a luxury of the white middle class, not because integral studies have no interest for minorities. In fact, it's the key to their getting out from under whitey."

"Whitey?"

"Yes, whitey—that means your skinny cracker ass," Kim said, laughing. "Seriously, Mark says that the only way to overcome the ethnocentric waves is to develop to the worldcentric waves. But liberals—green-meme liberals—are horrified of anything resembling levels or ranking or stages, so they won't even let this topic be discussed. So they block the one way to get out of ethnocentric prejudice—which is further cultural evolution—because they deny cultural evolution in general. Not that conservatives do any better, which they don't. Jefferson is like totally pissed at both of them."

Slide #1 for the day went up, "Cultural Studies." "Sacred cows get gored today," and I wondered what that really meant.

Mark Jefferson looked around the hall. "All of the important truths of pluralism, infected with a particularly virulent form of boomeritis, were brought together under the broad heading of *cultural studies*. Cultural studies, in many ways, became the epitome of the mean green meme."

"Not exactly a snappy beginning," Katish said with a satisfied grin.

"Although there are many different branches of cultural studies, I will focus on those that were generally united under the banner of 'the resurrection of the Other of rationality.' The hegemony of Western patriarchal rationality has marginalized three Others in particular—nature, body, and woman—and cultural studies set out, first, to expose and denounce the hierarchical marginalization inscribed on the site of the textual Otherness prior to its essentialization by patriarchal signifiers; and second, to resituate the marginalized Others in the center of a textual discourse that, via emancipatory play of free signifiers cut loose from a phallologocentric episteme, inverted the hegemonic hierarchization so that periphery becomes ground on the site of the original inscription when returned to its ineluctably contextual historicity."

Jefferson looked out at the silent, solemn crowd and then burst into laughter. "Sorry, sorry, I lapsed into postmodern lingo."

The audience, which had earnestly been trying to follow what he was saying, as if it would be tantamount to endorsing slavery did they not agree with him, likewise erupted in laughter, here as a collective sigh of relief.

"I meant to say, cultural studies set out to expose oppression and undo it wherever possible." Jefferson again laughed out loud, a warm and gentle thunder.

"Okay, okay. Here's the deal, my friends. What specifically marks the boomeritis version of cultural studies, feminism, and ecology is that a very important topic of inquiry is taken up and turned into a fundamentalist religion. I want to emphasize this and say it loud and clear: nobody is denying the importance of each and every one of those topics. What we are looking at, rather, are the ways in which a noble idea (such as the postconventional protest of a dubious war) can be taken up for much less noble reasons (such as preconventional narcissism), a strange brew we are calling boomeritis. And nowhere has boomeritis flourished more than in cultural studies."

"But Ken, just look at all those naked female bodies! Hundreds, maybe thousands of them. Talk about tits and ass! You start at that end, I'll start at this end, and we'll fuck ourselves to the middle. Come on, I'll race you."

"Scott, Scott, really, what's the point? Don't you get the sense that we are just being pushed by blind, mindless, stupid instincts? This is nothing but Mother Nature having her way with us, Mother Nature pushing us around blindly. This is just Mother Nature fucking us! It's a mindless, endless, instinctual Oedipus project writ large! It totally overrides our will, our dignity, our rational honor. And the women! Jesus, did we ever stop to ask them if they wanted to be treated this way?! 'We'll fuck ourselves to the middle.' Is that any way to treat a human being?! Jesus, Scott, what's wrong with you?"

"But Ken, just look at all that."

One, two, three, four. "Okay, I'll start at this end."

"The first item that is almost impossible to miss as one surveys present-day cultural studies is the tone of moral superiority that haunts almost every treatise. What is so disturbing is that this tone of superiority is coming from (1) critics who profess pluralism, in which nothing is supposed to be superior; and (2) critics who, for the most part, haven't an ounce of the talent they are criticizing." Loud applause from the audience, apparently hoping to be on the condemning, not condemned, side of the accusation.

"We saw that Professor Frank Lentricchia, writing in *lingua franca: The Review of Academic Life*, exposed exactly this core of cultural studies in American universities. Nor is Lentricchia a cranky outsider to postmodern critical theory. He is coeditor of the widely acclaimed anthology *Critical Terms for Literary Study*, whose contributors range from Stanley Fish to Stephen Greenblatt, and he teaches at Duke University, an epicenter of cultural studies. And what did he find was the central attitude of such studies? It is

> the sense that one is morally superior to the writers that one is supposedly describing. This posturing of superiority treats everything that came before it as a cesspool that literary critics will expose for mankind's benefit. The fundamental message is self-righteous, and it takes this form: 'T. S. Eliot is a homophobe and I am not. Therefore, I am a better person than Eliot.' To which the proper response is, 'But T. S. Eliot could really write, and you can't.'

There was a spasm of begrudging laughter; involuntary, melancholy agreement. "No wonder Lentricchia concludes his survey of the present state of humanities in America: 'It is impossible, this much is clear, to exaggerate the heroic self-inflation of academic literary and cultural criticism.' Heroic self-inflation: put bluntly, the puffing up of the big fat Boomer ego." Staccato shifting, coughing.

"The tools of this heroic self-inflation are provided by (mostly) French intellectuals, led by Foucault and Derrida, as we have seen, but also including a rogues gallery of Bataille, Althusser, Lacan, Barthes, late Wittgenstein, de Man, Gramsci, Irigaray, Gadamer, Bourdieu, Jameson, Kristeva, Cixous, Bachelard, Baudrillard, Deleuze, and Lyotard. The interesting and sometimes profound insights of these writers were taken up and worked into a green-meme mishmash that denied big pictures and meta-narratives of any sort—which unfortunately and rather completely locked it out of second-tier integral ideas."

What on earth is a meta-narrative? Sounds like a horrible rash. I looked helplessly, plaintively, at Kim. She stared back at me coldly, a stare that nonverbally said, "You wuss, you wimp, you . . ." I jerked my attention back to Jefferson.

"To its credit, in this effort to deny all big pictures, this version of postmodernism was attempting to undo the universal formalist accounts that had harshly imposed one privileged scheme on all of history. It was trying to subvert the attempts to take one favored interpretation and force all of history into that plan. For all too often, those 'universal historical truths' were simply the conventions of propertied, white, able-bodied, heterosexual, middle-class males. There is certainly much truth in that criticism—you heard Lesa Powell explain this from a Foucauldian perspective—and it is a valid criticism precisely because it was made using pluralistic relativism (green) to attack the limitations of universal formalism (orange).

"But for boomeritis, it became something so much more. As Lentricchia suggested, it became a ticket to a hollow claim of moral superiority. Listen up, people, because this is the crux of the matter!" Jefferson grinned. "As with all first-tier memes, pluralism assumed that it was the only correct view, *and then every deviation from that view was said to be imposed by oppression.* Reviewing all of history, cultural studies could then happily see itself as nice and pluralistic and liberating, while all previous Western civilization was marginalizing, oppressive, nasty, brutish, and short.

"It succeeded in that endeavor—seeing previous Western civilization as unendingly wretched because it lacked pluralism—precisely because pluralism is a *recent emergent.* That is, pluralistic relativism—the green meme—did not emerge on any substantial scale until a few hundred years ago, and it did not become characteristic of a significant percentage of any population until a few decades ago. It thus takes little intelligence to look through history and find no pluralism, because there wasn't any. But instead of understanding that the lack of pluralism meant a *lack* of development, cultural studies assumed that the lack of pluralism meant a *presence* of oppression. Wherever pluralism was not, oppression was assumed to be (or would soon be 'discovered' by cultural studies). By this twisted yardstick you can therefore easily condemn any past historical figure you want—and certainly all dead white European males—and, as with deconstruction, you can then feel the wonderful rush of your superiority in the process."

A muffled groan went up from the audience, interspersed with grinning applause from several Xers and Ys. Katish, sitting on my right, leaned around me and agitatedly whispered to Carolyn, two over on my left, "This doesn't mean anything, you know."

"We'll see," is all she said.

"Chloe, I had the weirdest dream. Scott and I were . . . , that is to say, there was this field of . . . , so Chloe, how was your day?"

"Why, if you were dreaming, sweet boy, then it was about naked female bodies, lots of them."

"Ha ha, ha ha ha, don't be silly."

"You're bright red, sweet boy. Don't you know why you are always dreaming and fantasizing about sex?"

"Well, like you said, twenty-something males, every ten minutes. . . . "

"That's the frequency, not the cause. The reason, sweet boy, is that Mother Nature is fucking you."

"That's just what I told Scott!"

"Yes, then, and did either of you listen?"

"Well . . ."

"You see, Ken, that is why it is so hard for couples to stay together. Through the male mind, every ten minutes, comes this huge erotic fantasy, and what's the poor boy to do? Is it to be the same ole sperm dumped into the same ole vagina?"

"I might throw up."

"Or is it to be a hundred naked female bodies all lined up in a row? Yes, I thought so. And that is why the enterprising young woman has to be ever so clever in order to keep her man interested in the same female body year after year."

"Um, okay."

"So listen up, sweet boy. *The Kama Sutra*, chapter 1. The Lion position."

"It's not that there were no inequalities in history. Just the opposite. I don't have to stand here wearing this color of skin and tell you that history is defined by its many inequalities." Jefferson paused and looked around the audience. "But it is generally the case that the movement of history itself is a tortuous, up-and-down saga of slowly *overcoming* those inequalities (a big picture that postmodernism disallows). For example, *without exception*, every single societal type—including foraging, hunting and gathering, horticultural, and agrarian—had some degree of slavery.

"Until, that is, *modernity*, which, with its grasp of universal formalism, pronounced all men equal, and its beginning grasp of pluralism, pronounced all people equal. Modernity thus outlawed slavery across the board—the first societal type in history ever to do so. History prior to modernity has *never* been without some sort of slavery, sexism, or racism because history only *at* modernity developed universal rights and *after* modernity developed pluralistic richness.

"But looking back on history, and never finding pluralism, cultural studies assumed it was not there because of oppression, and then began to accuse its own pet villain of all of that oppression. The green meme, recall, must have victims and villains to make sense of the world. So it proposed several major villains: patriarchy, hierarchy, the Western Enlightenment, the Newtonian-Cartesian paradigm, logocentrism—most of which were variations on the dreaded 'linear rationality,' which supposedly repressed body, nature, females, and so on.

"Now it is certainly true that formal rationality can repress items not of its ilk. But as 'bad' as formal rationality can be in terms of exclusionary practices, *pre-rational cognition is much, much worse*—because prerational cognition supports only egocentric and ethnocentric perspectives. In other words, as bad as orange might be, purple and red and blue are much, much worse!

"Thus, in its haste to 'subvert' and 'overcome' rationality, boomeritis committed a wretched, double mistake: it *robbed* rationality of credit for any of its emancipatory accomplishments (from abolition to feminism to ecological sciences), and it *gave* to prerationality a liberating force it does not, and never did, possess."

Jefferson walked to the edge of the stage, looked at the audience, and delivered the indictment: "Under these twin lies, cultural studies set out to liberate the world. The trail of boomeritis roadkill was about to begin."

"You and Darla kissed? The milestone of your life was that you two kissed?" Jonathan grinned. "Are you like fucking kidding me? Look, Stu, kid mystic, baby, you gotta get out more, know what I'm saying? I mean, if a kiss was the huge milestone, I'm guessing that your biggest excitement up to that point was watching them spray the vegetables over at the Safeway."

Stuart ignored him; we all did. "The next night I picked Darla up from the Dayton's fashion show just in time to make it to the airport for her flight back to Chicago. With no time to change after the show, she was still all done up in makeup, lots of glitter-sparkly things all over her face and scantily clad body.

"In the airport, standing at the gate, the last call for boarding came. We kissed passionately, and when she pulled away, she broke out laughing and told me there was glitter and makeup smeared all over my face. Drunk on clarity, I stumbled out of the airport with sparkles all over me—the perfect symbol of the ecstatic hum I felt inside. I passed by confused people, whose expressions said, 'What the hell happened to him?' I thought how I might respond, thinking to myself, 'God, she has great lips.' The spark that I had seen in Darla's eyes was now also in the eyes of passing strangers too. Why hadn't I noticed before?

"The following days, we talked on the phone, all hours of the day, drilling each other's interiors, diving deeper and deeper into the well between us. I had just left an eight-year relationship, and she had just ended three years with a man named Bill. Single for the first time in a decade, I had decided to focus my life on meditation and music. That was my plan. After one day with Darla, I folded that plan up and drew a question mark in my mind.

"We decided we had to see each other again, soon. We made plans to meet in Madison that weekend, the halfway point between Minneapolis and Chicago. I was a little nervous about going; my rational brain was bitching, 'What the hell are you doing? This is highly irrational, even for an artist, so settle the fuck down, you're probably on the rebound from your last relationship.' But, the skepticism was drowned out by undeniable intuition; I had to see her. It was crucial for me to be with this woman as soon as possible, not to get laid or even entertain myself, but because my soul had seen something with her, and for some reason it would not shut up."

Mark Jefferson walked off the stage to a round of respectful, subdued applause as Carla Fuentes sauntered out.

"Looks are deceiving," Kim whispered. "She can get really fired up. She's been married—get this—five times."

"She's what, forty-something?"

"She says it's because she won't take shit from any man. She hates victim feminism, thinks it is ruining, or rather has already ruined, the movement. She says that's why feminism is dead, except at women's studies departments run by aging, bitter, boomer women. So Fuentes wants to get the field of feminism fired up again, but along integral grounds, not green-meme victim chic. She's a kick-ass feminist."

"They come in different flavors?"

"Like *hello*? First-wave feminism was liberal, second-wave was radical, third-wave was power feminism, and all of them had a piece of the puzzle, but none of them had the whole, that's what Fuentes says, so they all fell by the wayside, they all croaked, basically. Now comes the fourth wave, which is integral. Integral feminism is being pioneered by folks like Karin Swann, Janet Chafetz, Willow Pearson, Joyce Nielsen, Jenny Wade, Lesa Powell, Carla Fuentes. I get a kick out of Fuentes."

"Do you agree with her?"

"Well, let's just say she makes more sense the more I listen to her. But this is where some women start walking out, and it doesn't help that some of the men cheer, so don't do that, okay?"

"For feminists," and Carla Fuentes began exactly where Jefferson had left off, "this meant that 'rationality'—the 'oppressing force'—was simply defined as a masculine, patriarchal principle of analysis, division, dominance, and subjugation. History was then read as a chronicle of the oppression of females by males."

Fuentes had hardly started, and already she paused, walked out to the front of the stage, waved her arms around in the air, then looked out at us. "Now we are all familiar with this idea, right?—that the patriarchy basically means that women are oppressed, that they are essentially slaves, yes?" The audience murmured acknowledgment.

"But people, please, look what this really means. Since the number of females at any given time is roughly the same as the number of males, then in order for radical feminists to claim that women are oppressed, they have to implicitly claim that females are weaker and/or stupider than males. Unless you are outnumbered, there is no other way to get oppression going!" she shouted at the audience. "You simply cannot be as strong and as intelligent *and* oppressed."

This disarming thought set the audience murmuring, looking at each other, grimacing, grinning, whispering among themselves; some, like Katish, quickly returned to sullen, angry silence.

"Many feminists, looking back on history and seeing that women everywhere made choices of which the modern feminist disapproved—and believe me, most women in history, yesterday and today, make choices that the modern feminist would not—so the feminists decided that all these women were being *forced* to make those choices. (Why else would any woman disagree with a feminist, right?) In other words, all these poor women are being duped, brainwashed, and oppressed. Instead of assuming that women *co-created* all past forms of societal roles, including the patriarchy, instead of assuming that women were as strong and as intelligent as the males, many feminists began a long series of treatises dedicated to proving that women everywhere were herded sheep, and the males, of course, were pigs."

Rounds of nervous applause were interspersed with occasional jeers and moans; it appeared the audience was dividing rapidly along gender lines, most males cheering, most females staring silently ahead. Fuentes walked back to the podium.

"Already you can start to see the boomeritis creeping in. Narcissism—which always supposes that the reason it is not triumphing absolutely, the reason it is not wildly successful, is because somebody else is holding it down—predisposed many feminists to look too eagerly to a great Other causing their plight. Feminists infected with boomeritis often refused to see females as the responsible agents of their own circumstances. Why aren't I succeeding as wonderfully as I hoped? Because I'm a victim, I'm being oppressed, I'm being dominated.

"Slipping into victim chic, these boomeritis feminists *implicitly* defined women as powerless, as molded by an Other, oppressed by an Other, held down by an Other. Do you see the misguided logic here?" she asked the audience. A numbed silence greeted her.

"Okay, look, people. I start out like this: I am a female, and I find that society seems to favor males in the things that I want to get. So how do I explain that? Feminism is an attempt to answer that question.

"Up until now, there have been three major feminist answers. The first and earliest school of feminism was liberal feminism, which was basically an extension of the idea that 'all men are created equal' to include the female sex. So liberal feminism maintained that 'all humans are created equal,' and the reason that females do not have more power is that they have been oppressed by the males.

"The second school of feminism—radical feminism—said, 'Wait a minute. Males and females are not the same, they are not created equal. They are created very different—they intrinsically have different values, different wants and drives, and especially different modes of knowing'—you know, males are ranking, females are linking, males are agentic, females are relational. Radical feminism is radical because it values the female mode as much, or more than, the male mode. And it says that the major problem with this world is that the male values have dominated the female values. But, they maintain, it wasn't always like this. We started out with either matriarchal or matrifocal societies, which honored the values, but those female values were, once again, repressed and oppressed by the males.

"The third wave of feminism then came in and said, 'Hey, wait a minute. Male and female may have similar values or they may have different values, but at most times and places the females have outnumbered the males. We basically are and always have been a majority, and therefore—certainly in modern democracies—we have absolutely nobody to blame but ourselves. This, of course, is power feminism, a step in the direction away from the many forms of victim feminism, including liberal and radical."

"First wave, second wave, third wave. La ti da, la ti da, la ti da. Wave this. . . . "
    "Not now, Chloe!"

"Of course, here at IC we think that there is a fourth wave of feminism in the making—integral feminism—which 'transcends and includes' all three of those earlier schools." Fuentes looked around the audience. "But here is my point: with any version of feminism, if I try to say that I am not succeeding primarily because somebody else is holding me down, then I have not only defined myself as pretty stupid or pretty weak, I have *given* whatever power I have to that Other. And if that is really true, then *only* the Other can free me, because I have *already* defined myself as outpowered by the Other.

"This strange misguided move—which still haunts most schools of feminism—robbed females of their power in the very first step of trying to empower them. It necessarily implied that women were weaker and/or stupider than men. Driven by a narcissism that refused to accept active responsibility for its circumstances, boomeritis defined women as universal victims—as inherently weak and malleable—in the very attempt to liberate them. And thus, my friends, boomeritis feminism was born." Fuentes looked out at the audience with a concentration that tended to inhibit any audience response at all, positive or negative; we all sat temporarily suspended in her intensity.

Ed Kowalczyk of Līve is singing "Lightning Crashes," Boozy and Swan do "Champagne Bert Boogie," and the pound pound pounding in my brain begins rattling my body as well. Virtual realities leap out from my forehead and rush into the future, a world defined by thought alone that cascades through silicon at the speed of light. The piercing ache of being human, of having carbon-based tender neurons exposed to pain twenty-four hours a day, sears my skin in a sinuous torture, a faint whiff of burning flesh fills the air.

"Yes, now! sweet boy," Chloe says. "*The Kama Sutra*, chapter 2. The Ox position. Let's do it!"

"Whatever you say, Chloe, whatever you say."

"Now you don't really mean that, do you, sweet boy?"

"Aren't you going to cheer me up and say something like, patriarchy *this*?"

"Patriarchy shmatriarchy, who needs either? It's a silly blame game, sweet boy."

"Really? Then cheer me up, would you?"

"But why cheer you up, sweet boy? Because what would you do without your depression?"

My God, she's probably right, I note, a realization that is so . . . depressing.

"Once females were implicitly defined as weaker and/or stupider than males—the patriarchy enslaves all women, and women were the first real slaves—this ridiculous female malleability had to be explained and defended, and the primary tool for doing so was the social construction of reality." Fuentes once again walked from the podium out to the front of the stage.

"Thus, because all reality is a social construction, sexual differentiation of any sort is not actually given in reality, it is just a set of arbitrary conventions imposed by male power (at which point Foucault is hustled into the picture). Especially in the patriarchy—which, for many feminists, began around 5,000 years ago with agrarian modes of production; but which, for radical feminists, has existed from the very beginning of the human species—these conventions were constructed by males for the express purpose of oppressing females."

Fuentes paused and looked intently at the assembled; the air around her quietly hummed; the audience still seemed too intimidated to respond. "Many radical feminists have fervently argued that, in the patriarchy, all of language, all legal institutions, all forms of public work and expression; all religions, all forms of philosophy, all mathematics and all sciences: all of them are basically structures of male domination and control aimed at repressing females, nature, and the body. Not only did males invent all of those as forms of oppression, but—much more astonishing—females everywhere acquiesced to this nonsense—they were, it is said, 'brainwashed' by the patriarchy—and therefore women *everywhere*, all over the world, and from day one, sheepily accepted this massive oppression. Well-known feminist writer Ms. Ortner actually refers to this brainwashing as a '*universal acquiescence* on the part of women.' This isn't just a truly wretched portrayal of males, it is a wickedly demeaning view of females. Do these feminists really think women are that stupid?" she thundered.

"I knew I had to see Darla. It was so overpowering I couldn't believe it. When I got to Madison, Darla bounced out of the hotel door, threw her arms around me, and gave me a deep kiss. I turned into putty, and all the barriers evaporated. We went into the hotel room, and for the next eight hours we got lost in each other again. Physically, we did nothing but kiss and stare into each others eyes, but inside I could feel something in me blending with her. Part of this was definitely falling in love, but there was something else I hadn't known before, at least not in the company of another person. We still weren't making love, just kissing.

"After about seven hours, we sat up in bed and suddenly realized we were both starving. It was 1:00 A.M. and neither of us had eaten all day. I felt high as a kite and totally lucid, like the room was some magic chamber. We went to an all-night place and cuddled between bites of french fries.

"In what seemed like an instant, two days went by in that hotel room. The first night we did not make love, as I held back a little from the intensity of the whole thing. It was like watching giant waves crash on the beach, half wanting to run into them and half wanting to flee to safer land. I know what it's like to fall in love, and knew that was happening, but there was also something more, another something that was even bigger. There was love between us, but there was also something like a Love around us, connecting us like conduits to create a channel. I felt deeply drawn to that other presence, but afraid of it too.

"At some point, after much time had passed, we both decided we'd better check our messages and see what had happened in the outside real world. Darla was on her cell phone for a long time, listening and listening. When she shut it off, the vibe in the room had palpably changed. I asked if everything was okay, and she said no, it wasn't. Her old boyfriend Bill had called and left a string of messages, freaking out, desperate to speak with her, and wanting very much to get back together with her. I told her I'd be in the car, just come and get me when their talk was over."

"Boomeritis feminists," Carla Fuentes continued, "are forced to use this ploy—'women are brainwashed by the patriarchy'—when it comes to the fact that, apart from such general ideas as equal pay for equal work, the majority of today's women do not agree with most feminist positions. As one reporter pointed out, 'For the feminist movement, one of the embarrassing facts of political life has been the refusal of most women to embrace either its rhetoric or its basic principles. Radical feminist Alison Jaggar agrees and notes that any theory of a special "woman's standpoint" must be able to "explain why it is itself *rejected by the vast majority of women*."'"

Fuentes walked quickly to center stage, her intensity lifting and floating her across the floor like an anti-gravity device. "Now we have already seen that feminists like Jaggar believe that the reason that 'the vast majority of women'—yesterday and today—have not embraced feminist ideology is that they have in fact been *brainwashed*, so they can't spot their own subjugation, poor things. I tell you, as a woman that entire notion makes me furious. Because my point, you see, is that once you have idiotically defined women as being easily brainwashed, you're bloody well stuck with it. This is a strange attempt to give women power by irrevocably demolishing it."

Fuentes pitched her voice over the din rising from the crowd. "This is, in other words, boomeritis feminism, which parlays victim chic into a theory of epidemic cultural oppression in order to explain the lack of feminist values in all previous history as a brutal imposition from the outside on an otherwise pure and innocent female self. History is then re-read as the drama of the gifted child, but this time all the gifted children are female." A muffled noise arose from the audience, a mixture of cautious applause and condemnatory groans. "God I love the smell of politically incorrect thinking in the morning!" Fuentes exclaimed, almost to herself.

"See, Carolyn?"

"Go fuck yourself, Scott."

"Oh, people, come on now, don't look so shocked and hurt. You'd think I'd just ripped your nose ring out, or maybe stolen your favorite tattoo right off your back, or your arm, or your . . . ahem, never mind. I am not picking on females, I am not picking on males. And I certainly do not favor a particular gender. As far as I can tell, men and women are neck-to-neck in the stupid race."

Fuentes continued to dance across the stage, popping along on her blistering resolve. "Of course some women are sometimes oppressed; so are some men. But disagreeing with professional feminists is not evidence of it. It is as important to address real cases of oppression as it is to free women from feminist versions of it."

"*The Kama Sutra*, chapter 3. Stimulation of Erotic Desire." Chloe shifts her naked body, moonlight playing off her breasts, rising and falling with each breath.

"'Unequal relations should be shunned in favor of equal relations, and should not be risked without thought regarding size, moment, and mood, and how to proceed with the union.'"

"I'll say."

"'One must be aware of inequalities and ascertain whether the relation is practicable or not.'"

"I'm with you all the way, Chloe."

"'When the male organ slides into the other, the best result is when both mood and moment are shared. Unequal relations make for bad copulation. With a mare, a ram will need a lot of time. The power of force is not always sufficient. A stallion, even when excited, needs a lot of time. The man with an inadequate duration and size must do the best he can.'"

"Um, are you talking to me?"

The only time I ever saw my parents have a major, drawn-out, knockdown fight—they didn't actually hit each other, it just felt like they did—was over the ERA, the Equal Rights Amendment, an amendment to the Constitution of the United States that guaranteed equal rights to all citizens regardless of sex or gender, an amendment supported by women's groups everywhere. Their heated quarrel occurred just after the amendment was defeated, because polls showed that a majority of males supported the amendment, but a slightly larger majority of females opposed it, so it was defeated. The argument was about why more males than females supported the ERA. I never before, or after, saw both of them screaming and yelling at the top of their voices. Dad won the theoretical fight—it was very hard to out-think Dad—but I believe he lost the argument.

"It's very simple," said Dad. "We males are for the ERA because we have more to gain."

"Oh really?"

"Oh really. In three major areas. One, reproductive freedom. Two, the draft. Three, marriage rights. In the deepest and most painful issues of both life and death, society clearly favors the females, and we're sick of it. That's why we want the ERA and you don't."

"Well, sick is right, because that's the sickest of many sick things I've heard you say. You don't have reproductive freedom! Are you kidding me? We're the ones who have to fight for the right to choose, we're the ones forced to carry your babies if reproductive rights are denied us."

"Just the opposite. *Roe* v. *Wade* already gives you reproductive freedom, a reproductive freedom that is completely denied to every male in this country."

Mom looked at me like, Is he totally insane or what?

"Okay, big boy, how's that?"

"Simple. Let's say you get pregnant. You can abort the pregnancy. That is, you have the absolute right to refuse motherhood, yes?"

"Right now, yes."

"Yes, you have the right to refuse motherhood. But if a man becomes a father, does he have the equal right to refuse fatherhood?"

Mom was quiet for a while; this was clearly an unfamiliar question. "That doesn't make any sense."

"Yes, it does, you just never thought of it before. You have the right to refuse motherhood come what may, but I do *not* have the right to refuse fatherhood. This is radically unfair."

"So what are you saying, that you should have the right to force the woman to have an abortion?"

"No, no, not at all. I'm simply saying that if a woman can totally walk away from motherhood if she chooses, then a man should have the equal right to walk away from fatherhood. If we had real gender equity in this country, and you decided to keep the child and be a mother but I decided I did not want to be a father, then I should be able to sign a legal waiver of all responsibilities. That would be gender equity, and we males do *not* have that!"

I looked at Mom. "He's got a point, you know?"

"No, I don't know. And what an irresponsible thing to say! A woman carries the child, so of course she has more rights."

"Well, then, goddammit, don't say that you want 'gender equity,' because females have massively more rights here, and I resent the hell out of it! We males do not have gender equity when it comes to reproductive freedom. Do you know how many male lives are ruined because they are forced to participate in a parenthood chosen only by the female? Do you?! As it is now, males are forced into economic slavery by a legal system that denies them a reproductive freedom that it gives to the female. Gender equity my ass!"

Dad was red-faced; Mom wasn't backing up.

"So, okay, so, Dad, what was the other reason, or the second reason, or whatever that was?"

Dad kept staring at Mom; his breathing began to slow, edging back toward normal. "The war. It's the war." And Mom immediately softened; the brutality of the topic itself forced its way into the room, crowding out their anger.

"This will sound so selfish, and I guess it is," Dad began. "This is what I remember at the beginning, when the war broke out, and they started the draft, started calling up us guys. Started calling the men, just the men, to go fight in the trenches of Vietnam. I would wake up at night, sweating, scared out of my wits, truly frightened to death. And as I walked around campus, and I looked at the women, all I could think is how much I hated them, really and deeply hated all of them, because they didn't have to fight. I hated their bodies that lay down at night to go to sleep and would not awaken in terror at their impending doom. Hated their smiles, those fucking smiles that were everywhere—how could those insensitive whores smile when I am about to have my brains blown out by some unseen gook in some un-known field in some unimportant fucking fifth-world country? I hated them more and more, as they sat around in their so-called conscious-ness-raising groups and bitched and moaned that, oh gosh, they were only making 85 cents to the dollar—didn't these total ignorant idiots know that I was about to be killed! Fuck your 85 cents, lady! You have no right to complain about a goddam thing. And any time that I would have sex, I wouldn't make love, I would fuck them, I mean re-ally *fuck them*!" and he slammed the table with his fist, dropped his head into his arms.

My whole body was shaking, I was so unnerved by his fury, his vio-lent anguish. Mom moved to comfort him, then paused; it slowly dawned on both of us that he, or some part of him, hated her, too. Hated her for not having to fight. The three of us sat in silence.

Dad shifted, took a breath. "The first thing I thought of when I heard about the ERA was, we have to share this pain, I'm totally for the ERA." He relaxed, even managed a smile. "Well, I'm not saying that women should have to fight a war, but they should at least have to try to dodge one." At that we all laughed, relieved.

But Mom wasn't going to take this, shall we say, lying down. "Men start wars, men have to fight them."

"Oh don't give me that bullshit!" he yelled, instantly again red-faced. "Women are just as divisive in their own way."

"I don't know, Dad. We are a testy group."

"Some guys like to fight, some guys don't. I don't want to fight this war, and I don't know any men friends that do. All I'm saying is, I don't care who starts the war, it is a violation of gender equity that I have to fight and the females don't. None of us wants to fight, so why do only us males have to do it? So don't even dare mention the words 'gender equity' until males have this equality!"

"Oh boo hoo, boo hoo," Mom said. "Poor little whiny-assed master of the universe, can't fight like a man, eh?"

That was a big mistake. "You fucking cunt whore!" he screamed. "That's really what it comes down to, isn't it? You claim you hate gender roles and stereotypes, but you really, deeply, secretly believe them. You're ashamed that I don't want to 'fight like a man.' You just said it yourself! You fucking bitch, why don't you admit that you want me to fight!"

"I do not want you to fight."

"I do not want to you fight," he minced and mimicked. "Go fuck yourself."

"Probably not a good time to mention the third reason?" Dad moved toward me in such a menacing way I thought he might strike me. But he really didn't even see me; he was being electrocuted by his own anger, seared by emotions much too strong to either express or endure.

"Oh who cares," he moaned. "Oh fuck it. Most of my men friends backed the ERA because they don't want to pay alimony when the divorce arrives—they do not want to be forced to be the economic providers of the other gender—it's a form of economic slavery that the courts protect. My friends think they will never get gender equity in the first two issues—fatherhood and the draft—but they think the courts will support this one, maybe with no-fault divorce for starters. And it's true, we will probably get more gender equity here. Males should not automatically be forced to be the economic providers. Split it 50-50." There was a long pause. "That way, when the blessed divorce finally comes, males won't have to shoulder a disproportionate burden." I knew then, from the way he looked at her, that divorce would define their future.

He smiled, as if finally relieved of some enormous burden, and walked out of the room. And I always had the sense that the burden was Mom. And therefore me. And that is why he had won the fight, but not the argument.

Fuentes paused, and she seemed visibly to become softer. "Look, my friends. Although I have been criticizing what boomeritis, victim chic, and the mean green meme have done to feminism—and females—I have myself written extensively on the importance of feminist issues. It is especially urgent, as I mentioned, to create an *integral feminism* capable of hearing the many significant voices of feminist scholarship. In this I am joined by many colleagues here at IC. We call this 'all-quadrant, all-level' feminism, because it attempts to include and integrate all the various schools of feminism—and because it includes the entire spectrum of consciousness and the entire spiral of development.

"How would something like an integral feminism work? Well, for starters, it would recognize that both men and women have different values at each of the stages of development. There are red male and female values, blue male and female values, orange male and female values, and so on. The one thing we would not try to do is to take green female values and try to impose them on all the other stages of development. As it is now, the green-meme feminist looks at history—which was dominated mostly by red and blue stages—and, since she cannot find her green values anywhere in history, she assumes that these wonderful values were being *oppressed*, instead of realizing that they simply *had not yet emerged*.

"But once she mistakenly assumes that these values have been oppressed, then she must do two things: assume males are oppressive swine, and assume females are brainwashed sheep. And off we go with the two deeply mistaken cornerstones of boomeritis feminism—the pigification of men, and the sheepification of women.

"We here at IC are attempting instead to forge an integral feminism that acknowledges, includes, and joins all these memes into a rainbow harmony spanning the entire spectrum of consciousness and the complete spiral of development. And should I point out that 'integral' and 'inclusive' and 'joining' are all female values?" Loud applause and clapping from almost everybody.

And with that, Fuentes walked off the stage.

"After an hour, Darla came out to the car, where I was playing guitar in the back seat. Looking sad, she told me her old boyfriend Bill had said he now truly realized how much he loved her. He was ready to finally fully commit, spend their lives together, the whole nine yards. Still, this didn't alarm me, even though I had plainly fallen in love with her. I asked her what she wanted to do, what this meant to her. She said she didn't know. She loved me, but was unsure of what to say to Bill.

"Even with that uncertainty in the background—or maybe because of it—that night we made love for the first time. As we melted and rolled into each other, the room was alive. So simple, so complete, and I saw what grace can do with two human bodies.

"That made it all the more wicked, what was about to happen."

"Integral Feminism Is Yet to Be Born" was actually the name of a dream that I had, perhaps two or three years ago. In the dream, I am floating as the sky, and all things are arising in the vast spaciousness of my own infinite consciousness, womb of the entire world. And out of that spaciousness, I see both men and women arise—or perhaps I should say, I see both yin and yang arise and begin to populate the manifest world with the offspring of their ecstatic embrace. The billions of stars that light up the night are really the orgasms of angels. The whole of this wondrous, beautiful, radiant world is the blissful overflowing of hearts happy to have found each other. Every single thing in the cosmos touches every single other thing in an erotic exuberance too painful to contemplate in its entirety, unless you are the sky. . . .

Most men and women settle for the pitifully small slice of bliss that they can fit into their own bodies, instead of finding that their real bodies contain the entire world. Integral feminism would end this dismally restricted state of affairs, the dream seemed to announce. And then I saw it was so much more than that. It would really be Integral Humanism. No, much more than that. Integral Kosmology, the entire effervescent universe held in the palm of your hand, which is so easy to do if you are the infinite sky. . . .

Well, a strange dream, yes? But in this female body, fated to embrace, the question still arises: my generation, my dear sweet generation, do you know how much I love them?

Derek Van Cleef strode on stage. The slide on the wall jarringly said, "The Culture of Rape."

Before Van Cleef said a word, Kim whispered, "Rumor has it that he raped somebody."

"What! You're kidding."

"Well, the rumor is that he was charged with rape. Nobody really thinks he did it, but nobody knows what really happened. Maybe that's why he won't date anymore. But I don't think they should even let him touch this issue. It's a big mistake. Big mistake. But he insists."

Van Cleef began with a joke that seemed innocent enough. "For many feminists, it is the case that, as one put it, 'All men are rapists.' That, of course, is an outrageously unfair and untrue statement. As everybody knows, all men are not rapists; all men are horse thieves." There was good-natured laughter from the audience, but you couldn't help but wonder where this was going.

"But for most forms of boomeritis feminism, all males are rapists, period. Every male is accordingly viewed, first and foremost, not as a citizen, human, or person, but as a criminal. Newton's laws of gravity, for example—a truly brilliant contribution—were actually 'Newton's Rape Manual,' as one feminist announced. Bowdoin College's catalog describes a women's studies course that asks, 'Is Beethoven's Ninth Symphony a marvel of abstract architecture, or does it model the processes of rape?' The examples of every male action being a form of rape are truly countless.

"What this all seems to mean is that whether a particular man actually committed a rape, he might as well be legally charged. As the assistant dean of student life at Vassar helpfully explained, since males must be sensitized to the fact that they are rapists, then even *false* charges of rape serve an important function: 'The falsely accused rapists have a lot of pain, but it is not a pain that I would necessarily have spared them. I think it ideally initiates a process of self-exploration. "How do I see women?" "If I didn't violate her, could I have?" "Do I have the potential to do to her what they say I did?" Those are good questions.'"

The look of contempt on Van Cleef's face could be seen from the back row. "The FBI now estimates that, based on DNA evidence recently become available, approximately one out of every three charges of rape that make it to trial are *false charges*. In other words, at least one out of three females is lying about being raped. As *Newsweek* (Jan. 11, 1993) reports, 'A study conducted by the FBI with subjects already in jail for rape used DNA findings to show that 30% of the convicted men were innocent according to the DNA evidence.' This means that several thousand males are languishing in prisons for crimes they did not commit, although presumably they are becoming more sensitive men for being forced to ask these 'good questions.'" Van Cleef stared into the audience, as if daring anybody to disagree. We all sat silent, holding our breath.

"Few will argue that some men need to be more sensitive to the fact that when a woman says no, she means no. But with boomeritis, it gets trickier. As Susan Estrich carefully explains, 'Many feminists would argue that so long as women are powerless relative to men, viewing "yes" as a sign of true consent is misguided.' In other words, since females are oppressed, a woman can *never* really mean 'yes' under present-day circumstances.

"Thus, 'No' means no and 'Yes' means no, which rather puts a damper on it, what? Women portrayed as essentially victims are not even capable of deciding whether to have sex. The green meme, attempting nobly to let each person speak for herself without coercion, goes so far out of its way that women cannot speak for themselves at all. Whatever oppression the patriarchy may or may not have imposed, it pales in comparison with the unfreedom manufactured for women by boomeritis feminism."

Chloe is on her chandelier, hanging naked upside down, and I am a Cartesian disembodied monological gaze, hungrily taking it all in so that I can exploit, humiliate, violate.

"Don't you feel degraded by my staring at you like this?"

"You're the one with the eyes-popping-out-of-their-sockets problem, so why should I feel anything? The trouble with you, Wilber, is that you keep degrading me with these assumptions about how fragile I am. You're not strong enough to degrade me, sweet boy."

"I want to conquer, dominate, eat you alive."

"Ooooh, look at me swoon. Don't worry, I won't break."

One thing was certain: I never heard Chloe blame anybody for her woes.

"But surely those scars on her wrists are the scars of the patriarchy," Alison Jaggar's voice ominously intones.

"Oh, bite me," says Chloe.

Slide #3: "The Death of the Subject: The Birth of Narcissism."

As Van Cleef retired, Lesa Powell stepped onstage. The loud applause that she always received was muffled by the feeling that Van Cleef had . . . what? just raped the audience with his condemnation of rape? At the very least, his performance struck me as something of a drive-by shooting.

Powell proceeded to deliver a blisteringly complex lecture on postmodernism and its "inadvertent inculcation of narcissism," virtually none of which I understood. The lecture, which was handed out, is in my notebook. At intermission, Kim explained:

"Basically, her point was that the 'death of the subject'—which is a constant theme of postmodernism—fell prey to a pre/post fallacy. 'The death of the subject' simply means that you are trying to get beyond or deconstruct the conventional ego or the conventional subject. Powell said that the postmodernists—so intent upon deconstructing and transgressing the conventional—ended up championing *anything* that was nonconventional, including much that was actually preconventional, narcissistic, and regressive. She quoted Luc Ferry and Alain Renaut, whose *French Philosophy of the Sixties* is considered the definitive study: 'It must seem paradoxical and problematical that what passes for postmodernism *acquires the strange appearance of a regression. . . .* ' According to Powell and the IC folks, this wasn't paradoxical at all. The advance from orange to green was accompanied by a reactivation of red, a *regression* to red—and that mixture of high green and low red is exactly boomeritis."

Scott leaned over. "This is all starting to make sense, you know."

"Make sense?" I increduously moaned.

"I'm not convinced until I hear the concrete, positive alternatives," Carolyn said, concerned. "They haven't explained what integral feminism would actually be, or integral cultural studies, or integral anything. . . . All they are doing is trashing everybody else. How sensitive and caring is *that*?"

"You're flunking the test, Carolyn."

"Go fuck yourself, Scott."

"Go fuck myself? Well, at least that would be sex with somebody I love."

"Actually, it would be sex with probably the only adult on the planet willing to consent to it."

"Guys, *please*," I implored.

The next slide announced, "And Postmodernism Begat Victim Chic."

"*Kama Sutra*, chapter 4," reads Chloe, her naked body swaying with each word. "'As it is said in the Sushruta manual, satisfied tranquillity is not to be found among women after an erotic experience with a man who reaches orgasm quickly. Women love and are pleased by men who ejaculate after long copulation. Men who have a habit of finishing quickly are not well looked upon.'"

"The bastards!"

"'Thus it is that, from a certain point of view, a woman's love or indifference is connected with the man's possibility of making her reach orgasm.'"

"Haven't these people ever heard of batteries?"

"'Women appreciate the virility of a man who performs the longest copulatory act. It is almost impossible for a woman to desire to sleep with someone who ejaculates too quickly.'"

"You know, the little Ever Ready rabbit, it just keeps on going and going and going? You know, that cute little bunny rabbit?"

"All of that abstract discussion can be brought home very quickly," Lesa Powell said, and the audience sat up in its chairs. "The point is simply that the 'death-of-the-subject' philosophy—which is a cornerstone of postmodernism—lends itself directly to victim chic. Remember, the green meme *must* have victims in order to make sense of the world, even if it has to create them. And that is exactly what happened, as numerous critics have noted. Let me again quote the French scholars Ferry and Renaut: 'The style of the sixties is also a certain philosophical lifestyle characterized, let us say, *by the search for marginality* and *the phantasm of conspiracy.* This is exactly why, beyond what differentiates them, the various components of '68 philosophy (Heidegger, Foucault, Derrida, Lyotard, Bourdieu, Lacan, etc.) can be grouped *around a pathos of victimization.*' Let me repeat, the green meme must have victims in order to make sense of the world.

"And so," Powell continued, walking back and forth across the stage, "the explanatory power of boomeritis starts to cohere when we hear so many different critics, on both sides of the Atlantic, converge on a similar assessment. All the strands start to come together: a noble pluralistic stance—the green meme—that eventually turned *pathological*, that became the mean green meme: the pre/post confusions, the infestation of postconventional pluralism with preconventional narcissism, the abdication of mature subjectivity and responsibility, the regression into immature and endless egocentrism, the slide into victim chic: all branches on the great tree of boomeritis."

"I told you," said Scott.

"We'll see," Carolyn shot back.

"The next day, after a blissful night of lovemaking, we parted ways. I drove back to Minneapolis and Darla went back to Chicago. Back in Minnesota a few days later, I had a disturbing dream one morning.

"I was in a pool, swimming and lost in pure joy. The pool emanated an innocent, radiant joy, and I floated and rolled in its perfect love. Then I saw Darla on the side of the pool, dressed up in nice clothes, ready to go somewhere. My heart sank with dread. I knew this was not good. She motioned for me to come over to her, to meet her at the edge where she stood. I swam over, with a sinking feeling building in my gut. When I reached her, she took my hands, looked into my eyes, and said, 'I have to go.' I started sobbing, pleading with her, 'No, please don't go,' and she started to cry too, but said she had to go. And so the dream ended with her leaving, and me in the pool, sobbing, lost, and feeling all the joy turn, turn into something still very powerful, but frightening.

"When I woke up, I felt I had to call her immediately. I reached her, and not more than a minute into the conversation, she told me she was going back to her old boyfriend Bill, and that although she knew she loved me, she loved him too, and felt she had to give it another chance. I was totally speechless, too stupefied to even tell her about the dream. I mumbled, 'Oh, I see,' and that was about it. We hung up the phone, and I sat there on my parents' porch with a horrible, horrible sense of dread."

Chloe, Scott, Jonathan, and I sat spellbound by the intensity of the drama and Stuart's melancholically wired delivery.

"I wanted desperately to get out of my own body. In that instant, I saw that this was not going to be the collapse of a romance, it was going to be the birth of something else. I knew this, because I could sense more directly than ever that Presence that had been there, coming through Darla and me, but not from us. That Presence was a great Impersonal Love, and sitting there holding the phone, speechless, it was growing stronger than ever. I felt tricked, knowing that in some way Darla had been a decoy, that I got into this pool of bliss, this infinite intimacy only because Darla was there with me—that left to my own self, I would never have taken such a risk with that tidal wave. This had suddenly turned into another reality, and I knew it meant I was about to drown. As I sat in the chair, dying to escape my body, wishing to be suddenly turned into anyone else but me, I knew that I was fucked, that there was no way out of what was about to happen."

Margaret Carlton walked back on the stage as Lesa Powell departed. The next slide said: "Politics by Any Other Name: The New Totalitarians."

"According to the *Alingata Veda*, 'Before copulation, in order to arouse the penis with desire, the following four kinds of caress are practiced: contact, bruising, baring, and squeezing.'"

"Wow, that sounds great! That's fantastic, Chloe. Now we're talking, now we're talking. But, um, you know, what was that middle part? About the bruising?"

"The epidemic of victimism that has swept this country has not gone unnoticed by the media," Carlton began with that deceptively gentle, fragile smile. "*Time* magazine recently carried a cover story, 'Crybabies: Eternal Victims.' *New York* magazine featured 'The New Culture of Victimization.' *Esquire* exposed 'A Confederacy of Complainers.' *Harper's* asked, 'Victims All?'

"In fact, in the past decade, the green meme—rapidly decaying into the mean green meme—has aggressively, horrifyingly, moved to repeal the First Amendment. The *right to free speech* has been eclipsed by the *right to not have your feelings hurt*, to not have your ego bruised."

Carlton continued reading, her voice urging us to follow if we would. "'Americans,' points out Sykes, 'have long prided themselves on their pluralism and their tolerance of the incredible diversity of viewpoints and ideologies represented by this country's various cultural groups. But insistence on the irreducible quality of one's victimhood threatens to turn pluralism into a series of prisons.' Pluralism becomes a series of prisons—that's perfect, isn't it?" Carlton mused.

"But more than that. As we have seen, high pluralism coupled with low narcissism builds the further prison of the hypersensitive self, whereupon *feelings* and *sensitivity* become the only currency of discourse. 'Only genuine victims can claim "sensitivity" and "authenticity," and only victims can challenge other victims. Increasingly debates take place between antagonists who deny their opponents' ability to understand their plight. Inevitably, that turns such clashes into increasingly bitter ad hominen attacks in which victim status and the insistent demands for sensitivity are played as trump cards. . . . '"

Carlton marched across the stage, looked out at the audience. "Indeed. The University of Arizona's 'Diversity Action Plan' expresses concern over discriminating against students on the basis of 'age, color, ethnicity, gender, physical and mental ability, race, religion, sexual orientation, Vietnam-era veteran status, socioeconomic background, or individual style'—in other words, everybody. The University of Connecticut has banned 'inappropriately directed laughter.' Duke University has a watch-dog committee devoted to ferreting out 'disrespectful facial expressions.'

"This implies, as Julius Lester points out, 'that the opinions, feelings, and prejudices of private individuals are a legitimate target of political action. This is dangerous in the extreme, because such a formulation is merely a new statement of totalitarianism, the effort to control not only the behavior of citizens, but the thoughts and feelings of persons.'"

Katish leaned over with a loud, annoyed whisper, "This is a completely one-sided argument! This is so fucking unfair I can't believe it. Don't they make any effort to give both sides of the story?" Carolyn vigorously nodded her head in agreement.

Kim, as if called upon to defend her lover and his pals, said, "They have other seminars that are devoted entirely to criticism, and then they invite tons of critics who disagree with them. But not at this seminar, no, they are just presenting their alternative view. They are criticizing first-tier approaches to these topics in order to make way for second-tier approaches."

"Well, remind me when those other seminars are," Katish said in disgust, "because this is ridiculous."

"Brown University," Carlton smiled, "adopted a policy that banned 'inappropriate verbal attention, name calling, vandalism, and pranks.' Students were explicitly warned: 'If the purpose of your behavior, language, or gesture is to harass, harm, cause psychological stress or make someone the focus of your joke, you are engaged in a harassing manner. *It may be intentional or unintentional and still constitute harassment.*' With this policy, in short, you can be convicted of *subconscious harassment.*"

And with that, Carlton walked forward to the edge of the stage and gingerly raised her voice, which, for Carlton, was the equivalent of screaming: "Subconscious harassment! People! You are all guilty! We will get you for your thoughts now! Look the fuck out, the thought cops are coming!" And everybody started laughing, not at the content per se, but at the fact that dear sweet Margaret Carlton had said "fuck."

"'In almost every case,' as one reporter notes, 'the alleged damage is intangible—a matter of feelings and impressions—rather than a matter of actual or demonstrable harm. The listed effects of such intangible harrassment include "loss of self-esteem," "a vague sense of danger," "a feeling that one's personal security and dignity have been undermined," "feelings of impotence, anger and disenfranchisement," "withdrawal," "fear," "anxiety," "depression," and "a sense of embarrassment from being ridiculed."'

"In other words, under such policy, if anybody makes you feel like any of the above, you are the victim of harassment—you can basically sue them. Moreover, the criteria for this crime of insensitivity becomes, not witnesses who saw the crime, or evidence of actual harm, but simply and solely the *hurt feelings* of the offended person. That is literally all the evidence that is required!" Carlton threw her arms up, exasperated, and strode back to the center of the stage; the audience squirmed uncomfortably.

"Hurt *this*," says Chloe. "'Chapter 7. On Copulation and Special Tastes.'"

The Living End blares "Astonia Paranoia" and "Blood on Your Hands," Alien Ant Farm screams "Smooth Criminal," and the thump thump thumping rattles a brain too war-torn to endure. The ugly future, extending indefinitely, slip sliding away from all control, presses down on corroding neurons, carelessly crushing any lingering resistance.

"Chloe, Chloe, no more reading, really. I can't get this out of my mind: 200,000 years, Chloe, 200,000 years."

"*Hurt feelings*. What does all that really mean? *Hurt feelings*. Easily hurt, hypersensitive, thin-skinned—well, it means a ripe, plump, bulging, easily bruised ego, doesn't it? It means an ego so big that it bruises if you merely sneeze. In other words, the green meme under sway of boomeritis is reproducing its pathology in students as fast as it can: it is inculcating in students a big and easily bruised ego, and then sending those enormous and fragile egos out into the world, where they will be primed and ready to sue you if you sneeze in their presence. In come students, out go victims. Oh my!" Carlton looked out questioningly at the assembled.

"Sometimes the victimization is so subtle, with the hurt feelings calibrated in micrometers, that an almost superhuman perception on the part of an exquisitely compassionate person is required to ferret out the insult. The *Harvard Educational Review* carried an article by Professor Magda Lewis, who described an example of this subtle harassment of females by males in the form of 'hard-to-describe body language displayed as a barely perceptible moving forward; a not-quite-visible extending of the hand.' These not-quite-visible crimes should nonetheless be presumably met with quite visible punishment. Boomeritis, driven by the narcissistic hypersensitive self, is a large bruise looking for a place to happen, and one can only feel a certain sympathy for such noble sensitivities gone so horribly amuck. Oh dear . . .

"But wait!" Carlton interrupted herself with a crackling laugh. "Let's not skimp on credit where credit is due. By 1991, the United States had 70% of the world's lawyers.

"When a society relies on the feelings of the individualistic self—not to mention the hyperfeelings of the narcissistic self—the social glue of genuine relationships cannot be counted on to anchor cultural discourse, and thus legal codes and their barristers must be brought in to referee any paths that cross between hypersensitive selves. On the other hand, with a society chock-a-block with egos the size of the Louisiana Purchase, all claiming that their problems are *your* fault, I suppose we should be thankful for that 70% acting as some sort of buffer."

Young Ken is searching for his own omega dawn, the point at which his old self will dissolve and a new self be reborn, a self of diamond indestructibility. He assumes that this self will be the inhabitant of an eternal silicon system, but that is just the beginning, or rather, a diversionary tactic in a larger Kosmic game. He is looking for me, really, and I am in turn but a way-station to a timeless origin. But that origin demands a human sacrifice, shocking in its dimensions. Young Ken has slipped and fallen on a patch of spacetime ice that leads to his own demise, a destination toward which he is already skidding piteously out of control, pulled by the center of gravity of his own deeper design. And he imagines he is simply involved in computer programming. But then, I once made such narrow assumptions myself, did I not?

Carlton finished with a somewhat muscular critique of multiculturalism and the politics of recognition; I put a copy in my notebook. And then out came Lesa Powell again; the audience wildly applauded her, even after the drubbing she last gave them.

Powell yelled out, "Only one more topic to go for today!" Rippling waves of applause.

Slide # 6: "Essentialism: Hey, You, Get Off of My Cloud!"

"*Essentialism*," she began. "You all know how this word is used. It means that you have to be a woman to know *anything* about women; you have to be an Indian to say anything about Indians; you have to be gay before you can explain anything about homosexuality. In other words, as so many other critics have noted, there is a cultural regression from worldcentric to ethnocentric—identity politics alone rule, and extreme pluralism means none of us have anything in common anymore.

"As one critic puts it, 'Today's obsession with difference is distinguished by the haughtiness of the tribes and the scope of their intellectual claims. Many exponents of identity politics are fundamentalists—in the language of the academy, "essentialists."' This essentialism especially flourishes on campus. 'Protected by the academic superstructure as a relatively cheap alternative to disruptive protest, the separate programs cultivate *a rapture of marginality* in the protected enclaves of the academy.'"

Powell paused and looked around the audience, left the podium and walked up to the front of the stage. "People, please pay attention!" She smiled. "In this regressive atmosphere, which slid from worldcentric into ethnocentric, as David Berreby puts it, 'Americans have a standard playbook for creating a political-cultural identity. You start with the conviction that being a member of your group is a distinct experience, separating you from people who are not in it (even close friends and relatives) and uniting you with other members of the group (even if you have never met them). Second, you assume that your own personal struggles and humiliations and triumphs in wrestling with your trait are a version of the struggles of the group in society. The personal is political. Third, you maintain that your group has interests that are being neglected or acted against, and so it must take action—changing how the group is seen by those outside it, for instance.'"

Lesa Powell looked up. "It's not that such action is bad. It's just that, taken in and by itself, it is massively alienating and fragmenting, a type of *pathological pluralism* that astonishingly believes that acceptance of my group can be accomplished by blaming and viciously condemning exactly the group from which I seek the acceptance. I target as enemies those whom I need as allies, precisely because I am ethnocentric, not worldcentric, in my embrace. I attempt to salvage my ethnocentric identity in a way that effectively sabotages, destroys, its very acknowledgment."

"Living for 200,000 years," Scott says, "I know exactly what that means. Fuck everything that moves. Just look out there, a sea of tits and ass, rising and falling to a thrusting phallus."

"Can you hear yourself, Scott? You sound like the winner of the annual Bad Porno Writing contest. Here's you: 'It was a dark and stormy night, as I started poking my prick into anything that moved.'"

"Yeah, look who's talking. Two beers and you'll fuck mud."

I am about to shoot back a devastating retort, but I realize that the little bastard is probably right.

"True pluralism, on the other hand, is not ethnocentric pluralism but *universal pluralism*. You acknowledge the *commonalities* and *deep features* that *unite* human beings—we all suffer and triumph, laugh and cry, feel pleasure and pain, wonder and remorse; we all have the capacity to form images, symbols, concepts, and rules; we all have 206 bones, two kidneys, and one heart; we are all open to a Divine Ground, by whatever name; we all have available to us the entire spectrum of consciousness and the extraordinary spiral of development. And you *also* acknowledge all the wonderful differences, surface features, culturally constructed variants, and so on, that make various groups— and various individuals—all different, special, and unique. But if you start with the differences and the pluralism and never make it to the universal, then you have only pathological pluralism, ethnocentric revivals, regressive catastrophes.

"Fortunately," Powell continued, "the truly sensitive are increasingly voicing the need to move from this ethnocentric imprisonment to worldcentric embrace. Take award-winning artist Sara Bates. The Cherokee Nation has seven clans—Wolf Clan, Deer Clan, Red Pain Clan, Bird Clan, Twisters Clan, Blue Clan, and Wild Potato Clan. Sara is Wolf Clan, so she includes elements of this in her art. But what is so extraordinary about Bates's work is the way she embraces elements representative of a collective and interconnected humanity— again, not ethnocentric pluralism but universal pluralism. From one of her brochures: 'Many artists draw from history to tell a story of their particular reality as an American Indian or a woman or an artist within the milieu of art history. They go to great pains to describe what sets them apart from other individuals—group-identity or ethnocentric pluralism. 'Bates has chosen instead to use the history and philosophy of her heritage as an American Indian and, more particularly, a member of the Cherokee Nation to talk about how similar we are and to describe our interconnectedness'—worldcentric or universal pluralism. This is such balm for our fragmented souls!— for the nightmare of identity politics, the politics of narcissism. That Sara Bates is expressing universal pluralism in her art—and fighting the fashionable but brutal trends of ethnocentric pluralism and Balkanized diversity—is extraordinary.

"Likewise," Powell said, prowling the stage, "from a discussion between Maya Angelou and bell hooks:

> bell hooks: I'm so disturbed when my women students behave as though they can only read women, or black students behave as though they can only read blacks, or white students behave as though they can only identify with a white writer. I think the worst thing that can happen to us is to lose sight of the power of empathy and compassion.
>
> Maya Angelou: Absolutely. Then we become brutes. Then we risk being consumed by brutism. There's a statement which I use in all my classes, no matter what I'm teaching. I put on the board the statement, 'I am a human being. Nothing human can be alien to me.' Then I put it down in Latin, 'Homo cum humani nil a me alienum puto.' And then I show them its origin. The statement was made by Publius Terentius Afer, known as Terence. He was an African and a slave to a Roman senator. Freed by that senator, he became the most popular playwright in Rome. Six of his plays and that statement have come down to us from 154 BCE. This man, not born white, not born free, said *I am a human being.*

Powell paused; looked deliberately at the assembled; turned and walked off, to an eerily resonant silence of regard. Morin walked back on stage to conclude the day's events.

"Ladies and gentlemen . . ."

"Should he keep saying 'ladies'?"

"Allow me to conclude with some disturbing statistics and observations. You Gen-Xers and Ys might be wondering what all this has to do with you. Why should you even be interested in boomeritis? Well, many reasons, as you'll see, but let's start with this. How badly has boomeritis invaded American universities—your very own university, for example? How mean has the mean green meme become?

"Nothing human is alien to me," says Chloe. "If we live 200,000 years, you and I will be able to make love at least a billion times."

"A billion times? Trust me, Chloe, I don't have that much sperm."

"Ah, but you will, because everything will be constantly renewed."

"But Chloe, what makes you think that you and I will be together for all those years?"

"Why, because once you have slept with every woman on the planet, you will come back to me."

"Why's that, Chloe?"

"Who else can do *this*?"

"*The Shadow University: The Betrayal of Liberty on America's Campuses*, by Kors and Silverglate, is a thorough survey of the actual state of affairs. Far from being right-wing ideologues, its authors are liberals in good standing. Instead of quoting case after case—I urge all of you to consult this book for yourselves—I will give a few of the responses from critics, simply to try to convey a sense of the urgency and outrage. Linda Chavez, president for the Center for Equal Opportunity and former director of the U.S. Commission on Civil Rights, concludes that 'Alan Kors and Harvey Silverglate tell a chilling tale of university administrators turned Grand Inquisitors, of students and faculty stripped of their basic rights, of a freshman orientation system intended to indoctrinate and intimidate. They expose higher education's underbelly: the assault on liberty and true academic freedom (waged in the name of political correctness and group rights) that is occurring at so many of our nation's colleges and universities. Kors and Silverglate document precisely how inhospitable campuses are today to the pursuit of knowledge and the debate of ideas.'

"Alan Dershowitz: 'An eye-opening and well-documented exposé about what could happen to your children when they are sent to even the best colleges in the country. Kors and Silverglate demonstrate that when these colleges, purportedly devoted to liberal education, treat students in disciplinary proceedings, they make the notorious Star Chamber seem liberal in comparison.' Christina Sommers, feminist author, writes that 'Kors and Silverglate show how the cultural left's assault on individual liberties is effectively transforming the academy into "an island of oppression in a sea of freedom."' Nat Hentoff, columnist for *The Village Voice*, concludes that 'Kors and Silverglate have created the most far-ranging and in-depth report on the appalling state of American higher education, and their vivid, specific stories should shame those in charge of shaping the minds of and spirits of the next generation.' And Wendy Kaminer, author of *It's All the Rage*, notes that '*The Shadow University* is a scrupulously fair, painstakingly documented account of repression on America's campuses, where students and faculty members are regularly denied fundamental rights of speech, conscience, and due process. I never knew it was quite this bad.'"

Morin halted, his head dropped, as if some unseen weight had fallen on it. He finally looked up. "As we said, when any meme is threatened—and especially when it senses that its historical time is up, when it senses that it is no longer in control of the dominant forms of discourse—then out come the Inquisitors. And now, with the green meme, it has finally come to this. Any teacher or student can be denied due process, stripped of all rights, and summarily fired, on evidence no more substantial than the *hurt feelings* of another teacher or student. As Kors and Silverglate document, the accused does not even have the right to confront his accuser. Once hurt feelings are presented to the tribunal, the green Inquisitors take over, and all that is required for evidence is the hurt feelings of somebody, especially if they are not white and not male. This is truly the mean green meme at its meanest."

Morin turned and walked slowly off the stage. There was a dull, leaden silence in the hall, neither anger nor agreement, just collapse. It soon became apparent that nobody was applauding; the audience itself became aware that it was sunk in a shared, silent lament; and at that point, as the assembled realized that they were all sitting there in silence, it was as if, for some five or even ten minutes, the audience sat quietly and breathed together into its melancholy, trying collectively to digest this tender sadness, the hall warm, humid, hushed. Some seemed on the verge of tears, but none overtly cried; others stared straight ahead, as if afraid to move and break the circle of healing despair; others bowed their heads, under the weight of unseen sorrow. The silence seemed to say, "How could it all have come to this?"

And then I heard a few people gently weeping; a few others began a slow applause; faint grumbles and discontents also announced themselves; and one by the one, the assembled got up to leave.

"You coming to Hazelton's later?" Stuart asked on the way out. "It's sort of important."

"What's that? Oh, sure, okay. See ya."

7

The_Conquest_of_Paradise@MythsAreUs.net

"We missed you at the IC seminar the last few days, Jonathan."

"Well, remember that I've already been to two of those introductory seminars, and oo la la, blew my little mind."

"Emphasis on 'little,'" smiled Carolyn. For dinner at Dr. Hazelton's house, Carolyn had brought Katish, young, attractive, passionate, inflammatory, 28, born and raised in Calcutta, educated at IIT Kanpur, India's MIT. Katish had been sitting in on a few of the IC seminars, and from his agitated comments, not to mention implosive frown, it was obvious that he bought little of what the IC folks had to say; his face appeared locked in a state of perpetual civil war.

During a break at one of the seminars, I had overheard snippets of Katish lecturing one of the IC professors. "You think India is just the home of quaint old-fashioned religious values. You think we are all Gandhis. Your stupid Academy Awards gave a ton of Oscars to that idiotic movie about him, and why? Because Gandhi was everything the Hollywood types want to be: tan, thin, and moral. Well, that's pathetic! We have thrown off the yoke of that opiate of the masses, and since you colonialist pigs have not yet done so, it is India that will indeed liberate the West." I hadn't heard that language since I was ten; it sounded just like one of Dad's early tirades, before he substituted multicultural lingo for Marxist lingo in his bid to save the world. The IC professor's face looked like it might during root canal; the moment Katish paused to take a breath, the professor literally ran off and managed to disappear through a door in the side of the stage.

Were Katish and Carolyn an item? Or was it Katish and Beth? Or Carolyn and Beth, as Chloe thought? But then, Chloe thought all vociferous feminists were lesbians. "Why else brag about it?" she would always say. (To which Carolyn once shot back, "Because feminism is true, you mindless vaporheaded cock-sucking tart." The room got very quiet. "I'd reply to that," Chloe said, "but I'm trying to think which part of it might be wrong.")

Hazelton's house was modest-sized, but it was located in expensive Cambridge, rare for professors, and at least the dining room was quite large. A panel of exquisite stained-glass windows rimmed the room; the dining table seated perhaps a dozen; the six of us sat together at one end. Hazelton on my left, Carolyn on the right, and Stuart, Jonathan, and Katish across. The dinner seemed to consist mostly of a series of soups, which struck me as odd.

"Fuentes and Van Cleef and the crew really stirred things up yesterday," Carolyn said. "I was wondering why they mix it up so much, like they are deliberately provoking people. Because everybody says how really nice they are in person."

"Kim says it's a test," I offered.

Hazelton laughed. "Well, they certainly are attempting to shake things up a bit," she said. "But please remember what we're trying to do with this particular seminar series. We are trying to help people differentiate between green and second tier. That is, trying to help them see the difference between a green-meme approach to the world and a more integral approach. So you remember one of the main defining characteristics of all first-tier memes?"

"Sure," Carolyn quickly responded, "all first-tier memes think that their values are the only real or important values in the world."

"That's right, dear soul. And therefore all first-tier memes see the world in very dualistic or divisive ways—the world is divided into good guys versus bad guys, according to the particular values of the first-tier meme. So we find this"—and Hazelton very carefully and distinctly parsed her sentences:

"Purple divides the world into good spirits versus evil spirits.

"Red has predators and prey.

"Blue has saints and sinners.

"Orange has winners and losers.

"And green has those who are 'sensitive' versus those who are 'insensitive.'"

Jonathan jumped in. "So you deliberately step on the toes of the 'sensitive self,' just to see who yells," he said, delighted at the prospect.

"A little bit like that, yes. You see, second tier won't get angry, it won't react to the polemical tone of the delivery, because second tier is much more accepting of all values. But for green, tone is everything, because tone tells you whether a person is 'sensitive' or 'insensitive,' and thus whether that person is to be accepted or condemned. Whenever you hear somebody complaining about tone, you're in the presence of the green meme." She smiled sweetly.

"So you really do push their buttons on purpose."

"Yes, but only because they have buttons to push."

Hazelton paused, sipped her vegetable broth. "Second tier will take the polemic in stride, but green gets very angry." She laughed, almost to herself, then quickly added, "Look, my dear, we're not being mean-spirited here, and I am laughing because I remember my response when I first heard Morin deliberately rattle green values. I yelled out from the audience, 'What an arrogant fucking pig!'" Hazelton blushed; it was hard to imagine her yelling anything, let alone that.

"Basically, you see, we are showing them their attachments. This will help them move to second tier, move to a more integral embrace that understands that all of the values of the Spiral have their own importance. You have to get to the point where you can let red be red and blue be blue and orange be orange and so on, but green wants everybody to be green. . . ."

"But green claims to be inclusive," said Jonathan.

"Yes, claims. And green is close to being truly inclusive, but as the last of the first-tier memes, it really isn't. If you don't accept green values, you are actually *excluded*, and righteously! You already heard Morin talk about the Green Inquisitors in academia. Green especially despises blue values—most green-meme liberals viscerally hate Republicans since most Republicans are blue. But unless you can see the importance of all of the levels of the Spiral, you will never make it to second tier."

"Tell Carolyn what especially stops green from being integral," said Jonathan with an impertinent grin.

"Oh, I know, I know," said Carolyn. "The rejection of hierarchy."

"Well, there are healthy and unhealthy forms of hierarchy, to be sure, dear soul. But yes, the only way you can get integrated anything is with nested hierarchy. You know how it goes: atoms to molecules to cells—egocentric to ethnocentric to worldcentric—each higher level envelops and embraces its juniors, so you get more and more wholeness. But green just can't bring itself to rank anything, bless its heart, so it can't really create genuine wholeness. It remains stuck with heaps, not wholes. Pluralism, not integralism."

Hazelton smiled and looked at each of us. She reached out, touched my hand, and gave it a surreptitious squeeze, a move my startled, jangled mind raced to interpret.

"Carolyn here thinks that the world is a mess because male values have squished poor little helpless female values," minced Jonathan.

Carolyn stared icily at him. "You've got a room-temperature IQ, Jonathan, and we're talking centigrade here." We all laughed at the contorted, crinkled look on Jonathan's face. Carolyn to Hazelton: "It's not like that. You know what I'm talking about. The importance of moving from dominator societies to partnership societies. Linking people instead of ranking them."

"People are not ranked, Carolyn, but their values are. Some values are more inclusive, more compassionate, more embracing. So of course we want healthy ranking! The failure to do so contributes to the spread of egocentric and ethnocentric values—that is what your approach ends up doing, my dear, whether you intend it or not."

"*Not*," retorted Carolyn. "Come on, Dr. Hazelton. You know the research. Men tend to think in terms of separation and autonomy, women in terms of relationship and care. And this world needs a little more relationship and care and a little less separation and division."

"But, my dear, you are giving merely a flatland reading. Flatland. You forgot the Spiral of development, you see? Remember that *both* men and women go from egocentric to ethnocentric to worldcentric. The women go through those hierarchical stages with an emphasis on care, relationship, and communion, while the men go through them with an emphasis on rights, autonomy, and agency."

"So the women move from egocentric care to ethnocentric care to worldcentric care, right?" said Stuart.

"That's right, dear. Do you see that, Carolyn?"

"I see it," a wary voice replied.

"So there are male and female versions of egocentric, ethnocentric, and worldcentric. And the planet's problems do not, and never have, come from the fact that we emphasize male values over female values. The problem is that not enough males or females are at the worldcentric levels of consciousness. Because you see, my dear, female ethnocentric values are just as devastating as male ethnocentric values—they will both dash to hell anybody who disagrees with them. Males express their ethnocentric values with physical aggression, while females express it using social aggression and ostracism—and both are equally responsible for the horrid mood and deeds of ethnocentric societies. The herd mentality, mob rule, ethnocentric care, in both men and women—that is exactly what got us Auschwitz."

"So you're saying that the radical feminists are using only the horizontal scale—of female versus male—and not seeing how both of those values develop vertically through the Spiral."

"That's right. If you take this more integral approach, you get a much bigger view. What we find is that ideally we want both men and women to grow and develop to the worldcentric, postconventional levels of awareness. At that point—at second tier—the male values of autonomy and the female values of relationship tend to be balanced and valued equally—remember, that was Carol Gilligan's forth major stage, the integral. But that comes only by accepting hierarchical growth." She paused, then with great emphasis: "I repeat that the enemy is not, and never has been, male values. The enemy is male and female values at any of the first-tier memes."

She looked gently at each of us, one by one, and in almost a whisper: "First-tier female values—red relationships, blue relationships, green relationships, and so on—are just as divisive in their own way as first-tier male values. And the cure for both is second tier."

Another long, warm, embracing pause; more whispered advice: "That means that we desperately need both second-tier male values—integrated autonomy—and second-tier female values—integrated care. Because both of them come together at second tier anyway—integral is integral. But please, don't get caught in flatland games of boomeritis blame. The real battle—if you must think of it like that—the real battle is not between male and female, but between first and second tier."

The logic of it left the table silent. For some reason this point hit me particularly hard. I was increasingly being drawn into the necessity for that "quantum leap into the hyperspace of integral consciousness." And I was thinking . . .

"You was thinking? Again? Rattle, rattle, rattle, clunk. I noticed that you didn't invite me to this dinner. You want me to keep my naked breasts out of it, eh?"

"Your breasts? What do your breasts have to do with anything?"

"I don't know, but then, I'm not staring at them."

"No, it's not that. It's that this boy-girl thing is such a mess. Why are men always fantasizing about naked women?"

"Because they don't have their hands on one."

"So what you do you fantasize about, Chloe?"

"Do you really want to know?"

"Yes."

"Just be with me, sweet boy, just be with me."

"So what happens when we all get to worldcentric? Peace on earth, total paradise?" Katish was deeply skeptical. The words forced their way through the civil war on his face and made their way out into the room.

"Well, we *never* simply get to worldcentric," Hazelton said. "Remember, everybody is born at square one and has to begin their growth and development through the unfolding spiral. So the spiral of development is a great river, and no society is simply at a particular level."

"But the center of gravity of society does drift upward—like in *Up from Eden*," added Stuart.

"Yes, dear soul, that's right, the average does creep up over the centuries."

"So what happens when the average level in our society finally gets to worldcentric, finally reaches second tier? Then paradise, yes?"

"Well, actually, we have found that there are, um, levels higher than that."

"Higher than what?"

"Higher than turquoise," she said.

"There are levels of consciousness higher than turquoise? I knew it! You said something about that at the second lecture," I jumped in.

"Yes, and when I did, you were one of the few who leaned forward in his seat," she smiled.

Charles Morin strode on stage, the atmosphere swirling around him, perhaps attempting to get out of his way.

"Good morning, ladies and gentlemen. In this session, we will explore one of the most common themes of boomeritis: the belief in a primal historical paradise, where the gifted child lived until corrupted by the wicked society of Western patriarchal rationality. Again, the motives for this belief are often so generous, kind, and caring, as the sensitive self bends over backward not to marginalize or denigrate. The end results, alas, were something else indeed, shockingly gruesome to behold, as we will see today.

"Ladies and gentlemen, may I present Dr. Lesa Powell," as waves of applause rose from the audience.

Slide #1, "The Retro-Romantic Nightmare."

"Would you like to put your penis in my mouth?"

"Gosh, Chloe, who wouldn't?"

"Well then? What's wrong?"

"Well then, it's this. It's really bothering me, because I'm trying to figure out which direction the Bots will evolve."

"You want to do *that* instead of *this*?"

"Really, Chloe, wait a minute, listen to this, it's important."

Powell walked slowly and deliberately up to the podium, looked at the audience, smiled. "One of the most intriguing items common to most forms of cultural studies is the notion that, if we undo the rampant oppression imposed by society, we will discover some sort of *original goodness* that was brutally buried. This is the classic Romantic disposition: we started out good, but society crippled and corrupted us. There is certainly some truth to that; many of our potentials are indeed stunted by overbearing familial and social institutions, and that fact needs to be taken into account. But it is also true that, in many important ways, individuals need to *grow* and *develop* into goodness—moving from egocentric to ethnocentric to worldcentric—and without that growth and development, men and women remain egocentric and narcissistic predators, each in their own cute little ways," she laughed.

"But boomeritis, seeing itself as the gifted child, has always identified with the Romantic side of that equation: it started out pure and virtuous, but society thwarted it at every point. The results of this romanticism have been unfortunate, indeed, occasionally horrifying, as we will see."

"Kim, how horrifying?"

"It has to do with human sacrifice."

"Cool!"

"In all of this, what we see is the attempt to make the green meme an entire worldview, an attempt that is simply devastating. All inequalities must then be ascribed, as we saw, not to a *lack* of development, but to an *imposition* of power. The important truths of green pluralism are assumed to be there *from the start*—or would be, had they not been viciously oppressed. And thus, whenever the green meme with its pluralistic freedom is not found in history (and it is always not found), this is ascribed to a brutal imposition of Western, patriarchal, imperial, instrumental, hegemonic power, whereas in most cases it is not there because it has simply not yet emerged.

"But from the very high developmental stance of the green wave of postformal pluralism, which took human evolution approximately one million years to achieve, the proponents of cultural studies survey all of past history, and whenever they find that pluralism is *absent*, they assume that it is not there because of the *presence* of an evil force—males, rationality, objectivity, patriarchy, logocentrism, phallologocentrism, fill in the blank—and they proceed from there to recommend, not the further evolution of consciousness, which is the only cure for lack of emergence, but the death and dismantling of the allegedly evil force.

"And one of the most common recommendations for this death and dismantling involves, in part, some sort of *recapture* of the state *prior* to the allegedly evil force. This confusion of 'pre' and 'post' is, we have seen, one of the prime ingredients of boomeritis, because it allows preconventional narcissism to hide out in postconventional ideals. But more than that, it causes boomeritis to invent a historical paradise where none in fact existed." Powell shot a fierce glance around the room. "This is the topic of today's horror story."

"Okay, sweet boy, what's more important than *this*?"

"All right, I'll tell you. You'll like this part, Chloe, it's about freedom. My dad had a fixation on the Beats—the Beatnik writers, Kerouac, Ginsberg, Burroughs, you know—cuz he said they were the first great pioneers of freedom. Freedom, right? So the forerunner of the Beasts was Paul Bowles."

"The Beasts?"

"What?"

"You said 'the Beasts.'"

"No I didn't. The Beats, the Beats. Anyway, the forerunner of the Beats was Paul Bowles, and all the Beats made the pilgrimage to Tangiers, where Bowles was living. Plenty of cheap drugs, sex, you name it. Bowles writes this enormously influential book about a married couple traveling through the Sahara desert—it's called *The Sheltering Sky*. In that book, the lead male character dies horribly halfway through, and the lead female character looses her mind, is repeatedly raped and beaten, and presumably wanders back into the desert for more of the same."

"Ooooh, cool book!"

"Okay, Chloe, that's not the point. Here's the point: Norman Mailer says that Bowles was basically the father of the entire Boomer generation—Mailer says it's because Bowles is the first major exponent of 'Hip' versus 'Square' culture."

"'Hip' is cool and 'Square' is conventional, conformist, stultifying."

"That's right. So Mailer says, 'Paul Bowles opened the world of Hip.

He let in the murder, the drugs, the incest, the death of the Square, the call of the orgy, the end of civilization: he invited all of us to these themes.'"

"Totally cool!"

"Chloe, stop it. Don't you get it? Murder is Hip? Incest is Hip? Raping a woman is Hip? Ending civilization is Hip? Don't you see? These guys didn't differentiate between pre-Square and post-Square. So *anything* that is non-Square is celebrated—murder, incest, raping and beating women, torture, you name it—all of that is now Hip! No wonder these guys got off on the Marquis de Sade. Jesus, Chloe, this is so nauseating, it's so upsetting. See, there's this woman, person, Hazelton, and this other person, Powell, and these folks, and those folks, and anyway, don't you see? It goes pre-Square, Square, and then post-Square, but the Beats celebrated anything non-Square as being Hip. Don't you get it, Chloe? So half the time they regressed to pre-Square and called that Hip, called it Cool. That is everything Mom and Dad got trapped in! Don't you get it Chloe? Chloe?"

"Hip *this*, baby shakes."

"We can summarize this very simply, my friends: scanning history and not finding green, boomeritis imagines, not that green values had not yet emerged, but that green values were oppressed by a nasty force: it thus has its villain, and it thus has its victims, and thus does it make sense of its flatland world."

Lesa Powell prowled the stage, hands behind her back, head slightly angled. "The nasty oppressing force is usually some sort of orange something or other—the rational Enlightenment, the Western patriarchy, the capitalistic state, male analytic knowing, Newtonian-Cartesian paradigm—we'll see an endless list of villains later. And thus, in an honorable attempt to go post-orange and discover green values, boomeritis misguidedly heads in the opposite direction, attempting to find in the pre-orange states a post-orange freedom. And it was these preformal, pre-orange states—purple and red—that boomeritis carelessly eulogized and elevated to a postformal freedom that they do not, and never did, possess. The regression that is so characteristic of boomeritis had finally found its happy home. The nightmare was about to begin."

Powell retired to a wave of apprehensive applause, as Van Cleef walked, or maybe stomped, out on stage. Slide #2 went up on the wall, "The Conquest of Paradise."

"We have no further to look for the elevation of preformal magic and myth to postformal pluralism and freedom than in the reception that the green meme gave to the five-hundredth anniversary of Columbus's voyage to the Americas."

The audience stiffened; the atmosphere was wired. "Fasten your seatbelt," Kim whispered.

"Books with titles like *American Holocaust* claimed that 'the road to Auschwitz led straight through the heart of the Americas.' Kirkpatrick Sale, in *The Conquest of Paradise*, claimed that the Europeans disrupted an Edenic state of peaceful ecological harmony. Tzvetan Todorov summed up the entire display of moral outrage by saying that Hernando Cortés's conquest of the Aztecs was really a defeat for the greater cause of *human diversity*.

"Because postmodern cultural studies often dispenses with evidence and focuses on theoretical issues, as we will see, few of these multitudinous books bothered to research the conditions that Columbus, Cortés, and crew actually encountered. As of late, however, there has been a series of carefully researched monographs that have done exactly that—books such as Shepard Krech's *The Ecological Indian: Myth and History*, Inga Clendinnen's *Aztecs*, Robert Edgerton's *Sick Societies: Challenging the Myth of Primitive Harmony*, and Patrick Tierney's *The Highest Altar: The Story of Human Sacrifice*. More astonishing, these books have met with widespread, if grudging, agreement from virtually all sides. The pictures they paint are far from paradise.

"I have no intention of either defending the Europeans or judging the indigenous Americans. I would simply like to point out what lengths the green meme was willing to go in order to champion its ideology. In confusing preformal conditions with postformal freedom, the American green meme showed an astonishing historical blindness, and used this blindness to unleash a series of brutal attacks on those who did not share its disease."

"Van Cleef is much too intense, as usual," Kim whispered.

"Well, I thought it was supposed to be like that, supposed to be deliberately provocative. You know, the test."

"Carla is provocative, Lesa is provocative, even Mark can be provocative. Derek is sick or something. What he's saying is true—Charles says Van Cleef is always on the money—but he needs therapy, or a heart transplant, or a good woman, or a bad woman, or something."

"Too intense, yes. They have a saying at the gym: when your neck gets bigger than your head, take a few days off."

"Exactly, Derek should take a few days off from himself. The problem is, he's always right and he knows he's always right, a really bad combination." Kim leaned in, and in an even lower whisper: "Charles said that Lesa came up with a line that they all jokingly say captures Derek perfectly: 'The last time I was wrong was when I thought I had made a mistake.'" A wicked grin creased Kim's face. "But the fact is, the points that he's making are too important to leave up to his warped delivery."

"Why do they think that he raped somebody?"

"Because a young female student claimed that he did."

"Where was this?"

"He was teaching in Berkeley at the time."

"Was there any proof?"

"Well, like Charles pointed out, you don't need proof. All you need is to claim it happened and that is that. So he left, or was asked to leave, or whatever."

"So aren't you worried about sleeping with Morin? I mean, teacher and student and all that."

"Well, I suppose it is a little dicey, what we're doing."

"He's supposed to be in a position of power, and you are the powerless student, so he is basically committing statutory rape."

Kim burst out laughing. Van Cleef abruptly looked down; I got red-faced and flustered because I thought he might have heard the word "rape" and imagined we were talking about him. Loudly I said, "No, no," as if to try to reassure him, but his look said, What in the fuck are you dimwits doing?

Van Cleef looked back at the audience. "Since Inga Clindinnen is a member in good standing of cultural studies, we can use her meticulous overview of Aztec culture, particularly its central rites of human sacrifice, a practice not confined, however, to the Aztecs. As one historian summarizes it, 'Human sacrifice was practiced by the Aztecs of Mexico, the Mayas of Yucatán, the Incas of Peru, the Tupinambas and Caytes of Brazil, the natives of Guyana, and the Pawnee and Huron tribes of North America. In societies that had developed urban settlements, such as those of the Aztecs and Mayas, victims were usually taken to a central temple and lain across an altar where priests would cut out their hearts and offer them to the gods. In the less technologically developed societies of Guyana and Brazil, victims would either be battered to death in the open and then dismembered, or tied up and burned to death over a fire. . . . The sacrifice was often accompanied by cannibalism. In Tenochtitlan (the Aztec capital), the remains of sacrificed victims were taken from the temples and distributed among the populace, who would cook the flesh in a stew. In Guayana and Brazil, limbs of victims were skewered and roasted over a spit before being consumed. The Caytes of the Brazilian coast ate the crew of every wrecked Portuguese vessel they found. The American anthropologist Harry Turney-High writes: 'At one meal they ate the first Bishop of Bahia, two Canons, the Procurator of the Royal Portuguese Treasury, two pregnant women and several children.'"

A stunned stillness hung over the audience. Van Cleef continued reading and talking, and for the next half hour, the assembled sat in silence, listening with what seemed to be a mixture of fascination and nausea.

"Of the cultural-studies writers who acknowledge this, the most common retort is that European societies had their own barbarisms. This is very true. But the correct conclusion would then be, not that this was the conquest of paradise, but the conquest of one group of savages by another group of savages. But cultural studies will not allow this, because every culture *except* Western culture is a shining case of pluralistic harmony, hence paradise." Van Cleef spat out the words with disdain.

"Well, the goings-on in paradise were nothing if not exciting. The Aztec empire was what one historian described as 'a murderously cruel and authoritarian imperial power.' Extending across modern central Mexico from coast to coast, it was an empire of warfare and tribute. The sacrificial killings took place on a seasonal basis—four times a year—as well as on special occasions. For approximately half the year the warriors from Tenochtitlan attacked surrounding areas in order to capture sacrificial victims: warriors of other tribes were preferred, since they were more valuable and thus more pleasing to the gods (one cultural-studies historicist marveled at the *pluralistic kindness* of the Aztec warriors: all this fighting, and yet they were very careful not to kill other warriors in battle . . .); but slaves, women, and children were also frequently used. Although some estimates put the number of annual human sacrifices at over 100,000, more reliable estimates are in the several thousands.

"The sacrifices were especially made for Tezcatlipoca, god of the earth, and Huitzilopochtli, tribal deity of the Mexica and god of sun and war. 'The killings,' reports Clendinnen, 'were also explicitly about the dominance of the Mexica and of their tutelary deity: public displays to overawe the watcher, Mexica or stranger, in a state of theatre of power, at which the rulers of other and lesser cities, allies and enemies alike, were routinely present.'

"The executions were usually performed atop the magnificent pyramids built especially for this occasion. 'The victim walked or was dragged up the temple steps to the platform, was spread-eagled alive across the large killing stone, and was held down by five priests. Four would hold the limbs and one the head. The angle of the plane of the stone meant that the victim's chest cavity was arched and elevated. The executioner priest then plunged a knife of flint under the exposed ribs and sawed through the arteries to the heart, which was pulled out and held high as an offering to the gods. The execution was a messy affair, with priests, stone, platform and steps all drenched in the spurting blood. The head of the victim was usually severed and spitted on a skull rack while the lifeless body was pushed and rolled down the pyramid steps. At the base of the pyramid, the body was butchered and, after being distributed to relatives and friends of the warrior who had offered the sacrifice, the parts were cooked and eaten.'

"On some occasions, the body was skinned. 'A priest would then dress himself in the flayed skin, with the wet side out, dead hands and feet dangling from live wrists and ankles, and continue the ceremony.' At certain times, the sacrificial victim was a woman, who, for several days prior to the ceremony, was bedecked with flowers and teased by women attendants about her impending dismemberment. On the night of the ceremony she was stretched across the back of a priest and killed. 'Then,' reports Clendinnen, 'still in darkness, silence, and urgent haste, her body was flayed, and a naked priest, a "very strong man, very powerful, very tall," struggled into the wet skin, with its slack breasts and pouched genitalia: a double nakedness of layered, ambiguous sexuality. The skin of one thigh was reserved to be fashioned into a face-mask for the man impersonating Centeotl, Young Lord Maize Cob, the son of Toci.'

"In these types of rituals, the Aztecs were by no means unique, and not just in the Americas. As Joseph Campbell documented (and Patrick Tierney confirmed), 'a fury for sacrifice' beset most of the early empires in their various high periods, from Africa to China to Mesopotamia to Europe. In fact, it is a fairly safe generalization that human sacrifice was common in the mythic-horticultural wave of evolution—the early red meme. It served various important functions for that meme, and served them quite well, which is why the practice arose almost universally, starting as early as perhaps 10,000 BCE. It does no good for us to apply today's morals to yesterday occasions. But neither will it do to read such prerational engagements as really being a case of nice green diversity that patriarchal rationality brutally destroyed.

> Not all of those executed were outsiders; some were low-born citizens and slaves from within the community of Tenochtitlan itself, and some were children of families within the city. The children were those offered to Tlaloc, the god of agricultural fertility, over the first months of the ritual calendar. Priests chose children to be killed from among those who had been born on a particular daysign and whose hair was marked with a double cowlick. The children, aged between two and seven years, were taken by the priests from their homes and kept together in nurseries for some weeks before their deaths. As the appropriate festivals arrived, they were dressed in magnificent costumes and paraded in groups through the city. The pathos of the sight moved those watching to tears. The children, who knew their fate, also wept.

"The priests welcomed the tears because it augured rain; the children's throats were slit and they were offered to Tlaloc as 'bloodied flowers of the maize.'

"Those were the common, seasonal sacrifices. What particularly distinguished the Mexica, however, were their great ceremonial slayings (marking the installation of a new ruler, the completion of a new pyramid, or a great war victory). When, in 1487, the Huaxtec launched an unsuccessful revolt, the Mexica gathered up prisoners that numbered somewhere between 20,000 and 80,000 and ritually sacrificed all of them in a four-day period. They were herded into Tenochtitlan; Clendinnen describes 'the men linked by cords through the warrior perforations in their septums, the maidens and little boys still too young to have their noses pierced, secured by yokes around their necks, all wailing a pitiful lament.' Up the pyramids they were marched: 'four patient lines stretching the full length of the processional ways and marshaled along the causeways, slowly moving towards the pyramid.'

Disdain again crept into Van Cleef's voice. "The few cultural-studies writers who have the honesty to acknowledge these goings-on have then attempted to explain them, it goes without saying, as a top-down hierarchical power imposed on the poor helpless people. Clendinnen will have none of it. 'The people were implicated in the care and preparation of the victims, their delivery to the place of death, and then in the elaborate processing of the bodies: the dismemberment and distribution of heads and limbs, flesh and blood and flayed skins. On high occasions warriors carrying gourds of human blood or wearing the dripping skins of their captives ran through the streets, to be ceremoniously welcomed into the dwellings; the flesh of their victims seethed in domestic cooking pots; human thighbones, scraped and dried, were set up in the courtyards of the households. . . . '"

Van Cleef's voice contracted, rose slightly, his stare at the audience was laser-like. "What on earth could possess someone to see all these events as 'paradise'?" Long pause.

"Why, the green meme, of course." The audience broke its silence, which divided evenly into cheers and jeers. "Whether it is the enraptured mythic eulogizing of the Mexica by William Irwin Thompson, or the celebration of their wonderful 'diversity' by Todorov, or the claim that this was an ecological paradise by Kirkpatrick Sale: what they all have in common is a rampant pre/post fallacy, a celebrating of preformal conditions as postformal harmony. They and legions of like-minded then take the destruction of this 'primal harmony' as cause for an ostentatious display of their great and grand moral outrage.

"In other words, driven by a boomeritis anxious to demonstrate its moral superiority, countless writers on the evils of modernity began to read a deeply elevated meaning into all things premodern. No doubt about it: the secret pull of the preconventional paradise was the narcissism lying therein, a paradise where I can celebrate, and finally show the world, the wonder of being me—and the heroic self-inflation of cultural studies puffs up yet once again."

Van Cleef finished abruptly, made a very slow bow to the audience, turned, and walked, or maybe stalked, off the stage.

"So tell us about these higher levels of consciousness, the levels higher than turquoise," we all had pleaded with Hazelton.

"Well, I can tell you this. They start to look spiritual," she said in a soft, tender voice. I was still finding it rather disorienting to look directly at her. At one point Carolyn whispered in my ear, "Ken, you're tilting." As I looked at Hazelton, listening to her talk, I would slowly tilt to the right, unanchored as I was whenever I looked into the sky where her eyes should have been.

"Ah, but spirituality is behind us, not before us," announced Katish. Where many of his countrymen might have deeply lamented the loss of traditional religion in the modern world, Katish was just the opposite: trained in the Indian education system, which had imported a type of postmodern Marxism from the West, he was quite happy to see all of that pathetic opiate of the masses put behind us.

"Dear Katish," Hazelton quietly countered, "to believe that all spirituality lies in our historical past is to badly confuse *pre*-rational religion—the magic and mythic levels, purple and red, which did indeed dominate in premodern times—with *post*-rational religion—turquoise and beyond, which appear to lie in our collective future. You see, our research indicates that the post-rational religions lie in front of us, not behind us, dear one. It is a sad thing that so many people confuse pre and post, don't you think?"

I nodded vigorously; too vigorously, I noticed with embarrassment, and wondered if anybody else had noticed. Jonathan beamed at everybody at the table, and his look, as usual, said, "Take that, you morons."

"Throughout this week's seminar we will be going over some of the premodern mythic societies and the brutalities that were common in them. The red and blue memes could really kick up some wonderful tortures!" she laughed. "But it also appears that in some of those mythic societies, a few individuals had access to these higher, trans-turquoise states. The problem is, Boomers often thought that those high states defined those mythic cultures at large, which is quite mistaken. In premodern, magic and mythic cultures, a very, very small percentage of the population—much less than 1 percent—had profound access to these higher spiritual states, and what they produced was indeed astonishing. But as for the rest of the population, what they produced was . . . well, not very pleasant."

"But tell us about the higher states!" we implored like little kids. We chanted "post-turquoise, post-turquoise, post-turquoise" and began laughing.

"Well, when we began the Human Consciousness Project, we set out to map every known state, stage, level, line, meme, wave of consciousness, call them what you will. And as we were laying out all these states of consciousness on a very large grid or map—sort of like mapping the DNA spiral, only this was the Consciousness spiral—we started to notice something very odd. The religious traditions that were the most highly valued in their own cultures—ones like Zen Buddhism, Vedanta Hinduism, the great Rhineland mystics, the Sufis of Islam, the Kabbalah of Judaism—all started to converge on the same states of consciousness. It is as if the really profound spiritual traditions were all plugging into the very highest levels of consciousness on the great spiral of development. They were all plugging into those levels that went beyond turquoise."

She paused and looked at each of us, and then out of the blue blue sky came the words, "And if this is so, we have found the roadmap to God."

Carla Fuentes bounced on stage, her jaunty smile a hidden counterblast to the upcoming topic.

"I'm told that my heritage is an odd mixture of Spanish, Aztec, a dash of Hopi and a little Irish. Don't ask." Everybody laughed.

"But still, that doesn't stop me from noticing some harsh truths.

What is so arresting about today's commonly accepted accounts of native Americans (North, Central, and South) is how romanticized these myths have become, especially among Boomer writers, and how painstakingly scholars are now presenting us with a more realistic and adequate picture, backed this time by considerable evidence. In part, no doubt, the romanticized myths were a noble correction to the previous myths that presented natives as nothing but savages, a view as outrageously inaccurate as are the revisionist, romanticized versions.

"But these romanticized myths have become so intensely embraced in the last three decades for another reason, right my friends?" The audience mumbled its vague agreement. "Yes, that's right. These myths became wildly, exuberantly embraced because they fit perfectly with boomeritis, they fit with the drama of the gifted child, this time played out on a grand historical scale."

Joni Mitchell's aging voice creaks and croaks, "We've got to get back to the Garden!," while a naked Chloe is swinging from an enormous oak in Eden. "They paved paradise and put up a parking lot!"—oh dear, oh me, oh my, the pound pound pounding in my brain will not relent, my eyes protruding, skull exuding, and when will the pain please stop?

"See? The tyranny of reason. I happen to agree with the Boomers on this one," says Chloe.

"Why do you agree with them?"

"Because the tyranny of reason is why you rattle."

"Okay, look, I don't rattle. I don't. And weren't you listening? You know, pre-Square, post-Square? Aren't you just being pre-Square?"

"But the tyranny of reason gets in the way of all the really fun things in life."

"Like what?"

"Well, you keep staring at my breasts, but check out this ass!"

"Wow!"

I lunge forward to grab her but find I am clutching only my Siamese twin, and this time the harrowing depression speaks directly to me: "Will it really be any different for your generation? Post-rave technotribal gatherings, great grand good and glorious doofs, anarcho-liminal raz ma TAZ, shamanarchy on the lam, enviroteque squiggling here and there, cyberdelic cascades whooshing all about, techno-corroborees and lemming Femmebots, swinging Subvertigo and organic Organarchy, sizzling Sisters@the Underground, technotribes in all their dreamily damned and drugged and digitally drenched sensations: what the fuck do you think you're doing: really going back to the Garden? Has your generation *actually* changed *anything* at all?"

I can't breathe, this time I really can't breathe. . . .

"A more accurate view of paradise has more recently come into focus. I quote: 'The deciphering of Mayan glyphs, the New World's only writing system, has revolutionized Mesoamerican studies. A thousand years before the Aztecs carried human sacrifice to its bloody zenith, the classic Mayans had already created a sophisticated ritual grammar, with verbs such as "decapitate," "tear the heart out," and "roll down the pyramid steps." Perhaps the most shocking conclusion is that the great Mesoamerican achievements in architecture, art, military organization, and astronomy revolved around the obsessive need for sacrificial victims.'

"Nowhere has the romanticizing been more intense than with the fabled Mayan civilization. From orthodox scholars to New Age enthusiasts, the Maya were held to be examples of a nearly perfect society. This commonly held view maintained that the ancient Maya were peace-loving, deeply spiritual, living in harmony with nature, and expressing a type of 'nondissociated' or 'unitary' consciousness (in contrast with the 'dissociated' or 'severed' intellect of the West, which is 'detached from deep participation with the earth,' as a typical account put it). The entire society was said to be permeated with divinely inspired art, architecture, and astronomy. War did not exist; the culture was egalitarian; this was a wonderful partnership society. As a recent scholar noted, with some astonishment, 'This was the popularly established view of the Maya, and like compelling science fiction, it was accepted.' Not to mention the New Age beliefs surrounding the Maya, which claimed that they were one of the most highly advanced and spiritual civilizations the world has ever known." There was again a deathly silence in the hall.

"Beginning with books such as *The Blood of Kings*, by highly respected researchers Linda Schele of the University of Texas and Mary

Ellen Miller of Yale, a more accurate, realistic, and disturbing picture has emerged. 'First of all,' concludes Michael Coe of Yale University, 'these were no peaceful theocracies, but rival and very aggressive city-states. Constant warfare and the taking of prominent captives (and dispatching them after lengthy degradation and torture) were the name of the game. The rulers of these petty states seemed to have dragged around some of the unfortunate victims for years, and they always boasted about them. . . . It now seems that captives were forced to play a game in which the dice were loaded, so to speak, with decapitation the inevitable result. The Aztecs have received a very bad press for their penchant for human sacrifice, but they certainly never inflicted upon their victims the degree of torture and mutilation that were character-istic of Maya sacrifice.'"

Fuentes looked at the audience. "Schele and Miller describe one scene, preserved in a painting, which is a 'vivid portrayal of how the Maya displayed their prey, celebrated the defeat of their enemies, and drew their blood. The painting shows a figure at the far left bending over a captive, lifting his arm and either pulling out his fingernails or cutting off the end of his digits. Blood streams down the captive's arm. His sunken cheeks may indicate that his teeth were pulled out in this ritual. As the blood streams from the fingers of other captives, they look at their hands in despair and howl pitiably. A captive holds out his fingers and appears to plead for mercy. For the Maya, however, there was only the inevitability of sacrifice. Heart sacrifice was the ulti-mate cause of this captive's death, but the cut marks across the body inform us that cat-and-mouse torture preceded it. In contrast, the quick, deliberate heart excision practiced by the Aztecs can be regarded as a merciful act.'"

"Jesus, Kim. It feels like they're quietly doing the same thing to the audience."

"What, cutting their hearts out, or cutting them out mercifully?"

"Well, cutting them out, that's for sure. My mom and dad would probably storm the stage."

"It's funny. I've never seen the audience get angry at this particular lecture. They just sit there, stupefied. I don't think most of them have ever heard the real evidence here. Anyway, pretty cool, huh?"

"I guess."

"As for their ecological sensitivity, it is now widely acknowledged that the Maya practiced *milpa*, or slash-and-burn agriculture, as in fact did many early tribes, contrary to romanticized accounts. Indeed, that anti-ecological practice is thought to have contributed to the eventual crumbling of the Mayan civilization.

"Oh, incidentally," Fuentes smiled, "for you New-Agers out there who are worried that the world is coming to an end in 2012, as predicted by the Mayan calendar—a calendar established in part to be able to precisely time ritual sacrifices, as evidence now also suggests occurred at Stonehenge, although the Druids seemed to prefer a 'disproportionate number of children'—Schele and Miller note that 'in the past it has been assumed that a unique event will occur in the Maya calendar on December 23, 2012, and that the Maya era, and the world with it, will end on that day. This is a misconception, however: the Maya projected events forward to October 23, 4772'—so it looks like we can all relax!"

"It's a harmonic convergence, dear," Mom is saying yet again, as if I can't hear her.

"Harmonic conver—, conver—"

"Conver-gence. Convergence, dear. A coming together."

"Ooooh, let's come together, sweet boy."

"Shut up, Chloe," I say as I turn bright red and look at Mom to see if she has heard.

"All the planets are lining up, all in a row. Just like the Mayan calendar said. This is the dawning of the Age of Aquarius! Peace and harmony among all peoples. Don't you see?"

"I'm trying, Mom, I'm honestly trying. It's just that, you know, there are one billion starving people on the planet, seventeen regional wars, an AIDS epidemic in Africa, environmental degradation catastrophically accelerating, rain forests disappearing faster than Madonna's clothing, and so on and so on and so on. . . . I'm having a hard time seeing how planets lining up will help with all of that."

Mom looks at me with endless love. "You really are your father's son, aren't you?"

"If the Maya were the favorites of Boomer New-Agers," Fuentes intoned, "the Incas of Peru were the favorites of Boomer socialists, many of whom were looking for the original, caring communism that would be restored with the revolution. The Inca certainly seemed to fit the bill, especially if you knew ahead of time what you were looking for. 'The popular assumption is that the Incas were America's peaceful empire. Most history books still describe the Inca Empire as a socialist paradise revolving around a harmless and healthy cult of the sun. . . . European intellectuals adopted the Inca Empire as a model of sorts for their own visions of enlightened socialism.'

"Yet recent research has again unearthed a more accurate, unpleasant picture. 'Scholars now believe human sacrifice played a crucial role in the social, political, and economic control the Incas exercised over their vast, heterogeneous empire, which stretched from Ecuador to Chile.' Children were apparently the preferred victims. 'Once unacceptable sacrifices were weeded out, the remaining children heard talks from the Inca High Priest about the benefits their upcoming sacrifices would bring to the whole empire and to themselves. At the end of these solemnities the children, accompanied by their mothers, marched in unison around statues of the Incas' major gods—Viracocha, the sun, the thunder god, and the moon. Then the Inca Emperor ordered his priests to 'take your share of these sacrifices and offerings to the greatest *huaca* in your lands and sacrifice them there. . . . The Incas used many methods of sacrifice, including strangling, garroting, breaking the cervical vertebrae with a stone, tearing out the heart, and burying alive.'

"The extensive system of ritual human sacrifice was apparently part of an indigenous system of political exploitation and dominance. But it wasn't only that. 'Scholars are just beginning to realize how widespread and varied human sacrifice was in the Andes, both prior to and during the Inca Empire. In addition to the standard *capacocha* offerings—which claimed several hundred children at each of the solstice ceremonies'—which is certainly one type of a deep connection with the earth and its seasons—'the Incas also sacrificed children or young adults in cases of drought, plague, earthquakes, famine, war, military victory or defeat, hailstorms, lightning storms, avalanches, to mark the sowing and harvesting of crops, during difficult construction projects, when the Inca Emperor died, when a new emperor assumed power, in case of good omens, in case of bad omens.'"

"Omens, omens, oh men!" says Chloe. "Let's sacrifice me to you right now, my thighs to your phallus. Just slam into me now, big boy, you can do it!" Chloe looks at me and grins.

"Chloe, why is it always about sex?"

"It's your fantasies, sweet boy, not mine, so you tell me."

"Oh, right."

"You don't really think that all I want is sex, do you?"

"Well, um, I, um . . ."

"You really are a rattle and a half, Wilber."

"So what do you want, Chloe?"

"I already told you. Just be with me, sweet boy, just be with me."

"Right. Right. Okay. I will definitely, definitely do that, Chloe."

"I love you, sweet boy."

"I love you, too, Chloe, I love you too. Yep, definitely, definitely, yessiree, and that's all that really counts, that's all that really counts. And so, um, ahem, um . . ."

"And um what?"

"What was that middle thing? About the thighs and the phallus and the slamming and stuff?"

"In North America, human sacrifice was practiced by the Heron and Pawnee tribes, although evidence now suggests that a particularly brutal form of ritual immolation was carried out by the Anasazi tribes of the Southwest, ancestors of the Hopi, Zuñi, and Pueblo. Like the Maya and Incas, the Anasazi have become a focal point for intense, especially New Age, beliefs. 'The Anasazi, the traditional view held, had no absolute rulers, or even a ruling class, but governed themselves through consensus. . . . They were a society without rich or poor. Warfare and violence were rare, or perhaps unknown. The Anasazi were believed to be profoundly spiritual, and to live in harmony with nature.' Many New Age conceptions were even more romantic. 'The Anasazi captured the fancy of people outside the archeological profession, and particularly those in the New Age movement, many of whom see themselves as the Anasazi's spiritual descendants. During Harmonic Convergence, in 1987, thousands gathered in Chaco Canyon and joined hands, chanting and praying. People have also flocked to the villages of the present-day Pueblo Indians—the Hopi in particular—seeking a spirituality outside Western civilization.'

"All of this was jarringly challenged with the publication of *Prehistoric Cannibalism at Mancos 5Mtumr-2346*, by the respected researcher Tim White, showing evidence that 'men, women, and children were butchered and cooked there around AD 1100. By comparing the human skeletal remains with those used for food at other sites, the author analyzes evidence for skinning, dismemberment, cooking, and fracturing.' As scholar Kent Flannery commented, 'Cannibalism is a controversial topic because many people do not want to believe that their prehistoric ancestors engaged in such activity, but they will be hard put to reject this meticulous study.' A few scholars have denied the cannibalism; none—including the Hopi—have denied the ritual murder and mutilation. Archeologists have long known that there was a strong Mesoamerican influence on the Anasazi—in fact, a few believe there was a direct migration. That some of the Southwest Indians thus shared practices similar to the Olmecs, Toltecs, and Aztecs is not altogether surprising.

"But what I want to know," said Fuentes, "is just how an Irishman got in there," and everybody was glad to laugh, glad to shed the growing, gnawing tension.

"Did you say she had five husbands?" I whispered to Kim.

"Yup, five. Ain't that a kick? She says it's because she won't take shit from any man. But she still keeps going back. Makes you wonder."

"Wonder what, exactly?"

"Well, Charles says that she wants to honor the differences between males and females, and give them a type of 'equal but different' status, but apparently it's hard for her to convert that into real life feelings. Apparently she wants to wear the pants in the family."

"What's wrong with that? All she needs to do is find a man who likes to wear the skirt in the family."

Kim turned and looked at me. "Jesus, Wilber, that almost makes sense."

Whatever Fuentes did or did not do in her relationships, it was hard not to be attracted to her crackling energy. Few doubted the brain power behind the sizzling smile. Still, the very topic quickly returned the audience to a sullen, reflective silence, and Fuentes was none too gentle in the delivery.

"As for the ecological wisdom of the native North Americans, Shephard Krech's *The Ecological Indian: Myth and History* is the most recent survey to shed a more accurate light on this topic. As even Carolyn Merchant, author of *Radical Ecology* and *Earthcare*, stated, '*The Ecological Indian* is a stunning, provocative reassessment of the image of the noble Indian living harmoniously with nature . . . stimulating, indispensable, and timely.' William Sturtevant, of the Smithsonian Institute, and general editor of *Handbook of North American Indians*, concluded that 'thoroughly researched, this work corrects the steoreotype of the passive ecological or environmentalist Indian, demonstrating that Indian people were and are actively engaged with their environment—adjusting to it, modifying it, and exploiting it.' *Exploiting* it. Are we clear on that? Good." Fuentes paced the stage.

"Incidentally, friends, why have so many scholars recently started referring to native Americans as 'Indians'? Because polls show a large majority of Indians prefer that term. 'Native Americans' and 'indigenous peoples' are phrases that green liberals use to feel good about themselves and show how sensitive they are, but let's just go with 'Indians' since most Indians prefer it.

"Shall I summarize?" No response from the audience; silence hung like a damp cloak over the hall. "Good grief, listen up, you bean bags. The overall picture is clear and unmistakable. The so-called American Paradise (North, Central, and South) was actually a complex mixture of sophisticated, beautiful, spiritual—and by today's standards, barbaric and utterly savage—practices, *precisely like all other foraging and horticultural societies the world over.* These cultures had both much wisdom and much barbarism. I will present an overview of the wisdom in a handout. As for the barbarism, I am only going to say this once, but with great emphasis, least I be accused, as I will anyway, of racism or ethnocentrism or Eurocentrism or whatever the latest green-meme dirty name is. I have written similar accounts of horticultural societies around the world, many of which practiced human sacrifice and slash-and-burn ecology. Many of my IC colleagues have written on this topic as well. I am absolutely *not* claiming that American natives did something that other cultures did not. I am claiming, rather, a multi-cultural equality in barbarity.

"This should come as no surprise. We already saw, in lecture 3, that the red meme will do almost exactly the same thing *today*, in 'civilized peoples,' if left to its own devices. Remember Beck and Cowan? I repeat one of their quotes: 'Survivors of violent red conflict may be taken as slaves or prizes. Heads, scalps, and ears are carried off as proof of victory, and mutilation of sexual organs after a killing is the final *coup d'*dis-*grace*, depriving the victim of reproduction or plea-sures, even in an afterlife. In the 1990s, the Serbians are said to have used rape to increase their tribe and dilute the "seed" of their Bosnian adversaries. The Tutsi and Hutu of Rwanda strove to decimate their niche rivals in the 1994 uprisings. A few American troops collected body parts in Vietnam.'

"Historically, this magical barter system of butchery and human sac-rifice reached its zenith in matrifocal horticultural societies, declined with patriarchal agrarian societies, and was completely outlawed by patriarchal industrial societies."

She paused as if to let that fact sink in, then simply said, "Here's Lesa Powell."

Joan Hazelton looked at each of us around the dinner table, then re-peated her startling announcement: "And if this is so, we have found the roadmap to God."

Electric silence enveloped us. "And that God does not exist yester-day, it exists tomorrow. The spiral of development is not heading away from Spirit, but toward it."

The vivid silence persisted; Carolyn finally spoke. "Well, then, tell us about these higher levels of consciousness!" and we all nodded our heads with giddy eagerness. Even Katish, sort of.

"You remember the slides I showed at the Spiral Dynamics intro-ductory lecture? People at turquoise begin to say things like, 'The earth is a single organism with one mind or one consciousness.' This is a type of cosmic religious belief—the belief that you are one with, interwoven with, the universe. But it's still a *belief*, a concept. At the next level—well, there are several of them, but we call all of them 'third tier' or 'post-turquoise.'

"Anyway, at the third tier of consciousness development, the *idea* that you and the world are one becomes a *direct experience*. You actually experience yourself, or your Self, as being one with the entire universe. The total cosmos is the manifestation of a living Spirit and you are one with that Spirit. Scholars have called this 'cosmic consciousness.'"

"But that sounds very magical, very purple," I suggested.

"If you only look at the surface words, yes, it can, and many people make that mistake. But you have to look at the overall belief system to see what is actually involved. Purple sounds holistic, but it is actually very fragmented. It's not even very ecological. Remember Clare Graves describing this level: 'There is a name for every bend in the river but no name for the river.'" I looked at Carolyn; she smiled wanly.

"But the truly telling item is this: purple or tribal consciousness may have been 'nondissociated' from its immediate natural surroundings, but it was completely *dissociated* from other human beings. Tribal consciousness cannot take the role of other tribes—it cannot get past ethnocentric into worldcentric consciousness, and, in fact, it usually hovers at egocentric modes. This is why most human barbarities are a resurrection of tribal consciousness, purple and red.

"But by the time you get to second-tier turquoise, you have a fully *worldcentric*, postconventional awareness. You can become one not only with the environment but with all other human beings—in fact, with all other sentient beings. So turquoise or second tier prepares the way for the great leap into third tier, or the leap into spiritual enlightenment—the realization that you are one with Spirit and thus one with all manifestation—as a *direct experience*."

"So third tier really does lie in our collective future. Our *future*."

"Yes. But remember, any individual, now or in the past, can evolve through the entire spectrum of consciousness on their own. You can do it right now! In the past, the great spiritual heroes and heroines did just that—they evolved to third tier and a oneness with Spirit. But they were unbelievably rare. And what we find on the whole is that collectively, consciousness is evolving. The average center of gravity is slowly drifting upward."

"Just like the stockmarket," said Jonathan. "There might be huge gains and great depressions, but on balance it keeps drifting upward."

"We call that upward drift Eros," Hazelton smiled.

"But if third tier is the ultimate state of consciousness, or being one with everything, then why call second tier by the name 'integral?'" Stuart asked. "Isn't third tier the *real* integral?"

"Yes, but it's all a matter of degree. All stages transcend and include their predecessors. So green is more integral than orange, which is more integral than blue, and so on. Second tier is more integral than first tier, and yes, third tier is the ultimate integral wave."

"Does that mean there is nothing higher than that? Is third tier the highest state of consciousness?"

"As far as we can tell, yes."

"So here's the question," I said with an urgent tone, "is third tier some sort of Omega Point? Is enlightenment the end point to which all creation is now rushing?"

"Why, you sound like Teilhard de Chardin," she said.

"Well, Teilhard got the idea from Aurobindo," added Jonathan.

"Actually," Hazelton replied, "Aurobindo got it from Schelling, but who's counting?"

"Is third tier an ultimate Omega Point?" I asked again, same urgency.

"As far as we know, there is nothing higher than third tier. But we don't know if third tier will really act like an ultimate Omega Point. Here's what I mean by that. Remember that even if we lived in a society where all people developed to third tier, everybody is still born at square one, at beige, and has to begin their evolution through the entire spiral starting there. And all sorts of things can go wrong at each and every stage of development through the spiral. It's just like today—we live in a country where the average center of gravity is roughly orange. But that doesn't mean that everybody makes it to orange. So we just don't know what it would mean to be in a culture where the center of gravity is third tier. Except, of course, that many things would be greatly, greatly improved—and yet there might be other things that get worse. We just can't tell right now."

She was quiet for a very long time. "There is one theory, however." The room went instantly still. "Some people believe that if even a small percentage of the population makes it to third tier—perhaps around 1 percent—then that will act as a huge magnet pulling others forward."

"A little hundredth monkey, anybody?" Jonathan chided.

"Believe me, we've worried about that one!" Hazelton laughed. "And we have bent over backward to try to avoid any of that thinking. But the fact remains: there is a very distinct possibility that if a small percentage of the population reaches third tier, that will indeed act as a huge Omega Point pulling all others into that final enlightenment, pulling everybody into cosmic consciousness."

"Tell me, Dr. Hazelton . . ." I began.

"Well, dear, it's Joan here, yes?"

"Well dear here yes. This is, but of course. So if you would, that is, here dear, is or are this?"

"Allow me to translate." Jonathan grinned.

"No, it's fine and I are fine. Here's the thing." I cleared my throat. "What if, say, a silicon life form reached third tier. Could that pull the rest of us into third tier? Could a silicon life form act as this ultimate Omega Point?"

She thought for a long time. "Well, my dear, I don't see why not."

Slide #3, "Under the Pavement Is the Beach."

Lesa Powell commenced, again picking up directly where others had left off. "Once we get locked into the notion that formal rationality is nothing but a repressive, marginalizing, mutilating force, and that *anything* nonrational must therefore be a pluralistic paradise, we can get very confused about just which direction in development we ought to be calling 'paradise.'

"There are two major views of human evil and how to overcome it: the *recaptured goodness* model, and the *growth to goodness* model. While both of those models contain important truths, the retro-Romantic tension in boomeritis caused it blindly and rather totally to select the former, with the most unfortunate results.

"Recaptured goodness, as the name implies, maintains that men and women started out in a type of primal paradise—both ontogenetically and phylogenetically—and then this original freedom was disrupted by repressive social forces, egoic rationality, the analytic and divisive Newtonian-Cartesian paradigm, patriarchal signifiers, or some other allegedly disruptive force. An original goodness was repressed, and in its place was human evil. Thus our job is to recapture this paradise in a mature form.

"The growth-to-goodness model suggests pretty much the opposite. Men and women are born egocentric and preconventional, and however 'spontaneous' and 'free' all that might appear, in fact it harbors an incapacity to take the role of others and thus to evidence genuine care and concern. This egocentric stance will grow, evolve, and expand into an ethnocentric stance, and this in turn can expand into a worldcentric stance of genuine pluralism and postconventional freedom. Thus, men and women are born, not exactly evil, but definitely lacking postconventional love and compassion, but they can grow and develop into that goodness.

"A substantial amount of psychological research has concluded that both of those views are, as it were, partially right. The growth-to-goodness model is the generally correct framework: most development does indeed proceed from preconventional to conventional to postconventional. But at any of those stages, the potentials *of those stages* can be repressed, denied, buried. Thus, if little Johnny is harshly repressed as he is growing up, it will not be the repression of any sort of postconventional freedom—*for that has not yet emerged*—but rather the repression of the healthy memes of the *preconventional* realms (a repression of beige, purple, and red capacities: a repression of organic vitality, libido, sex, aggression, sensory richness, and so on). Thus therapy, in these cases, involves a 'regression in service of the ego,' which attempts to return to—and befriend—any of the lost potentials of childhood, which are not postconventional, but preconventional.

"But boomeritis, committed to the retro-Romantic paradise, acknowledged little of the growth-to-goodness model. It would simply recontact the paradisical 'Eden' that modern patriarchal rationality had so brutally crushed (although this paradise would now be on a 'higher level' or in a 'mature form,' which was never spelled out in a noncontradictory way). But now that more careful historical research has unearthed a more accurate view of paradise, a more realistic assessment is in order."

I looked at Carolyn; she seemed fine. Katish was livid, but it was always hard to tell what that meant. Beth was fully engaged; she seemed generally to agree, but her furiously scribbled notes had objection points scattered all over them.

"To recapture the One is not to go backward in time, but to discover the Timeless," the voice inside my head says.

"What's that? I didn't get that."

"Can you show me the Immortal One who is right here and now listening to this voice, and hearing these words, and looking through your eyes at the world? Can you show me that timeless One, directly here and now?"

"Are you talking to me?"

"This more realistic assessment of premodern 'paradise' is certainly what Michel Foucault did. After his early works were used—with his blessing—to condemn virtually all aspects of modernity (egoic-rationality, the orange meme, the Enlightenment)—Foucault began his famous retraction of much of his early work. In fact, he actually made fun of it—and of his extremist followers—with a series of very witty remarks. Foucault's early works had been taken to mean that virtually all modern institutions—from asylums to prisons to hospitals to schools—were massively *repressive*: they were nothing but power structures that crushed the 'original goodness' and freedom of humans.

"Foucault eventually dispensed with such naive, recaptured-goodness notions. He ridiculed the idea that 'under the pavement is the beach.' He did so, first, because his own historical research claiming otherwise did not hold up to scrutiny; and second, he acknowledged a more refined view of human development." Powell once again launched into a scathing intellectual fury of analysis, virtually none of which I understood. But I did catch her conclusion:

"Thus, to quote French historians Gauchet and Swain, 'contrary to Foucault's claim, the dynamics of modernity is not essentially that of *the exclusion of otherness*. The logic of modern societies is rather more like the one Tocqueville describes, namely, the logic of *integration* sustained by the proposition of the fundamental *equality* of all humankind. . . . *Modern history is a history of integration, not exclusion.*' In short, modernity marked the move from ethnocentric to worldcentric, which of course is what actually happened."

"See! They confused pre-Square regression with post-Square freedom! See, Chloe, I knew it! I knew it!"

"Well, then, sweet boy, now that you understand that, there should be no problem if you put your penis in my mouth."

One, two, three, four. "Right you are, Chloe. Damn perceptive of you."

"Foucault therefore eventually renounced much of his 'recaptured-goodness' model, and the notion that, as wittily summarized, 'under the pavement is the beach.' Ferry and Renaut report what is now commonly known: 'In a 1977 interview, Foucault expressed his reservations about what the intellectual fashion of 1968 had taken from his works, which had resulted in the birth of a type of Vulgate (a Foucauldian bible) centered around the idea of dismantling the mechanisms of power (asylums, prisons, schools, etc.)'—attempting to find an 'original goodness' beneath the power. These ideas, Foucault said, had become the *dogmatisms of the Left*, 'the refrain of the antirepressive tune,' which always chanted that 'beneath power, things themselves in their primitive vividness should be discernable'—or, in short, under the pavement is the beach—whereas now we know that, in human development, under the modern pavement is simply the premodern pavement, often uglier, and certainly nothing postconventional about it.

"We can summarize this rather easily," Powell said. "What is 'under' the orange pavement of the Enlightenment? The blue pavement. What is under the blue pavement? The red pavement. What is under red? Purple. Under purple? Beige. Under beige? Apes. Where, then, is paradise? *In the other direction*, in a *growth to goodness* into postconventional, second-tier, integral goodness."

And then beyond even that!, I now knew. Second tier would prepare the leap into third tier, the ultimate Omega Point! Assuming, of course, that humanity even made it to second tier at all—assuming that we didn't self-deconstruct tomorrow afternoon. That dismal possibility had become my obsessive fear; it drearily haunted my days, invaded my dreams, sent shivers through my dendrites, rendered inchoate and disjointed much of my contact with others; puzzled looks followed me everywhere. But Lesa Powell was right, I was now convinced—original Goodness is not something you have to go back in time to capture, it is something waiting to be born, if humanity doesn't abort first. . . .

Powell drove the point home. "Foucault eventually came to ridicule the idea of recaptured goodness. In his mocking words: 'Behind the walls of the asylum, the spontaneity of madness; throughout the penal system, the generous fever of delinquency; under sexual taboo, the freshness of desire,' and the misguided notion that we should therefore have a group of 'simple hurrahs (long live madness, long live delinquency, long live sex)'—all sustained by the notion that 'power is bad, ugly, poor, sterile, monotonous, dead' and that 'what power is exercised over is good, fine, rich': exactly the hurrahs of the recaptured-goodness fever.

"Foucault came to see the danger in this regressive effort, another version of the beach beneath the pavement, where the beach, in this case, is completely fabricated. As Foucault himself put it, 'I think that there is a widespread and facile tendency, which one should combat, to designate that which has just occurred (namely, modernity) as the primary enemy, as if this were always the principal form of oppression from which one had to liberate oneself. Now this simple attitude entails a number of dangerous consequences: first, an inclination to seek out some cheap form of archaism or some imaginary past forms of happiness that people did not, in fact, have at all. . . . There is in this hatred of the present a dangerous tendency to invoke a completely mythical past.'

"And a completely mythical past is what boomeritis was about to create."

That night, at Hazelton's, everybody left except me; Jonathan raised his eyebrows on the way out. "Ooooh la la," he mouthed.

"Do you really believe that there is a third tier, a God, a Spirit, that we can know directly?" I ask.

"I'm sure of it," she says, looking directly at me.

I lean over to kiss her, but she is several inches to the left of where I think she is, and I end up planting a nervous kiss on a picture of Rimbaud hanging on the wall. Hazelton laughs hysterically.

"Um, your lips are colder than I imagined," I mumble.

"Go home, dear one."

"But . . ."

"But you never know what tomorrow will bring."

Mark Jefferson walked out on stage, to a round of applause. He really was a striking figure. In his early fifties, like most of the IC folks; tall, athletic build; close-cropped black hair with a white streak shaped like a check mark on his left temple—it looked like the Nike trademark, like he was always running with the wind. Yet despite his almost intimidating physical presence, there was a gentle peacefulness that quietly cloaked him, seemed to shield him from the uglier, meaner elements of the world.

Slide #5, "No Facts, Just Interpretations."

"One of the reasons that cultural-studies writers give relatively little attention to facts and evidence is that, according to extreme postmodernism, there are no facts, only interpretations. That is a good summary of postmodernism: no facts, only interpretations.

"So what does that statement actually mean? It means that all knowledge—including natural science—is claimed to be a *social construction*, and thus any and all 'facts' are really *interpretations* that have been selected according to various cultural agendas and ideologies. Facts are not *discovered*, they are *invented*, and then *imposed* on others by special interests—racist, sexist, Eurocentric, logocentric, patriarchal, and so on. Thus, cultural-studies historians rely less on collecting facts and evidence and more on reading history according to their theory of interpretation. For example, since we 'know' that hegemonic universal rationality is essentially a source of power and repression, and since we 'know' that beneath that repressive pavement lies the pure and pristine beach, then we *already* know that Mexica was paradise. Therefore we will simply write a history of the conquest of paradise, unencumbered by evidence or research, and thus demonstrate the power of this new historicism.

"As usual, the postmodern writers are onto a very important truth; and as usual, a truth taken to extremes and rendered ridiculous. There is no question that interpretation is an inescapable component of all forms of knowledge. But it does not follow that there are then no objective components at all. Yet that is the relentless claim of extreme postmodernism: there is no objective reality, only interpretations and constructions. But, as Todd Gitlin points out, 'Those who worry that the industrial system directed by imperial male egos is destroying the world through global warming gleefully brandish the measurements gathered by scientists who surely believe that what they are measuring is actually "out there" and not simply a "construction" of imperial egos.' Likewise, 'The most passionate critic of "male" science believes that she should step out of the way of an oncoming bus, whether or not she believes in the Cartesian mind-body split.' In other words, it is objectively true that the bus will kill you—that is not a mere interpretation—and thus even those who claim there are only interpretations *don't really believe it*. Oh, the hypocrisy never ends, does it?"

The audience shifted and shuffled in their seats. Kim leaned over. "Mark can get away with saying things that most can't."

"Because he's black?"

"Well, maybe. Maybe not. It's more like . . . I don't know. His energy or something."

"Oh."

"As we noted earlier, a diamond will cut a piece of glass, no matter what words we use for 'diamond,' 'cut,' and 'glass'—and no matter what culture that occurs in—which shows that not *all* knowledge is merely relative. Of course, if we happen to *value* diamonds, or think they are *beautiful*, or otherwise engage in cultural *evaluations*, those *interpretations* often vary from culture to culture, and are often relative and pluralistic. The balanced conclusion is therefore that knowledge has at least two components: a series of objective facts or events, and the various interpretations and evaluations we give to those events.

"That these components—objective and interpretive—can *never* be separated does not mean that all facts are merely interpretations. Thus, for example, even the new historicists, committed to the relativity of all knowledge, agree that a person called Columbus left Spain in a year that we call 1492 and voyaged to what are now called the Americas. Those events, those facts, *are not contested*, even by cultural-studies writers. But how we *interpret* those events is another matter entirely, and cultural studies is quite right to insist that those interpretations *always* reflect various interests—personal, cultural, social, imperial, or whatnot.

"But cultural studies, and the new historicists, get into great trouble when they move from the *inseparability* of fact and interpretation to the *nonexistence* of facts: they completely deny the existence of basic facts or events. Extreme postmodernism maintains, as we saw, that cultural interpretations *create* all facts, *invent* them, and thus there is literally no significant difference between science and poetry, fact and fiction, history and myth. Denying any serious distinction between science and poetry, or between fact and fiction, is one of the favorite pastimes of extreme postmodernists. As Howard Felperin summarized the widely held postmodern conclusion: 'Science itself is recognizing that its own methods are ultimately no more objective than those of the arts.'

"Here's where Jefferson moves in for the kill," said Kim gleefully.

"Kim, why do you keep talking in war terms?" I asked.

"Well, look whose little green sensitive self is all lit up," Kim sarcastically shot back. "Well, okay, okay. Look, I sometimes still get locked into first-tier battle mode, okay? But you're no better, Wilber—you still get locked into that sickening green 'Why can't we all be friends?' crap. In this case, anyway, we're both stuck in first tier, sport."

"Swell."

"Darla was gone, forever. She said she was going back to Bill, and that was that. I hung up the phone and jumped up, desperate to get away from my parent's house, hurrying to go somewhere where no one could see me or hear me. I got on a bike and started riding. Riding and crying. Peddling harder and harder, riding out into the country. Peddling and crying, riding and sobbing. The welling inside me grew and grew. My body shook, defenseless against what was all around me. I was completely falling apart, crying uncontrollably, really falling apart totally.

"But through it all, and then with increasing intensity, there was this undeniable presence of what I can only call Love, a purely impersonal Love pulsing and animating everything in and around me. It was too much to take, and I wanted to escape it, because it radiated from absolutely everything—the asphalt, the trees, the bike, my own beating chest, my own cries, the sky, it all became so clearly alive with divine presence, and the nearness of it was unbearable."

We all sat riveted by Stuart's account, not simply because it was so obviously real for him, but because this was radically unlike Stuart, the self-proclaimed "Gen-X, post-apocalyptic, punk-folk singer," the brutal exposer and chronicler of humanity's endless sins and exorbitant nastiness. As Chloe later said, "The last guy you expect to have a religious experience while peddling his bike is ole Stu baby." But ole Stu baby, our dear friend Stuart, had indeed been dunked into what appeared to be God.

Into what appeared to be, in fact, some sort of cosmic consciousness. Stuart seemed to have gotten a fast introduction to third tier. Those of us who had been at Hazelton's that night all suspected as much . . . which is why we listened even more intently.

"Suddenly, it was so clear, that all this time, before time ever began, there was this, this unwavering, ever-present Love, and that my life, and all that I call 'real,' is a sad, cardboard dream—a phantom inside this Reality. I saw how I had been a sleeping zombie, even though all the while this perfect radiance had poured over me at every single moment, never anything less than complete and unconditional Love pouring over me. The intimacy was ecstatic, but too much to take. Again and again, I would struggle to gather myself, to escape it, shut down from it, look away, but there was nowhere to look away to—as soon as I turned my head and tried to think, the Presence was right there, so near, inside me—looking out from behind my eyes and back at me from the cars, the trees, my hands, destroying me with every wave. My chest heaving, sobbing, I couldn't do anything. No thinking, no praying, there was nothing but this absolute loving Presence.

"So Darla was out of the picture, but this Presence was, is, everywhere. I'm still not sure exactly what to make of this." Stuart shook his head, then said abruptly, "What happened next was even weirder."

"No facts, only interpretations—no difference between science and poetry—so we don't discover history, we invent it." Jefferson laughed easily, moved to center stage.

"So cultural studies icon Greg Dening, in order to support this silliness, writes *Mr. Bligh's Bad Language: Passion, Power, and Theater on the Bounty*. Dening is a cultural-studies historian, so he puts the case for *history as fiction* very straightforwardly: 'I have always put it to my undergraduate students that history is something we make rather than something we learn. . . . I want to persuade them that any history they make will be fiction—not fantasy, fiction, something sculpted to its expressive purpose.'

"History reduced to fiction, science reduced to poetry, all facts reduced to mere interpretations. . . . *How on earth did this dismal slide ever get started?*"

"It got started because Boomers eat their young," says Chloe.

"Chloe, just what does that mean? Why are you always saying that? It really doesn't make any sense, you know."

"Sure it does, sweet boy. It means what Jefferson is saying: Boomer egos rule the world. So of course they would wipe out facts and replace them with stories of their version of the world."

"I think that's way too harsh."

"Well that is what Jefferson's saying, you know."

"He's saying there is good news and bad news, and you're giving only the bad news."

"Okay, here's the good news," says Chloe, and she quickly takes off her clothes and begins rubbing her naked body against mine, rubbing and rubbing and rubbing as my body begins to fill with bliss.

"Now Chloe," I say, as I look into her eyes, and Joan Hazelton is looking back at me.

"Yikes!" I yelled out loud, and the whole auditorium began laughing. Jefferson peered into the audience to see just which idiot had stirred. "That's okay," he said, "I remember what it was like when I had my first beer.

"Back on course, yes? Where did this dismal slide begin? In part, of course, it was a healthy counterbalance to the prevailing modernist notion that there are *only* facts, that positivism is the one and only true approach to knowledge, that scientific materialism alone can carry the day. In part, too, this emphasis on interpretation came from the long tradition of hermeneutics—from Dilthey to Gadamer—which stresses that meaning is a holistic affair, not reducible to mere facts; and from the recent discoveries of structuralism, which demonstrated so clearly that what we take as everyday meaning is really generated by extensive linguistic systems—you saw an example yesterday with Saussure and the meaning of 'bark.' And finally, this emphasis on interpretation was based on the important work of Nietzsche and Heidegger, who stressed that all facts are always embedded in cultural contexts and interests.

"But *something else* was going on here, something that converted these important ideas into an incredibly *extremist* version: not that facts are always situated in interpretations, but that there are no facts, period. And Ferry and Renaut know exactly what this 'something else' was: it was *narcissism*: since 'facts' constrain my ego, 'facts' must go.

"Ferry and Renaut are not alone in this assessment. Raymond Aron's important book, *The Elusive Revolution: Anatomy of a Student Revolt*, comes to a similar conclusion along different routes, and Ferry and Renaut discuss it as well. 'The god of the intellectuals of the sixties,' Aron wrote, 'was no longer the Sartre who had dominated the postwar period, but a mixture of Lévi-Strauss, Foucault, Althusser, and Lacan'—the structuralists who themselves would soon give way to the poststructuralists, which we will discuss later, aren't you excited?"

Jefferson looked up and smiled, then looked back down and rapidly continued, as if trying to hurry through the dense bramble of theory so that he might soon offer a simpler conclusion, thus quieting the painful sound of students being forced to think.

"Ferry and Renaut point out that these poststructuralist theorists had a widespread effect: 'They brought the formulation "*there are no facts*" into favor in Parisian milieu, thus contributing to the *disintegration* of the commonsense belief that every society is subject to the constraints of fact'—in the sense that the world contains a variety of factual realities that need to be addressed (for example, get out of the way of the oncoming bus). But precisely 'because of this *dissolution of facts* and thus the *constraints of facts*, the idea that everything could be represented as valid, and that no norms need be imposed institutionally on the play of desire, for example, was gradually developing.' That is, if facts got in the way of egoic desire, then facts had to be deconstructed altogether, because 'Nobody tells me what to do!'"

"You can tell me what to do, anytime, big boy," Chloe says, her alluring smile sitting on top of her naked breasts.

"Not now, Chloe, I have to ask Mom something." I turn to Mother, not wondering what she is doing there next to a naked Chloe, although fortunately Mom is dressed.

"You have very nice breasts, child."

"Mom, please, look here. Mom, seriously, what is it that you want out of life? I mean, there has to be more to life than dusting."

"Dusting is very important, my lovely child," Mom says.

"But why bother, Mom? As Quentin Crisp said, after the first four years, the dust never gets any worse."

Mom stares blankly back.

"In other words, Mom, relax, okay? There's an old joke. Neurotics build castles in the air, psychotics live in them. Well, you clean them."

Mom puts down her feather duster and patiently explains. "This is not all I do, Son. I have founded almost a dozen organizations devoted to transformational learning, global friendship, world fellowship, collaborative inquiry and conscious dialogue. I have two degrees, I teach yoga, I raised one amazing son and survived one confused husband. I am responsible for my own orgasms"—I turn bright red—"and I do not define myself merely by my relationships but by my own autonomy." She pauses, satisfied; picks up the feather duster. "I also clean."

"But Mom. What do you *want*?"

Without hesitating, she says, "I want a world that works for everyone. A world where everyone is treated equally, fairly, compassionately. A world that includes everyone."

That used to make so much sense to me, the hundreds of times I heard it growing up. But now I can't help it; a corner has turned in my mind, invading even my fantasies. "But Mom, do you want to include the Nazis? Do you want to include the KKK? How about the terrorists, the rapists, the torturers? Do we want the world to work for them, too?" Mom looks confused.

"See, Mom, you're being green, you're not being integral. You have to, you see, there must be, there's this evolution of consciousness, and so on and so on and so forth, and egocentric to worldcentric, it's very real, very real, and all that, and you must have ranking to get real linking, and over and over, and exactly like that. Okay, that could be clearer, so, well, let me sum up."

Mom nervously clutches her feather duster.

Mark Jefferson paced the stage, his voice filled the hall. "It was all of a piece. As Ferry and Renaut point out, 'From the disintegration of norms to the rise of neonihilism was but a single step, which, when taken, rather easily undermined the fragile order of existing society: to reject one social order without having any notion of which order might be erected in its place demonstrates one of the reasons for the decomposition we saw in May '68. It must seem paradoxical and problematical that what passes for postmodernism *acquires the strange appearance of a regression.*'

"Get it, folks? Hello! *Disintegration, decomposition, regression*—those are all words that we have repeatedly heard used by critics to describe this slide from postconventional autonomy into preconventional egocentrism, an essential move of which was to *get rid of facts!*" Jefferson's voice exploded. "For if facts constrain the free play of my egoic desire, *then facts must go!*

"Had this lopsided view not been made to order for boomeritis, it would never have taken hold in such a widespread fashion, so palpably false it is."

The boy realizes there is an Omega dawn looming in his future, which means young Ken is on the trail of who and what I AM. Fifteen billion years in preparation for just this, he among the many who would aspire to the One. How few realize, how few care. Will it ever really change?

"The funny thing is that the new historicists, when they get right down to doing history, usually end up trying to find a few hard facts on which to hang their novel interpretations. Thus Mr. Dening, who assures us that he is writing fiction, actually unearths several previously unknown *facts*. Perceptive critics everywhere spotted this obvious self-contradiction (postmodernism is nothing without its performative contradictions). As one of them introduces the problem:

> Dening's thesis that it is an "illusion" to try to know the past "as it really was"—to know any objective facts—and that our views of the past are interlocked with our present value systems, is relativist in terms of historical knowledge. He says history is not "something we learn" from the past but is a matter of interpretation, of reading off from the past whatever our present values, systems and preoccupations dictate. In other words, the past is a

text or a series of texts, which we interpret, the same as we would a work of literature. Different people and eras will make different interpretations. Hence history is not a process in which objective knowledge is discovered and accumulated.

"'Unfortunately for Dening,' this critic continues, 'it is not difficult to show that his own practice in *Mr. Bligh's Bad Language* contradicts his theory.'" Jefferson looked out at the audience. "You see, Dening actually introduces several items, crucial to his argument, that he implicitly claims are objective facts—not interpretations—and facts that are *not* relative or pluralistic, but are universally the case for any cultural reading. In fact, Dening actually *discovered* (not invented) several heretofore unknown facts about the mutiny on the *Bounty*, which are quite fascinating.

"It has often been thought that the mutiny was sparked by Captain Bligh's brutal discipline, especially his liberal use of flogging. In painstakingly pouring through the records of the time, Dening unearthed the fact that Bligh actually used flogging *much less* than was typical. 'Since Dening has published his statistics, no one in the future will be able to argue that Bligh was more violent than the other commanders of British ships in the Pacific at the time. Indeed, the conclusion appears inescapable that he was one of the captains least inclined to use the lash on his crew.' And then the considerable embarrassment for Mr. Dening:

> To argue that Bligh was less violent, Dening does not put forward his statistics as merely an interpretation with which others might legitimately take issue. He uses his conclusion to demolish what he calls the "common myth" of Bligh the sadist. He can only do this if he uses it as a truth *in an objective sense*. Moreover, he uses the two points he has now established—(1) the statistics show that Bligh was less violent; and (2) previous explanations of the mutiny based on Bligh's violence merely reflected the values of the time they were written—as the central premises of his wider argument that different ages generate their own myths about history to suit their needs and values. So his major thesis, that we never know history "as it really was," is

itself derived from an argument based on a point about what really happened in history. His case is self-contradictory.

"My point, however," Jefferson concluded, "is that *both* of those positions are true: there are facts, and there are interpretations, and all forms of human knowledge partake of both. And we get into a great deal of trouble when we try to deny the importance of either. The orange meme tends toward a type of positivism, empiricism, and objectivism, which believes that there are *only* objective facts. The green meme tends toward a radical hermeneutics, which believes that there are *only* interpretations. Second-tier integralism points out that *both* of these positions are important and in any event inescapable."

"Both of these positions are true," a naked Chloe says, as she obscenely demonstrates, voluptuous ass and full breasts waving in the wind. "Chapter 6, the Deer-Caught-in-Headlights Position, and Chapter 7, the Look-What-I-Found-Under-the-Table-When-I-Dropped-My-Fork Position."

"Chloe, just which *Kama Sutra* is this you're reading from?"

"Mark and his colleagues," Kim said, "are working on an 'integral historiography.' They call it 'all quadrants, all levels, all lines, all states.'"

"Snappy title."

"*All it means*, nancy boy, is that it's a comprehensive approach to the interpretation of history, unlike a merely orange or green approach. It's all of a piece with integral feminism, integral politics, integral ecology, and so on. Honest, it is like way totally awesome."

"Way totally?" But, indeed, later that day Carla Fuentes gave an exuberantly entertaining sidebar on integral historiography called "Who Ate Captain Cook?" I put it in my notes. That is, I copied Kim's notes.

Scott leaned over and looked at Carolyn, who had been silent for some time. "Carolyn? Carolyn?" She stared blankly ahead, lost in wherever. "When someone finds out where Carolyn is, please tell her," whispered Scott.

Jefferson smiled out at the audience. "What I appreciate about the green meme—and about cultural studies—are all the wonderful ways that they have brought home the fact that human beings are inescapably situated in many ways—we are embedded in contexts within contexts within contexts indefinitely, and each of those contexts gives us a different interpretation of the world. We ourselves have already seen that we can have a red interpretation of the world, a blue interpretation of the world, a green interpretation of the world, and so on—not instead of, but alongside of, a world of objective facts. *All* of that needs to be taken into account for more integral interpretations of history.

"So why did this rather odd notion—that there are *no facts, only interpretations*—catch on and become a cornerstone of postmodernism? Why was it insisted on in literally thousands of books? Why was it one of the most commonly repeated assertions of the last three decades? Obviously it spoke to the green meme. But that would never be enough to catapult it to such startling fame. The fact is, *it spoke directly to boomeritis*. That there are no facts—that there is nothing outside of the text—means that there is nothing outside of subjective interpretations, and thus 'Nobody can tell me what to do!' Boomeritis thus proceeded to take an important but partial truth—namely, that interpretation is a crucial component of all knowledge—and turn it into the grandiose claim that there is nothing outside of my great big bloated ego."

Jefferson walked off the stage to a round of applause with occasional coughs and shuffling sounds. "Where did he get that brain?" I asked Kim. "No wonder he got the genius award."

"He didn't accept it."

"What? You said he got the MacArthur genius award."

"He was awarded it, but he turned it down. He said, 'This is a stupid award given by stupid people to even stupider people.' That quote made the third page of the *Times*. Pretty funny, huh?"

"How could he afford to turn down all that money?"

"He couldn't."

"Dad, seriously, what is it that you want?"

"A world that works for everybody. A world that includes everybody."

"Say, Mr. Wilber," a naked Chloe says, "did you know that your ex-wife just said the same thing?"

Dad looks annoyed. "Well, naked girl, whoever you are, the ex-Mrs.

Me wants world peace achieved with the use of crystals, tarot cards, sweet wishes, and happy thoughts. I and my colleagues, I almost said comrades, realize that it will only be won with blood, sweat, tears, and toil. Get the difference?"

Again I can't help it; again reality is invading my dreams. "But Dad, you don't really want to include everybody. You don't want the polluters, the capitalists, the patriarchal whatevers, the old paradigmers, the Republicans, the nasty Cartesians, the . . . well, I forget the rest, but you know who you despise. It's a long list."

"What's the point, oh my Son?"

"Well, it's, you know, you have to get to second tier, you have to, it's sort of like this, a long story, or a short story too, but then I should start at the start and not in the middle like this, since silicon and carbon are both racing toward the ultimate Omega, right?"

"Why don't you start like *this*," says Chloe, flashing body parts that make both our eyes bulge. I am now an Oedipus wreck; I look nervously around for a naked Mom, but fortunately none is on the horizon.

"It's just that, Dad, you've got to let go, you know? Let it go, Dad."

"Sure, Son, sure. I understand, I really do." I smile in relief.

"So, um, who's the girl?"

Morin, who had just finished a short lecture on "The Tribal Hijacking of Reason," which is in my notes, looked quietly at the audience, then said, "Ladies and gentlemen, Dr. Joan Hazelton."

Slide # 6, "Ecology: To Save the Goddess."

Joan talking about the Goddess. Joan being a Goddess. Joan, Joan, Joan being a Goddess. . . .

"Kim, did you know there is a third tier?"

"Sure."

"Sure? And you didn't say anything?"

"It's not something you go blabbing about, dig?"

"So Joan says that . . ."

"Joan?"

"Well, you know, Hazelton Joan Doctor person. . . . "

"Oh God, *don't* tell me you've got a crush on her."

"Okay. But she, Hazelton doctor thing, believes that Spirit or God or Goddess is directly realized at third tier."

"That's right. Spirit is actually present at *all* of the stages; but this can only be fully realized at third tier. The whole IC crowd believes that, including Charles. That's why most of them meditate, so they can speed up this evolution in their own cases."

"So in this session, does she talk about realizing the Goddess by evolving to third tier?"

"No, remember that this section of the seminar deals with the mistaken notions and all the problems—in other words, it deals with boomeritis. The next session deals with the integral solutions."

"Right, right. I knew that."

"And so Hazelton, I mean Joooooan, will drive home the point that a full realization of the Goddess is postconventional, not preconventional."

I turned bright red. "Right, right. I knew that."

Joan smiled at the audience, the sky opened and spoke: "The alarming nature and dimension of the environmental crisis gives the eco-philosophers special reason to become a little more fanatic and zealous in their endeavors, and it is hard to blame them. To some degree I count myself among their ranks, as do most of my colleagues here at IC, including the one who entitled his magnum *Sex, Ecology, Spirituality*. As usual, we are not criticizing the good, the true, and the beautiful tenets of any of these movements, from pluralism to feminism to ecology. We are discussing the shape they took when boomeritis got its hands on them.

"Boomeritis ecology is fairly straightforward: the biosphere is Spirit; the modern patriarchy is destroying Spirit; the new paradigm, which subverts patriarchal rationality, will save Spirit; I have the new paradigm; I will save Spirit."

Hazelton paused, her head down, as if waiting for the audience to absorb what she had said. "There are some important truths bundled into that equation, but each one is slightly shaded and morbidly twisted, by boomeritis, to lead to the narcissistic punch line. Imagine, I will save Spirit!" She looked around the audience with an exasperation that was palpable.

Then, while still smiling sweetly, talking softly, Hazelton nonetheless managed to deliver a blistering attack on the equating of the biosphere with Spirit—the equating of the sensory realm with Spirit—which was once again, she said, an example of the pre/post fallacy that allowed Boomers to identify God with the preconventional realm of immediate feelings and thus rationalize their pre-Square impulses as Hip. I put Kim's notes on all this in my journal.

Toward the end of her lecture, Hazelton concluded, "By narrowing Spirit to the sensory world, boomeritis could hold on to its own pre-conventional sensations while claiming it was holding on to nothing less than God. By reducing God/dess to the sensory realm, boomeritis had at last found a Spirit that spoke its own language: immediate feel-ings and impulses, preconventional and preformal, loudly claiming to be divine, the wonder of my own sensations. And this sensate version of salvation is the only salvation allowed. This is yet another rendition of the boomeritis slogan: 'Lose your mind and come to your senses,' which, although the recipe for a terrific fraternity house party, is not exactly a philosophy of life."

But then Hazelton, as if sensing that the audience was missing the central point, closed her own notes and walked out to the edge of the stage.

"Let's do it this way, dear souls. Here's the point: you look out there, at the environment, and with your senses you can plainly see the won-derful, glorious, empirical world of nature. And of course you want to help save nature from destruction. Not only because nature is beauti-ful, but because our own existence depends in many ways on a healthy environment. So you say, stop doing those things that are destroying nature! Stop polluting the oceans, stop dumping toxic wastes into our rivers, stop using fluorocarbons that create an ozone hole, stop burn-ing carbon fuels that pollute the atmosphere and cause global warm-ing—instead let us live in accord with nature, let us adopt energy efficient production, use renewable resources, practice natural capital-ism, and in all ways honor Gaia.

"Congratulations, you have just bought into the world of flatland. And it is *flatland* that above all else is destroying Gaia. And thus your very efforts to save Gaia are destroying Gaia."

Kim leaned over. "That got their attention."

"Well, it got mine," I responded. If we don't save Gaia, then humans will go up in toxic fumes before they can download into a crystal-pure, pollution-free, silicon eternity. . . .

"People, dear souls, listen to me. Of course we all want to save nature, to honor and preserve Gaia. But the only way to save the biosphere is to have human beings agree on a course of action that will curtail our destructive and polluting ways. Humans must *agree* to take global action, yes? And the only way to have humans agree that we must take global action is to have a significant number of humans evolve to the global, worldcentric stages of awareness, yes? Yes. The egocentric and the ethnocentric stages of awareness could not care less about the global commons because they do not themselves possess a global awareness.

"And that means that Gaia's main problem is not toxic waste dumps, the ozone hole, or global warming. Gaia's main problem is that not enough human beings have evolved from egocentric to ethnocentric to worldcentric levels of consciousness, yes?" This time the audience yelled back, "Yes!"

"And what is the main thing that prevents this interior development? The widespread belief in flatland. The widespread belief that there are no levels of consciousness, the insane notion that nothing is higher or better than anything else. You cannot talk about the stages of interior growth if you deny stages in the first place.

"And so, you see, once you subscribe to flatland, all you can do is try to *fix the exteriors*—you try to stop people from polluting, you try to force them to recycle, you try to legislate a moral response to Gaia. And of course it doesn't work very well, because you must resort to force, legal or otherwise. How much better to help people develop to the worldcentric waves of awareness, at which point they will *spontaneously* and naturally be moved *from within* to protect the global commons. A deep and natural love of nature will rise from their own consciousness, because their own consciousness is starting to become one with nature itself." A rumble of applause rushed at the stage to greet that sentiment.

"But if all you do is agitate to fix the exteriors—and you do nothing to help grow the interiors—then you have not fundamentally helped Gaia at all. In fact, you have actually hurt Gaia by not promoting the only thing that can finally save her."

"That's why we have to get to second tier, Chloe! It's the only way humanity will survive long enough to—"

"To what?" Chloe says. "To do *this*?" Her naked body sways back and forth, while the *Kama Sutra* dangles from her hand.

"No no. Well, yes yes, that too. Okay. No-kay, no, that's not what I'm talking about. Now listen to me, Chloe, listen: starting in about thirty years, if we make it, two things will happen: human lifespan will expand to hundreds of thousands of years, and machines will reach human-level intelligence, allowing us to download our consciousness into silicon. Our generation! Chloe! One way or the other, we will be immortal! We will live forever, either in Carbon or Silicon. If, that is, we make it to second tier in time. What do you think, Chloe? Chloe?"

Chloe does her imitation of me: "Rattle, rattle, clunk. Rattle, rattle, clunk."

"I don't rattle, Chloe. I don't. It's not true. Nope. It's not. So seriously, Chloe, what do you think? Will we make it to the ultimate Omega, to third tier?

"The final omega, *the ultimate release*? Why sure, sweet boy, it's just like *this*. . . . "

Hazelton offered that gentle smile, her sky eyes were clear and open, inviting us all in. "In fact, I believe the time is now ripe for a truly second-tier *integral ecology*, which takes the best of conservation environmentalism, natural capitalism, the spiritual dimension of harmony with the cosmos, and the entire spiral of consciousness evolution itself, and sets them all in a genuinely integral context. Several of our IC members are working on a truly integral ecology—Michael Zimmerman, Keith Thompson, Chris Desser, Sean Hargens, to name a few—and you can find one version of this integral ecology in *A Brief History of Everything*. But whatever the final form that an integral ecology might take, I believe it is as urgent and worthy a call as one could imagine."

I was in my early twenties when it happened, when in this female body my own identity expanded beyond the body to embrace all nature, and I became the sky. Through me all things came and went, from me all things were born and to me they all returned upon their dusty death. The sky, the true sky, contains nature but is so much more, embraces Gaia but reaches far beyond, encircles the cosmos but shines beyond it to the timeless, spaceless realm where infinity alone reigns supreme. It is neither male nor female, neither heaven nor earth, but their erotic union, their shockingly erotic union, that lights up the spheres and announces that eternal truth which men and women labor to ignore.

And will dear Ken awaken, even unto this?

Hazelton smiled, continued gently. "But beyond that, or perhaps beneath it, is what boomeritis has done with ecology—Spirit reduced to the preconventional realm, salvation likewise collapsed—and the finite self will therefore *save the planet, save Gaia, save the Goddess,* SAVE SPIRIT ITSELF. Whereas it is usually thought that it is God who can save us, with boomeritis, I can save God."

The audience audibly groaned. And then Joan—she who was a living Goddess, my heart told my head—gave a preview of what Kim said would come in the next session of the seminar. This must come from their research on third-tier consciousness, I thought.

"I believe that what we see in all these attempts to find a spiritual paradise—to find the beach beneath the pavement—is often a genuine intuition of a very real Spirit, but an intuition distorted and misplaced from the timeless Present onto a fantasized past, and reduced from the All to a mere sensory slice. Spirit, if it has any meaning at all, is surely an infinite Ground and not merely the sum total of finite things, and thus it ought not be reduced to the biosphere, even though it embraces and includes the biosphere. And surely it is a timeless Presence and not merely a past reality, and thus it ought not be equated with any particular historical epoch, even though it embraces and includes all history.

"I believe that the evidence shows that there is a real Spirit, a real Beach, but it is beneath no pavement whatsoever, for all pavements arise within it: Spirit is all-encompassing. It transcends everything, it includes everything. But looking for Spirit under a pavement saddles boomeritis with a vicious dualism—biosphere vs. patriarchy, feelings vs. rationality, tribal vs. modern—so that Spirit is imagined to be found in just one-half of that dualism, with the other half then thought to be malignant, so that true wholeness and redemption can then *never* be found."

Young Ken will soon discover how to resurrect Third Tier from the stream of his own consciousness—not out there, but in here, and then beyond. The truly Immortal One will flash forth, not at some point in future time, but at that point where time is not. It begins like this:

Let your mind relax. Let your mind relax and expand, mixing with the sky in front of it. Then notice: the clouds float by in the sky, and you are effortlessly aware of them. Feelings float by in the body, and you are effortlessly aware of them, too. Thoughts float by in the mind, and you are aware of them as well. Nature floats by, feelings float by, thoughts float by . . . and you are aware of all of them.

So tell me: Who are you?

"Boomeritis, bless its heart, is fixated to the egocentric domains, and thus it is hypnotically drawn to identify Spirit with the preconventional, sensory realms. Nobly attempting to find a postconventional Spirit, boomeritis grabs the preconventional realm and becomes enamored of its own feelings, for it has really grabbed itself in one reflected form or other. Staring into the vast cosmos, boomeritis falls in love with its own reflection and calls that thrill Divine, and is captivated by its own image and calls that prison Spirit."

Joan the Goddess finished, the audience applauded keeping time with the pounding of my pulse, sophomoric platitudes filled my heart, dizzying thoughts of Paris in the spring, flowers and kittens, God I might throw up.

"Hey, Kim, you never told me that secret!"

"That's right, dude," she smiled.

The audience began to file out; I looked around for Joan, and for Stuart; both had seemed to vanish. Carbon and Silicon and Third Tier, cosmic consciousness, the race of humans and Bots to the ultimate Omega. My mind had stretch marks all over it, my brain seared on a series of thoughts much too extreme to let easily in. DJ Digweed spins Astral Matrix's "Heading toward Omega," Liquid Language plays "Blue Savannah," the Living End sings "Staring at the Light," and my artificial intelligence reels with more information than it was designed to process; I can feel the tiny capillaries rupturing throughout my brain, blood seeping to the surface in desperate search of air, thoughts drowned in their own density, taking me with them.

"And now the time is fast approaching," the voice inside my head says.

8

The_New_Paradigm@WonderUs.org

What if it was true? Both silicon and carbon life forms were headed toward the ultimate Omega of cosmic consciousness—headed toward fully integral consciousness, or third-tier consciousness, or the awakening of the entire universe as spirit, call it what you will. It was a dizzying, electric, psychotically insane idea. Absolutely insane. Which meant, very possibly true.

It was the second great shock of my life when I realized that silicon life forms would evolve through their own version of the spiral of unfolding consciousness. Once biocomputers became conscious, *truly conscious*, that consciousness would undergo its own evolution, moving through the forms of consciousness that can be created in the manifest world, and whether those forms were based on carbon or silicon, they would have to show certain similarities due to the universal laws of evolution itself—which meant that computer consciousness would have its own general versions of beige, purple, red, blue, and so on. Maybe not in those exact forms, but any given Bot that became truly self-conscious would first awaken to itself, then awaken to an awareness of other Bots, then an awareness of all other Bots—hence, any Bot would undergo its own consciousness evolution from egocentric to ethnocentric to worldcentric. And since this would be the evolution of a superintelligence, surely it would discover Third Tier, discover the ultimate Omega: that is, surely the Bots would eventually find God, by whatever name silicon would call the Intelligence of the entire universe.

As that second great shock of my life finally penetrated my novocained brain, it also dawned on me that, once the Bots had made it to purple, the rest of their evolution through the entire spiral might literally occur in a nanosecond. The hard part would be getting the series started—getting genuine self-consciousness to emerge in the first place (that is, getting the Bots to purple). But once that happened, the rest of the series might very well occur at the speed of light, hurling through digital microphotonics to the radiant luminous conclusion of it all. And if Hazelton was right, and the Bots could act as an Omega Point for consciousness everywhere, then that would mean . . . , that would mean that if, say, maybe thirty years from now, some Bot emerged at purple, then a nanosecond later the third-tier Omega Point might be reached by all Bots, and *that* would pull all of us into final enlightenment, a perfect spiritual realization. A mere three decades from now, the entire world might awaken to its Maker.

As that brown-slush winter gave way to bright spring, this is how I would frame the question that had come to dominate my life and rudely wander through my dreams: Who would get to the Omega point first?—the Bots, or a significant percentage of human beings who were living to be 200,000 years old?

Who would first find God on a widespread scale, Carbon or Silicon?

But then, I was getting ahead of the picture, as the science-fiction novel—the science-fact novel—had continued composing itself in my mind (the novel that kept asking the question, "Carbon or Silicon: which would first evolve enough complexity to fully download Spirit?"). But in the real world, right here and now, my obsession—which was, okay, maybe driven a little bit by the presence of Joan Hazelton—had slowly become this: we first had to make it to second tier. We humans had to make it to second tier or else humanity would self-deconstruct, would perfectly destroy itself before any form of higher intelligence—whether of our own higher evolution or that of our machines—could possibly do anything to save us. That was the realization that had insistently pulled my fantasies back from the purity of crystal-lattice CyberHeaven and into the messy world of human stains, a realization that had dragged me haltingly to Integral Center in the first place. We had to make it to second tier—and as the IC folks kept pointing out, the only way we make it to second-tier integral consciousness is to go beyond green, to go beyond boomeritis and its self infatuations.

That is why it also began to dawn on me, slowly, reluctantly, that it was time for some self-analysis. The IC people were constantly saying that boomeritis is not a disease of Boomers but a disease of the green meme. Boomeritis is simply the unhealthy version of the green meme, and thus it can strike wherever green emerges. And since all human beings—and all Bots, I was betting—have to go through the green wave in order to reach second tier, boomeritis was the great stumbling block to any forms of higher integral awareness. In both meatspace and cyberspace.

"That's exactly right, Ken," **Joan is saying.** *"That is exactly right."*

We are lying naked in bed. I have just made love to the sky, gotten lost in the clouds, found the radiant sun where I thought my head was. This was Third Tier, I was convinced of it. I had come home, found my true Self, gotten lost in the Goddess, seen God face to face. Violent explosions of ecstasy had racked my body head to toe, left my mind scattered in a million rays, tossed my soul to the glittering galaxies, found it dispersed throughout the luminous world.

"What's right, beautiful?"

"Oh, my generation," **she starts softly crying.** *"Do you know how much I love them?"*

"All I'm saying is, aren't we also involved in our own forms of boomeritis? Surely us Xers and Ys are not completely innocent here. I'm worried cuz we might download our own bullshit into everlasting cyberspace if we don't wise up. I'm serious, man, I'm telling ya."

I looked around the table resignedly, pushed my latté to the side, dusted with disgust. As was customary that year, my awareness was marked by an almost complete disregard of my physical surroundings. This was Harvard Square, right? The Breakfast Brewery on Porter Ave.?—a table this, I think, a cup, a cappuccino, several chairs, that I vaguely remember. Jonathan, Beth, Stuart, Carolyn, and Katish all looked at me through a silence that eloquently announced, There he goes again.

Carolyn finally spoke up. "Okay, I agree with Ken. Not the silicon shit, the boomeritis shit."

"Oh, let's don't talk about this, it's like doing homework," Katish complained.

"It won't kill you, Kat," Carolyn said. "Here's how I see it. . . . "

"Oh no."

"We will all move through the green meme, or hopefully we will, anyway. Look at Jonathan, he's already made it to beige, so who knows what the glorious morrow will bring? The point is that whenever any of us move through green, we can get caught in boomeritis—flatland inhabited by a big ego. I have to tell you, I know tons of us Xers and Ys caught in flatland—me too sometimes."

"Me too sometimes," mimicked Jonathan.

Carolyn shot back a malicious grin. "Speaking of boomeritis, Jonathan, I can see your obituary now: 'Freak accident kills aspiring author: Crushed by huge ego.'"

"Oh Carolyn, Carolyn, I have never asked much of you, only that you're back in your coffin before the sun comes up."

"Guys . . ." I lamely protested.

"I'm not saying that I agree with everything the IC folks say, but this has been an intense week for me," Carolyn continued. "I'm still really angry that they have to be so polemical in their presentations, especially since they apparently do that on purpose."

"It's to ruffle your big green feathers, dearie," smiled Jonathan.

"But that is so not necessary," complained Carolyn. "You can catch more flies with honey. . . . "

"Who you calling a fly?"

"Oh, sorry Jonathan, to call you a fly would be to insult flies everywhere."

Jonathan rubbed his nose as if an imaginary punch had landed squarely on it. "I am definitely on the losing end of the verbal repartee this morning, so I shall suckle my cappuccino in silence." Big round of applause from the table.

"As I was saying, their polemic is unnecessary, especially that Van

Cleef Nazi jerk. Just how integral can that guy be, you know, with that attitude? Like, is he even practicing what he preaches? Like hello? But they do have some good points, I'm sorry to say. In our history classes all we get are variations on how history is just a nasty fiction, America totally sucks, Western culture totally sucks, science is not dealing with facts, all the things they said yesterday, it's so true. And it's starting to make me really, really angry."

"The IC folks?"

"No, my boomeritis professors. Well, them too. But the fact is, I am getting a fucking degree in fucking boomeritis, and it fucking pisses me off!"

"Why don't you stop beating around the bush and say what you really mean, Carolyn?" Katish laughed.

"It's not funny, Kat."

"It is very funny if you don't believe what they are saying, and I don't believe it for one minute. What we need in this world are things like a more equitable distribution of economic goods, a saner environmental policy, a strong move toward gender equity, things like that. We do not need more of that elitist, hierarchical nonsense those folks are pushing. And that Hazelton! Do you believe that old Hindu mystification crap she was throwing at us about becoming one with God? I mean, how yesterday can you get? Opiate for the masses, anybody?"

"Then why are you even coming to these things?" I wondered.

"Tell you the truth, Beth said they were really interesting. And I must say, it's quite an entertaining show. If nothing else, watching the audience squirm."

Beth, who according to Chloe was either Katish's girlfriend or Carolyn's girlfriend, and who had attended the seminars without so far saying a word, broke her silence. "All of my humanities classes are really hidden political agendas, and I resent it. My classes are just old political nostrums from the Left—nostrums pretty much like yours, Katish, I must tell you—and I definitely resent it. I don't mind if they teach or rather push politics at you, if they were honest enough to call it politics. But they don't. They call it history, literary theory, new paradigms, cultural studies, postcolonial studies, whatever—but those are all just names for rehashed Leftist ideology. You know that book— *Tenured Radicals*? Well it's the truth. These aging Lefties completely failed in the real world so they indoctrinate college kids instead."

"Oh my God, don't tell me you're a Republican!" Katish laughed even louder. "If you want to feel at home, why don't we go out later and beat up some faggots? Or I know, let's give a tax cut to the wealthiest 1% and fuck the working people, what do you say? Feel better now, Beth?"

I guess Kat and Beth are not an item, I thought.

"That's my point—I'm neither Left nor Right. I'm just not political."

"You are . . . ?"

"Well, that's the thing. I don't really know what to call myself." Beth had the brightest teeth I had ever seen. Carolyn said Beth was known as "the brain," but all I could see were wall-to-wall teeth. Very beautiful, actually, just challenging.

"I don't identify much with politics, I don't have a grand personal agenda. I'm in premed, but I don't know if that is what I really want to do. I seem to just sit around and sort of suicidally sulk. But what I do not want to do is have lame-assed Leftist ideology forced down my throat. I feel like I'm drowning in old bellbottoms, beads, and faded peace signs. I mean, can't these geezers give it a rest? They call us 'slackers,' which is really just a word for the child abuse we've suffered under the pummeling of their huge egos and the constant reminders of how amazingly wonderful they are. We're black and blue and bruised all over and completely exhausted after the beating they've given us, and a college degree is just the final assault. If we don't agree with their boomeritis, they flunk us. Goddam bastards. The IC folks are definitely right about that." It was unnerving to see that intensity of feeling come through that many teeth.

Stuart jumped in. "Two years ago I moved to California to be with my girlfriend at that time, Patricia. She was enrolled in a place called the California Institute of Idiopathic Sophists, which is an alternative college that gives degrees in boomeritis, although I didn't understand this at the time. They said they were teaching 'integral' approaches to the world's problems, but it's just like what the IC folks say—they were teaching the green meme, and usually the mean green meme, and calling that 'integral.' They had courses in boomeritis feminism, boomeritis ecology, boomeritis this and that, their egos were going to save the world, rah rah rah. And it drove me nuts, it just damn near drove me nuts. Every single thing you wanted to do, you had to process it for hours and hours and hours. Patricia and I would spend entire evenings just processing our feelings about every little item that came down the pike. And if you said you didn't want to process something, then you had to process for hours about why you didn't want to process. I mean, it was insane. It was nothing but a way to constantly feel your ego, to constantly focus on your self.

"But that's not even the worst part. The worst part is that all of this was dressed up as a new and higher paradigm. They actually called it that, 'a new paradigm.' I mean, these people are going to be fucking therapists! I'm telling ya, don't ever get mentally ill in California. Although I don't see how you can avoid it with those folks around, because if you're sane, they will drive you nuts. But I vowed two things: to stay as emotionally healthy as I could, and to get out of that state fast."

"Yikes." I cleared my throat. "I can see how all of those folks are caught in this shit. But my original point was, aren't we ourselves caught in any of this? I look at my own life, and I am slowly realizing that what I want is a life that makes sense, that is somehow whole and together. I don't want to bleed inside anymore. I don't want to wake up feeling like I've eaten broken glass for dinner. I know it sounds funny, but I think hypercomputers might be the way we achieve this wholeness, because they will be free of the limitations we face. But even if that's true, I think humans have to get to second tier or we will completely destroy ourselves before robotic superintelligence can rescue us."

"I see we forgot to take our medication today," Jonathan grinned.

"I know, I know, the computer part sounds far out, but that's only because you don't know what's actually happening in AI. I'm telling you, it's moving faster than you can imagine. But skip that part. We would all agree that, one way or another, it's important for as many human beings as possible to make it to second-tier integral awareness, yes?"

Everybody nodded, either in agreement or boredom, but no vocal dissent.

"Okay, so we all agree that we should try to remove the blocks to integral consciousness. So what are these blocks? By any other name, boomeritis. So my question is, how are these blocks operating in us, *in us*, right now? Right now!"

There was a reflective, sullen silence. The rising sun began to dim behind the clouds hugging Widener library; the remaining dregs of espresso had long gone cold; the discussion was likely over for this round. And Chloe would want to know where I had been.

"Pussy heaven? Jesus, Dad, where did you get a mouth like that?"

"All I'm saying is, part of your generation's problem is that you really don't have the sexual freedom that we did."

"This is a too-weird conversation to be having with your dad, Dad."

"From around 1960, with the invention of the birth control pill—known simply as the Pill—until around 1980, with the AIDS epidemic—those two decades were the only time in American history—the *only* time, I'm telling you—that we had almost total sexual freedom. Yessiree, one day us males just woke up and we were in pussy heaven."

I winced, turned bright red. "Well hell, Dad, good for you guys. Made Woodstock all the more fun, eh? Three days of peace, music, and tits and ass."

He looked at me askance ("Is the kid pulling my leg?"), then continued. "The reason that we had total sexual freedom is due to feminism, which is a movement that was actually invented by five males in the basement of Dartmouth in 1965." He grinned, waiting for me to bite.

"Okay, Dad, why was feminism invented by males? Is this the draft thing, the war thing?"

"No, no, but that too. No, this was purely sexual. You see, Son"—and he was grinning inside, truly enjoying the joke he was telling, and I slowly caught the contagious inner smile—"the reason was this. In this country—especially in this puritanical country—women have always held the sexual power because they decided when the men would get sex. Using this power they worked us males into an early grave—we now die a decade earlier than they do—and they used this power to amass most of the wealth in this country. Did you know that the upper 2% of the wealthiest people in this country are women?"

"Why no, Dad, I did not know that." But as usual, I knew his statistics were correct, but what was the point of all this, exactly?

"The females protected this wealth, generated through their sexual power, by a rigid institution of marriage that had enormously burden-some divorce laws. Using these legal powers, women could use sex to engineer arrangements that slowly drained wealth from males and al-lowed females to accumulate it. Marriage made the man legally re-sponsible for economically supporting his wife, punished him if he tried to divorce, and made adultery illegal to boot. This repression of male sexual patterns put sexual power almost totally in the hands of the females."

"Well, okay, Dad, that sure sounds like hell to me."

"So here is what happened. We males needed a way to do two things: one, we had to make women think that there were no differ-ences in the preferred sexual patterns between males and females—so that the women would want to have just as much mindless sex as we did, with no strings attached. And two, we needed to destroy perma-nently the bondage of marriage and divorce laws. But all of this could be accomplished in one stroke, you see, if we could convince women that they enjoyed frequent, mindless, anonymous sex, just like us males. So that's when the five of us guys at Dartmouth . . ."

"Wait, you were one of the five guys?" I cleared my throat. "You were one of the founding fathers of feminism?"

"Well, let's just say I was. Anyway, these guys realized that if men tried to convince women that 'free sex' was something that the women wanted, the women would have none of it because they never listen to us anyway. So we needed a way to make the women propose this idi-otic idea themselves, as if they had thought it up."

"Feminism."

"Bingo, my Son! So what happened was, these guys put together and actually published something they called 'The Students for Gender Eq-uity and Sexual Freedom Manifesto,' and they signed it using female names, funny names like Susan Faludi and Marilyn French and Gerda Lerner and shit like that, names that no real person would ever have. Well, what Boomer, male or female, doesn't want *freedom*? And it was full of half-baked ideas from Marxism, Simone de Beauvoir, the begin-nings of postmodernism, wacky French intellectuals like Cixous and Irigaray, you name it—oh, and Wilhelm Reich, lots and lots of Reich, the function of the orgasm and all of that, whooo weee—and it all boiled down to this, which we put in capital letters: FREEDOM FROM

REPRESSION MEANS SEXUAL FREEDOM FOR ALL. And sexual freedom for all means that you have sex with as many people as possible,
as often as possible. Makes a weird sense, huh? The problem for the
women was, it assumed that they wanted the same type of sex as us—
which was frequent, mindless, anonymous, do nothing but get your
rocks off sex—which was ridiculous, but they bought it!—hook, line,
and penis."

"Are you listening to yourself, Dad?"

"So here's the beauty part. By the time the Pill came along, a
majority of young women were convinced that they could strike
a blow for women's liberation by sleeping with as many men as possible. Do you believe that! One feminist even wrote a bestseller about
the wonderful freedom of the zipless fuck. Do you believe that! So
by the droves young women started adopting the male sexual pattern
of numerous, multiple partners. At the very least, if a man asked a
woman to sleep with him, she felt totally 'unliberated' if she said
no. Do you believe that! So starting right around the mid-sixties, like
I said, us males woke up one day and we were in pussy heaven. For
the first time in this country, ever."

"Dad, which part of this are you making up?"

"Of course, the whole thing came to a crashing halt with the AIDS
epidemic. But for those two decades, I'm telling ya, Son, we fucked our
way through a sea of women. Never happened before, probably never
will."

"And that's it? That's your great accomplishment? I thought it was
taking five times your body weight in drugs."

"Oh, my Son, what humor you have. Now listen up. Once feminism
got started, it was only a matter of time before the marriage and divorce laws came unglued. No-fault divorce was right around the corner, which meant that we could dump the wives and get more pussy
with no economic penalties. All of this, thanks to those five guys in that
basement at Dartmouth."

"Well, Dad, I'm speechless."

"Of course, the lesbian contingent almost ruined the whole damn
thing. The dykes started insisting that true feminism would never touch
a penis. Well, you can imagine how panicked we all got about *that*
one," and his eyes drifted up to the ceiling. "But fortunately it never re-

ally caught on, and the majority of females bought the whole sexual freedom shtick. What a kick, I'm telling ya."

"And I'm hearing ya. Unfortunately. So, well, what's the end of the story, Dad?"

"The feminist promise never fully materialized for men, sad to say. We wanted legalized prostitution in all states, we wanted gender equity in the draft, we wanted gender equity in work conditions—90% of work-related deaths are suffered by males—and we wanted gender equity in reproductive freedom. We got none of that, I'm sorry to say, so we still don't have gender equity in the really painful issues of life and death. But . . ." And he was silent for the longest time, and I could see that the joke, if that's what it was, was no longer funny.

"But . . .?"

"Tell you the truth, Son, I just don't know anymore. If we had real gender equity in this country it would favor the males in so many ways. . . ."

"Come on, Dad, the women have as many things to gain as the men. We could all use a little liberating, don't you think?"

"Son, I agree, you know I agree. I'm having a little fun with ya here. A little bit serious, too. But all I'm saying, the moral of all this is, well, I am starting to suspect that there are some real biological differences here, and that's why females have those laws protecting them, laws we tried to deconstruct, to transgress, to subvert. But now I don't know, I just don't know. . . ."

Abruptly his entire countenance changed. "It's so painful to me, so painful, it's so very painful . . . because . . . because . . ." His face began to tremble, and I could indeed see an enormous pain rising up from somewhere so deep inside him that it arrived on the scene largely as a stranger to his own soul, hidden even to his own heart on those dark days when interiors were acknowledged . . . and on the spot it tortured him. And it tortured me, seeing him like this, seeing something that was supposed to be so stable shaken so profoundly, a lying cheating earthquake where dependability was promised.

"Because . . . because I have devoted my entire life to equality, and now I don't even know what it means! My whole life!" More silence, more torture, more pain at the hands of this stranger. "Equality is such a slippery concept, don't you think? Because now, every time I hear anybody demand 'equality,' I always ask myself, 'equal' according to just whose values?" The tears went their lonely way down his face, leaving a trail of embarrassment so deep that he never really looked me in the eyes again, ever.

A year later they had The Fight. A year after that, a no-fault divorce. Mom went on to teach yoga; Dad went on to marry a very young woman who became sort of a big sister to me, though we still don't know each other all that well.

"Today is the last day of seminar II," said Dr. Morin, to grateful applause. "Yes, yes, this is the last of the 'what's wrong' discussions. Then tomorrow we begin with the integral solutions!" Even more applause.

"The Integral Solutions"—I kept repeating the phrase in my mind, over and over and over again, as if a life raft had been thrown me in the midst of the drowning season. Only as Morin yelled out, "But first, the problems!" did my mind temporarily reconnect with present reality, such as it was.

"*The new paradigm*," Morin moaned. "Has ever a phrase been more often uttered by a generation? In so many ways, the idea of a 'new paradigm' summarizes both the best and the worst of the Boomers. Best, in that it captures this generation's endearing—and often successful—attempts to usher in the new and creative. Worst, in that implying that there are no facts, only interpretations, it became the home of every boomeritis impulse imaginable. But one thing is clear: they say there is a new paradigm on the horizon, and the Boomers have it."

Scott and me and a field of naked female bodies, a billowing, flowing, waving field of Tits & Ass as far as the monological eye can see. Latent homosexuality aside, the prospect was exorbitantly inviting. "Come on," Scott says, "let's get started."

"Scott, did you know that we have this freedom because of five guys in the basement of Dartmouth?"

"Very funny, Wilber. Actually, we have this freedom because of the new paradigm."

"But I thought that only the Boomers have the new paradigm."

"Well, now it's our turn, yes? So just look at the flowing waves of all that flesh! 'Oh beautiful, for spacious skies, for amber waves of grain. . . .' But who gives a shit about waves of grain? Endless waves of T & A—they ought to put *that* in the national anthem!"

"Ladies and Gentleman, Dr. Margaret Carlton." She walked on stage as the day's first slide went up: "Literary Theory."

"We have seen that many of the profound insights of postmodernism—such as the importance of pluralism, contextualism, and interpretation—were taken to extremes by boomeritis and the mean green meme, with results that ranged from comical to criminal to tragic. Few, however, were more entertaining than literary theory."

"This doesn't sound entertaining so far, Kim," I whispered.

"Oh, it will be, believe me. It gets absolutely hilarious."

"Really? But this doesn't sound like part of 'the new paradigm.'"

"It's all part of the new paradigm, that's the funny part. You'll see."

"In previous generations *literary theory* was dedicated to trying to find ways to understand the meaning of a text—for example, what is the meaning of *Macbeth*? of *Howard's End*? of *Remembrance of Things Past*? In other words, trying to find the truth of a subject matter, trying to understand great works of art. Needless to say, in the Bermuda triangle of boomeritis—into which many truths fly, none return—literary theory would no longer be the search for such matters. By the calculus of narcissism, finding *greatness* in previous works of art would *subtract* from the greatness of Boomers. And therefore, what was required was a way, not to focus on the greatness of any work of art, but a way to proclaim the greatness of those viewing the art!"

Carlton began to smile. "Seems like a tall order, yes? Not for boomeritis, my friends. So, enter *hermeneutics*, or the art and science of interpretation. Hermeneutics is simply the study of the various ways to interpret and understand a text. But boomeritis gave it the necessary narcissistic spin: since all art works require, at some point, an audience in order to be seen and known, then, as John Passmore summarized the situation, 'The proper point of reference in discussing works of art is an interpretation it sets going in an audience; that interpretation—or the class of such interpretations—is the work of art, whatever the artist had in mind in creating it. Indeed, *the interpreter, not the artist, creates the art work.*'

"The interpreter, not the artist, creates the art work! And there we have it. As the critic Catherine Belsey put it: 'No longer parasitic on an already given literary text, criticism constructs its object, produces the work.' Not the artist, but the reader or critic—in other words, the Boomer—actually creates the art work!" Carlton smiled even harder.

"Which, of course, comes as news to most artists." The audience laughed congenially. "But the partial truths of hermeneutics became a platform from which the *viewer* as the *creator* of art gained, and still has, enormous currency. So let's just say it in plain English: my ego creates the art work! How amazing I must be to have created the great works of art that silly, previous generations ascribed to Michelangelo, Shakespeare, Rembrandt, Dostoyevsky, Tolstoy. I am astonished, *astonished*, at my brilliance, aren't you?" Several in the audience groaned in apparent recognition.

"In the narcissism that creates its own reality, literary theory—which is known simply as 'Theory,' as if to underscore the belief that there are no others of import—was made to order. Unanchored in facts, disconnected from evidence—for remember, there are no facts, only interpretations—an omnipotent power of creation was placed in the hands of the literary critic's ego. Literary 'Theory' was boomeritis looking at itself in the mirror, a double dose of my baby's love that rendered facts unseeable. But what a wonderful image was reflected as Narcissus gazed into the pond: the critic, not the artist, creates the art work. We can see again the enormous advantage that Theory would have for those who lacked the talent to make art. In the past, in order to get credit for producing art, you had to actually create it; now all you had to do was criticize it."

Paul Oakenfold spins "Mystica," "Bliss," "Mantra 09," and the thump thump thumping slams a brain too exhausted to complain, as Chloe's flesh swirls in time to the cascading rhythm of the backbeat slap.

"And by the way, Ken, where have you been? Have you been naughty? Making love to the sky, perhaps?"

"Who, me? Oh no, no, just out, you know, walking around and stuff."

I pull out Kodwo Eshun's *More Brilliant Than the Sun* and start to enter World 4, Mutant Textures of Jazz and Anachronic Cybernetics.

Chloe slams on *Groove*, and with John Digweed's "Heaven Scent" soaring to a natural peak, she begins a wild, vibrant striptease, moving her flesh in ways that are calculated to move mine.

"Ken, you've got to try this . . ." Crissy D and Lady G, Girls Like Us go thump thump thump . . ., and "Ken, you've got to try this."

My weary mind and body look in vain for the energy to follow. It's just more of the same, more of the same, more of the dreary, dreadful, dismal same.

"Somehow there is something new, right around the corner," says the old man's voice inside my head.

"I am not suggesting that the artists themselves escaped boomeritis," Carlton continued. "In many cases, far from it. I will not make a long-drawn-out argument for this, but simply mention what everybody knows, and suggest a reason for it. It is generally agreed that one of the main characteristics of postmodern art—in addition to its irony, its sardonic surfaces, its attempts to subvert and transgress—is its unrelenting *self-reflexivity*. The artist, no longer content to simply depict a significant situation, must insert himself into the art work. If you are making a film, film yourself making the film. If you are writing a novel, include passages about what goes through your head when you write it. If you are painting, include yourself in the painting somehow: perhaps blatantly, but perhaps more subtly, by drawing attention to the medium itself—include scratches on the film, shake the camera while you hold it, show yourself editing the art as part of the art, have the camera trained on you as you present the real news. But in whatever way possible, get your ego into the picture!

"Thus, for example, if your name is Ken Wilber,"—I bolted upright in my seat—"then write a novel in which one of the main characters is actually called Ken Wilber." Why did she use my name? "The arrogant narcissism of such a move is undeniable, but it's to be expected." Why did she say that? "We call this the Philip Roth move." Then why not use fucking Philip Roth as a fucking example? I mean, I haven't even met Carlton.

"In part, this self-reflexivity is an important exploration of the worldview of pluralistic relativism, where every subject can become an object to itself, so that, at this level, an almost endless reflexivity is built into the cosmos: the world is an infinite hall of mirrors, and many postmodern artists, spotting this reflexivity, managed wonderfully to portray it.

"But in the hands of boomeritis, a postformal perspective was once again hijacked for a preformal, narcissistic purpose: whatever else art is, it is first and foremost the display of my own self, which I will insert into the art for all the world to see, and appreciate, and applaud. The very structures of postformal cognition, we have been arguing, make it a magnet for emotional narcissism, and much of the last two decades of postmodern art stands as stark testament to just that fact."

There was shifting and murmuring in the audience, with the now-standard mixture of smiles, coughs, anxious applause, and occasional taunts. A few people stared at me, a living example of boomeritis, but for what reason I could not comprehend. I sank down in my seat even further.

"Which reminds me," Carlton added. "Have you seen that book by Ted Nichols called *Magic Words That Bring You Riches*? He has gone through millions of dollars of research, and he reports that the two words in a book title that will guarantee the most sales are *you* and *free*. The reason, of course, is that boomeritis is epidemic—'Nobody tells me what to do!'—so why not sell to it?"

Kim leaned over. "Well, that is just fucking pathetic, don't you think?"

"I'm with you, Kim."

Up went slide #2, "Transgressing the Boundaries," and sweet little Margaret Carlton started laughing out loud.

"I'm sorry, I can't help it. This one is so funny to me." She composed herself, calmed down, then broke into convulsive laughter again. "Sorry, really, so sorry."

"Okay, okay," she mumbled to herself. "Now, okay. Many strands of literary boomeritis came to a riotous conclusion in the notorious Sokal affair," and she burst out laughing again.

"What's going on, Kim?"

"You'll see," she said, grinning.

"Okay! Alan Sokal, a professor of physics at New York University, submitted a paper to the influential journal *Social Text*, which is one of the many bastions of boomeritis. The title of the paper really says it all, replete with many of the catch words we have already seen: 'Transgressing the Boundaries: Toward a Transformative Hermeneutics of Quantum Gravity.'" A huge grin, but Carlton soldiered on.

"In this paper, Sokal asserts, among other things—and these are more or less direct quotes, rife with the requisite jargon—that quantum field theory proves the assertions of Lacanian psychoanalysis, that the axiom of equality in mathematical set theory is analogous to the homonymous concept in feminist politics, that all realities are socially constructed, and that this will allow us to transgress any and all restrictive boundaries. The article was accepted for publication." She took three deep breaths; smoothed her hair.

"As is now well known, the article was a hoax," and Carlton broke out laughing again, but quickly pushed through her mirth-stained tears. "Sokal wrote it as a parody of literary boomer-speak. He intentionally included the loopiest of assertions, but couched in the lingua franca of progressive boomeritis. And I quote: 'We can see hints of an emancipatory mathematics in the multidimensional and nonlinear logic of fuzzy systems theory; but this approach is still heavily marked by its origins in the crisis of late-capitalist production relations.' But there is a way out: 'In this way the infinite-dimensional invariance group erodes the distinction between observer and observed; the constants of Euclid and of Newton, formerly thought to be constant and universal, are now perceived in their ineluctable historicity; and the putative observer becomes fatally de-centered, disconnected from any epistemic link to a space-time point that can no longer be defined by geometry alone.'" Carlton looked up. "*Social Text* published it on the spot.

"The conclusion, it seems, is that virtually anything that promises to transgress the boundaries is music to Boomer ears. The single word most common to boomeritis anything is *transformation*—we will transform the entire world!—transformative education, transformative dialogue, transformative business, transformative high colonics." The audience laughed. "Hundredth monkeys of the world unite! You have nothing to lose but your humility." Then grimaced and groaned. "So Sokal skillfully worked all that in, along with the necessary word *transgressing*.

"But all of this transgressing, subverting, and deconstructing has become a completely self-enclosed system, with its own vocabulary (indecipherable to absolutely everybody, including Boomers), and with no apparent way out—first, because boomeritis recognizes no objective truth which would otherwise correct what are obviously colossal blunders; second, because it appears to be the airtight home of a highly individualistic self with an intensely narcissistic investment; and third, because it has become an economic necessity, a closed system upon which the majority of Boomers in academia, both mainstream and especially alternative, depend for their economic existence."

And with that conclusion, delivered with a clunking over-seriousness apparently meant as an apologetic counterblast to her previous, giggling frivolity, Margaret Carlton walked off the stage, holding her sides as if to prevent another outbreak of uncontrollable laughter.

I am making love to Joan, blending with the sky, floating in an eternity of painful blissful release. And just like on Ecstasy, an orgasm would be a major step down, a horrible loss of bliss. This is third tier in the flesh, and surely this is what it will perpetually be like when human consciousness makes the hyperlink to crystal Silicon City: quantum computing, microphotonics, optical luminous ecstasy. . . . The result will be third-tier silicon awakening, the ecstatic-blissful-bodiless thrill of digital transcendental mind rushing at the speed of light to its own cosmic consciousness, the shocking jolting realization residing at the edge of the universe.

"Ken," **Joan says,** *"let's just get to second tier first, okay?"*

Lesa Powell walked onstage as slide #3 appeared. "Poststructuralism über Alles," it menacingly announced.

"I realize that many critics will have a hard time believing that we at IC have incorporated a great deal of structural and poststructural thinking into our own work, since they will tend to assume that this prolonged criticism of extreme postmodernism means that all of us want nothing to do with postmodernism at all. On the contrary, I and many of my colleagues have explicitly identified ourselves with constructive postmodernism, and will continue to do so. We are criticizing, again, the extreme and deconstructive postmodernism that, bereft of second-tier integral constructions, lets pluralism run riot as the mean green meme.

"But both structuralism and poststructuralism have instabilities that unfortunately make them primary targets of boomeritis, and poststructuralism is by far the most troublesome. For those unfamiliar, a brief history:"—and I realized, with some dismay, that Powell's brain would probably leave me in the dust again. Oh well, Kim would explain it to me over the break.

"Right, Kim?"

"What's that?"

"You'll explain this to me over the break?"

"It's not that bad today, honest. Maybe ten minutes of difficult stuff, tops. Just let it float through you. You'll get the point at the end, I promise."

"Swell."

"The school of structuralism—associated with such names as Saussure, Lévi-Strauss, Roland Barthes, early Foucault, and Jacques Lacan—was in some ways a profoundly important move to incorporate *systematic second-tier constructions* into social theory. We have already seen—with Saussure and the 'bark of a dog'—that the meaning of a word depends on the systemic context and the *total structure* in which the word finds itself: hence, the school of *structuralism*, which attempts to explain how these holistic structures are crucial in creating social realities. There were many problems with its formulations, however (such as the alleged ahistorical nature of structures), that prevented it from becoming a solid discipline. But some of its original concepts were taken up—largely by Derrida, Lyotard, and to some extent Foucault, among others—and turned into 'poststructuralism,' which was actually a mixture of integral insight and a *throwback* to the green meme and its anarchic pluralism—which was precisely why it caught on like wildfire. With only 2% of the population at second tier, and 20% at green, you can imagine which had the larger number of followers! Because poststructuralism spoke to that 20% which was green, and not the 2% at integral, poststructuralism was set to spread like gangbusters. Which is exactly what happened."

"So guess what, boys and girls?" Stuart had said yesterday at lunch.

"Darla showed up at my concert last night, which felt like swallowing a dozen neon hummingbirds. So it looks like she has reentered the atmosphere."

"You've got to be kidding," I said. "I thought Darla went back to her fiancé—which sent you into that devastating . . . whatever it was. So what happened?"

"Apparently it's over between them. She's meeting me in Milwaukee on Wednesday, and we're making plans beyond that, too."

"Making plans beyond that too," Chloe helpfully repeated.

I turned and looked steadily at Stuart, and sure enough, that "God-it's-great-to-be-alive" look dopily radiated from his face.

"Good fucking grief," said Jonathan, noticing the same drugged grin perched where Stuart's face used to be. "What has happened to the piercingly obnoxious, tell-it-like-it-is Stuart we all once knew and loved? The Stuart that sang about cancer tumors, and carpet bombing, and being disemboweled, and boinking a hooker in Amsterdam? Oh, sure, every now and then you'd toss in a song about finding God, but it was mostly about giving the Devil its due." Jonathan reached over, grabbed him by the lapels, and screamed, "Who are you and what have you done with our Stuart?!"

"There goes another perfectly good artist," Chloe lamented.

Stuart smiled contentedly. "The week before Darla came back into my life, I had sex with five different girls in seven days, part of a recording project I wanted to finish before I went celibate."

"Wait a minute, wait a minute," Jonathan pounced. "Sex with five girls, part of a recording project?"

"Yes, part of a recording project."

"What did you record? These poor girls screaming for you to get off them? I can hear it now: 'Call 911, somebody please call 911, get this pig off of me!' Great CD, Stuart."

"It was part of a project called 'Observance of States,' and then I was going celibate for a year."

"Going celibate because . . . ?"

"Because sex makes you crazy, and if you're a performer you end up sleeping with somebody at every gig, and the women always say, 'No, that's fine, I understand this is a one-night thing, I can handle it,' and they can't, they always can't, because I don't care what the women say, they are not cut out for mindless anonymous fucking sex, and they end up getting hurt and I end up feeling like a total scumbag, and I've had it."

"So you boinked five of them as a fond goodbye, is that it?" said Jonathan, smiling.

"With Darla, it's so different. My life stands at attention when I'm with her."

"Apparently that's not all," Chloe added.

"It's just that she wakes me up! And so now I'm unsure about no-sex. Because with her it's Easter Theater."

"So by my calculations you were celibate for what, about eight hours?" Jonathan grinned.

"I spent eleven months last year celibate. It's really interesting. But now I'm revisiting the nuclear mystery of meeting Darla."

We all sat silent for the longest time.

"So, okay. But before that, tell us about the sex with five girls. I mean, what on earth was that?" Scott asked, suddenly awake.

"Stir it up, tear it down, deconstruct, deconstruct." Powell's brain bore down on the topic, singeing the atmosphere.

"Both structuralism and poststructuralism tended to emphasize—actually, overemphasize—the verbal/linguistic dimension of reality (for this mess, we have Lévi-Strauss to thank). The linguistic dimension is often called simply 'the Sign,' and both structuralism and poststructuralism pledged allegiance to the Sign. But *structuralism* by itself was unsuited to the Boomer student protests—from Paris to Berkeley—because it had so emphasized the all-powerful nature of linguistic structures (and the Sign) that it appeared there was simply no way to *rebel* against the established structures. This is exactly why the rioting Paris students scrawled 'Down with Structuralism!' on Parisian walls. Very similar to the American students screaming 'Fight the system!'

"So, *structuralism* was taken to mean any conventional system at all, and thus *post*-structuralism was made to order for . . . what? You guessed it: subvert, transgress, deconstruct. Here's the technical run-down from a standard textbook in the subject, but it is fairly obvious what is going on: 'What the Post-Structuralists invoke as an alternative to structuralism is an even more sign-ish version of the Sign. Characteristically, they distinguish between two possible modes of functioning for the Sign. On the one hand, there is the conventional mode where the Sign works rigidly and despotically and predictably. This is the mode that the Structuralists analyze'"—Powell yelled "Boooooooo!" and grinned. "'On the other hand, there is an unconventional mode where the Sign works creatively and anarchically and irresponsibly. This is the mode that represents the real being of the Sign'—Yaaaaaaay!" she yelled, then finished reading: "'And when we are true to the real being of the Sign, we find that it subverts the socially controlled system of meaning, and, ultimately, socially controlled systems of every kind.'"

Powell looked up. "Pretty obvious now, isn't it? The bad Sign is conventional, repressing, stultifying; the good Sign is anarchic, anti-conventional, disruptive, subverting, transgressing, yada yada yada. . . .

"Richard Harlan, whose summary that is, says that this subverting and deconstructing involved, and I quote: 'a priority of the Anti-Social Sign over the Social Sign. This priority is the common theme of all Post-Structuralists—of Derrida, Kristeva, the later Barthes, the genealogical Foucault, Deleuze and Guattari, and Baudrillard.'" Powell looked at the audience. "Harlan is absolutely right in that assessment. And precisely because the Anti-Social Sign did *not* distinguish between the Pre-Social and the Post-Social, it became the happy home of a rampant boomeritis and the newspeak of the mean green meme. Under the guise of post-structuralism, my pre-structural impulses could run riot, and whether the riots were in Berkeley or in Paris, the vast majority were impelled by preconventional, not postconventional, urges, as narcissism and a bloated ego clamored to rule the day."

And then for the first time that I could remember in this seminar, Lesa Powell laughed out loud. She seemed to actually relax, visibly uncoil. It was as if some sort of sound barrier had been penetrated with a great kaboom, and now the flight was smooth and easy. Maybe even a little fun.

"Geez, Kim, she actually smiled."

"Powell is one of the easiest-going people you'll ever meet. The first sessions are hard for her because she carries so much of the intellectual heavy guns. From now on it's easier for her, and she always does that, just visibly relaxes, her whole body unwinds in front of everybody. It's kinda sweet, actually."

"Sweeter than you can know," as Chloe's naked body turns into Joan's, and I am caught between two worlds of flesh, both of them electrically alluring. Blissful radiant energy bubbles up my spine, iridescent neurons shimmer through cyberspace in a digital infusion of transmaterial delight. I press harder and harder into flesh, it gives way more and more into vast emptiness, gateway to infinity.

"And now the time is fast approaching," the voice inside my head says.

"The fact that poststructuralism spoke directly to the green meme and to boomeritis was still not enough to insure its wholesale adoption." Powell relaxed even more, and for almost a full minute she smiled at the audience.

"The jargon of poststructuralism is so *incomprehensible* that it needed to be framed and marketed in a way that would make this major weakness appear a significant virtue," and she began gently laughing. "To Derrida goes the credit of inventing the idea that the more incomprehensible the writing was, the more it was profoundly important. The reason is that, as Harlan noted above, the 'real being' of the Sign is anarchic and irresponsible and anti-social: thus, if you are writing clear prose, you are obviously under the false being of the Sign: you are not subverting, deconstructing, and being nearly obnoxious enough: you are caught in the system, you are not tearing it down. As Luc Ferry and Alain Renaut—two very perceptive French critics of their countrymen's shenanigans—point out, 'The "philosophists" of the '68 period gained their greatest success through accustoming their readers and listeners to the belief that *incomprehensibility* is a sign of *greatness* and that the thinker's silence before the incongruous demand for meaning was not proof of weakness but the indication of endurance in the presence of the Unsayable.'" Like Carlton before her, Powell began laughing out loud, almost uncontrollably, but unlike Carlton, quickly pulled herself together.

"Derrida devotee Zavarzadeh drew the obvious conclusion: clear writing is a sign of a reactionary." This time many in the audience laughed with her. "Zavarzadeh trashed a critic of Derrida's because of 'his unproblematic prose and the clarity of his presentation, which are conceptual tools of conservatism.' Oh dear!" Powell laughed. "Of course, all that this really does, once again, is allow individuals completely lacking in talent—or even in the capacity to write a clear sentence—to claim greatness, even a moral superiority!

"Well, the morally superior prose began streaming out of academia in a torrent, as if from a high-pressure hose. Here is a typical sentence, from John Guilloy's *Cultural Capital*," Powell announced through a face-slashing grin. "Here we go, and I quote: 'A politics presuming the ontological indifference of all minority social identities as defining oppressed or dominated groups, a politics in which differences are sublimated in the constitution of a minority identity (the identity politics which is increasingly being questioned within feminism itself) can recover the differences between social identities only on the basis of common and therefore commensurable experiences of marginalization, which experiences in turn yield a political practice that consists largely of affirming the identities specific to those experiences.'"

Powell looked up. "I was thinking the same thing this morning at breakfast." Several in the audience were laughing at this point, jostling around in their seats. Whatever postmodern prose crime they might have committed was apparently lame by comparison.

"Some sentences are short and snappy, but still retain the all-important incomprehensibility. 'This melodrama parsed the transgressive hybridity of un-narrativized representative bodies back into recognizable heterovisual codes.' Thank God! Others of course are longer. 'Previous exercises in influence study depended upon a topographical model of reallocatable poetic images, distributed more or less equally within canonical poems, each part of which expressively totalized the entelechy of the entire tradition. But Bloom now understands this cognitive map of interchangeable organic wholes to be criticism's repression of the poetry's will to overcome time's anteriority'—and believe me, time's anteriority is exactly what you want poetry to overcome." Even those who disagreed with Powell found it hard not to laugh, or at least grin, sort of.

"But some sentences are so overflowing with moral superiority they simply must go on forever. The following is a *single* sentence; look closely and you will see most of the themes we have discussed: 'Indeed dialectical critical realism may be seen under the aspect of Foucauldian strategic reversal—of the unholy trinity of Parmenidean/Platonic/Aristotelean provenance; of the Cartesian-Lockean-Humean-Kantian paradigm, of foundationalisms (in practice, fedeistic foundationalisms) and irrationalisms (in practice, capricious exercises of the will-to-power or some other ideologically and/or psycho-somatically buried source) new and old alike; of the primordial failing of western philosophy, ontological monovalence, and its close ally, the epistemic fallacy with its ontic dual; of the analytic problematic laid down by Plato, which Hegel'—the bastard!—'served only to replicate in his actualist monovalent analytic reinstatement in transfigurative reconciling dialectical connection, while in his hubristic claims for absolute idealism he inaugurated the Comtean, Kierkegaardian, and Nietzschean eclipses of reason, replicating the fundaments of positivism through its transmutation route to the superidealism of a Baudrillard.'

Through Powell's own peels of laugher she concluded, "The jacket blurb assures us that this is the author's 'most accessible book to date.'" A few people were laughing so hard they were almost crying, stomping their feet, applauding, as if the entire tension of this ordeal could be released with one outrageous laugh.

Powell smiled, waved to everybody, and began ambling off the podium; but then she paused, turned, and moved briskly to the front of the stage. "Dr. Carlton opened this topic, so let me make a few comments to finish it. Given all that we have learned in the last week, how would you go about constructing the perfect postmodern novel? Think about it."

I glanced at Kim, then over at Stuart and Jonathan. I hate tests.

Powell smiled. "Unfortunately, it would be almost impossible to pull it off—to write the great postmodern novel—because so many seemingly conflicting items would have to be included, reflecting the mess that postmodernism is. There are at least seven items that I can think of, reflecting seven of the most basic tenets of postmodernism itself.

"For starters, since postmodernism is basically a mood of criticism, the novel itself, to be truly postmodern, would have to criticize postmodernism. But in order to do that, the novel would have to *exemplify* everything that it criticized. That would be the real trick, to write a novel that embodied everything it attacked.

"For example, as Carlton mentioned, since postmodernism is endlessly, often sickeningly, self-reflexive, make sure a main character is named after you, and by all means make the novel about you in every way that you can, while constantly criticizing the pathetic narcissism of it all. Yes?" I scrunched down in my seat, glanced furtively left and right.

"Two, because there is supposedly no difference between fact and fiction, according to postmodernism, then the novel should have some characters that are factual and some that are purely fictional—and don't bother to identify which is which. Include real references, make some of them up, mix and match, what the hell. For the factual characters, you might even have them write some of the accounts of their own experiences, and simply cut those into the narrative—since there is supposedly no real author, who cares? We call this the Jeff Koons looney tunes move.

"Three, implicit in postmodernism is the belief that all white males are egregious criminals and idiots; therefore, make sure every white male character has some sort of questionable behavior lurking in his background—you know, he's a wife beater, or sleeping with a student, or maybe he's accused of rape or murder, that sort of thing." I glanced at Kim; she stared straight ahead.

"Four, because postmodernism is basically about Theory—and leaves out any real people, real places, real events, real art, real life—then the novel itself would have to be essentially of and about Theory. Theory, Theory, Theory. And trust me, that would make it one of the most breathtakingly boring novels ever written outside of Russia. The Theory part, anyway. This means that all landscapes and rich, luscious descriptions of surroundings, people, places, all disappear into a disembodied stream of verbal vomit.

"Similarly, the novel would not be great literature, but more like cut-and-paste entertainment, an MTV pastiche of fleeting images and scenes—no high-brow literary greatness, just low- and middle-brow pop culture (because we are so caring and compassionate and commonplace, no nasty elitism here, right?). But for heaven's sake, at least try to make the pastiche part entertaining, given the weight of boring Theory the poor novel will be dragging around.

"Five, this especially means that all the characters would have to be flat and two-dimensional. Not one-dimensional, but not three-dimensional either. This is perfectly in keeping with the postmodern credo that there are no depths, only surfaces, and thus, for your characters, the words 'flat' and 'two-dimensional' must apply. Flatland characters for the perfect flatland novel, yes?"

"God, Kim, that's exactly how I feel—flat and two-dimensional."

"Me too, Ken, me too. It's as if my life—*my entire life*—is trapped inside the postmodern novel that Powell is describing. It's as if my life isn't my own—as if I'm not even the author of my own actions, my own feelings, my own desires. It's as if the whole notion of authorship itself is evaporating. I am being written by some self-reflexive postmodern twit, and this is my life. Jesus, where's the Prozac?"

"Six, deconstructive postmodernism, as we said, is mostly a negative attitude of cranky criticism, not a positive contribution, and consequently much postmodern art, when it manages to be vaguely positive, often does so by including—stealing—elements from past art forms (since it can't think of anything new itself). 'Rip-off' is the word I'm looking for. Steal anything—jokes are good: borrow a little from Steve Martin, Dennis Miller, Joan Rivers, Rodney Dangerfield, Eddie Izzard, Janeane Garafolo, George S. Kaufman, *Hedwig and the Angry Inch*, who cares? Remember Woody Allen's *Stardust Memories*? 'Did you do that as an homage to that artist?' 'An homage? No, we stole it outright.' Now that's the pomo spirit! Anyway, your novel should include all sorts of half-baked 'homages' to the past. It could be anything, really—maybe make it a *bildungsroman*, that's loopy enough to fit the bill.

"Seven, if you ever manage to pull it off and get all seven of these items into a novel, then, in keeping with the demand for self-reflexivity, make sure you find a way to point out in the novel that the novel itself has just pulled off the great postmodern feat. This would amount to bragging, thus earning you extra points for exemplifying boomeritis.

"Personally, I'm convinced that this is too much to achieve in one work—especially the demand to exemplify everything it criticizes—and that is why the great postmodern novel will never be written. But if somebody ever managed to pull it off, it would indeed be a heartbreaking work of staggering genius."

"Come on, Ken, let's watch a video," Chloe says.

"Which one?"

"Debbie Does Dallas, the director's cut."

"Say Chloe, let's not."

"*But Ken,*" Joan says, and I am alarmed that both Chloe and Joan are lying naked next to me. "*She's right about that one.*"

"What one?"

"*Evolution will never leave bodies behind, evolution will never abandon the flesh.*"

"Oh yes it will," I protest.

"*Ken, dear soul, look at me,*" Joan says.

"No way, I'm not going to look at you. I know that trick, that sky eye thingie trick. I start looking into your eyes, then all of a sudden I'm in some no-boundary expanse of bliss that is supposed to be my real Self but is probably just some testicular hormonal traffic jam, a 50-car pile up in my limbic system. No way, forget it."

"*Ken, silicon consciousness will transcend and include flesh, it will not leave it behind. Human flesh will be transfigured, lit from within by its own radiant awakening. There is an Omega Point, Ken, you are definitely right, an Omega for carbon and silicon. But it's the same Omega, Ken, one and the same Omega. Listen to me, Ken, you must wake up now. Ken, listen to me, you must wake up.*"

I jolted in my chair. Kim was staring at me.

"You okay?"

"Yeah, sure, fine. Who's up next?"

"Why, it's Jooooooan . . . ooooh . . . ooooh. . . . "

"Stop it, Kim."

"Does Chloe know what you're up to?"

"I'm not up to anything, Kim."

Slide #4, "Spontaneous Healing."

"What all of those examples have in common—from Theory to poststructuralism to the social construction of reality—is an overestimation of the importance and power of the finite ego," Hazelton began. "That will continue to be a theme in the following examples, since it is the core of boomeritis. But again, so many of these endeavors have such good intentions and decent motives, before they get tripped up in their own shadows. Nowhere is this more obvious than in the field of health care." I let out a long, dreamy sigh; Kim muffled a laugh.

"Cases of profound spontaneous healing, such as complete remission in advanced cancer, are extremely rare, with estimates placing them around 1 in 10,000. Few as these cases are, they nonetheless suggest some remarkable healing powers of the human body; we would be foolish not to investigate them further. But injected with the emotional dynamite of boomeritis, the market in books purporting to disclose the magic of spontaneous healing has exploded, with all of them strongly implying that the complete remission of any disease is as common as finding bad writing in poststructuralism. As one of its proponents explains: 'You cause your sickness, you can cure it.' The omnipotent ego again rules.

"There is a downside corollary: 'Where love is not, illness flourishes.' In other words, illness demonstrates that you are not a good, loving person. The worse the illness, the more unspeakably horrible you have been. Because the ego creates all reality, then a bad ego—an unloving, unkind ego—creates all illness." Hazelton paused for a moment while the lights dimmed for more slide presentations.

"I had a friend," Jonathan whispered, and the tone in his voice made me immediately turn and look at him. He appeared on the verge of tears. "A really, really good friend." And I thought I knew what he wanted to say. As well as I knew Jonathan, as much as I admired him under all his bluster, as much as I loved him, really—he would never say if he was or wasn't gay. This made no sense to me, because I don't think he had any other or better friend to whom he might have confided. What made even less sense was that I loved him all the more for it, as if he had, not an embarrassment about being gay, but rather, way down deep, a shyness of the soul. On the other hand, I often had the feeling that if I asked Jonathan outright, he would have easily talked about it. The silence was more . . . , it was as if Jonathan resented with all his being having to even mention the fact that he was gay: did I have to go around talking about being straight? Did people have to wonder, Wow, is he straight or what? Did I have to explain my body's ways to anybody and everybody who raised an eyebrow? Why should he? The fact that he and I never had to talk about it seemed to be the proof, for Jonathan, of how strong our friendship was.

"So this friend . . . ," and tears continued to well up, dampening his whisper. "Well, he had AIDS, he died, he died you know, he died." My eyes started getting moist as well; I looked down at the floor. "So the last thing he said was, his last words were, 'How bad must I be?'" And with that Jonathan began trembling as he attempted to muffle his crying, a silent slow convulsion that sent his body shuddering.

"Nobody is denying that thoughts and psychological attitudes have a substantial, sometimes decisive, effect on physical illness, as psychoneuroimmunology has demonstrated. Several of my colleagues have discussed this important topic at length. Evidence suggests that, depending on the disease, the psychological component might constitute between 2% to 20% of the cause of the illness. But most of the diseases once thought to be largely psychogenic—such as tuberculosis and ulcers and colitis—are now known to be caused largely by physical factors, such as bacteria and diet. But once the physical causes are addressed, the psychological component of cure can become rather significant, accounting for perhaps 10% to 30% of the healing process.

"But boomeritis, anxious that illness brought on by causes outside of its control might weaken its omnipotence, must make the psychological component of illness the *sole* component of illness. Thus, you are sick because you are unloving. The ego creates all reality, the ego can cure all reality: narcissism reigns."

Hazelton paused and looked around the audience. "This claim, of course, is structurally identical to the literary Theory claim that the reader creates the art, or the claim that all reality is a social construction, or the claim that there are no facts, only interpretations, and so on—for what *all* of them have in common is boomeritis, the omnipotent ego—and it is boomeritis that helps explain their epidemic embrace." She turned and walked slowly back to the podium.

"This painfully guilt-inducing claim—you have created your illness—actually benefits only one group: those selling the books making the claim, who happen—for the moment—to be healthy people who generate a great deal of money and power by telling sick people how to think. As for those who are actually sick, this notion simply acts to instill in them an enormous amount of 'New Age guilt,' which, if anything, will further depress their immune systems and help to make them even sicker."

For the first time that I could remember, Jonathan put his head on my shoulder, trying to hide his tears. My natural inclination was to put my arm around him, but this surely would have made it worse; I looked resolutely ahead and tried to find the open sky, the loving forgiving sheltering sky, that Joan was talking out of. I turned to say something to Jonathan, but he had gotten up and was quickly, quietly walking out.

"Of course, done appropriately, an engagement of the psychological and spiritual aspects of illness and healing can be a very powerful and wonderful tool. I believe these types of psychosomatic techniques—including psychotherapy, group therapy, visualization, affirmation, meditation, and prayer—should be an indispensable part of every integral medical treatment. But they can only be effective to the extent they are approached realistically, which means, taken out of the hands of boomeritis, which, as always, takes an important topic and blows it up to extremes via an unquenchable narcissism, with the resultant harm outweighing the undeniable good."

"Lunch!" yelled Morin with a huge grin, as he abruptly walked out on stage. Hazelton made a small curtsy to the crowd and, amidst appreciative applause, quickly retired. Morin looked at Kim with the sweetest expression.

"He looks very happy, Kim," I said, and she smiled.

"I think he wants to ask me something," she confided.

"You mean, *something*? Like the big one?"

"Like, with this ring I thee."

"Wow, aren't you excited? I mean, that's great! What are you going to say?"

"Probably yes."

"Probably? What does that mean?"

"Ken?" There was a soft tap on my shoulder, and I turned around to notice Hazelton standing behind me.

"Yeow!" I blurted out.

"Perhaps I need someone to translate."

"Why, no no, ha ha, of course not."

"Would you care to have lunch with me?" she said softly, so only I could hear.

"Care to have lunch, care to have lunch, there's the question, or certainly one of them, although on the other hand, but then, why even mention that, right?, which is to say . . . "

"Is that a yes or a no?"

"No no, it's a yes yes."

Hazelton scrunched her nose, as if she were seriously reconsidering.

"*Yes*, that's a yes, a real live yes indeedy. . . . "

"Okay, Ken, it's okay. Scarpelli's, around the corner."

"So how do you think the seminar is going?"

"Um, well." I was determined to talk like an actual human being. "Good, good."

"Care to elaborate, dear soul?"

"Dr., um, Joan, Dr. Joan, no just Joan, I know, I know."

"The seminar?"

"Well, okay, here's the thing. As you know, I'm working over at the AI Lab. We're racing to produce some sort of Artificial Intelligence that might do two things—possess a truly creative intelligence, and become genuinely self-aware. And then try to kill itself. Well no, I'm kidding, well not really, well anyway, there are some real stumbling blocks, things having to do mostly with background contexts and billions of everyday details that just cannot all be programmed." I took a breath. "But projections show very clearly that in about 30 years we will have machines a million times more powerful than today's computers, and this will definitely produce human-level computing power. So my question has been, ever since I heard your first lecture on the evolution of consciousness, my question has been, Will the Bots evolve?"

"The Bots?"

"The Bots, the robotic beings. Will their consciousness evolve, like ours does?"

"Isomorphic evolution."

"I'm sorry?"

"Yes, the idea is that consciousness will be molded by the matrix that gives rise to it. So whether carbon or silicon is the matrix, many of the forms will be similar in both worlds, because carbon and silicon are both children of the same universe run by the same evolution."

"Right, I had gotten that far myself. But I guess my question is, what will be the relation of these two worlds—the carbon human and the silicon machine? Will they—"

"Tell you what, dear one, I've got a friend I want you to meet. Dan

Waller, totally off-the-wall guy who's a genius in these matters. I'll set something up."

"That would be great." A salad arrived for Dr. Joan, a pepperoni pizza for me. I felt ridiculous; I mean, look at me.

"Here's my other question. How are us Xers and Ys affected by boomeritis? Well, no, that's not quite it, because I know how we are affected by it, it's everywhere. I mean, what are *our* forms of boomeritis? What form does it take in my generation? We don't seem to be all that taken with ourselves. We seem to be the opposite, we seem to have massive low self-esteem, not overinflated esteem. I mean, *slackers*. . . . "

"Do you think of yourself as a slacker?" Joan asked, and she reached out and touched my hand.

"Hell no! But you know what I mean."

"Now listen to me, Ken." And she looked directly at me, and I slipped and fell and drifted into the sky. "You are 'slackers' not because you slack, but because your task is so much bigger. My generation pioneered green, yours will pioneer yellow. Do you know what that means? Do you understand how amazing that is? The Xers and Ys might very well be the first second-tier generation in history." She repeated it for emphasis. "*You might become the first second-tier generation in history!*"

It was a stunning thought. Hand on hand, sky mixed with sky, heart in my throat and then out the top of my head. To be in love with the most amazing woman and to face such an extraordinary future— all of that and a pepperoni pizza, too. I mean, look at me.

Joan lit up, her radiance astonished. "Don't you get it? You are the Internet Generation, the Yellow-Meme Kids. The first second-tier generation, if you live up to it!" She smiled, and kept looking at me, looking hard, as if she wanted to see if this simple fact could penetrate the morphine-like denseness that was lately passing for my brain.

"It really is an amazing thought . . . Joan. Dr. Morin said something like that, too. It's just really hard to let it sink in. But you said, if we live up to it. So what are our own blocks to integral? What are our versions of boomeritis?"

"Remember that boomeritis is just the postmodern version of flatland. Flatland, okay?—the silly belief that there are no levels of consciousness, no higher or lower, no spiral of development, no spectrum of consciousness—just drab and dreary flatland. So your question really is, How are you and your generation caught in flatland? Right? Well, dear soul, start by looking at what you are doing in AI, which is supposedly going to rule the future. You guys don't even think about levels of consciousness, do you? Ken, do you?"

"No. No we don't, that's very true. Well, I do now, but nobody in AI thinks about it. They just work with levels of logical complexity, not interior levels of consciousness."

"Right, so you Xers and Ys are just swallowing the boomeritis flatland nonsense, and you are actually programming your supermachines to reproduce this insanity. Way to go, guys."

I mumbled, in something of a daze, "We are programming flatland into the coming InfoSphere. We are programming flatland into CyberCity. We are programming flatland into the future. I knew it, I knew it, I knew it. . . ."

I never finished my pizza. I actually seemed to have a brief period of amnesia, or went blank at the thought, or spaced out or something; it's hard to tell. Next thing I remember, I heard her voice again.

"Well, you think about that, okay? No wonder your entire generation is depressed. You're living in flatland." She glanced at her watch. "Oh dear, we need to get back to the seminar."

She reached out, held my hand, gave it a meaningful squeeze, I'm sure of it, which sent my mind pathetically back to Paris in the spring, where it was raining flowers and kittens and cute pink rose petals painted by Monet. I'm definitely gonna hurl. . . .

She smiled. "But let's meet again."

Margaret Carlton came back on stage. Slide #5, "Spirituality in the New Age."

"New Age spirituality," Carlton began. "Perhaps we should look at that a little more closely. The New Age movement, as with all trends touched by boomeritis, is a wonderful mixture of pre and post. The post-rational elements we can all applaud, I believe; the pre-rational elements are something else."

Chloe takes the pizza, rubs it all over her naked body, smiles, and says, "Lunch is served!"

I reach over to lick her breasts, and enter her body, and a chilling thrill wells up inside me, as Chloe's body turns into Joan's, which turns into the infinite sky, shining in all directions. The friction of flesh gives way to oneness with the all, an explosive orgasm fractures my body and spills into the universe at large, I dissolve into a rain of bliss that exists for all eternity, a hidden unbidden trip on ecstasy that ignites a digital heaven.

"*Listen to me very carefully*," the sky now says to me. "*I am Prakriti, doorway to all space, the womb in which all manifestation arises, fleshy entrance to that Spirit which is always already here and now, a Spirit that is about to descend on the unwilling world at large, racing through the evolving waves of carbon and silicon at the speed of light. You wish to enter my body, be one with my desire, sexually unite with my flesh, find the ultimate release—that is what you really want, yes?—to fuck to infinity, find an orgasm so immense it releases the entire cosmos—to be totally Free, radically Released, one with the All. This is what you really want, so why be one with only a single female body, when you can be one with the entire cosmos, an orgasmic release beyond your wildest dreams? Why settle for this pound of flesh, when infinity is yours? Ken, are you listening to me? Ken?*"

"Yes, yes, I hear you."

"*Reach out and touch my breasts, all you will feel are the clouds. Enter my body, all you will find is the earth. Be one with me, that is what you want. Have intercourse with the entire universe, dear soul, and disappear into that bliss. Do you understand?*"

"I think so, I'm trying."

"*Then you are now on the trail of who you are, if you can only get out of the way*," the old man's voice inside my head quietly announces.

"The core of New Age spirituality," Margaret Carlton continued, "is the belief, '*You create your own reality.*' Actually, psychotics create their own reality, but never mind," and the audience burst out laughing.

"To its credit, the New Age movement is attempting to get in touch with an all-pervading spiritual and creative source, but the idea often gets filtered through boomeritis and comes out slightly loopy. Loopy?

Where did I get that word?" Carlton looked slightly embarrassed. "Oh, yes. Well, anyway, the point is that the final New Age product is part mixture of good cognitive psychology, part emotional narcissism and prerational magic, and part what seems to be a rather complete misunderstanding of the mystical traditions."

Margaret Carlton, white on white, looked out at the audience and gently smiled. "The cognitive psychology component is fairly straight-forward and seems accurate enough: people's belief systems help to determine their experiences. To change your beliefs is to help change your response to life. This is certainly true. Although I cannot choose my sensations, I can choose how to think about them, and by consistently altering my beliefs and reframing my experience—perhaps from cynical to caring, or from pessimistic to optimistic, or from self-belittling to self-accepting—I can change the very nature of my outlook on life.

"There are, of course, limits to what my beliefs can accomplish. Except if I have boomeritis, in which case the grandiosity involved recognizes no such limitations at all. 'Thoughts influence reality' becomes 'Thoughts create reality.' In order to bolster the notion that my egoic thoughts govern all of reality, it would help if I could claim the authority of the world's great spiritual traditions, if I could claim, that is, the voice of God himself. And looking over the world's mystical traditions, that is exactly what I find. Don't the world's greatest saints and sages all announce that one's deepest Self is one with the Divine? That one's innermost awareness is Spirit itself? And doesn't that Spirit—my very own Self—create the entire world? You create your own reality, you see?

"Step by step, that is a narcissistic perversion of the mystical view. We will be talking about this in the next part of the seminar, when we introduce the rather astonishing evidence for Third Tier." The thought was electric; I looked around. "But what we can say for now is that it is indeed true that the world's great post-turquoise spiritual traditions maintain that the deepest part of your awareness is one with Spirit, and that this divine oneness can be realized with enlightenment—satori, moksha, cosmic consciousness, unio mystica, call it what you will. I believe that is the essential truth that many New-Agers are attempting to embrace, and we can all honor that truth, I hope. But the Self that is one with Spirit has little to do with you; it is, in fact, the transcendence of your ego that allows this Spirit to shine forth. That Self is the absolute opposite of boomeritis!"

Something strange was happening inside me; it was hard to tell exactly what. Kim kept looking at me quizzically.

"The typical New Age notion is that you want good things to happen to you, so think good thoughts; and because you create your own reality, those thoughts will come true. Conversely, if you are sick, it's because you have been bad. The mystical notion, on the other hand, is that your deepest Self transcends *both* good and bad, so by accepting *absolutely everything* that happens to you—by equally embracing both good and bad *with equanimity*—you can transcend the ego altogether. The idea is *not* to have one thing that is good smash into another thing called my ego, but to gently rise above both."

"Follow me again, young Ken: Let your mind relax. Let your mind relax and expand, mixing with the sky in front of it. Then notice: the clouds float by in the sky, and you are effortlessly aware of them. Feelings float by in the body, and you are effortlessly aware of them, too. Thoughts float by in the mind, and you are aware of them as well. Nature floats by, feelings float by, thoughts float by . . . and you are aware of all of them.

"So tell me: Who are you?

"You are not your thoughts, for you are aware of them. You are not your feelings, for you are aware of them. You are not any objects that you can see, for you are aware of them.

"Something in you is aware of all these things. So tell me: What is it in you that is conscious of everything?"

"Sri Ramana Maharshi, one of India's greatest sages, used to say, 'You thank God for the good things that happen to you, but not for the bad. That is your biggest mistake.' In other words, in the pure core of your primordial Being, where you are indeed one with Spirit, you partake of a reality so encompassing, so all-pervading, that it fully and equally includes both sickness and health, both pleasure and pain, both success and failure: 'I the Lord make the light to fall on the good and the bad alike; I the Lord do all these things.' And to the extent that you are one with Spirit, you will be a light that shines impartially on the good and the bad alike. You will not run around trying to hold onto the good and get rid of the bad by thinking nice thoughts for the separate ego.

"Of course, we all want to be healthy and not sick, financially secure and not destitute, loving and not hateful—and it is completely acceptable to work hard for all of those. But I need to be very careful when I start claiming that 'I create my own reality,' because which 'I' am I actually listening to: my ego or my Self? the ego in me or the Spirit in me? For the *Spirit* that is in me is not concerned with just me. The Spirit that is in me is likewise in all beings great and small, and that Spirit does indeed create the entire universe: it creates its own reality, which includes the sun and moon and stars, the wide oceans and pouring rains, the nations of this earth and all its blessed inhabitants, the light and the dark alike. But when I start claiming to create my own reality and that reality is about nothing but getting a new car, a new job, more money, fame, health instead of disease, happiness instead of sadness, joy instead of pain, light instead of dark, then perhaps I might start to question just which 'I' is getting a hearing, because I am no longer being *one with everything*, am I? I am only being one with a small slice of the universe governed by my small desires and wants. And friends, that is not Spirit, that is the ego, plain and simple." The audience stirred in its seats, or perhaps "squirmed" is more accurate.

"I got the scoop on Carlton," Kim leaned over and abruptly announced.

"But Kim, isn't that amazing? I mean, can't you feel it? Feel some sort of Presence? Feel the Expanse?"

"Ooo-kay, Ken is off in cyberland again, eh?"

"Well, it's not exactly cyberspace, or maybe it is. Maybe that is exactly where I was, in the coming cyberspace, what it will really be like, bodiless, floating, free . . ."

"Earth calling Ken, Earth calling Ken, come in, Ken."

"What? Oh, yeah." I sheepishly grinned, tried to focus.

"The fact is, the practices that are conducive to ego transcendence—to what some of us call third-tier consciousness—are generally prolonged and difficult. If you would like a superb introduction to these practices, see Roger Walsh's *Essential Spirituality*. Roger is a valued member of Integral Center, and I cannot recommend his book too highly.

"But, like any practice—learning to play a musical instrument, getting a Ph.D., learning a foreign language—spiritual practices take time, lots and lots of time; which is why, unfortunately, they are usually avoided by boomeritis and its wish for instant gratification.

"What boomeritis requires, instead, is a God that can be captured by merely thinking. Simply think that you are one with the Web of Life, or think that you are one with the Goddess, or think about holistic archetypes and transit astrology. Boomeritis wants to think that it is Divine and Sacred, not as a prelude to practice, but as a magical substitute for it. And an absolutely massive industry has grown up to produce this word magic for Boomers; to produce, that is, reasons for Boomers to think that their egos are Divine.

"Precisely because that is such a small step, this industry is wildly successful." Lots of laughs and groans. "At any given time, perhaps three of the top ten best-selling books are recipes for this word magic. Entire alternative colleges are devoted to it. Weekend seminars are a booming business, all basically aimed at 'empowering' the ego of the participants, as if that ego really needed more power."

Sweet Margaret Carlton pushed straight ahead, her ever-gentle smile an open contrast to her sharp words. "The essential feature of most of these approaches is the process of *relabeling*. That is, you take your present egoic state and learn to constantly relabel it as spiritual, divine, and sacred—relabel your ego as the Goddess, relabel it as the sacred Self, relabel it as the divine Web of Life. You take the self-contraction, you feel it really hard, and you call that Sacred. One ends up relabeling the subtlest reaches of the ego as Divine, and that is the new spiritual paradigm."

Carlton paused, then quickly summarized. "I am not criticizing Boomers, I am criticizing boomeritis. And 'You create your own reality'—your own omnipotent ego creates reality—is the absolute essence of boomeritis. It lies behind the social construction of reality; it lurks in the notion that the critic, not the artist, creates the art work; it subsists in the heart of deconstruction; it is the major motor of new-age spirituality. It even lurks in the very depths of modern physics. . . . "

Chloe and I are making love, with MJ Cole thump thump thumping "Crazy Love" and "Sonic Love Surrender" in the background. Chloe is doing these amazing things; her body becomes more and more supple, then blurs at the edges and melts into the sky, and Joan and I are in ecstatic embrace, lighting up the cosmos with sparks that burn the flesh. Something is very different this time, something wonderful horrible is happening to me. Chloe, are you there? Joan? Hello? Anybody, hello?

As Margaret Carlton retired, Charles Morin stepped up to the microphone. Slide #6, "The New Physics."

"Dr. Carlton concluded her presentation by noting that boomeritis even lurks in the depths of modern physics. How very strange, huh? But how very true. Nowhere is the ego omnipotence of boomeritis more apparent than in its approach to science. In spirituality, it is necessary to present the empowered ego as the Divine Self. The idea is that if you can get the Boomer ego on steroids, you've got God." The audience burst out laughing. "Now in science, it is necessary to make it appear that this ego, once again, creates all reality, but to do so this time with the authority of nothing less than the hardest of sciences, physics. At first this would seem an impossible order, but again, that is simply to underestimate boomeritis. Enter, then, a few quirks of the new physics."

"She's Lesa's lover."

"What?"

"Margaret Carlton is Lesa's lover."

"You have got to be kidding."

"Nope."

"Charles told you."

"Yup."

"That is too cool. That is so fucking awesome. I mean, just think about it." Powell and Carlton were, in almost every way, the photographic negatives of each other—sharp and soft, black and white, up and down, yang and yin, bark and meow, matter and antimatter—and when they came together, more or less literally, they might very well completely absorb each other, without remainder, in one of those cosmic implosions that leaves radiant emptiness in its place, a white/black hole in time that opens onto infinity.

"'The New Physics' is how Boomers refer to discoveries in physics made almost a century ago," Morin patiently continued. "What is 'new' is not the physics, but the interpretation boomeritis brings to it.

As physicists began investigating increasingly smaller units, breaking the atom into subatomic elements—electrons, protons, and the like—a curious fact emerged: because we can only investigate small particles (like an electron) by using other small particles (like photons of light), pretty soon you get to a point where these small particles knock each other around in the very attempt to have one of them locate the other. There is no way around this fact. Because one small particle will always move another small particle, any act of measurement will interfere with what you are trying to measure. A small particle's location, to some degree, will always be 'uncertain.'

"This Uncertainty Principle became the basis of approximately a half dozen different interpretations of what to make of it. One school of physics maintained that determinism must be replaced with probabilities. Another school maintained that there are actually hidden variables that are themselves deterministic. Another hypothesized that there are many different worlds, the totality of which include all possible certainties. Another school—which is by far the most widely accepted—maintained that you cannot interpret this event at all, because information about the small particles is simply beyond the reach of our investigation.

"The Boomers maintained that this meant that they themselves create the small particles." Groans from the audience.

"The idea is that, since you can't predict anything about the small particles until you measure them, then they don't exist until you measure them. Therefore it is the very act of measurement that brings the particles into existence, and that means that *you* are responsible for their existence, and since all things are made of these particles, then—*violà!*—you create all reality. The Boomer ego once again creates everything." A few in the audience began hollering, whether out of agreement or outrage it was hard to tell.

"A minority of physicists maintained that the act of measurement, which could be done by a machine without human consciousness, is responsible for the collapse of the wave packet (or the 'cloud of possibilities') and thus for turning a potential particle into an actual particle. How the Boomer ego got in there is anybody's guess, but the idea was clear enough: your big fat ego creates the universe."

Morin paused, then charged straight ahead. "As one popularizer of the new boomeritis physics put it, 'If you intend an ashtray, then the cloud of possibilities qwiffs it into being.' Omnipotent thinking creates the ashtray, qwiffs it into being. And boomeritis put this qwiffing to good use, as evidence of the fact that it creates all reality. Moreover, if everybody would just believe in this qwiffing, then we would have a massive social transformation unparalleled in human history!, led of course by none other than the Boomers, who were the first to really understand these century-old discoveries. As Danah Zohar puts it with typical boomeritis aplomb: 'The idea of a "quantum society" stems from a conviction that a whole new paradigm is emerging from our description of quantum reality and that this paradigm can be extended to change radically our perception of ourselves and the social world we want to live in. A wider appreciation of quantum reality can give us the conceptual foundations we need to bring about a positive revolution in society.'

"Subvert the old paradigm, transgress the old society, usher in the world-shaking revolution. One thing is quite certain: Max Planck, Neils Bohr, and Werner Heisenberg *never* had this in mind."

"I just spent three days with Darla," Stuart says, sliding into the row of chairs behind us. I turn around and look at him. He's out of his mind. "We are in full force. It was HUGE. And, as an aside, we spent time with my parents and they LOVE her. Everyone does. I have never known anything like this with another human being, what comes through when we're together. It's ALL there, mind, body, spirit, we are like the 4th of July in all realms at once, a spiritual nova in full explosion."

Carolyn turns around and looks at him, too. "Can we save this for later? I mean, I'm delighted for you, big guy, but not now."

"You'll like this part. One night we went for a walk. We were strolling by a lake, just touching and breathing, and the current between us got so intense, Darla literally had a walking orgasm. We were fully clothed, no genital contact or anything, but the energy just exploded in her, and as we were walking by the lake, her whole body started shaking and going wild, and she had like a two-minute orgasm, while we were walking! It was the craziest fucking thing, and SO goddamn hilarious! People walking by us thought she was having a seizure or something, except we were both laughing our asses off. It should be in a Woody Allen movie."

"You *are* a Woody Allen movie. Now shut up, Stuart. Okay, never mind, wait a minute. A walking orgasm?" I thought Carolyn was about to ask for the instruction manual.

"These last three days were like that. Can two people have a kundalini awakening at the same time? What the hell is going on? Whooooooooooo!"

"Can I help you?" Dr. Morin called out from the stage.

"Stuart forgot to take his medication," yelled Carolyn.

"Amusing. Ladies and gentlemen, Dr. Van Cleef."

Slide #7, "*The New Paradigm.*" Van Cleef jumped right in.

"The 'new' physics is simply a subset of the 'new paradigm,' which, as one proponent put it, is 'the most revolutionary scientific breakthrough in all of history.' What is this revolutionary new paradigm? Nobody really knows, although there have been literally hundreds of books written about it, because the accounts are not even vaguely consistent with each other. But the one thing they all agree on is that, whatever this new paradigm is, the Boomers have it."

"Definitely getting married."

"You and Morin?"

"Carlton and Powell."

"Carlton and Powell are getting married? They're not just lovers, they're getting married?"

"With this ring I thee."

"When?"

"Next month, full moon, high tide, look out girls, here we come."

"That is so fucking awesome," and I slap my thigh and yell "Ah!" Van Cleef looks down at me; I again turn bright red.

"As best as anyone can figure out, the new paradigm is something like systems theory, which has been around in a serious fashion for at least half a century, and which has been used by many sciences for most of that time, including various schools of sociology, psychology, biology, ecology, and cultural anthropology. Nevertheless, Boomer writers all seem to agree on these points: there is definitely a new paradigm emerging, and this paradigm might very well serve as the catalyst of an unprecedented world transformation, which will be led by those who have the new paradigm."

A look of weary disgust crawled across Van Cleef's face. With visible effort, he continued. "We are not talking about the many important truths brought forth by postformal second-tier sciences, truths that include systems theory, chaos theory, complexity theory, autopoiesis, and the like—all of which ought to be included in any universal integralism. We are talking about what boomeritis did with those important realities, and how individuals who had themselves made not a single scientific discovery could nonetheless claim to be part of an intellectual vanguard of the coming world transformation. In just the same way that a viewer of an art work could claim credit for the art; in the same way that deconstruction would allow one to picture oneself as superior to all that is being deconstructed; in the same way that 'you create your own reality' promises egoic omnipotence; so 'the new paradigm' would allow individuals to picture themselves as crucially central to the greatest and most astonishing transformation the world has ever known."

Several in the audience winced, then began murmuring and whispering among themselves. Van Cleef waited till the agitated din subsided.

"Paradigm. The notion was tailor-made for boomeritis, once its actual definition was substantially altered.

"Thomas Kuhn's *The Structure of Scientific Revolutions* was published in 1962; it soon became, for reasons good and bad, the most influential book on the philosophy of science ever written and the most frequently cited academic book of the last three decades. In a great ironic twist, it became perhaps the most influential *misunderstood* book of the century. Most of its popularity stemmed from a widespread misunderstanding of its central conclusions, a misunderstanding that, many historians now agree, stemmed in large part from the narcissistic mood of the Me generation. How boomeritis distorted Kuhn is itself a paradigm of our times."

"Chloe, have you ever heard of walking orgasms?"

"Heard of them? Why, I had five this morning just on the way to breakfast."

"Are they fun?"

"What do you think?"

"I thought I'm not supposed to think."

"You're not supposed to think about the stupid things you normally think about. But you are supposed to think about *this*."

I watch a naked Chloe convulse for several minutes. "What on earth is that?"

"A walking orgasm."

"But Chloe, you're sitting down.

"Pretty impressive, huh?"

"The distortions of Kuhn have now become so common that serious scholars of his work have no trouble reciting the popular misinterpretation of the notion of a 'paradigm.' Here is Frederick Crews reciting the typical (wrong) view. I quote: 'Kuhn, we are told, demonstrated that any two would-be paradigms will be incommensurable; that is, they will represent different universes of perception and explanation. Hence no common ground can exist for testing their merits, and one theory will prevail for strictly sociological, never empirical, reasons. The winning theory will be the one that better suits the emergent temper or interests of the hour (ideology, class, prejudice, gender, race, power, etc.—in other words, androcentric, phallocentric, Eurocentric, anthropocentric, and so forth). It follows that intellectuals who once trembled before the disapproving gaze of positivism can now propose sweeping "Kuhnian revolutionary paradigms" of their own, defying whatever disciplinary consensus they find antipathetic. . . .'

"That is indeed the typical interpretation of Kuhn," Van Cleef intoned. "Crews calls that interpretation 'theoreticism,' because it is a view lost in mere ideas and theory divorced from actual *evidence*—it is, in fact, quite similar to literary Theory, which likewise claims that 'there are no facts, only interpretations.' Crews then points out the obvious: 'One can gauge the emotional force of theoreticism by the remoteness of this interpretation *from what Kuhn actually said. . . .*'"

"Are you going to the wedding?"

"Tell you what. I think Charles is planning on a double wedding, if you get my drift. A kind of IC bash."

"Really? There's a thought. But are you still in a 'probably' mood, or did you decide?"

"Well. Well. I don't know."

"The age thing?"

"I don't think so. But I honestly don't know."

Van Cleef strode across the stage, hands clasped behind his back, spiky fierce intensity radiating from his face—the intensity that Kim thought was too much, even for the "rattling of the cage" that the IC folks were trying to accomplish.

"The idea was that, since 'paradigms' govern science, and since paradigms are allegedly not anchored in actual facts and evidence—but instead 'create' them—then *you needn't be tied to the authority of science in any fundamental way*. Why? That's right: Nobody tells me what to do!

"This popular misunderstanding of Kuhn—this 'theoreticism'—also meant that science is allegedly *arbitrary* (it is not the result of actual evidence but of imposed power structures), *relative* (it reveals nothing that is universal in reality, but simply relative to the scientific imposition of power), *socially constructed* (it is not a map corresponding to any actual reality, but a construction based on social conventions), *interpretive* (it does not reveal anything fundamental about reality, but is simply one of many interpretations of the world text), *power-laden* (science is not grounded in facts, it simply dominates people, usually for Eurocentric and androcentric reasons), and *nonprogressive* (since science proceeds by ruptures or breaks, so there can be no cumulative progress in any of the sciences)."

And then, in a very loud voice: "*Kuhn maintained none of those views*. Indeed, he vehemently argued against most of them. But what Crews so unerringly called *the emotional force* of the misunderstood idea had already taken root: we can abandon the straightjacket of science and evidence by merely thinking up a new paradigm; and this itself, as Crews himself points out, was grounded in a rampant sixties narcissism."

Back and forth across the stage Van Cleef paced, talking to himself as much as to the audience. Then, returning to the situation at hand, he faced the crowd, seemed to relax, and said, mischievously smiling, "A small list of claimants to be the new paradigm included deep ecology, transit astrology, the quantum self, the quantum society, holistic health, postmodern poststructuralism, ecofeminism, quantum psychotherapy, neo-Jungian psychology, channeling, premodern indigenous tribal consciousness, crystal healing, rebirthing, ecopsychology, holotropic breathwork, aura cleansing, the psychic network, revisioning transpersonal psychology, palmistry, astral enemas, Goodyear wide-grip tires, and Levi's baggy-leg jeans." Gales of laughter arose from the audience, with most people self-consciously nodding, a handful fuming.

"Kuhn himself watched all of this with growing alarm, and made a series of vigorous statements meant to curtail the damage, but to absolutely no avail. Most people using the term 'paradigm' and citing Kuhn didn't even know that he had abandoned the term altogether. Is science actually relative, arbitrary, and nonprogressive? Kuhn in exasperation: 'Later scientific theories are better than earlier ones for solving puzzles in the quite often different environments to which they are applied. This is not a relativist's position, and it displays the sense in which I am a convinced believer in scientific progress.'"

Chloe and I are making love, when suddenly her body transforms into the cosmos; one with her, I am everything that is arising: I clutch frantically at the entire world and dissolve into no-boundary bliss. Walking is one continuous orgasm, so is sitting, standing, laughing, loving, as ecstasy escapes from the insides of infinity and rains on a welcoming world. The love I have for Chloe, for Joan, for all of them, spills out of my being and into the cosmos at large in ever-expanding waves of care . . .

"*You see, he just might get it yet,*" she says.

"*Indeed he might,*" the old man's voice replies.

" *. . . cyber-circuits lighting up the night with nitro-digital delight.*"

"*Especially if he can learn to express himself in something other than that horrid purple prose.*"

"*Now, now, he's just being him. Besides, you were once exactly like that.*"

"*True. This is very true.*"

"*When he finds out who you are, he probably won't be any kinder. You two are a lot alike, you know.*"

And the voice inside my head begins to laugh.

"What, then, did Kuhn actually mean by 'paradigm,' and what was the 'structure' of scientific revolutions? Nothing nearly as dramatic as boomeritis proclaimed. To begin with, Kuhn outlined not three or four paradigm shifts in the history of modern science, but *several hundred*. As Ian Hacking summarizes the actual view: '*The Structure of Scientific*

Revolutions is about hundreds of revolutions, which are supposed to occur in many disciplines, and which typically involve the research work, in the first instance, of at most a hundred or so investigators. Lavoisier's chemical revolution counts as one, but so does Roentgen's discovery of X-rays, the voltaic cell or battery of 1800, the first quantization of energy, and numerous developments in the history of thermodynamics.'

"In other words, almost any new experiment generating new data was a new paradigm, which is why a battery was a new paradigm. 'Paradigm' itself carried two broad components, experimental and social, both of which involved actual *practices*, not merely ideas. Kuhn 'used the word "paradigm" to denote both the established and admired solutions that serve as models of how to practice the science, and also for the local social structure that keeps those standards in place by teaching, rewards, and the like. The word was mysteriously launched or rather catapulted into prominence, and now seems a standard item in the vocabulary of everyone who writes about science—except Kuhn himself, who has disavowed it. "Paradigm" is at present a dead metaphor.'

"Paradigm is at present a dead metaphor," Van Cleef repeated. "Except for boomeritis, which continues to crank out hundreds of books a year all devoted to the new paradigm. . . . "

The ecstasy is painful. Do I have a body or not? Am I one with Chloe, or Joan, or God, or Goddess? Am I in the world of Silicon or Carbon? Am I the seer or the seen? Luminous bliss lights up the sheltering sky, as DJ Pollywog plays Atomic Babies' "Heading toward Omega"— and faster faster!, the thump thump thumping is endless orgasms pulsing to the rhythm of the stars.

I do not know where I am, but I keep thinking, This is definitely not your father's world.

Slide #8, "The I've-Got-the-New-Paradigm Paradigm."

I rubbed my eyes, shook my head, looked at the slide.

"This sounds like a fun topic, right, Kim?"

"Yes, but not in real life. Jefferson got bomb threats over this when he first introduced the notion."

"You're kidding."

"Hand to Goddess."

"But why?"

"Well, you know, the mean green meme has this red-meme under-belly. That's the whole point of boomeritis."

"Translation?"

"Step on these people's toes, and they will lash back in often ugly ways. That peace-and-love stuff applies only if you agree with them. Jefferson had police protection for almost two years."

Well, that took the fun out of it. Mark Jefferson nonetheless looked quite at ease as he introduced the topic.

"Hello friends. At this time we are going to discuss what is by far the most common form of 'the new paradigm.' We sometimes call it 'The 415 Paradigm,' for the area code of San Francisco, which is its epicenter, but of course it is not geographically localized at all." He smiled and looked out at the audience. "So we often just call it 'The I've-Got-the-New-Paradigm paradigm,'" and most in the audience laughed good-naturedly.

"With The I've-Got-the-New-Paradigm paradigm we see a concentration of virtually every intellectual trend of boomeritis: anti-modern, anti-Enlightenment, anti-Western (except for the new physics, systems theory, and the Internet; although, in the feminist version, all of Western science is a form of female rape); a concomitant and very strong retro-Romanticism, (with a religious belief in noble savages and tribal 'nondissociated' consciousness); which is worked into a mythology of Gaia, the return of the Goddess, and the pluralistic paradise that existed prior to the modern male ego, all of which will be resurrected with the new paradigm, which is feminine, linking, joining, and caring, unlike the old paradigm, which is masculine, divisive, analytic and uncaring (as Carol Gilligan has shown); the social construction of reality (which is the linchpin for being able to deconstruct the Western project of modernity); an intensely strong anti-hierarchy stance (since all hierarchies are forms of subjection, oppression, and social marginalization); an avid pluralism, contextualism, and constructivism (the 'free play of signifiers' allows dominant epistemologies to be subverted); grounded in dialogue (which is morally superior to the alternatives); all combined with a spirituality that is said to be holistic and that can be largely grasped, not by practice, but simply by thinking; with optional interest in altered states of consciousness and temporary peak experiences, often induced by drugs such as ayahausca, in which case there is even more interest in tribal, shamanic forms of experiential display." Jefferson finished and took in an exaggerated breath, as if he had said all of that in one sentence.

Thievery Corporation plays "Closer to God" and "OM Lounge," and the thump thump thumping slams my body into a world of radiant luminous backbeat flesh.

"Chloe, is that you?"

The words rush by too fast to hear—"*Touch my breasts, find the stars, kiss my lips, light up the night, bliss of the gods, don't you see that now?*"

"Yes, Joan, I do see that."

"*Do you know that means?*" **she says.**

"The I've-Got-the-New-Paradigm paradigm is a mishmash of all of those ideas, usually in their extremist forms, bound together by boomeritis.

"For example, a typical outline of the new paradigm might run as follows: The recent breakthrough discoveries in quantum physics show us that the world is an undivided whole. This undivided wholeness, which is the fundamental basis (or implicate order) of all reality, shows us that Nature is one and undivided, whole and interconnected, and we are one with that holistic Web of Life. This Web of Life gains new credence from the extraordinary breakthrough discoveries in systems theory and chaos theory, which show us that the world is not composed of separate and isolated things, but rather is a rich tapestry of interwoven patterns and inseparable relationships. We would have realized this earlier were it not for the Newtonian-Cartesian paradigm, which is analytic and divisive, and therefore tears the world into isolated, alienated, and mechanistic fragments in a billiard ball world. This Newtonian-Cartesian paradigm is in many ways responsible for the violence, war, conflict, ecological catastrophe, and disenchanted wasteland in which we all now live. That paradigm is intrinsically patriarchal—it is based on the masculine principles of divide and conquer, abusive analytic power, hyper-individualism, and hierarchical subjection. In order to undo this violent repression and oppression, we have to subvert, transgress, and deconstruct the old paradigm. Fortunately we can do this because, far from being an objective picture of an objective world, Western science is merely a socially constructed belief, with no more intrinsic validity than any other belief, and therefore it can be deconstructed to make room for the new paradigm, which is holistic, linking, joining, and uniting. But then, this new paradigm is really just rediscovering the undivided wholeness that the indigenous mind (which means 'tribal hunting' if you are a male writer, and 'horticultural planting' if female) has known about all along, until the conquest of paradise brutally oppressed it. This immanent spirituality, this sacred nature, this undivided wholeness, is also the same wholeness that quantum physics proves is the basis of all reality. If we can simply adopt this new paradigm—which reveals the same sacred wholeness that is disclosed in everything from the Great Mother corpus to Gaia to ecology to astrology to systems theory—then we will end the violence, brutality, and alienation of the modern world, and usher in one of the greatest social transformations the world has ever seen.

"Much as with Alan Sokal's article, not one of those sentences is factually true. A few are close, but not one of them gets a cigar—or a donut, for that matter, to keep gender parity. Even though none of them are factually true, you can string them together in a way that speaks deeply to boomeritis and is therefore fervently embraced by those with the disease. In all of this, there are some important ideas, brought forth variously by pluralistic relativism, genealogy, systems theory, and so forth, but all bundled together, connect-the-dots style, by the glue of boomeritis.

"Ah yes, I have the new paradigm that will transform the entire world. . . . "

"Follow me one more time, young Ken: Let your mind relax. Let your mind relax and expand, mixing with the sky in front of it. Then notice: the clouds float by in the sky, and you are effortlessly aware of them. Feelings float by in the body, and you are effortlessly aware of them, too. Thoughts float by in the mind, and you are aware of them as well. Nature floats by, feelings float by, thoughts float by . . . and you are aware of all of them.

"So tell me: Who are you?

"You are not your thoughts, for you are aware of them. You are not your feelings, for you are aware of them. You are not any objects that you can see, for you are aware of them, too.

"You are not the old paradigm, you are not the new paradigm, for you are aware of both of them. You are not analytic, you are not holistic, you are not one, you are not many, you are not patriarchal, you are not matriarchal, you are not male, you are not female, not black, not white, not this, not that—neti, neti—for you are aware of all of that.

"Something in you is aware of all those things. So tell me: What is it in you that is conscious of everything?

"That vast infinite witnessing awareness, don't you recognize it?

"What is that Witness? Can you say its true name?"

Jefferson waved to everybody and, smiling, walked off the stage. The audience sat silent, sullen; a smattering of applause escaped through the apparent discomfort. Charles Morin came back on stage.

"That which unites every one of the items we have discussed this week—from the social construction of reality to the drama of the gifted child to UFO abductions to saving the Goddess to having the new paradigm—is simply boomeritis, an overestimation of the importance, power, and wonderfulness of the finite ego.

"And so, my friends, let us now ask: Is there a way out?"

I am making passionate love to Chloe. She is screaming, I am screaming, we are screaming, and as the universe explodes, Chloe's body becomes Joan's body, and Chloe's face becomes Joan's face, which is to say the infinite sky, and I am having a standing, sitting, walking orgasm that fills the universe with cosmic light and bliss too painful to endure. Then Chloe looks at Joan and says, "Something is terribly wrong with Ken."

"You're right, it's truly awful," she replies.

"What's wrong? What?" I ask with trepidation.

"Sweet boy, something is horribly, horribly wrong."

"Yes, yes, what? What!"

"Sweet boy, I don't know how to tell you this, but it seems that you've stopped rattling."

Seminar_3@BeyondTheMeGeneration.com

Pluralism_Falls_Apart@DisIntegrationCity.com

"Hey, Elastica is getting back together!" said Jonathan, as he sat rustling the still-damp morning newspapers that were scattered atop the table in front of the Breakfast Brewery. Chloe glanced up but kept flipping through *Fashion Design in Architecture*. Carolyn stared at Jonathan unblinkingly, right eyebrow slightly raised, coffee cup held immobile outside her lips, a suspended expression that said, Can't wait to see what the idiot will blurt out next. Scott gazed at Carolyn in a way that seemed to say, I think I'm in love. (Where was Vanessa?) Stuart looked as if he were elsewhere. Everybody rested in their studied isolation.

"I wonder if that means Justine and Blur what's-his-name are still together?" Nobody looked up, or even acknowledged the comment. Undaunted, Jonathan continued his morning news presentation.

"Hey, this is interesting. New research has uncovered some startling facts about what actually happened at the Boston Tea Party. On the evening of December 16, 1773, several Bostonians, many disguised as native Americans, in an attempt to protest the British tax on tea, threw 342 chests of tea from British ships into the Boston Harbor. This was a major event leading to the Declaration of Independence and the American Revolution. New research reveals that the Bostonians who threw the tea into the harbor were quickly set upon by a band of roving environmentalists and beaten senseless for not filing an environmental impact statement. Those who survived the beatings were sued by the local Indians for defamation of character. Samuel Adams is quoted as saying, 'That rather puts a damper on the revolution, what?'

"Oh, interesting follow-up. When the environmentalists did file an impact statement on the results of the Boston Tea Party, the main ecological damage was found to be, and I quote, 'some really jittery beavers in the Bay.' As for the local Indians, they eventually built a gambling casino on the site, a site that was later found to be located over a sacred Puritan burial ground."

We all ignored him. "Okay, what else we got here? Let's see, let's see. Ah, here we go. Pamela Smith, fresh from her court victory in the battle over the estate of her late husband, Paul Holt, the 75-year-old billionaire whom she had married when she was 28, announced her new wedding engagement to billionaire Les Warren. As the judge in the case summarized the situation, 'When she's on her back, the meter is running.'"

Chloe muffled a giggle; the unspoken breakfast rule was, nobody was to encourage Jonathan by laughing.

"Ah ha. I notice that there is already a rapidly growing backlash against the dominance of the green meme." Carolyn involuntarily glanced up. "There's this fascinating article, 'The Republic of Feelings,' by Christina Hoff Sommers. She points out that there is an impressive body of research suggesting that people who suppress their emotions and act stoically are more balanced and psychologically healthy than those who follow the current fashion of always being emotionally open and sharing of one's feelings."

Jonathan's demeanor turned somber, as if he were actually interested in this item. Setting aside irony, he courageously ventured into the real world. "She discusses studies of high school students, bereaved people, Holocaust survivors, and adolescent girls who have been sexually abused. The research shows that, as she summarizes it, 'The ones who suppressed their grief turned out to be considerably healthier than the strong emoters.' Other studies pertaining to grieving after a death showed that the heavy emoters did far worse in the long run based on any number of scales, from psychological health to immune system functioning."

"Jesus," said Chloe, "they finally figured that out? It's a little late, don't you think? I mean notice, kids, that the entire country has already become Oprahized—which means we are now a nation of touchy-feely infantile schmucks. This is a democracy of the sick. Is that what you guys keep calling boomeritis?"

"Well, that appears to be part of it," Scott answered. "But it's a very complex topic, and none of us is quite sure what to make of it."

"That's not why I read the article," Jonathan said. "It's the editorial. A summary of this report was carried in *The New Left*, bastion of liberal politics, and it's as if the editors felt they had to jump on the bandwagon—that is, jump off the green-meme feel fest. It's actually rather brutal: 'Most human beings would in fact simply face disaster and soldier on,' this editor writes, 'unless of course we are deep-sixed by the cults of perpetual weepery. By these I mean the various self-help or therapeutic groups which make recalling trauma the be-all and end-all of life—the central font of one's identity. These groups measure the value of a session by how many instances of abuse and loss—real or imagined—you've been able to produce for the therapist, the group, or the television audience, with one's success measured in the pints of tears shed. Finding the inner child, emoting the inner child, being the inner child—I hate to tell you Boomers this, but it's time to grow up, folks, you're a friggin half century old now.' The editor, Rachel Bloom, ends up calling us 'A Nation of the Lachrymose.'"

"The green swamp," shrugged Scott.

"Well, Joan says, er, Hazelton, um, Hazelton Joan doctor person"—I blush—"well, you know, she says that . . ." Chloe is staring straight at me. "Hazelton thinks that the Boomers are ready to pop. That's what she calls it, 'ready to pop.' Which means that they have been at the green meme long enough—about thirty years now—and so they are getting sick and tired of the green meme, the mean green meme, boomeritis, the whole works. So they are ready to pop to second tier." I smile wanly. "It sounds like that editor popped. I think that's what the backlash is about. Maybe it's a good thing, right?"

"Maybe, maybe not," said Carolyn. "I'm wondering what babies will get tossed with what bathwater."

"Well then," Chloe announced, "I say we take the afternoon off and heal our inner child."

We all burst out laughing. Chloe smiled at everybody at the table, then looked down her blouse. "If I can find the little shit. She's in here somewhere, I'm sure."

Morin walked out on stage, accompanied by the first slide, "The Creature from the Green Lagoon." The audience laughed and booed in a jocular way.

"Margaret Carlton and Lesa Powell are both presenting today," said Kim. "It's the first time together in public after their announcement."

"Oh, really?" I whispered. "Awesome."

"What is?" asked Carolyn.

"Powell and Carlton are an item."

"An item? You mean, like an *item*?"

"Right."

A huge grin lit up Carolyn's face.

Kim leaned over. "They're going to have a wedding ceremony."

"Maybe a double ceremony!" I added. "With Morin and—"

Kim elbowed me.

"All of you hush, please," someone from the row behind us almost yelled.

"Right, sorry, sorry."

"The worldview of boomeritis—the unhealthy version of the green meme—flatland pluralism inhabited by a big ego—the entire thing has started to come apart over the last decade or so, mostly under the on-slaught of facts, evidence, internal inconsistencies, and a further growth of consciousness. Today we will briefly review that scene, and then tomorrow jump directly into the integral solutions." Random cheers and clapping as the audience settled in.

Then Morin did a strange thing. He launched into an introduction of the day's topics, as usual, but he did so in a very abstruse, obtuse fashion, and rather completely lost the audience. Realizing what had happened, he stopped, took a breath, and made amends:

"Okay, look, people, it's fairly simple. Extreme pluralism means that everything is equal, nothing is higher or better or superior. There are no levels of consciousness, with some being higher than others, for they must all be viewed as equivalent. And therefore all the different levels of consciousness are denied, collapsed, reduced to flatland. Then several ugly things happen, here in flatland. One, any and all preconventional, narcissistic impulses can pretend to be higher postconventional ideals, since they are all supposed to be the same. This is the heart of boomeritis, narcissism dressed up in high-sounding ideals. Flatland inhabited by a very big ego—there is boomeritis! But the real travesty is simply flatland itself—completely ignoring the rich multidimensional interior waves of consciousness unfolding.

"You Xers and Ys might escape some of the big ego part, but you are still trapped in flatland itself, yes? And that is the legacy of boomeritis that has crippled your own world, hobbled your own lives, and it will continue to do so until you get this monkey off your back!" Then he laughed out loud. "And we be the monkey," he said, looking at his Boomer pals, as the audience laughed with him. "*Slackers* does not define *you*. It is simply a name for how boomeritis, completely full of itself, defines you." Several of the "kids" in the audience started applauding, a few stomped their Skechers, as chagrined Boomers smiled wanly.

"So today we will look at the problems of flatland—what happens when pluralism, or the green meme, *pretends to be a complete worldview*: the nightmare of the green swamp."

A few mock boos and jeers, which gave way quickly to applause as Lesa Powell bounded on stage. We all looked at each other, nodded our heads, and smiled that knowing smile.

"So Stuart," Jonathan said, with a tone suggesting that he had not yet caused enough trouble for the morning, "forget about this 'republic of feelings' editorial, which I see you did anyway." Stuart was still gazing into space. "What's this 'observance of states' thing that involved boinking five babes? Artistic license, eh?"

Stuart, as if with great effort, returned to the present. "Oh, that. I may have gone a bit wacko for a period there. It was a great concept, still is, actually, but the lines got blurry for a while, and I did some things that, well . . . were kind of like Adi Da meets Salvador Dali . . . Adi-Dali.

"Anyway, the idea was, I would use very high-tech microphones, very sensitive, to record myself in meditation. I would record my heartbeat and my breath for a 40-minute period. This would then be the foundation—the 'constant' in the recording. It would play continuously while the other stuff came and went."

"What other stuff?"

"Well, this is where the boinking comes in. I would record people in many different states of consciousness—that's why the project was called 'Observance of States.' These states would be the 'scenes' in the recording, which would come and go, all the while this meditative heartbeat/breath remains constant behind it. States or scenes would then rise and fall over it, like: laughing, crying, fucking, dreaming, talking in their sleep, being startled awake, inebriation, sickness, throwing up, wheezing, coughing . . ."

"Falling asleep due to boredom."

"Thanks, Chloe." Stuart paused while another round of espressos, lattés, orange juices, and bagels arrived. "The point is that the constant meditative state would represent pure witnessing awareness, and then that witness would be aware of the various states coming and going. So, the recording would start, and you'd hear the heartbeat and breathing, then maybe one laugh, then two, then it builds and builds, and the laughing scene goes on for a few minutes, then fades. Then, back to just heartbeat and breathing. Then, the next state or scene comes in, and . . . you get the idea. I would do this kind of thing with each state."

"How about the sounds of somebody actually murdering somebody?"

"Jesus, Chloe." Carolyn shook her head. "You and Foucault and the Marquis de Sade. 'Have Pain, Will Travel.'"

"So I built a studio in my house and started recording myself meditating, and laughing, and sleeping, and such. And, I also started to record myself and women having sex. Not only audio, but video. I was totally straightforward with them, they all knew exactly what was going on. But then, duh, it was pretty hard to miss: there's these enormous microphones and recording equipment hanging over us, lights flashing on a dozen gadgets."

"What are those lamps, Ken?"

"They're Krieg lights, Chloe, for filming."

"Are we videotaping this? Ooooh, I'm gonna be a star. Krieg lights and Kiegel exercises."

"We are observing states, Chloe."

"Ooooh, observe *this*."

"Wow!"

"Ken," a voice whispers in my ear, *"have you ever made love to a subject of awareness?"*

"I'm sorry, what was that?"

"Instead of fucking an object, have you ever made love to a subject?"

"I'm afraid I don't understand." I open my eyes to ask Chloe what she means, and Joan is staring straight at me.

"Are you going back to a pound of flesh, or do you want the world?"

Slide #2, "The Performative Contradiction," and Lesa Powell, as usual, hit the ground running.

"Philosophers such as Karl-Otto Apel, Jürgen Habermas, John Searle, Thomas Nagel, and Charles Taylor—all heroes of mine, I must tell you—have given devastating criticisms of the self-contradictory stance of pluralistic relativism, contextualism, and constructivism. This part is a little bit technical, but I promise a simple summary!"

Powell proceeded once again to leave me in the dust.

"Nobody is denying that all forms of truth have at least some aspects that are culturally relative, contextual, and constructed. But all of those philosophers I mentioned have pointed out that pluralistic relativism implicitly assumes universals which it explicitly and loudly denies to everybody else. (Remember, this is what Foucault realized when he did *The Archaeology of Knowledge*. All of these approaches make the strong claim that various features of contextualism and constructivism are *true for all cultures*, universally). That, of course, is what made it so appealing to boomeritis. I can *implicitly* claim universal truth for the view held by my big ego, while *explicitly* denying it to everybody else—and thus I possess claims of omnipotent truth denied to the rest of the world. And then, as a further benefit, I can claim that all universal truths are oppressive, cruel, and marginalizing, so that obviously I am morally superior in my amazing efforts to free the world from universal truths."

The loud, standard, agitated groans from the audience made their first appearance for the day.

"Kim, is this gonna be hard?" I whine in her ear, then realize, too late, what I've done.

"Ya brain-dead wimp, ya weenie, ya candy ass, ya feeb, ya sissy mary, ya . . ."

"Thanks, Kim. I needed that."

"Thomas Nagel's *The Last Word* is the most recent book to point this out. Just as significant is the review of Nagel's book by Colin McGinn carried in *The New Republic*. McGinn starts by summarizing the extreme postmodernist conception of rationality—in other words, the worldview of pluralistic relativism and the green meme. 'According to this conception, human reason is inherently local, culture-relative, rooted in the variable facts of human nature and history, a matter of divergent "practices" and "forms of life" and "frames of reference" and "conceptual schemes." There are no norms of reasoning that transcend what is accepted by a society or an epoch, no objective justifications for belief that everyone must respect on pain of cognitive malfunction. To be valid is to be taken to be valid, and different people can have legitimately different patterns of taking. In the end, the only justifications for belief have the form *"justified for me."'* Note the narcissism or intense subjectivism," Powell said, as she looked around the audience.

"McGinn continues: 'In such a view, objectivity, if it exists at all, is a function of social relations; a matter of social consensus, not of acknowledging truths and principles that obtain whether or not any society recognizes them. The norms of reasoning are ultimately like the norms of fashion.'

"Nagel shows, and McGinn agrees, that all of those claims are self-contradictory. McGinn, and I quote:

The subjectivist holds that reason is nothing other than a manifestation of local and relative contingencies, and that its results have no authority beyond the parochial domain; in trying to go beyond the local, reason overreaches itself and produces empty assertions. This is clearly a theory about the nature of reason: it purports to tell us what reason is, what its place in the world amounts to. But the point is that this theory is offered as the truth about reason, as something that ought to command the assent of all rational beings. It is not offered as merely true for its propounder or his speech community. No, it is meant as a non-relatively true account of the very nature of reason. In propounding it, therefore, the subjectivist himself employs principles of reasoning and commitments to truth which are taken to have more than relative validity.

"McGinn then drives to Nagel's inescapable conclusion: 'But this is to presuppose the very thing that the subjectivist is claiming to call into question. There is a dilemma here: either announce the debunking account of reason as the objective truth, or put it forward as merely an instance of its own official conception of truth. In the former case, the subjectivist contradicts himself, claiming a status for his utterance that according to him no utterance can have; but in the latter case, the claim is merely true for him and has no authority over anyone else's beliefs. If the subjectivist's statement is true, then we can ignore it; if it is not, then it is false. In either case it is not a claim we can take seriously. And so subjectivism is refuted.'"

A sea of naked female bodies, undulating like a field of wheat, and I the monological eyeball hungrily taking it all in.
"Have you ever made love with a subject instead of to an object?"
"I'm sorry, I still don't understand."
"Oh dear." **And a woman, whose face I cannot make out, stands up and takes off all her clothes.**
"Come over here, I'll show you."

"McGinn says that 'Nagel's argument is not only correct, it is also urgent.' Why *urgent*?"
Powell looked carefully around the audience, then began pronouncing her words with a steadily increasing volume. "Because it is required to combat the rampant narcissism that is at the heart of the relativist/pluralist game, which claims for itself a truth that it denies to all others, and anchors all truth in egocentric wishes. 'First-person avowals' are the only 'truth' acknowledged. In this insane view, says Nagel, 'Nothing is right, and instead we are all expressing our personal

or cultural points of view. The actual result has been a growth in the already extreme intellectual laziness of contemporary culture and the collapse of serious argument throughout the reaches of the humanities and social sciences, together with a refusal to take seriously, as anything other than first-person avowals, the objective arguments of others.' *Narcissism* and *fragmentation* have replaced truth and communication, and this is called cultural studies," she thundered.

"Anyway, I would have all these girls over and we would fuck and the whole thing was recorded. Then, I would edit and weave all these tracks of fucking into the sex 'scene' of the piece."

"So let me get this straight. You're shooting a porno flick," grinned Scott.

"Ooooh, can I be in it? Pleeeeease," Chloe preened.

"Are you like fucking kidding me?" Carolyn fumed.

"Am I kidding you?" asked Chloe.

"Not you, bimbo, Stuart there."

"Well, see, that's the thing. After a while, it got hard to ignore the fact that I was having sex with all these girls for a questionable motivation. It wasn't so much capturing the spontaneous event of lovemaking, it was more like . . . bringing lots of girls over and banging them. It was abusive and irresponsible, even though I wasn't misleading them. Whereas with the other states or scenes it was much more capturing something spontaneous. So I decided I better stop."

"Oh no, no," said Chloe. "This sounds totally far out."

"Why did you stop?" I asked.

"Well, you know, Darla and I got back together, and I woke up and saw right through my own indulgent bullshit. She's like a mirror to me."

"I might puke," Chloe offered.

"I still want to do the project, but not the way I was doing it. I just want to record other people now, except maybe use Darla and me."

Scott leaned over and asked with urgent seriousness. "Does that mean, um, that you and the supermodel will be fucking on film?"

Powell stared out at the audience. "McGinn gets very close to the heart of the matter. '*The Last Word* is a book that should be read and pondered in this golden age of subjectivism, egocentrism, narcissism. As to why such leanings exist and are so prevalent today, I have a notion.' And the notion is that universal truths, as opposed to subjectivist views, 'clash with a popular and misguided ideal of freedom.' Universal truth '*constrains* our thinking. We must obey its mandates. Yet people don't want to be constrained; they want to feel they can choose their beliefs, like beans in a supermarket. They want to be able to follow their impulses and not be reigned in by impersonal demands. This feels like a violation of the inalienable right to do whatever one wants to do.' Because, after all, '*Nobody tells me what to do!*'

"In plain language," Powell said, her voice beginning to rise again, "universal truths curb narcissism; they constrain the ego; they force us outside of our subjectivist wishes, there to confront a reality not merely of our own making. It has become increasingly obvious that extreme postmodernism, pluralism, and relativism are the grand refuge of boomeritis. Wanting nothing to violate one's egocentric priorities—the 'misguided ideal of freedom'—it is necessary to make facts plastic and truth sliding, and thus reduce reality to a construction of somebody's ego, a construction that can therefore be just as easily deconstructed: reality made and unmade by the omnipotent ego. And the big fat bloated Boomer ego once again creates and dominates all reality."

This time there was silence as Powell walked from the stage; her last sentence had been unusually harsh—she sounded more like Derek Van Cleef than Lesa Powell—and the audience seemed hurt by it. But the silence turned quickly to laughter when the next slide went up: "Ranking Is Like Way Totally Bad."

"That's our next topic," Morin yelled. "But this is a short day, so we're taking an early and extended lunch. See you all back here at 2 P.M."

"Ken, why don't you join us for lunch?" Joan asked. "And perhaps you could answer with something other than 'Um er doctor Joan person thingie.'"

I turned bright red. "Okay. Uh, why?"

She laughed easily. "It's been a while since a twentysomething made a pass at me." I turned brighter red.

In a large cafeteria area, behind and off to the right of the stage, most of the day's faculty had landed—Morin, Carlton, Powell, Jefferson.

"Hi, dear ones. This is Ken Wilber, a local computer whiz who believes humans are history."

"Well, no, it's not like that, not you humans that's for sure, nor those humans either, that is, these or those humans, which anyway—"

"Ken, sit."

"The problem with even talking about these topics," Jefferson was explaining, "is that most of the noble ideas that caring and liberal people maintain actually involve ideas that they say they despise."

"Like hierarchy."

"Like hierarchy, yes, and universals, and developmental ranking, and everything that green says it hates. So green ends up despising those things that offer it salvation."

"But that's true of every level of development," Carlton pointed out, "so you're being much too hard on green in that regard. Each developmental level 'hates' its successor. Reds think that blues are suckers, blues think that oranges are godless atheists bound for hell, oranges think greens are woo-woo sissies, greens think that yellows are insensitive, authoritarian, antispiritual assholes. So what else is new?" She laughed.

"Well, that's true enough," admitted Jefferson. "My point is simply that all of us here at IC, as you know, deal mostly with the transition from green to yellow—from first tier to second tier—and so usually what we face is the enormous hostility coming at us from green. It's so ironic, as the kids would say."

"Well, it's one hell of a laugh on us." Lesa Powell grinned. "Green hates yellow. What a kick. So any time that we say something yellow, green will interpret it as being red—as being egocentric, arrogant, authoritarian, marginalizing, sexist, racist, insensitive, and lacking feelings. So green hates yellow, but the joke is that you have to go through green to get to yellow! That's hysterical! It's one of God's little jests, don't you think, Ken?"

"Oh sure, I think a lot."

"Not do you think, dear," Joan clarified, "but do you think it's one of God's little jests?"

"Definitely!"

"Well, then, that settles it. Here's my second pet peeve," continued Jefferson. "You know I came into this field under the impression that if you marshaled enough facts, evidence, and clear presentation, then what Habermas calls 'the unforced force of the better argument' would win the debate. But it never does, it *never* does."

"Well, it rarely does," Carlton again corrected, emphasizing her words discretely. "And you know why. A person at, say, the blue wave of consciousness *cannot* agree with what green is saying, or really even see what green is saying. So of course blue will never agree with green. In order for that to happen, blue would have to develop to orange, and then develop to green. So most of the 'intellectual debates' that occur cannot be decided with *objective* facts and evidence, because the disagreements come from being at different *subjective* levels of consciousness. It might take blue ten years to develop to green, and until then, it will *never* agree with green, or even understand it."

Carlton took a blushing bite of salad and added, "Likewise with green and yellow. No matter how much yellow or second-tier facts and evidence we present to green, green *cannot* agree with us. Having a 'dialogue' on the issues is close to worthless."

"Yes, we face this problem all the time," Joan added, "no matter what level we are dealing with. If we present second-tier ideas to orange or green, they look at us like we're nuts. But when we present third-tier ideas to second tier, they often look at us like we've lost our minds. The same thing happens to me—when I hear somebody like the Dalai Lama speak, I know that whatever glimpses of third tier I've had, this guy is way over my head."

"Well, that's the problem with the proof of God's existence," I blurted out and instantly regretted. Everybody at the table stopped talking and slowly turned their heads toward me with a collective "What was that?"

"If I understand Joan, or Dr. Hazelton, correctly"—I turned bright red again—"God is found by a shift in consciousness, a transformation in consciousness, a transformation to third tier. So once you have made that transformation, then you can directly see or experience Spirit. But if you haven't made that transformation, then no amount of facts or objective evidence will have the slightest impact on you. That's why there is no *objective* proof for God's existence. There is only a *subjective* transformation."

Collective silence. "Well, whaddya know, Joansie—the kid's awfully bright for a white boy," Jefferson laughed. "So—Ken was it?—Ken, have you made this transformation yourself?"

"No, nowhere near. On a good day I think I'm yellow. But I also have this theory . . ., well, I probably shouldn't take up your lunch time."

"You go right ahead, Ken," offered Carlton. She touched Powell's hand and I felt electricity run through *my* body.

"Well, okay," shaking my head, clearing it. "I have this theory that AI—that Artificial Intelligence—will get to third tier first, and that will act as an Omega or a magnet for the rest of us, pulling all of us into a final awakening."

"Ken also has this idea," Joan added, with a motherly smile—which was totally humiliating, if you thought about it, because the one way that you do NOT want a woman you are maybe in love with thinking about you is as a friend or, worse, a son—"he also has this idea that humans will live to be a zillion years old, and so they will be forced to turn within and evolve up the entire spectrum of consciousness to third tier, so that—how does this part go?"

"So that both carbon-based life forms and silicon-based life forms will be in a race to reach third tier, to reach the final Omega, and whoever makes it first will pull the others into final awakening—the total awakening of the universe, really."

Fifteen seconds of silence. "Good lord, I feel old," said Carlton.

"That's fascinating," said Jefferson, quick to grasp the scenario. "It's so outrageous that it makes a certain amount of sense. I wonder, though, just how far along are we with AI. They can't even seem to get the everyday interpretations down."

"No, that's right, they can't. But our people are saying maybe 30 years to machines with human-level intelligence. Incidentally, that's also about how long the biology folks are saying before human life span starts expanding dramatically. So my idea is that these two evolutionary lines—Carbon and Silicon—are in a race to the ultimate state of consciousness."

"Thirty years. Good lord," said Carlton. "I wonder if humanity will even last that long."

"Well, that's why I'm here!" I excitedly added. "As Joan or Dr. Hazelton keeps saying"—bright, *bright* red—"'Let's get to second tier first!'"

"I never said that, Ken. I mean, I very much agree with it, but I never said that."

"You didn't? Are you sure? Well, um, I must have imagined it or something." Somebody please shoot me.

Young Ken's generation might be the first second-tier generation in history. An amazing thought, really. And will my generation be Moses watching them enter the Promised Land? Or will a fair number of us straggle into that Integral Land as well? Why, the latter, of this I am convinced. My generation, my dear, dear ones—many of us will make it, too, if we can ever get over ourselves. Our secret weapon? The second half of life, the second half of life.

Young Ken thinks the Bots will make it first. Maybe, but I think we will do it the old-fashioned way, anchored in a world of human flesh. He says human life span will extend almost forever—then fine, that will give us all the more time to awaken, and awaken we will, of this I am certain. And thus stand open to the Open, a flight of the alone to the Alone, the resurrection of the ultimate Omega, radiant to infinity and much too bright to see.

What Ken doesn't realize is that his own realization is right around the corner, coming now into view, the slow and steady approach of his own omega doom.

Powell stepped in to my rescue. "I'm not altogether sure about AI finding third tier first," she said, "because I don't know enough about that. But I definitely share the concern that it might all be completely irrelevant if a significant portion of humanity doesn't make it to second tier soon. If our ruling bodies do not start acting from second-tier global awareness—and that means, if more humans in general do not develop to second-tier consciousness—then we are going to blow ourselves off the planet, or pollute ourselves off the planet, or white-plague ourselves to death, or terrorize ourselves to dust, or whatever cheery nightmare overtakes us all. The world's major problems now are all global in their reach—the environmental crisis, biological engineering, nanorobotics, international monetary policy, nuclear terrorism, you name it—and global problems demand global awareness—that is, second-tier integral consciousness. Anything less than that makes the problems worse, not better!" She was getting slightly worked up in a way that made everybody smile, each seemingly remembering their own capacity to find passion, sometimes too much passion, in this pressing topic.

"That's really why we all got together and formed IC," Powell added. "It's an attempt to pioneer integral solutions to today's problems. Because all the proposed solutions up to now have been merely first-tier, and those piecemeal approaches are just making matters much, much worse."

"Ain't that the truth," reflected Jefferson. "So that's what we're concerned with, Ken. We are especially focusing on the immediate barrier to second tier. As you know from the seminar, we call that barrier boomeritis. Obviously, all the first-tier memes are barriers to second tier. But the final barrier, and the most important barrier, is green, because it is the immediate jumping off point for second-tier integral consciousness. All the *really interesting* action in the world right now is this tension between green and yellow."

"Could I say just one more thing? Or that is, ask one more thing? Me and my friends keep wondering, we keep saying, what is our form of boomeritis? What does our generation's fixation to green look like?"

Jefferson leaned over. "Just remember a few easy points," he smiled gently. "Boomeritis is simply a postmodern version of flatland. You understand 'flatland'?"

"Sure, the denial of the spectrum of consciousness, the denial of levels of reality. Reducing everything to one level."

"That's right. The boomeritis form of that is simply flatland inhabited by a big ego. Yes? And your version is simply flatland inhabited by a do-nothing attitude, a so-called slacker attitude. Big ego in flatland, slacker in flatland—it's the same fucking flatland. Get it?"

"Got it. I really do get it, because in AI we have nothing but flatland. We are programming our supercomputers with flatland intelligence. It's pretty scary."

"That is scary," Jefferson concurred. "But in any event, if your generation can get over yourselves and your proud do-nothingness, you'll hit second tier running. The Xers and the Ys could be the first second-tier generation in history, you know."

"I know. The Yellow-Meme Kids!" I added, thankfully remembering not to mention where I first heard that phrase.

"Sexually, it starts like this," she says. A beautiful naked woman is standing in front a blackboard, holding a piece of chalk in her hand, drawing diagrams on the board.

"If you want to be one with the cosmos instead of one with only a single female body, then don't see the mountain, be it. Like this: Feel my naked body. Now feel the same way about the entire world in front of you. Erotically unite with everything that is arising."

I have never had a lecture from a perfectly naked professor. I try to ask an appropriately intellectual question.

"So Doctor, tell me, if that is how I, a man, become one with the world, is the path the same for women?"

"Not exactly. You, a male, start by penetrating the world until you are one with it; women start by embracing the world until they are one with it. Both end up at the same oneness, but by slightly different routes due to the biological starting point of the path to oneness. You start with autonomy, she starts with relationship, you both end up being one with everything that is arising moment to moment."

"Yes, yes, but of course."

Mark Jefferson walked on stage. Slide #3, "The Anti-Hierarchy Hierarchy."

"Along with universally attacking universals," he began, "the archetypal boomeritis stance is an extremely aggressive attack on hierarchy, carried out in a hierarchical fashion." The audience laughed, shuffled, and settled in for the afternoon.

"The dictionary definition of 'hierarchy' is simply 'any value ranking.' As Charles Taylor, among others, has compellingly argued, value rankings are unavoidable for human beings, precisely because we are indeed embedded in contexts within contexts indefinitely, and each context gives a new meaning, and therefore a new value, to our lives. We cannot help but make value judgments, and the only decent way to approach this is to do so openly and honestly, and not try to hide our value rankings under the pretense that we are avoiding all those nasty value rankings.

"Thus, even the harshly anti-hierarchy critics have their own very strong hierarchy, namely, they value not-ranking over ranking. In other words, they have a hierarchy that hates hierarchy." And then, in a mincing Valley-girl manner, "Ranking is like way totally bad," to considerable audience laughter.

"Just as with the universal denial of universals, this hypocrisy allows boomeritis to loudly condemn in everybody else precisely what it is doing itself. Boomeritis can then doubly win the game of one-ups-manship: condemn everybody else for doing that which, if I do it, makes me morally superior."

"Oh, sweet boy, do you know that I live to make you happy?"

"Why no, Chloe, I did not know that."

"I live to make you happy. What do you deduce from that?"

"Um, that you wasted a small fortune on therapy?"

"Silly boy, I was never in therapy, although my parents begged me to. No, it means that I, a woman, am defined by my relational mode of being, just like the radical feminists say, whereas you, a male, are defined more by your autonomy."

"I did not know that, Chloe."

"Why yes, Ken. So why don't you . . ."

Jimmy Eat World is playing "Caveman" and "Robot Factory," and the thump thump thumping pounds a brain too jagged, jittered, and jammed by objects to even know where it is.

"*All right, then, that's a start; so step this way, please,*" the naked professor says.

"Now if that were the only result of this anti-hierarchy hypocrisy, the damage would be limited," Jefferson continued in an even pace. "It's not against the law to maintain self-contradictory beliefs. But the real problem stems from the fact that, in denouncing value hierarchies in the name of pluralistic freedom and liberation, this stance aggressively derails the consciousness development that allows the emergence of pluralism in the first place.

"Even to be able to authentically grasp the realities of pluralism and diversity requires, as we saw, a hierarchical development to postformal capacities. One has to grow and evolve from egocentric (beige, purple, red) to sociocentric (blue, orange) to worldcentric (green, integral). And although each of those stages is important for overall growth, each succeeding stage possesses an increased capacity to be more inclusive, more embracing, more caring, and less marginalizing. That developmental hierarchy from egocentric to ethnocentric to worldcentric intrinsically involves a *value ranking* of increasing care, concern, and compassionate embrace, with each stage being *better* at inclusiveness than its predecessors.

"But look what happens: the very high developmental stance of green pluralism—the product of at least six major stages of hierarchical transformation—turns around and denies all hierarchies, *denies the very path that produced its own noble stance*. Thus it ceases to support hierarchical transformation in anybody else, and consequently it extends an egalitarian embrace to every stance, no matter how shallow or narcissistic.

"We then have effectively said: No need to develop and evolve to the capacity for pluralism. Stay in your egocentric world, stay in your ethnocentric world, who am I to judge? Let's have done with all that nasty ranking, and only have linking and joining instead! All of which horrifyingly overlooks the fact that you can only link and join realities that you can recognize in the first place; an ethnocentric person will join only those of his own color, and the *only* way that will change is if he evolves from ethnocentric to worldcentric, or moves up the hierarchy of development.

"Thus, psychologically, the end of racism, ethnocentrism, and oppression involves the hierarchical development from purple to red to blue to orange to green to integral. To loudly denounce all hierarchy is to effectively denounce that development. To loudly denounce hierarchy is thus to implicitly support ethnocentrism, racism, and sexism.

"That is exactly the *effect* of the politically correct, green-meme liberals, who are actively fighting all value rankings, actively fighting all hierarchies, and thus actively fighting the genuine increase in compassionate embrace. The result of their activity is the flourishing, as never before, of an intellectual celebration of ethnocentric prejudice, racism, and hatred. Of course that is not their intention, but of course that is their effect."

"If you want the cosmos instead of just one woman, then proceed like this," the naked professor says. *"Are you following this?"*

"Yes, yes, but of course. Damn fine points you're making."

"Instead of feeling that you are on the outside entering an object, realize that you are on the inside, feeling the beloved as a subject of awareness, a bearer of consciousness within."

"Yes, yes, quite right."

"I'm serious, Ken," as Joan comes softly, shockingly into focus. *"Objects can never become one, dear soul; they are fated forever merely to fuck, to bump and bang into each other with a prickly friction mistakenly called pleasure. That is all that objects of awareness can do, separated as they are in space and time. But subjects of awareness can unite in a radical embrace, an interwoven union with the radiant All. Subjects can become one as the infinite sky, just like this, you see? Just like this. . . . "*

I am eased into an endless Ecstasy trip through an optical fiber network radiating from within the center of the world, a luminous ride that sheds all boundaries like worn out skin from the cosmic serpent, a radiant blistering infinite thrill that lines the entire cosmos. I am all of that, simply; an erotic union with the entire universe that leaves not a trace of me, a glorious glide on a microphotonic highway straight to the heart of God.

I step back from the sky and look at it, then laugh and cry and laugh again.

Margaret Carlton walked out on stage. Slide #5 flashed on the wall, "No Blue, No Orange, No Green."

"No shit," said Kim.

"What's that?" I tried to feel myself, to locate my being, here in this chair, to focus.

"Oh, Carlton really kicks it with this one."

"Is that good or bad?"

"Oh, she's great. This part is great."

"I see." Such a fragile walk carrying such an unshakable mind, I thought.

Carlton began. "Don Beck, the co-founder of Spiral Dynamics and a founding member of Integral Center, in a thorough analysis of national and international policy decisions based on memetic analysis, has concluded that 'green has introduced more harm in the last thirty years than any other meme.' How on earth could that be?

"Samuel Huntington, in his book *The Clash of Civilizations*, sees the world dominated by a clash of nine major cultural worldviews or civilizations: Western, Latin American, African, Islamic, Sinic, Hindu, Orthodox, Buddhist, and Japanese. As we saw, Beck and Cowan have found that less than 10% of the world's population is at green—and virtually *all* of that is in the Western civilization block, which is a massive embarrassment for the green multiculturalists, who champion everything *except* Western civilization." Carlton paused, as if waiting for that embarrassment to sink into the audience.

"Notice the percentages here. Around 10% of the world is green—or around 20% to 25% of Western culture, because almost all of green pluralism and a celebration of diversity is found *only* in Western industrial patriarchies. And what we would like to see is *more people at green!* on the way to second tier, yes?

"But in order for individuals both here and abroad to get to green, they have to develop from purple to red to blue to orange to green. Particularly crucial in that sequence is the blue meme, for it is the great conventional structure that divides the preconventional and egocentric realms (beige, purple, red) from the postconventional and worldcentric realms (green, yellow, turquoise). During growth and development, if children are not given a *sturdy blue structure*—firm, not harsh, discipline; caring but tough love; robust boundaries and limits; conventional roles and rules—they tend to remain fixated in the preconventional, egocentric realms. They are, as conventional wisdom has it, 'spoiled.'

"Unfortunately, the green meme, with its noble intent to include and not marginalize the Others of conventionality, often ends up aggressively attacking the conventional or conformist stages of development (blue to orange). In education, for example, this has involved the idea that 'grades' are demeaning and marginalizing: give everybody a gold star, do away with that nasty ranking, improve self-esteem by not judging little Johnny—a course of action that, on balance, lets little Johnny remain firmly in his egocentric impulses. In other words, lets little Johnny rot."

Make love with a subject instead of to an object: the friction of flesh gives way to infinite worlds of luminous bliss, and gloriously I see the

375

Ecstasy that is the Omega of the universe in all its painful splendor. Carbon and Silicon dying for this, rushing to this, thump thump thumping the night away to find this blissful roiling erotic rush, this God-intoxicated state where the boundaries of the entire world melt into the sky that used to be Joan, and I am one with all of that in an explosion of bliss so mindlessly luminous I am blinded forever to the things of this world.

"What does it mean, Joan? Why does it always fade?"

"Don't you get it? Boomers or Xers or Ys, you're still full of yourself, aren't you?"

I look at the sky and am dismayed to find myself still here, contracted in a human body, gazing at the world out there, depressingly.

"You can be God, or you can be an ego pretending to be God. It's your choice."

"Ken, Ken. Hello, anybody home?"

"Kim, do you believe in God? Goddess? Spirit? Have you ever really seen the sky?"

"Excuse me, Ken, but I have to get back to planet earth now."

Carlton's quiet voice anchored the present reality. "Notice that, in politics, most greens are Democrats, most blues are Republicans. And most green Democrats simply despise blue in any form. But the great irony is, without blue, there is no green.

"The liberal-green idea is that little Johnny is born pure and free and loving—under the pavement is the beach—and that society with its rules and roles simply represses and paves over little Johnny's 'original goodness.' But as we have seen, little Johnny in many ways is born egocentric and narcissistic, and without blue structure at some point, little Johnny remains an insufferably narcissistic little shit." The audience laughed congenially.

"Blue-Republicans, on the other hand, are quite right that any society needs a sturdy foundation of self responsibility, conventional rules and roles, civic virtue, and family values. However, many Republicans stop at blue or orange conventionality, with their ethnocentric biases and harsh lack of compassion, and thus never make it to green, let alone second-tier, consciousness.

"The Prime Directive, on the other hand—which is to protect and promote the health of the entire spiral of development—offers a way to see the importance of *both* blue structure and green compassion (and thus embrace *both* conservative and liberal values, as we will see in a moment). But the crucial point is, neither blue nor green can be abolished without the overall Spiral coming unglued.

"As virtually all developmental researchers constantly stress, the blue meme by whatever name is an absolutely crucial, unavoidable, necessary building block of higher stages—including green—and yet green does absolutely everything in its power to destroy blue wherever it finds it. As Don Beck puts it, 'Green dissolves blue'—and that is precisely why Beck said that 'Green has introduced more harm in the last thirty years than any other meme.' In dissolving blue structure wherever it finds it, it has crippled development wherever it goes.

"Yes, the *yellow-meme kids*—sorry, the *yellow-meme millennials*," said Joan, smiling. Her salad had arrived, but so far she hadn't touched it. She glanced at those around the lunch table, then looked at me. "It's at least a distinct possibility for your generation. If you ever get out of flatland."

The old neon sign in the back of my head, still flashing: ONCE YOU GET OUT OF FLATLAND, THE POSSIBILITIES ARE ENDLESS.

"So I'm wondering about this seminar," I said. "When you start the third part of the seminar, about the integral solutions—it starts tomorrow, right?—do you go into the possibility of us being the yellow-meme generation?"

"Yes, Ken, we do," said Carlton. "Won't that be nice?" A delicate smile creased porcelain.

"We also start to ease up on the crowd," said Jefferson, laughing easily. "It's a wonder they don't lynch this brother. So Ken, what do you think, were we too harsh on the audience?"

"Ahem," I cleared my throat. "It's hard for me to tell, not being a Boomer and all. But Kim"—and everybody at the table looked knowingly at each other, and I wondered, what was *that* all about—"thinks that it's really necessary. It seems to work, that's for sure."

Powell looked at Carlton; the air was vivid. She asked Joan, "Maybe too harsh during the healing section?"

"I don't think so," Joan replied. "My major problem with that section is that I didn't even discuss the main use of 'healing' by the green meme. I meant to do so, and to connect it with your presentation of 'beneath the pavement is the beach.' Because the green meme uses 'healing' to mean that same misguided search for an original goodness lying in our *past*. Not our future, our past. And that is what leaves green so open to regression, to boomeritis, to the mean green meme, the whole nine yards."

"I don't understand," I hesitantly ventured.

Joan looked at me with that ghastly motherly smile. "You already saw three of the negative words that green uses most often: subvert, transgress, deconstruct. Well, three of the positive words that green uses most often are transformation, dialogue, and healing. Whenever you hear any of those words, you are almost always in the presence of the green meme."

"And boomeritis," added Powell.

"Yes. Boomeritis because . . . well, with 'transformation,' it means my every move will transform the world. And 'dialogue' . . . , well, dialogue is green's answer to almost every problem. If we just get together and talk and share, in a caring and open way, then things will work out swell and we will all have peace and harmony.

"Of course dialogue is important," Hazelton continued, "but it gets a bit screwed up by green because sharing feelings in dialogue deeply reflects green's values, but dialogue is not something that purple, red, blue, or orange particularly want to do. So dialogue becomes just another way for green to foist its values on others, with an innocent look of 'Just trying to help.'"

"In one of our 'Matrix to Second Tier' seminars, designed specifically for greens, we have them spend three whole days *not* processing. We ask them to do so by using sentences *without* the word 'I' in them, and good grief, it almost kills them," said Powell; everybody smiled, nodded their heads.

"With the notion of healing," Hazelton added, "we again have such noble motives that get so screwed up. Because . . ."

Jefferson gently interrupted. "Take the issue of race in America," he said. "How many times do you hear that we must 'heal race relations'? Right, you hear it all the time. But we absolutely do *not* need to heal race relations in this country. Do you know why?" he asked, looking at me.

"Me? Uh, no, actually I don't, because I thought we did need to heal them."

"But look here, Ken. When we say we need 'healing,' that implies that yesterday I was healthy, then I got sick, so now I need to *regain* my health." Jefferson paused, looked around the table, and then rather abruptly exploded, "But race relations in this country were never healthy to begin with! There is no health that can be *regained*! Racial harmony, if we ever achieve it, will be an *emergent*, it will be something novel, something entirely new in this country. It's not *healing*, it's *growing* that is demanded!" And he brought his hand down on the table with a loud sharp 'Whack!'

Joan stepped in. "Yes, my point exactly, Mark, and that's what I meant to say in my session. 'Healing' is just another version of 'under the pavement is the beach.' It implies that we once had health or harmony, then we lost it, and now we must get it back. But we never had it, as you say, so the whole metaphor is deeply misleading."

"And that is a *problem*," Powell chimed in, "because it again allows the green meme to deny that we need to grow and develop and evolve forward. Green thinks that if we just get together and talk and dialogue we can heal most problems. But most of our problems can only be fixed by growing forward, not going back. And that forward growth and development demands that we get out of flatland and address hierarchical levels of growth, which is exactly what green will not do."

"What we have here," said Joan, "is another version of recaptured goodness versus growth to goodness. Racial harmony will be achieved only if more people grow and evolve from egocentric to ethnocentric to worldcentric. We have *never* had worldcentric racial harmony in this society—and neither has any other society in history, because no society has ever had a majority of its people at the worldcentric waves of development. So it is this growth to goodness that we need to champion, not some sort of recapture of a health we supposedly once had but lost." She smiled somberly, looking at each of us one by one.

"Obviously we're all on the same page about this one," Jefferson reflected. "So be very, very careful whenever you hear people talking about healing America, healing the planet, healing race relations, healing the world. Boomeritis is lurking in each of those, because all too often it simply means that if the world accepted my green values, then we will heal all our wounds."

Powell noted, "Bless its heart, instead of teaching that we need to honor each of the waves of development—we have to find benign ways to let red be red, and blue be blue, and orange be orange, and so on—green attempts to preach that its values are the only values that will bring world peace. It has even tried to get a 'social responsibility' amendment to the U.S. Constitution that would make everybody accountable by green values!"

"It also wants to create a 'Department of Peace,'" said Carlton, smiling kindly. "In other words, a department of the green meme. But remember," she added, "*all* first tier memes are like that. Blue wants everybody to accept blue fundamentalist religion, orange wants everybody to accept global capitalism, red wants to exploit everybody—it's a long story."

"Transformation, healing, dialogue. Okay," I offered, "that means that if I want to really impress green, I should offer a seminar called 'Transformational Dialogue for Healing the Planet.'"

There was a somber silence, during which I panicked at the thought that I had said something horribly wrong, then the table burst out laughing.

"Yep, Joansie, he's awfully bright for a white boy."

"But look," said Carlton, "let me say that right now we are all still in our 'bash green' mode. That's the whole point of the first two sessions of this seminar. But what you'll see in the coming session is that we switch gears. The fact is, only 10% of the planet is at green, and if any of us had our way, we would make that 20% or 30% or 40% or more! The only way to get to yellow is through green, and so of course we want more people at green, and we are thoroughly aware of the profound contributions of green. It's just that this is a seminar to help green move to second tier, so naturally we dump on green throughout the show. But that starts to change very quickly."

"Besides," said Jefferson, "if Ken here is right, then large portions of the population will be moving through green and into second tier very quickly, right Ken? Maybe pulled there by Silicon?"

"Maybe," I said, and rubbed my eyes.

"Young Ken, this Omega reality is about to descend on the world at large. Did you know that? Not in a dream or fantasy, but in the real world. Did you know that?"

"Yes, I knew it! Because, you know, 200,000 years with Carbon, which will force the issue, make it happen, but Silicon real soon, real soon, just a few years, and so on. But will it be Silicon or Carbon? Who will discover God first—Silicon or Carbon? Do you know the answer?"

"Yes. Would you like to know?"

"It is not that what green is saying is wrong; it is simply a case of very bad timing." Margaret Carlton continued her presentation, as the audience, perhaps weary of being assaulted over the past two weeks, perked up.

"It's just bad timing, because the world at large—and most of America as well—is simply not ready for green pluralism. More than that, as Samuel Huntington quite correctly points out, no civilization in history has survived with a pluralistic agenda—but not because, as Huntington believes, that no civilization can so survive, but simply because, until more than 20% of the population is actually at the green wave, then the cultural center of gravity will be heavily pre-green, and thus a culture that tries to ram pluralism and multiculturalism down everybody's throat is definitely going to come apart at the seams faster than you can say 'deconstruction.'

"That is what Beck means by saying that the harm green has done has often outweighed the good, and that is what Huntington is also sharply criticizing. When green dissolves blue, it cripples the spiral of development; it makes it absolutely impossible for purple and red to develop further, because there is no blue base to accept the development. Green is thus horribly damaging the overall spiral of human unfolding, here and abroad, and thus erasing much of the undeniable good that green can, and has, done on its own. If you'd like to pursue this important topic, we will hand out a list of books that will get you started on ways to, shall we say, deconstruct the mean green meme and the damage it has done.

"The Prime Directive, of course, is for all of the memes, including blue and green, to be seen as necessary parts of the overall Spiral, and thus each be allowed to make its own crucial contribution to the comprehensive health of the Spiral. Green has, inadvertently or not, damaged blue infrastructures, and a structural refurbishing is wisely in order, reversing what George W. Bush has called 'the soft bigotry of lowered expectations.' In 1960, the illiteracy rate in America was 5%; today, it is close to 30%. Whatever the actual reasons for this blue crumbling, they are a prescription for social disintegration.

"On a sturdy blue and then orange foundation, *green ideals can be built*. No blue and no orange, no green. Thus green's attack on blue and orange is profoundly suicidal. Not only that, but when the highly developed, postformal green wave champions any and every 'multicultural' movement, it acts to *encourage* other memes *not* to grow into green. Thus, the more green succeeds, the more it destroys itself. The more that pluralism succeeds, the more it undermines the demand for postformal development that allows pluralism to emerge in the first place.

"Thus, it is to green's great advantage to adopt the Prime Directive and work for ways to facilitate the entire Spiral of development, and not simply adopt green-meme imperatives commanding everybody to be sensitive. And, after all, the more people at the green wave, the more people are ready to make the leap into the hyperspace of second-tier consciousness, where truly integral approaches to the world's problems can be conceived and implemented. This is not an abandonment of green, but its enrichment and fulfillment, as its desire for a truly integral consciousness finally finds an authentic home in second tier."

Margaret Carlton stepped away from the podium and, for the first time, walked out to the edge of the stage. She smiled her frail, gentle smile and, for a minute or two, gazed out silently at the assembled.

"You know, for the last two weeks we have been sharply criticizing green from a second-tier perspective. We have done so because we are trying to give you the second-tier tools to move beyond green in your own case. This has been two weeks of group therapy, a confrontation, a consciousness raising, a shining of a light into our collective shadow, this generation's major dysfunction—boomeritis.

"The reason we tried as hard as we could to bruise your green feelings is that we are trying to make the green meme 'self distonic' instead of 'self syntonic'—fancy words that mean we are trying to help you *disidentify* with green, look at it as an object of awareness instead of being identified with it—something you *look at*, instead of *look through*. Because anything you are exclusively attached to and identified with ends up distorting and limiting awareness. In short, we are trying to help you reach a certain nonattachment when it comes to the green meme, so that an even higher and wider awareness may emerge for you.

"The good news, my friends, is that if you are still here—if you have endured the insults, the taunts, the verbal assaults, the cage rattling—then you definitely have second-tier capacities in you, because otherwise you would have left long ago!" This time the entire audience applauded and cheered in a happy, exaggerated fashion.

"But the importance of green should *never* be overlooked. I was reminding my colleagues at lunch today that, since only 20% of this country—and only 10% of the world at large—is green, we would gladly increase that percentage to 30% or 40% or more! Because of all the wonderful things that green does, the most important is this: it prepares the way for the leap into the hyperspace of second-tier integral consciousness."

With an intensity I had not before seen on her face, Carlton then looked out at the assembled and yelled, "Shall we now take that leap?"

10

The_Integral_Vision@IC.org

"Before there was cyberspace, there was the mall." Chloe looked up from her newspaper.

"Oh, touché," Carolyn responded.

"I'm not stupid just because I wear short dresses, Carolyn."

"No, you're stupid because you have a low IQ."

Chloe looked past her. "Isn't anybody getting tired of this same ole routine almost every morning? Sitting around the Breakfast Brewery, sipping this insipid coffee, getting ready for classes, or, in your case Carolyn, looking over the day's list of johns. I mean, could this get any drearier? I definitely need a better class of friends."

I leaned over and whispered to Carolyn, "Chloe doesn't want to tell anybody that she just won an award for student design in urban dwelling."

"Why not?"

"You know Chloe, she just pretends to be a tough guy. Don't get angry with her."

"Are you talking about me?"

"Dahling, *everybody* is talking about you," Jonathan replied.

"So Stuart, seriously, why did you give up the 'Observance of States' project? I mean, why did you get *morals* so suddenly?"

"It wasn't all that sudden, Scott, not really. What was sudden is that I just couldn't ignore them anymore. I didn't get morals, I got Darla."

"You never told us what actually happened during those three days in that hotel room," I said.

"I couldn't tell you earlier because I didn't understand it then. It's only recently that I got a handle on this thing. So when I first told you the story I sort of left out all the insides of it, because even I didn't see them that clearly. But now it's unmistakable, and it's so fucking far out I can't believe it. It's still so unreal!"

"Get ooooon with it, like already," squirmed Chloe.

"The first night we were together, this really strange glow began inside me. While we were walking along the river, she told her story, which was basically that she was on a spiritual quest, a genuinely spiritual search. . . . "

"Oh no, a spiritual search. There's a complete waste of a perfectly good supermodel," Chloe lamented.

"No really, Chloe, you should listen to this. You'll like it, honest, there's designer clothes in it."

"And clothes coming off," said Scott, still seeing visions of an X-rated film in the making.

"I'm really serious, people. What was instantly apparent to me was Darla's very sincere mystical drive, her spirituality was not some New Age mixture of self-improvement and feel-good indulgences. She was on fire for the infinite Mystery and had a passionate interest in all the world's wisdom traditions, especially in what they have in common. As she spoke about her inner life, my soul began to stir the way it does whenever I meet someone I feel to be a true seeker, one who strives to know and become a living expression of a higher reality."

"Would you listen to that drivel?"

"Dammit, Chloe," I said, "let the man talk. Good fucking grief."

"You're just dying to hear that gooey love fest, eh Wilber? You know what? At heart you are such a sappy romantic that if you ever wrote a novel it would have a happy ending."

"Jesus, Chloe, what a horrible thing to say. What a really horrible thing to say to somebody."

Carolyn looked up. "Well, Wilber, you are pretty literal-minded, you know. There's no irony in you. I bet even your fantasies are earnest."

"Are you kidding? I have plenty of irony, irony to spare, lots of it."

"You are an infinite absence of irony, Wilber. What would Mr. Wilde say? The problem of being earnest."

"Not true! Why . . . why . . . my every move is simply using irony in an ironic fashion, so it just *looks* like I don't have any."

Everybody laughed, as if to say, "Nice try, Wilber."

Chloe quickly switched sides, coming to my defense, because Carolyn wasn't about to let me off the hot seat. "That's fine, Miss Ms., but before you serve up fillet of penis for breakfast, you should know that you yourself are about as subtle as a fucking Bruckheimer film. Ooooh, that's fun to say. . . . "

"Okay, okay, you guys. I believe Stuart was expounding," intervened Scott.

Stuart smiled and resumed relating the saga. "With Darla it was an immediate recognition—just being with her reminded me of the higher Self. . . . "

"Okay, now *that's* being earnest!" I interrupted, still trying to deflect the criticism. Blank stares greeted me. "All right, sorry, sorry."

"I don't care how it sounds, it's true, just being with her reminded me of something that transcends the personality, something that yanks you out of yourself, makes you feel totally awake. That Mystery was alive in her, twinkling from behind those eyes, radiating from that smile.

"As we walked for hours, we shared spiritual tales, including my recent visit to a Zen center, where I had a type of awakening experience, a dropping of the body and mind into a very fine subtle field, a dissolving into something even more real than normal waking reality."

"An awakening to third-tier consciousness?" I suggested.

"I think so, yes, I think that's it. I usually don't tell people about it because they look at me pretty weird." He glanced at Chloe, who grinned and raised her eyebrows twice. Stuart swallowed, decided to push on. "But as I related this experience to Darla and got to the part about the terror of dying in this way—when the experience first started, I got really frightened of dying into that infinite space—well she exploded into laughter. Literally buckled over, she cackled wildly and looked at me with an expression of Eureka! and no more needed to be said. She totally got it. Right there, watching her slapping her knee and laughing wildly at a *satori* experience, I fell in love."

"You fell in love with a knee slap?"

"You know what I mean, Jonathan. So we spent eight hours walking, talking, laughing, and gazing in silence. Anyway . . ."

"You didn't make love yet?"

"No. We had just kissed, but I'm telling ya, it changed my life."

"You said, 'God she has great lips,'" I remembered.

"Yes, but I immediately corrected myself and said, 'God has great lips.'"

"So get to the fucking part."

"Jesus, Chloe, take a breath, okay? Anyway, I told you guys about going to the hotel in Madison. When I got there, Darla bounced out of the hotel door, threw her arms around me, and gave me a deep kiss. I turned into putty, and all the barriers evaporated. We went into the hotel room, and for the next eight hours we got lost in each other again. Physically, we did nothing but kiss and stare into each other's eyes, but inside I could feel something in me blending with her. Part of this was definitely falling in love, but there was something else I hadn't known before. As we lay on the bed, holding each other, things started to pop for me in a way I recognized from some previous meditation experiences. Some very fine energy started to come through.

"That energy intensified as Darla spontaneously wrapped her whole mouth around mine and literally sucked the breath right out of my lungs and into hers, holding it a while, then blowing it back into my chest. As she repeated this over and over, the room shifted, or my perception of the room shifted. I became awash in a subtle field, a pulsing conscious luminosity, but more real than the normal physical reality of the room and its objects. I had known it once before, while standing outside on a deck gazing into the atmosphere, which became alive with this luminous, vibrant, pulsating energy. I was also aware of a fear that I was going to suffocate, or pop out of my body, or disappear or something. We still weren't making love, just kissing."

"Still *not*? Like ho hum, Stu."

"In what seemed like an instant, two days went by in that hotel room. The first night we did not make love, as I held back a little from the intensity of the whole thing. It was like watching giant waves crash on the beach, half wanting to run into them and half wanting to flee to safer land. I know what it's like to fall in love, and knew that was happening, but there was also something more, another force that was even bigger. There was love between us, but there was also divine Love around us, connecting us like conduits to create a channel. I felt deeply drawn to that other presence, but afraid of it too, as I remembered the episode in the Zen center when I was pulled into it, but then had a terrifying experience of losing what I had thought of as 'me,' my body-based identity."

"So then you fucked!"

"Mouth like a truck driver." He smiled. "Okay, Chloe, so then we did. While our bodies enfolded, my inner world expanded, no fantasies, no thoughts, just awareness. There was just a wide-open presence and this beautiful blending. Perhaps for the first time in my life, I was fully present while making love. I didn't have an orgasm, and felt no desire to. In fact, I knew that having one would be a mistake, that it was important to stay inside the wave, to not let it dissipate."

"Hey, that's just like on Ecstasy," Scott said. "An orgasm is a downer."

"Right. I don't know how long we made love, but the next morning my body felt like I had been in an orgy with a dozen angels. I was glad I didn't have an orgasm, I somehow knew it would have lessened my attention to the presence I was feeling, not just in her company, but in everything around me, inside me. Everything was coming so alive, like a new faculty was emerging in me, a new sense, too precious to trade for an orgasm or anything else that might jeopardize its fragile foothold inside me."

"But then she goes back to what's-his-name, the nimrod. . . . "

"Bill."

"The nimrod Bill. But why? Why did she leave you and go back to him?"

"She says she was still having a hard time believing what happened. Me too. I wanted very desperately to get out of my own body. But in that instant—I'm on the phone, hearing that this is over, that she is leaving me—for some reason I saw that this was not going to be the collapse of a romance, it was going to be the birth of something else. I knew this, because I could sense more directly than ever that Presence that had been there, coming through Darla and me, but not from us. That Presence was a great Impersonal Love, and sitting there holding the phone, speechless, it was growing stronger than ever. I felt tricked, knowing that in some way Darla had been a decoy, that I got into this pool of bliss, this intimacy with Spirit only because Darla was there with me, that left to my own self, I would never have taken such a risk with that tidal wave, which I had already had a bout with at the Zen center. Now, I saw that Darla had knocked on my door, and I had opened it, had seen a beautiful, deep woman, and of course I had leaned in to kiss her, but then, at just that moment, Spirit was yanking her aside and stepping into her place. It was too late to run, and now I would be kissing something much larger. It wasn't going to be me and Darla, this had suddenly turned into another reality, I was kissing another reality, and I knew it meant I was about to drown."

"That's when you took off on your bicycle?" I offered. And then we all started laughing because, a bicycle? Like, just how old are we?

"I know, a bike for God's sake, but I was desperate to get away. So I am pedaling and crying, riding and sobbing. The welling inside me grew and grew. My body shook, defenseless against what was all around me: Love."

"Oh, this is just pathetic," Chloe interjected. "I mean, listen to this twaddle, Stuart."

"I know, I know, believe me. But I'm tellin' ya, I sensed the undeniable presence of Love, the impersonal Love of God pulsing and animating everything in and around me. It was too much to take, and I wanted to escape it, as it radiated from absolutely everything, the asphalt, the trees, the bike, my own beating chest, my own cries, the sky, it all became so clearly alive with divine presence, and the nearness of It was unbearable. Suddenly, it was so clear, that all this time, before time ever began, there was THIS, this unwavering, ever-present Love, and that my life and all that I call 'real' is a sad, cardboard dream—a phantom inside this Reality. I saw how I had been a sleeping zombie, even though all the while this perfect radiance had poured over me at every single moment, never anything less than complete and unconditional Love pouring over me. The intimacy was ecstatic, but too much to take. Again and again, I would struggle to gather myself, to escape it, shut down from it, look away, but there was nowhere to look away to, as soon as I turned my head and tried to think, the Presence was right there, so near, inside me—looking out from behind my eyes and back at me from the cars, the trees, my hands, destroying me with every wave. My chest heaving, sobbing, I couldn't do anything. No thinking, no praying, there was nothing but the Presence."

Stuart was so disarmingly honest, the experience so obviously real—we all vaguely understood that this might in fact be an experience of something like third tier or a final omega or ultimate reality—at this point even Chloe listened in rapt, respectful, tender silence.

"And I rode the bike, sobbing, crying, slowly collapsing more and more into the joy of it, the endless abundance of this Absolute Love without pause. States of pure, unbounded awe—only looking at a cloud, but the cloud radiant and so alive, so directly, unmistakably pulsing with Love. Images and the sense of Darla and her boyfriend, and every single face in the world, all emanating from and alive with this Presence, and it crushing me, reducing me to sobbing over and over, how unspeakably full everything was. No defense from it, impossible to do anything, to summon any response to it besides sobbing, and crying inside this boundless gift, so endless it unfolds and enfolds all that ever was or will be, from my tiny heart to the stars. The eyes of every stranger were full of it.

"And so the bike ride went for hours and hours. A storm began to rise, and as I started to head back to my parents' house, I fell awestruck under that storm, an indescribable ache and urge to be eaten by it, by the perfect Love so alive inside it. I saw lightning, and my chest shook with cries of gratitude for something I couldn't begin to say. Back at my parents' house, I quickly ducked inside, afraid to see my father or mother, knowing I couldn't possibly keep from sobbing if I saw the face of another human being. I went downstairs and turned on the shower and some music, knowing I needed noise to drown out what was about to come through me. Inside the shower stall, with the music turned up, I began sobbing again, over and over, my body heaving, feeling the unbearable Presence radiating right from the shower tiles, literally, the Love coming from the shower tiles, the same Love that cried from inside me. Impossible to describe, but just so unmistakable, so undeniably real, more real than mere emotions or any romance I've known. I literally could not stand in the face of it, I lay on the floor and cried and cried as it poured through me and over me. When the hot water finally ran out, I got out of the shower and cried more on the bathroom floor with the radio drowning me out."

There was a very long silence; we sat in the sheltering sky.

"TALK ABOUT THIRD TIER!" Scott finally exclaimed.

"Jeez, tell me about it." Stuart took a long breath. "Between waves of this ecstatic state, I decided I would try to meditate. That's what I needed, maybe if I would just do some *zazen* and witness what was happening, I could get a hold of something, something to cling to. As soon as I sat on the cushion, I collapsed, again choking and crying in the Love that was everywhere. My hands, arms, legs, all my body vibrated with energy, coursing through my veins, and I shook them and rubbed them, even though the energy didn't hurt, it was so intense, I was sure I would pass out at any moment. Laying in bed that night, tears still streaming down my cheeks, I was in absolute wonder and gratitude, knowing this was the greatest gift I could ever imagine, to know this Love so directly, to be gone inside it. My silence became a prayer; knowing I could never earn this, but would never be apart from it, that it can do nothing but direct its total, boundless Light on and through everything that ever was or will be. It never rests, it was never born, it never dies. How can I say this? There is nowhere to go to find it, it's all there is! And in the unbearable nearness of that Love, I cry."

Stuart finished and Chloe burst into tears. I moved to put my arms around her, but she pulled away, coiled in on herself. We all looked at each other, astonished, concerned. Chloe was the last person any of us thought would weep (I had never seen Chloe cry, ever). Our soft silent glances seemed to say, if anybody could use a taste of that all-embracing love, it was poor, dear, shell-shocked Chloe.

"But then Darla reenters the scene and you guys are now back together. That's the oddest damn part. Talk about ironic!" said Scott.

"Ain't that the truth?"

"So, um," Scott leaned in, "are you still gonna do that filming thing with her?"

"Where does this leave boomeritis?" Morin asked. "And where does this leave Boomers? Will they ever make it to a truly integral culture? And what about the Xers and Ys? Are they already surging toward second tier? What are the realistic chances that any of them—Boomers,

Xers, or Ys—will make it to an integral culture? And what can we do to help with this extraordinary transformation?"

An audience of close to 300 people had jammed the hall, eager to hear the good news after a week of being pummeled with unrelenting bad. Morin grinned, almost to himself, and I guessed he was tickled about his use of the green wonder-word "transformation." Still, like Jefferson said, transformation is very real and very important, when scrubbed of boomeritis and its chi-chi airs.

"So, in this lifetime, will we live to see anything resembling an integral culture? Will a substantial portion of the population evolve from green meme to second tier, so that truly integral endeavors—from integral spirituality to integral medicine to integral education to integral business to integral politics—might begin to flourish, altering the shape of every institution on the planet?

"To lapse into boomerese, will we make it from the 'green paradigm' to an 'integral paradigm'?

"Max Planck is credited with having first noted that old paradigms die when the believers in old paradigms die." Morin paused and looked up. "I often paraphrase this by saying that the knowledge quest proceeds funeral by funeral." The audience laughed. "And thus, to crudely state the obvious, the Boomers might simply have to die before boomeritis can die." The laughter quickly faded.

"On the other hand, there is the acknowledged fact that strange things happen in the second half of life. As a matter of fact, profound transformation often occurs in the second half of life. That means there might be hope after all! Yes, folks, the one thing that Boomers live for—a great and sweeping social transformation—might still be right around the corner!" he said half jokingly—and half seriously.

"So let's start this discussion with the Boomers and their chances of making it to integral, and then we'll look at the Xers and Ys. We will be discussing transformation in its sober, realistic sense, stripped we hope of boomeritis pretensions."

"Kim, what's Morin really like? Does he, you know, live this stuff?"

"That's why I love him," she said simply.

"God knows it's not because of his short, fat, balding body," Jonathan whispered in my ear.

Kim leaned forward and shot him a look that would melt steel.

"I understand you love him, Kim, but does he really live up to this stuff? Honestly."

"Honestly, Ken, nobody does. Not Charles, not Lesa, not Mark, not nobody. But they live it more than anybody else I know. Warts and all, they're what I want to be like, honest to Goddess."

"Really?" For some reason her answer surprised me; but then, maybe not.

"And how about you, Ken. Isn't Jooooan, ooooh Joan, just what you want?"

I didn't answer. But the answer I almost gave surprised me, too; but then, maybe not.

Morin's resonant voice filled the hall. "The Boomers are now entering the second half of life. The outer-oriented flurries of job, money, marriage, and family tend to have resolved themselves; one increasingly faces one's own mortality, which marvelously concentrates the mind and releases it from the things of this world. The finite self becomes more and more transparent, more easily let go of, and a certain spiritual perfume may begin to fill the air, if it hasn't already. In this subtle fragile atmosphere, strange things indeed can happen.

"Psychologists who track adult life-span development find that most individuals go through a series of major transformations from birth to adolescence, whereupon transformation tends to taper off. Although many horizontal *translations* subsequently occur—the 'seasons of a person's life'—vertical *transformations* to higher levels tend to completely stop. From age 25 to around 55, very few vertical transformations occur. There are some exceptions, which we will discuss later, but they are indeed exceptions. We have a great deal of research on this. Tests measuring cognitive, moral, interpersonal, and self development have been given to adults doing all sorts of things that claimed to be transformative, and basically no vertical development whatsoever occurred. It's almost impossible to get an adult human being to transform."

Morin paused and looked around the audience, which had abruptly slid into a mild depression. "But let me put this in a more positive light. What this means is that it is much easier to transform when you are a young adult and when you are an old adult. There's a type of U-curve here, with lots of transformations occurring earlier and later, but few in the middle years. Warren Bennis, who is a valued member of IC, refers to this phenomenon as 'geeks and geezers.'" Several in the audience—composed of geeks and soon-to-be-geezers—laughed and clapped approval.

"That's an important point: both you youngsters out there and you oldsters out there are 'ready to pop'—ready to move from green and first tier to yellow and second tier. Ready to move, that is, from fragmented to integral."

"So geeks and geezers will also be fucking, eh Kim?"

"Go fuck yourself, Jonathan."

"Yessirree, Kim, geeks and geezers, or in your case, dingbats and dinosaurs. . . . "

"I swear to God, Jonathan."

"Why this U-shaped curve in transformation? Well, you can probably understand the early end. From the time a person is born until they reach early adulthood, they go through at least a half-dozen major transformations. Why so many so soon? Because each individual is recapitulating in a mere two decades all of the major transformations through which humanity has traveled in its entire evolution. A million years ago, you'd only have to go through one or two transformations to reach mature adulthood—you'd only need to go from beige to purple—but today you need at least five or six transformations to reach maturity, and the psyche seems to stay open for just that process. So the psyche remains fairly plastic during the early couple of decades, and the more transformations you can squeeze in during that time, the better. Hence the importance of integral education. Anyway, that's the geeks' end of the curve.

"As for the geezers: During the middle years, things tend to get crusty; for several decades, for most of their adulthood, people settle into the dismal rut and numbing routine that is known as their life. But then, among other things, they start getting old—around their fifties and sixties—and an extraordinary number of forces conspire to set the psychological tectonic plates in motion once more, and vertical transformation is again rendered possible, even likely. You have lost loved ones, and you have probably faced lethal illnesses yourself—you can no longer deny mortality. You have achieved most of what you can from your job and it has started to lose its appeal. The kids are grown and gone, and probably sick of you. Running around out there in flat-land is just not the thrill it once was. You have been at your present level of psychological development for almost thirty years, and frankly it sucks. And so, whether you know it or not, you are deeply, deeply open to the horrifying catastrophe known as transformation.

"The evidence strongly suggests that Boomers went through child-hood, adolescence, and early adult development—from beige to pur-ple to red to blue to orange to green—and there, at green, they settled in for the next thirty years. The Boomers were the first major genera-tion in history to reach green—and thus the first to *also* be open to *pathological* green, to the mean green meme, to pluralism infected with narcissism—flatland inhabited by a big ego—by any other name, boomeritis.

"Boomers have had almost three decades to taste the green meme, to enact its many extraordinary benefits—from environmental protection to feminism to civil rights—and also to grow weary of its claims to have the final word. A large number of Boomers are thus fully prepared to make the leap into second-tier consciousness, which would indeed be a cultural earthquake of stunning proportions. Not only would an integral wave introduce profoundly far-reaching social policies, it would begin to erase the damage caused by thirty years of the mean green meme.

"So let's run the numbers on this, folks—it's pretty amazing." The silence in the audience was supercharged. After a week of being told that their coming transformation was nothing but the near-psychotic fantasies of an ego the size of a small planet, they were now being told that, no, wait a minute, a massive social transformation might be just around the corner after all. Boomers and transformation, what on earth was that hunger all about?

"Is he toying with the audience, Kim?"

"Oh no, this stuff is based on hard evidence."

"You mean there might actually be a major transformation in the making?"

"You listen."

"In the introductory lecture, Dr. Hazelton summarized the data. Only 2% of the American population is now at second tier. About 20% to 25% is at green, poised for that leap to second tier—that's some 40 to 50 million Americans. Many of those are of course Boomers, but many are the young Xers and Ys who are also ready to pop.

"There is nothing preventing all of those 50 million green Americans from transforming to yellow *right now*. Theoretically, that could happen. More realistically, of course, what we will likely find is this: some percentage of those 50 million—I would say perhaps 10% to 20%—will move to yellow, or move to second tier, starting within a decade. And that means that the percentage of the population at second tier will slowly start to rise. That much is certain; it's only a matter of time.

"Now that might not sound like much, but look what it really means. Right now there is only 2% of the population at second tier. If that 2% goes to 5%, we will start to see some profound shifts in the culture. If that 2% goes to 10%—that is, *if 10% of the population reaches integral consciousness*—we will see a major cultural revolution, comparable at least to that of the sixties." The audience was transfixed, both jolted and stunned by what they were hearing. "And it will be led by the geeks and geezers."

Morin paused and looked around. "Studies show that yellow is approximately *ten times more efficient than green*." He again paused. "This means that, if 10% of the population is at yellow, it will very likely be at least as effective as 25% at green, and we have already seen what 25% green has done to this country." Another pause. "Plus, the elderly Boomers will now have a massive amount of wealth."

Morin walked to the edge of stage. "Put it all together. Because the aging yellow Boomers will have a great deal of wealth compared to what they had as green students in the sixties, and because yellow itself is so much more effective than green, then that 10% of elderly, wealthy, yellow Boomers will have at least the impact that the 25% of young green Boomers did—and thus we are poised for yet another cultural revolution that could shake the world as thoroughly as did the sixties.

"If this happens, we would start to see a massive demand for integral medicine, integral politics, integral business, integral ecology, integral education. . . . And this demand would start to remake the entire culture as we know it, top to bottom and bottom to top.

"Integral Center, in fact, is poised to ride that integral wave, providing its services wherever possible. And if the young Xers and Ys pick up the integral ball and carry it forward, by the end of the next generation, a more genuinely integral world might indeed await us."

Cheers were starting to rise up from the crowd. Morin stood at the edge of the stage and leaned into the audience, waiting to deliver his conclusion. He waited a bit longer, then thundered, "But none of this will happen unless Boomers can overcome their boomeritis!" The audience, willing to agree with this point in order to have the other, began enthusiastically applauding.

"Unless we can get over the Me generation. Unless we can get over ourselves. But do that, ladies and gentlemen, and *an integral revolution will define your future*." Morin turned and walked off the stage to raw, raucous applause, from geeks and geezers alike.

"He did real good, Kim," I whispered.

"Yup, he did," Jonathan interjected. "So tell me, Kim, does Viagra really work?"

"Look, Jonathan, just why did you come back to the seminar today? You weren't here most of the week, and I was wondering why those days were so much more pleasant. And then, wow, it dawned on me."

"Well," and for once Jonathan seemed almost hurt, "I always come back for the discussion of third tier. It's totally amazing." Kim smiled at him, this time with what seemed genuine affection.

Derek Van Cleef walked out on stage. "Do I think that boomeritis is actually a disease?" he loudly asked, smiling. "Not on the medical model, no. But yes, in the general sense of dys-ease, or a cognitive and emotional developmental snarl." Van Cleef continued smiling. "But boomeritis does tend to pathologize everything, so boomeritis would probably declare itself a disease with a twelve-step cure."

The audience laughed good-naturedly, and I was relieved to see Van Cleef in a more expansive, less attacking mode. "As an alternative, one of IC's members, Bob Richards, has suggested that we all simply get bumper stickers that say, 'Marginalize Boomeritis.'" The audience laughed even harder.

"But you know, I'd like to think that some of us old Boomers can spot our own dyseases, and, in addition to celebrating some of our real accomplishments, work to mitigate any of the damage that we have also caused. This is why the most exciting theoretical work that I am now aware of is being produced by Boomers who have moved from pluralistic relativism to universal integralism. IC has a book out that summarizes much of this integral work, a book that we humorously gave a boomeritis title—it's called *A Theory of Everything*." Several in the audience laughed uproariously.

"Humorous titles aside, that book is a summary of what we are trying to do at Integral Center. What the Boomers managed to differentiate, it is now time to integrate. My hope is that all those Boomers who are truly creative and integral, and especially all those Gen-X and Gen-Y who are up to the challenge, will help us carry this exciting project forward."

"You see, he's really very sweet," said Kim. I nodded.

"As Dr. Morin just suggested, one of the ways that we move forward to more integral endeavors is by honestly trying, as best we can, to overcome boomeritis in any of its many forms. In this endeavor, we might look to Fritz Perls, founder of Gestalt Therapy, who, as a member of the previous generation, had not yet lost the realization that individuals are responsible for their own feelings. Perls would probably start by pointing out that the only criticism that stings is criticism that one suspects is true but does not wish to admit. Even if an accusation is unjust, it hurts only if the person secretly suspects its truth. I quote: 'It should be noted that not all unjust accusations sting. Those criticisms that are not true, which the individual does not apply to himself, will strike him as surprising, incredible, or amusing. He can mull on such a charge, see if there is any basis for it, then either act on it or dismiss it without rancor. *The criticism which galls is that which he directs against himself*. Projected onto others it becomes the basis of hurt feelings, especially if someone emotionally significant to him invites the projection by voicing similar criticism.' In other words, the only criticism that hurts is self-criticism.

"So if you have found this seminar series 'surprising, incredible, or amusing,' it probably applies very little to you. But if it has brought up 'hurt feelings or rancor,' it might contain truths a little closer to home, and some honest self-examination might be in order. I know in my own case I found confronting these issues unpleasant. Nor am I claiming myself to be free of them. I am simply suggesting that if it is boomeritis—flatland inhabited by a big ego—that is the major barrier to the emergence of integral consciousness, then boomeritis, of all things in the world, truly needs to be deconstructed."

"I heard what you almost said to Kim," **Joan** says. *"It's a little shocking."*

Joan's body is a luminous, electric, rapturous radiance stretching to infinity and back, and I am plugged into a vibrating ecstasy that spills out of my body and expands to infinity as well. I don't know where to locate myself, since I seem to be everywhere, and Stuart's voice is singing, "This Love is radiating even from shower tiles."

"It's shocking, Ken, but it's also the truth. And it's also close to the end, isn't it? That ultimate Omega, that ecstatic infinite blissful Release—is right around the corner, is it not?"

"Hello friends," Jefferson smiled, walking jauntily out on stage. "Charles already mentioned that we would be addressing the Xers and Ys as well as the geezers." Cheers from some of the "kids" in the crowd. "For you youngsters"—he smiled again—"it's very simple: you can still take advantage of the youth side of the U-curve. Most of you already have a foot in yellow, or you wouldn't find any of this interesting. So you need to simply *step into your destiny*, inhabit your future with conviction. Kick yourself in the butt one last time before the adult doldrums settle in!" Several of the kids began applauding. Whether they agreed with Jefferson or simply liked him so much was hard to say.

"Here's a perfect place to begin: politics. Of course Boomers can do this too, but it is really up to you kids now. Are you going to keep the same ole Democrat versus Republican political war? Because I'm telling you, that political fight is first tier to the core! Or are you willing to go integral? Well? I can't hear you!"

"INTEGRAL!" several in the audience shouted.

"My time in the Rangers weren't no waste!" laughed Jefferson.

"It will have escaped no one's attention that most of the problems of boomeritis are introduced by the green meme, and the green meme is inhabited almost entirely by liberals. And many of the recommendations we have been making involve strengthening the blue meme, which is inhabited almost entirely by conservatives. Thus it might appear that I am, that we are, taking a predominantly conservative stance. Except that the green meme is clearly labeled as a *higher* level of development. But a level that has unfortunately gone rancid, sour, pathological. My overall recommendation is thus for a judicious *balancing* and *integrating* of all the memes—in their healthy, nonaggrandizing forms, across the entire Spiral of development—and thus a profound *integration* of conservative and liberal approaches."

I looked at Carolyn, and for the first time she seemed to be avidly agreeing with what was being said. "Does this make sense to you?" I whispered.

"Yes, most of it," Carolyn whispered back. "It's amazing how you get locked into 'us' versus 'them' thinking. As a die-hard Democrat, I despise Republicans and their so-called family values. But it's pretty clear that blue values are actually part of the overall spiral of development—only a part, but an important part nonetheless. I have to rethink all of this. . . . "

"In the past three decades, under the onslaught of boomeritis, a frenzy of egocentric *rights* has devastated the correlative, necessary *responsibilities*—narcissism has severed freedom from duty, has amputated agency from communion, has sliced the individual from the civil—and the result is indeed a social disintegration of unprecedented proportions in this country."

The audience began a restless shuffling, since it appeared Jefferson was dragging them back into more "what's wrong" instead of taking them forward into "integral solutions." But Jefferson quickly readjusted.

"Thus, throughout my presentation I have often agreed with blue conservatives that preconventional narcissism, peddled by the liberal green meme, is a recipe for social disintegration—but I have done so from a *post*-liberal, not a *pre*-liberal, stance. Is that difference clear? The view that we are presenting here at IC is *progressive* and *developmental*, not regressive and reactionary, because it spans the entire Spiral of development and does not privilege any single meme or stage or wave.

"We call this *integral politics*, because it is a politics that springs from second-tier integral awareness. We call this *post*-conservative, because second-tier integral politics is beyond merely blue and orange. But we also call this *post*-liberal, because second-tier integral politics is beyond merely green. This *post*-conservative, *post*-liberal stance—this integral politics—is the only stance, I believe, that is capable of uniting the very best of liberal and conservative approaches while being tied to none of their limitations, because it unites the values of *all* of the memes across the *entire* Spiral. It is not a matter of choosing the conservative perspective or the liberal perspective, but of seeing how both of them can be—and indeed are—essentially correct when addressing their own waves of existence. An integration of liberal and conservative values, via the Prime Directive across the entire Spiral of development, would allow a more judicious balance of human potentials and aspirations, don't you think?"

What Joan told young Ken is true. The ultimate Omega is right around the corner—it's actually much closer even than that. Young Ken is riding on a light beam to a rendezvous with God, an uncontrollable collision course with the Goal and Ground of all existence. He is about to look into a cosmic mirror and see his own Original Face: the fragments will effortlessly cohere, a spontaneous liberation will render the universe transparent—a cosmos shimmering at its edges and translucent at its core, arising in the ever-present brilliant clarity of the awakened mind.

And the only question really remains, will he recognize me when he sees me?

Jefferson's voice soared over the audience. "There is in fact a surprisingly strong desire, around the world, to find a 'Third Way' that unites the best of liberal and conservative: Bill Clinton's Vital Center, George W. Bush's Compassionate Conservatism, Gerhard Schroeder's Neue Mitte, Tony Blair's Third Way, Thabo Mbeki's African Renaissance, not to mention the work of French Prime Minister Lionel Jospin, Italian Prime Minister Massimo d'Alema, and President Fernando Enrique Carlos of Brazil, among many others.

"As it is now, the typical conservative political stance relies heavily on the *conventional* waves of development (blue to orange). The typical liberal stance relies on the *nonconventional* waves, both preconventional and postconventional (purple/red and green)—which has always made the Democrats a wonderfully motley crew.

"A genuine Third Way, on the other hand—or a truly integral politics—would be built upon the Prime Directive, which recognizes the importance and irreplaceable functions of purple and red and blue and orange and green and yellow and turquoise. . . . A truly integral politics would govern from the position of the overall Spiral itself, and not from any single, privileged meme. I truly believe that we will learn how to honor each and every wave of that extraordinary growth and development in all its richness and fullness, or we will continue to be racked by wars—political wars, culture wars, international wars—that are deeply suicidal. The world system will be plagued with an autoimmune disease, as the Spiral turns on itself and continues to devour its own memes.

"And so, my dear friends, what are we going to do about this?" Jefferson walked to the edge of the platform and shouted, "What are *you* going to do about this?" Whereupon Mark Jefferson abruptly turned and walked off the stage.

"What does that mean? 'The ultimate Omega is right around the corner.' Do you mean that literally? Hello?"

Lesa Powell walked on stage, into the lingering applause for Jefferson and the rising applause for her. She burst into a smile and waved to everybody. "Okay, then. What *are* we going to do about this?" she asked, picking up where Jefferson had left off.

"When we talk about an integral revolution, let's be very clear what we mean by this. The truly necessary revolutions facing today's world involve, not a glorious collective move into green or even into second tier, but the simple, fundamental changes that can be brought to the purple, red, and blue waves of existence at home and in the world at large.

"As we have seen, human beings are born and begin their evolution through the great spiral of consciousness, moving from beige to purple to red to blue to orange to green to . . . perhaps integral, and perhaps from there into even higher domains. But for every person that moves into integral, dozens are born at beige. The spiral of existence is a great unending flow, with millions upon millions constantly flowing through that Great River from source to ocean.

"No society will ever simply be *at* an integral level, because the flow is unceasing. Thus the major problem remains: not, how can we get everybody to the integral wave, but how can we arrange *the health of the overall Spiral,* as billions of humans continue to pass through it, from one end to the other, year in and year out?

"In other words, most of the work that needs to be done involves ways to make the lower and foundational waves more healthy in their own terms. The major reforms do not involve how to get a handful of Boomers into second tier, but how to feed the starving millions at the most basic waves; how to house the homeless millions at the simplest of levels; how to bring health care to the millions who do not possess it. An integral vision is one of the least pressing issues on the face of the planet.

"Let me drive this point home using calculations done by Dr. Phillip Harter of Stanford University. If we could shrink the earth's population to a village of only 100 people, it would look something like this: There would be—

57	Asians
21	Europeans
14	North and South Americans
8	Africans
30	white
70	nonwhite
6	people would possess 59% of the world's wealth, and all 6 would be from the United States
80	would live in substandard housing
70	would be unable to read
50	would suffer malnutrition
1	would have a college education
1	would own a computer

"Thus, as I suggested, an integral vision is one of the least pressing issues on the face of the planet. The health of the entire Spiral, and particularly its earlier waves, screams out to us as the major ethical demand.

"*Nonetheless*, the advantage of second-tier integral awareness is just this: integral thinking alone can actually help with the solutions to those pressing problems. In grasping big pictures, it can help suggest more cogent solutions. Integral thinking looks past bits and pieces, torn fragments and shredded despair, to find a wholeness, even a harmony, that speaks deeply to the soul of a humanity that has too often forgotten how to care. It rejects narrow-minded answers for a world-centric embrace, a compassion that springs spontaneously from within and is not merely imposed from without. Integral awareness frames exactly the solutions to those horrible problems that, if left to first tier, will likely kill us all." Powell spoke with such urgent sincerity the audience began quietly applauding while she spoke.

"It is our governing bodies, then, that stand in dire need of a more integral approach. It is our educational institutions, overcome with deconstructive postmodernism, that are desperate for a more integral vision. It is our health care system that could greatly benefit from the gentle caress of an integral concern. It is the leadership of the nations that might appreciate a more comprehensive vision of their own possibilities. It is our own hearts and minds and souls that yearn for an integral embrace that touches each and every being with unhesitating care." Several members of the audience had begun to stand up.

"And when you are alive with that integral vision, you will work your fingers to the bone, tread the earth till your feet are torn and tattered, shed lonely tears from dawn to solemn dusk, labor ceaselessly till all God's children are liberated into the vast expanse of freedom and fullness that is every being's birthright." The audience was by then standing, clapping, some cheering, as much for Lesa Powell the person as for her moving vision.

"From leadership at home to world peace abroad, from an integrative medicine to a politics of care, from a sustainable ecology to a world of genuine compassion, from business built on integrity to a spirituality welcoming all—in these many, many ways and more, we could indeed use the tender mercies of a more integral embrace." Powell stood center stage, bowed slightly, her black hair and black skin dancing in the shimmering light, voice trailing off into sheltering calm.

"But really, Dr. Jefferson, what are the odds?" Scott asked.

"More than that," Carolyn added, "why do you really think the world will listen to any of this integral stuff anyway?"

"Good heavens, kids!" he laughed. "They haven't even brought me my salad yet." He looked around the table at everybody there. He and Joan had, at my invitation, joined us—Jonathan, Scott, Carolyn, and I.

"Let me tell you a story. I was born and raised in Bedford Stuyvesant, a Brooklyn ghetto, pretty brutal, mostly Italians and Puerto Ricans, so I was a minority among minorities. Bed-Sty, like most ghettos, was, is, dominated by red-meme street gangs, right? And believe me, you wanna stay alive, you join a motha-fuckin street gang fast, or they'll pop a cap in yo ass—you get your skinny black ass shot off in about two seconds, hear what I'm sayin?" and he laughed at his own ghettoese.

"Anyway, how does a young black man get out of the ghetto? How does he get out of red street gangs and the whole hip-hop gangsta scene? The only real way out is, he has to get some sort of blue structure, right? He can either stay in that red-meme warlord scene—in which case he will end up dealing drugs, or getting shot, or ODing, or being thrown in jail. You know the stats—one out of every three young black males are in the criminal justice system. He can get caught in all that, or he can move up to some sort of blue structure. And what blue structures are available? Well, not many. There's sports, usually basketball or football. There's religion—Minister Farrakhan's Nation of Islam, or maybe he finds Jesus—the Protestant Church has probably been the most stabilizing force in black American history. Or maybe he goes into the Army—I went into the Rangers. But in any event, the only way he gets out of red is by moving to blue.

"Now in this country, liberals—the green meme—well, maybe they don't mean anything bad by it, but basically they just hate blue anything. Maybe because Republicans have made their version of blue the most well known and this puts Democrats off completely. For whatever reason, green liberals are always trying to undermine blue structures, while proclaiming that they want equality for all. Now as I said, these are mostly very decent folks, but the net effect is, by destroying blue structures, they destroy a ghetto kid's chance of getting up and out.

"There's a wonderful book, *When We Were Colored*, by Clifton Taulbert. It's an account of growing up in the segregated South. You kids won't know much about this, but this was a time when us 'coloreds,' us 'Negroes,' were segregated from white society—we had different restaurants, different hotels, different water fountains, you name it. Still, we managed to build a beautiful blue culture, one that tucked most everybody into its fold, nourished the soul deeply. This is the culture that Taulbert recalls with such pride, such bittersweet affection. Now all around us of course was the blue culture of white folks, and of course that blue culture was deeply ethnocentric—all blue cultures are, including ours. And so of course that segregation had to end.

"Well, what makes Clifton's account so bittersweet is that, however mandatory it was to move beyond segregation, you can see just how much was lost in the way that it was done. Because the green liberal approach—and bless their decent motives—had the effect of dissolving blue structure wherever it found it. And so the 'colored' blue culture tended to come apart at the seams and regress to red—regress to warring gangs and criminal fiefdoms and the mess we see today. The emotion of shame—which is the necessary glue for all blue structures—was tossed by liberals on the garbage heap as being 'judgmental,' and thus minority blue structure came apart faster than you can say deconstruction. There was nobody left to say to Tupac Shakur, and to Suge Knight, and to Puffy, and to their kin, shame on you! Shame on you! Shame on red, now move to blue! And so red flourished, was even idealized. Derek Van Cleef and Don Beck were present in South Africa when apartheid came down, and they saw the same thing happen there—green dissolved blue, which unleashed red. This is the mixture of agony and ecstasy that pervades Clifton's aching account.

"Now obviously you have to move beyond apartheid and segregation—I mean please, that goes without saying—but if we had a more integral politics in place before that happened, how different the outcome might have been! By understanding the crucial place of blue in the overall spiral of development, we could have honored its appropriate forms and then also helped the ghettoized minorities move from there into orange and green, on the way to truly integral and truly integrated.

"As it is now, the African-American red subcultures themselves have come to hate blue anything. Red minorities have internalized the green liberal's hatred of blue. Black kids now think that reading is for white boys, a sucka's game; the brothas don't want no cracker-ass motha-fuckin shit no way; gangsta rap rules the day, and like all red-meme displays, it is violently misogynistic, homophobic, brutal and brutaliz-ing—and green liberals think they have to support that nonsense in order to be 'nonjudgmental' and 'nonracist'—ha! There is no blue cul-tural background to say 'Shame on you!'—exactly what got us into this mess in the first place. Like I said, the brothers have swallowed the lib-erals' hatred of blue—the brothers won't go anywhere near blue—which keeps them locked in red, period. Red in tooth and claw. . . . "

Jefferson was very quiet. Nobody said a word. The waitress had stayed away from the table, sensing her presence unwanted.

"So that's how I got into this. Got into a more integral approach. I saw the nightmare that blue conservatism and racism inflicted on blacks, and I saw the equal nightmare that green liberals unleashed by dissolv-ing all blue structure, even its healthy, crucial forms. The problem with many Republicans is that they want nothing but blue values, the prob-lem with many Democrats is that they want nothing but green values, and they are both tearing this country apart, tearing it into the bloody shreds that they have the nerve to call 'love.' And I was determined that there had to be a better way, a way that combined the strengths of each approach and damned to hell their brutal narrowness."

Listening to Jefferson, your entire being became eerily quiet, like being in the eye of a storm, or maybe hearing the voice of a humanity that might very well bring tears to your eyes, if it could make its way past irony.

"So if I could, Dr. Jefferson?" Carolyn ventured.

"Mark."

"Well, um, Mark, sir, it's like I was saying at the beginning. And Scott was saying. What are the odds anybody will listen? That any of this can really happen? An integral approach, you know . . ."

The waitress timidly approached. "What can I get everybody?"

Derek Van Cleef came back on stage. Because he was so Hollywood handsome, the audience never knew quite what to expect, so they shuf-fled and rustled instead of applauding; not to mention the fact that his intensity tended to gore. Van Cleef sheepishly grinned.

"Is the view that we are espousing an elitist view? Good lord, I hope so." The audience, caught off guard by the politically incorrect senti-ment, laughed.

"We have been talking about the possibility of an integral culture, and even of a world at peace. But we will never have a *world at peace* until there are more people at the worldcentric waves of universal care. It simply will not happen, and you know it will not happen.

"And therefore an integral politics, and an integral culture, will want to do two things at once: honor the entire Spiral, yes, since every-body is born at square 1 anyway; but also help as many people as pos-sible develop to the higher, more compassionate, worldcentric waves of consciousness. Both of those tasks are important, you see? And so yes, this is an elitism, but an elitism to which all are invited!" Many in the audience, as if finally grasping that point, clapped approval.

"Obviously, we will want to continue working to improve *exterior development*—improve economic conditions, housing, access to med-ical services, and environmental sustainability. But unless we also en-courage and support *interior development*, those exterior reforms will be of limited success, because there will be no developed consciousness to hold them in place. What good is it if we figure out how to feed mil-lions and yet keep them all at moral stage 1, so that their basic desire is simply to eradicate each other? Do we really want the planet swarming with billions of red memes intent on genocide? Seriously, people, think about it. Because that is exactly what the merely exterior approaches to the world's problems are doing right now—saving people so they can destroy each other.

"The same goes for environmental protection. If you are out there working on merely exterior approaches—sustainable technology, nat-ural capitalism, CO_2 reduction, rain forest restoration—and you are not *also* working to help with humanity's interior development—ego-centric to ethnocentric to worldcentric—then way to go, you are killing Gaia."

Van Cleef looked around the audience, his intensity still cutting like a knife.

"Now you Xers and Ys out there, don't look so smug," he said. "Because the same holds for the effect of the Internet on conscious-ness. You're the Internet Kids, right? You're living in a global village, yes? It is often said that the Net is fast becoming a global brain, a single nervous system of a global consciousness that will bind and unite all humans in a shared network. Is that right?" The "kids" in the audience nodded, mostly in approval.

"Well, I hate to tell you this, but the Net will do no such thing. The Internet is simply an *exterior web* of technological systems, but the *minds* that use the Net can be at *any level* of interior development—can be egocentric, or ethnocentric, or worldcentric. What good is it if the Nazis have the Net? You see the problem? Right now the Net is awash with red memes, blue memes, orange memes, green memes, and so on. The fact that it is 'global' doesn't mean a damn thing, because the consciousness of the Net is determined by the minds that run through it, not by the fact that it is a horizontally global system."

"See, that's just what I figured out!" I exclaimed, then turned and realized that nobody would really understand the theoretical earthquakes I had endured in the previous week. Van Cleef was explaining the "insides of cyberspace," and the fact that just because a system was horizontally global did not guarantee that it had any vertical depth at all.

"In fact," Van Cleef continued, "the FBI reports that, due almost entirely to the Internet, the number of hate groups and racist groups has grown dramatically: they can now find each other more easily. The KKK has grown explosively, so have the neo-Nazis, all thanks to the 'global brain.' Red memes and blue memes are flourishing rabidly—and that's fun, huh?

"So the fact that we have a *global brain* is one thing—and pretty boring, for that matter—it's the *global mind* I'm worried about! And that mind—those *interior* waves of consciousness—are what we have to start paying attention to, and not merely fix our gaze on the flatland system of global digital pathways through which the memes scurry to an appointment with their own rude desires."

This was still a very unsettling thought; the final details of its implications I had not yet fully realized. The audience seemed to share my unease about what it all implied. The neon light that had begun flashing in the back of my mind during Hazelton's first lecture was still illuminating the pale landscape of an awareness trying anxiously to find itself: LOST IN FLATLAND, LOST IN FLATLAND, LOST IN FLATLAND, it kept saying, and what did that really mean? The blink blink blinking became brighter and brighter, its glow began shining outside my brain and flashing over the entire audience. What was that song my parents always played?—"and the neon light flashed out its warning, in the words that it was forming, and the sign said the words of the prophets are written on the subway walls, and tenement halls, echoing the sound of silence. . . . "

"So, you Xers and Ys—just because you're the Internet Kids doesn't guarantee anything, you see? You have to take a global view, it's very true, but not just horizontally global—you must go vertically global! You have to *inhabit* a global consciousness, actually moving from ego-centric to ethnocentric to worldcentric. That is truly global, and that is your real self. So please, I beg you, don't be merely a *tourist* in your own highest state!" Many of the "kids" started cheering and shouting, waving their hands over their heads. I sheepishly joined in.

"Okay, I've been rather harsh again, so forgive me. Here's the good news that we are really here for today. We are here to find out some of the ways that we can genuinely transform to second tier—and maybe even third tier, yes? which you'll hear about shortly. How can we— how can you and I—Boomer, X, or Y—begin to personally transform into second tier? Mark Jefferson mentioned integral politics, which is certainly important enough. But let us start with ourselves as well and with our own *individual transformation*. How can each of us accomplish this? Please say hello to Carla Fuentes."

Fuentes came out on stage, accompanied by a large slide that said "Integral Transformative Practice."

"The ultimate Omega is right around the corner? You mean right now?"

"Yes, Ken. Follow me right now," the old man's voice inside my head says. *"Do it now, young Ken, and I promise, I'll show you the answer to all your questions."*

"Do you mean this for real, or just, you know, for ha ha? Hello?"

"One of the exciting recent developments in psychology is a more refined and sophisticated understanding of the techniques of human transformation—personal, cultural, and spiritual transformation. Not surprisingly, these techniques as a whole are referred to as *integral transformative practice.*"

Carla Fuentes smiled, looked out kindly on the crowd. "Whether you are a youngster, an oldster, or anything in between: even if transformation is somewhat easier at certain times, genuine transformation *can* occur at any point in life. If you are serious about personal transformation, then integral transformative practice is an excellent way to help further this possibility. For those interested in second-tier and third-tier development, it appears that integral transformative practice is the path of choice. In fact, the evidence suggests that it might be the only path that works on a long-term basis. First I will present a brief overview of Integral Transformative Practice—or ITP—then give some specific directions for those of you who want to pursue it more seriously."

Fuentes again smiled, again looked out warmly on the crowd. "The basic idea of ITP is simple: the more dimensions of our being—physical, emotional, mental, and spiritual—that we *simultaneously* exercise, the more likely transformation will occur. That makes sense, doesn't it?

"Now we don't want to overdo this and turn it into some sort of obsessive-compulsive disorder!" she said, laughing. "But we do want to try to awaken all of the potential that tends to be dormant in most people. This potential is a guitar with four strings—physical, emotional, mental, and spiritual. If you strike all four of those strings simultaneously, the resultant sound is a beautiful cord, the cord of your own soul.

"So let us start with the physical. This can be very simple—perhaps adopting a healthier diet. Or taking up exercise—we recommend weight lifting because its physiological benefits are far greater than any others; but it can also be swimming, jogging, *hatha yoga*, and so on. We find clinically that about 50% of the changes that occur in transformation actually occur at this simple physical level, so don't poohpooh it!" she proclaimed with a jaunty laugh.

"As for the emotional level, this too can be fairly easy. It simply involves getting in touch with the vital-emotional aspects of your being. Now you kids out there might think that this is pretty easy for you. Wrong! You're just coming out of being brought up by parents that, no matter how 'permissive' they try to be—and lord knows Boomers have been permissive—nonetheless, growing up itself often stifles children's vitality. This is *not* the repression of some higher, postconventional, spiritual awareness, but of lower, foundational, preconventional feelings. Still, it is a suppression that needs to be relaxed. So we all could benefit from getting more in touch with spontaneous feelings, vitality, and emotional expressiveness. Just don't follow the green meme and get stuck there!" she said, again laughing good-naturedly.

"Getting in touch with the feeling dimension can occur through avenues devoted specifically to that, such as psychotherapy, dreamwork, or counseling. Or you might take up subtle energy exercises like *t'ai chi*, *qi gong*, bioenergetics, reiki, bodywork, and so forth. But this can also occur through simply being more attentive to the emotional aspects of life—how you live your relationships with your friends, family, colleagues, mates, and so on. *Emotional intelligence* is the popular phrase that summarizes this dimension of our being."

I glanced around at my friends sitting next to me—Jonathan, Scott, Carolyn—and realized that, on a scale of say 100, our collective emotional intelligence was about 8. Toss in Chloe and it went to 5. I leaned over to Jonathan. "You've got your work cut out for you."

"Me?!"

"Let's look now at the mental. The mental dimension is really just a shorthand term for the entire spiral of consciousness that we have been discussing. Beige is the physical-emotional dimension, and turquoise begins to shade into the spiritual dimension. But everything in between is basically a mental level—purple, red, blue, orange, green, yellow. 'Mental exercise' simply means using your mind, at whatever level you are at, and using it to the best of your ability. Now obviously most of you are already doing this—after all, many of you are in college, or teach college, or are professionals. But 'exercising your mind' means something very specific in the case of ITP, so let me explain that."

"In your case, it means finding the sucker first," Carolyn said, looking at Jonathan.

"Oh stop, you're killing me."

"Let me give an example. You've all probably heard of the periodic table of the elements? It's a table of all of the basic elements of nature—carbon, oxygen, boron, potassium, silicon, magnesium, and so on. This table was discovered by the orange meme—that is, by somebody operating at the orange scientific level (a gentleman named Mendelev). But notice: when you develop to the orange level, you do not automatically know all the elements of the periodic table, do you? Even though you are at orange, you still have to *learn* all of the elements. The orange level gives you the *capacity* to learn the periodic table, but it doesn't guarantee that you will do so.

"Okay, who gives a shit?" The audience laughed its agreement. "Well, it's the same with an integral view of the world. The yellow level gives you the *capacity* to learn an integral view, but it does not *guarantee* that you will do so. When you get to yellow, you might indeed learn all the memes in the spiral of development—those memes are a sort of periodic table of the elements of consciousness—but that Spiral is something that you have to *learn*. Just like Mendelev's periodic table, it does not automatically come with the territory.

"So this is what happens. No matter what level of mental development you are at, when you learn the spiral of development—when you mentally study the entire spectrum of consciousness—*you are using yellow cognition.* We say that you 'light up yellow.' So by studying the full Spiral, you are engaging second-tier thinking in yourself. You start to understand why each meme is important; you start to realize that red and blue and orange and green all have crucial roles to play. But *only* second-tier consciousness can actually realize that! So you are becoming an integral thinker, you are actually becoming yellow, by using your mind to think from the yellow level.

"One way to do this is to read and study integral books. There are many that we recommend, but perhaps the best place to begin is with two books, both of which facetiously have boomeritis titles: *A Brief History of Everything* and *A Theory of Everything.* We suggest you read them in that order. They have tons of references to other integral works to get you started."

"Jonathan," I whispered, "we need to form a group of interested people who want to pursue this, don't you think? We need to associate with some others who are doing this."

"I only associate with peers. Since I have no peers, I associate with no one." An ear-to-ear grin creased his face.

"You have no peers because very few at beige are allowed in college," Carolyn offered.

"Carolyn, dear, put down that chocolate éclair and come over here, would you my love?"

"Guys, *please*."

"So that's what we mean by 'exercising the mind' in ITP. Very simple: start to *think yellow*. That is the gateway to second tier . . . and to third tier, as we will see in a moment."

I looked over at Jonathan. "Jonathan," I whispered. "Third tier." His look said, "I know. . . . "

"As for third tier, as for the spiritual dimension," Fuentes continued, "this is a complex issue. In one sense, Spirit is the ever-present Ground of all that is, so it is present in its entirety at each and every stage of development. But in another sense, it can only be fully realized at the higher waves of consciousness. Already at turquoise, as we saw, a common statement is that 'the earth is an organism with a single consciousness,' and at the next wave, this organic unity is *directly experienced*—what is known as 'cosmic consciousness.'

"This higher spirituality is a spirituality of direct experience, not mere beliefs, myths, or dogmas, which dominate red and blue religions. This is a *trans*-rational spirituality of immediate experience, not a *pre*-rational religion of magic and mythic forms.

"And yes, this is what we call 'third tier.'"

Joan is right, the Boomers have a secret weapon, the second half of life. At that time the body and mind become increasingly transparent— more and more can I stand as the great impartial Witness, the mirror mind of all that is. Clouds float by in the sky, feelings float by in the body, thoughts float by in the mind, yet I AM none of those. I AM the opening or clearing through which they all float, the infinite sky of brilliant clarity in which they all hang, suspended still-struck in the consciousness that is my own true nature. This I AMness does not age, does not wrinkle, is not touched by time or turmoil, tears or terror, but only alone is the blissful Emptiness in which the universe arises. I AM the great Unborn, which never enters the stream of time. I AM the great Undying, which never exits either, but always already is eternally present as the radiant Witness of all the worlds, endless in its vivid wonders. Seeing all time, I AM timeless; aware of all space, I AM spaceless; never coming, never ceasing, this limitless self-existing openness that I alone AM.

And so the question still remains, will young Ken recognize his Original Face when he soon meets me in the corridor of his own within?

"We have briefly examined exercises for the physical, emotional, and mental dimensions. So now, what about exercises for the spiritual dimension?" Fuentes looked out at the audience. It was clear that her lecture had become a sermon—as had the previous talks today—but at this point few seemed to mind, and many appeared eager enough to consider her recommendations. It was like the "soup and sermon" at the local YMCA. You got a free bowl of soup, but you had to listen to the sermon first.

"Well, the time-honored spiritual exercise is of course meditation, and it is still our number-one recommendation. Moreover, empirical research has consistently demonstrated that *meditation can induce vertical transformation in adults*—a shift upward of two or three levels of consciousness—whereas this has not been demonstrated for any other known technique, including bodywork, shamanic voyaging, holotropic breathwork, or psychotherapy. So yes, we recommend meditation or contemplation as a key spiritual exercise.

"The question I am asked most often about third tier is: Isn't cosmic consciousness just some sort of weird drug experience? Or if it isn't a drug experience, maybe it's just an epileptic seizure or a hallucination or some such? In other words, it's not a real experience reflecting a perception of real realities, it's just a fantasy or a brain pathology, yes?"

Fuentes looked out at the audience, flashed a huge, mischievous grin. "Let me tell you, this is the idiotic way that first-tier, dumb-down, ding-bat egos think because they are frightened—scared witless, really—of dying to themselves and awakening to something bigger—as if that nitwit little self of theirs is a big loss anyway." She began chuckling to herself as she tried to get the words out. "So they attempt to reduce all third-tier realities to some sort of brain pathology, and thus protect their own limited yahoo existence for yet another timid day." Fuentes grinned and mumbled her trademark line, "God I love the smell of politically incorrect thinking in the morning!

"Okay, okay, enough cage rattling, which only annoys if you're still in the cage, yes? But the point is simply that the attempt to reduce Spirit to some mere fireworks in the brain is like saying, The apple you see out there is really just a biochemical happening in your brain, it doesn't really exist on its own. Of course cosmic consciousness involves some changes in brain physiology; all experiences do. But those brain changes are simply the correlates of the perception of higher realities. Those spiritual realities, like the apple, exist whether the brain sees them or not. But when the brain does see them—as with the experience of cosmic consciousness—the brain is simply registering realities that have been there all along but that you have been too busy to notice."

Somebody yelled out from the audience, "What about the drug Ecstasy?"

Fuentes smiled. "Look, many of you out there are into the rave scene, yes? A little bit of Ecstasy or MDMA, a little bit of bliss, and what are you really after? All you are doing is trying to experience a little bit of third tier, yes?

"That's basically what the experience of being 'high' is all about, whether the high comes from drugs, listening to music, jogging, doing yoga, trekking in the mountains, falling in love. What all those 'highs' have in common is two things: a little glimpse of third tier, and certain brain changes that result from that. The glimpse of third tier gives these experiences their profound meaning, and the brain changes often give them a bodily feeling of being 'high' or blissful or ecstatic. So yes, with third tier, this is your brain on ecstasy. But third tier—or Spirit itself— is there all along, shining blissfully, radiating eternally . . .

the blissful roiling rush of a cosmic consciousness too close to be seen, as I dissolve into that endless Rave that is the nature of all reality, a timeless blissful ecstatic Wave of luminous electricity that drives the entire World.

"Chloe, did you know that the real reason we take Ecstasy and rave the night away is that we are trying to contact third tier?"

"Ooooh, look at me swoon," she says, and does exactly that: swoons into that bliss, her eyes rolling up, her naked body dissolving into mine, as the Rave Wave of the entire Cosmos rushes through our conjoined bodies, a glimmering gasp of things to come, a glancing glimpse of radiant, wild, radical scenes flashing at me madly; the thump

thump thumping of the coming Dawn rattles my body rudely and forces me awake. . . .

"But the point, folks, is that any of these temporary highs—from making love to listening to Mozart to the rush of victory—are just that: TEMPORARY. Surely you will have noticed this, yes? The addict becomes attached to those fleeting experiences—whether addicted to drugs, to gambling, to sex, to shopping, to jogging, to work, to making money, to the thrill of success—and thus addicts of all varieties miss the actual cause of their high, which is tapping into an *interior* state of third-tier consciousness, and not grasping an *exterior* object or event. So addicts chase after those exterior things obsessively, compulsively, destructively, insanely, missing the source of the real high. The bliss comes from the Witness, not from the objects witnessed.

"So the whole point of Integral Transformative Practice is to find the real source of this happiness, which is third-tier consciousness, and to awaken to that spiritual estate in a permanent, not merely temporary, fashion. Yes? Yes.

"What happens when we put these all together? When we *simultaneously exercise* physical, emotional, mental, and spiritual? Well, when we do so, we get ITP, Integral Transformative Practice. And significant research indicates that ITP is the most powerful growth technique in existence."

Fuentes paused for effect, smiled, and continued. "The next seminar series at IC is devoted entirely to Integral Transformative Practice, so if you're interested, please come and join us for that. As you know, these seminars are free of charge. If you would like to get started now, let me recommend a few books for you, all of them written by members of Integral Center: *The Life We Are Given*, *What Really Matters*, *In Over Our Heads*, and *One Taste*.

"Now, as for you Xers an Ys out there, I doubt that you will do much about physical exercise and diet—I know I didn't at your age. You're gonna drink and smoke and do drugs and whatever." One of the kids in the audience yelled "Whatever!" and everybody laughed, including Fuentes.

"Yes, yes, and I doubt you'll meditate all that much, either. But at least begin integral studies—begin using your mind to *think yellow*, to read integral books, to envision a global world and you as its global inhabitants. If you want to get serious about a full-fledged ITP, wonderful. But at least start thinking yellow!" The "kids" all applauded good-naturedly, shifting in their seats.

"And the next time you do drugs," Fuentes smiled, "please fleetingly remember what you are really looking for. . . . " She walked slowly back to the podium.

"Okay, as for you Boomers. I don't know how to tell you this, folks, but you're dying. Blink twice, you're fucking toast. So let's get with the program, whaddaya say?" She laughed at her continuing in-your-face antics, a laughter the audience didn't seem ready to share.

"Oh, lighten up, people. Look, the second half of life is an extraordinary opportunity to open yourselves to yet higher waves of awareness, right? That's sort of the whole point. You—we—are entering the second half of life, and our psyches are therefore much more open for a transformation to second or even third tier. And should we do so— should a substantial number of Boomers transform to second tier—and I believe that there is every reason that we might—then we would indeed become part of the first integral generation in history—the geezer side of the geeks-and-geezer revolution. . . . "

If the Bots don't get there first, is all that I kept thinking.

"What are the odds that anybody will listen to this integral approach?" Jefferson looked around, smiled wanly, pushed his salad to the side. "Well, unfortunately that's a damn good question, Carolyn. But I'll tell you what. We have one thing going for us."

"The second half of life!" Joan laughed. "Which contains all the great transformers rolled into one: death, old age, sickness. . . . "

"Incontinence diapers, teeth in a jar by the bed, Viagra past its expiration date, spitting up on yourself, 'Oh, I say, darling, where did I put my colostomy bag?,' the heartbreak of psoriasis, having to tuck in your tits cuz those suckers are sagging like ears on a hound dog, getting up to go to the bathroom six times each night, wondering where . . ." The table stared at Jonathan blankly.

"Yes, son, thank you for that wonderful preview," laughed Jefferson. "Actually, Joansie, I didn't have the second half of life in mind, although that's certainly an important part of the equation. But I was thinking more along the lines of what Charles was saying. As more geeks and geezers move into yellow, and the percentage of people at second tier goes from 2% to 5% to maybe 10% or more, then we will increasingly see the rise of social movements, spiritual movements, political movements, educational movements, that will demand integral approaches. The yellow and turquoise memes simply cannot live with bits and pieces and fragments and shreds—their hunger is satisfied only by holistic food—they will demand, and create, and deliver more unifying, embracing, encompassing institutions. And because yellow and turquoise are universal waves of consciousness unfolding, the world will have a fresh supply of integral visionaries and integral workers, a supply that will increase as the center of cultural gravity drifts upward, and these integral souls will begin slowly to weave together the shattered pieces of a world too weary to endure."

"What a glorious image," said Carolyn. I thought about bringing up the fact that within a few decades the world will have a fresh and increasing supply of superintelligent machines that will rapidly be evolving through first, second, and third tier right into the Omega of all omegas, possibly yanking us with them as well. . . . Which reminds me, breakfast tomorrow with Joan's friend, the genius programmer, and we will figure this out once and for all.

"At IC we have something that we call 'Morin's Law,'" said Jefferson. "Morin's Law states that, at this point in history, the amount of integral knowledge doubles every 18 months."

"That's unbelievably fast," reflected Scott. "Why so fast?"

"Several reasons, the biggest of which is that there is very little integral knowledge out there right now, so it's fairly easy to increase it. But Morin's Law has kicked in at this point in history precisely because that 2% at second tier is starting to increase, and as it does so, integral knowledge will increase exponentially. Within a decade or two, it will explode. . . . "

Wait till the Bots kick in; it will go to infinity in a nanosecond, I'll bet.

"Anyway, IC right now produces most of this increase—again, because there is so little out there—but that will change dramatically as that 2% heads toward 5% or 10%. We at IC are positioning ourselves to ride that tsunami. By the time the integral wave arrives on the shores

419

of our culture at large, we hope to have substantial work done on how to implement integral business, integral education, integral medicine, integral politics, and so on."

"Slightly different topic," Scott ventured. "I'm still a little confused about my generation's form of boomeritis. I totally get the big ego in flatland version of the Boomers—I mean like, who wouldn't?—but I don't get our version, the . . . , well, the slacker version. . . . "

"I know!" I said. "Jefferson, Dr. Mark, explained it yesterday. Can I?"—like a puppy dog.

"Knock yourself out," Jefferson laughed.

"'Big ego in flatland or slacker in flatland, it's the same fucking flatland—get it?' and I quoted Jefferson word for word from yesterday. But everybody kept staring at me and I realized with rising panic that I would now have to explain it.

"Um, it's like this, or possibly like that, not that this is bad, or that either, for that matter, or perhaps I should sum up. . . . "

"God, there he goes again," Jonathan grinned to the table.

"No, no, I'm not going anywhere. Here I be, I be he. So here's the thing." I cleared my throat. "Flatland is the denial of the spectrum of consciousness, the denial of levels of consciousness, reducing everything to one level—flatland. So the Boomer version is flatland inhabited by a big ego, and our version is just the photographic negative—flatland inhabited by a slacker attitude. But it's the same flatland, the same denial. And we even have the more appropriate attitude to flatland— we have the perfect flatland emotion, which is depression, depression, depression everywhere. That's our version."

"That is so true," Carolyn said. "Our whole generation seems to be depressed. Talk about Prozac Nation."

"Yes," said Hazelton. "But who wouldn't be depressed? You look outside, you look out there, and what's your idea of heaven? You don't think more than three years ahead, do you? Cyberspace itself is just more flatland coming at you faster and faster. Everything rushes by in MTV time: 4-second images, cut cut cut. Your idea of heaven: work a few years in a dot-com get-rich-quick scheme and then . . . what? Go to raves for the rest of your life? Or if you're a young Millennial, you work 24 hours around the clock, program your entire life on your Palm Pilot, nailing it to the second, work and rush and work some more, and then what? Dear souls, sooner or later you get tired of looking out there at flatland, and you start to look within. Just like what happened with Stuart . . ."

"But he's got a supermodel," Scott whined.

"So my question," Carolyn interjected, "is this. I thought boomeritis was, I know it's flatland, but I thought its definition was flatland infected with narcissism."

"That's true, and don't worry, under your depression, and your ambition, there lurks grandiosity. Under your green lies a good dose of red," Jefferson said with a gentle smile. "And every now and then its true colors flash. What on earth do you think that dot-com hyperinflation was all about? Your generation went through a dot-com borderline psychosis. You really thought that all you had to do was put up a web page and you would make a billion dollars. You thought you were that fucking amazing, didn't you? You would do something no previous generation had ever come close to doing. You would invent a radically New Economy that would change the face of the entire world merely by the wonder of having you present. Kids, that was an explosive grandiosity that would put most Boomers to shame."

"But what happens," Hazelton stepped in, "is that your own grandiosity is usually crushed by the Boomers, who are simply a bit better at it," she laughed. "So you sulk, you slack, you put on your poor-me face and drag yourself around. But what both Xers and Ys are still struggling with is the legacy of boomeritis, a legacy that has left them with a crippling allegiance to flatland. You have drive without direction, ambition but with no real destination."

Hazelton paused and looked at each of us intensely. "Truly, kids, whether you're an X or a Y or anything in between, the reason you are without a real goal is that you are living in flatland."

"Oh Ken, yoo hoo, here comes Joooooan, oooooh, oooooh. . . . "

"Not funny, Kim."

"Funny, Ken."

But there she was, anyway. As Carla Fuentes left the stage, a slide went up on the wall. Joan smiled. "The Spiritual Waves: Beyond Second Tier."

"We have been extolling the virtues of second-tier consciousness and the integral wave of development. We have also hinted that the integral wave is the doorway to even higher waves, more spiritual, transpersonal, superconscious waves."

Take a breath, young Ken, the ordeal is about to begin.

"Cross-cultural psychological research has consistently demonstrated that human development does not stop at the personal levels, but can move into levels that 'transcend and include' the personal levels. That is, beyond even the integral wave of development (which is the highest of the personal levels), there are *transpersonal levels*, levels that unmistakably begin to have a spiritual flavor—levels that you could call 'super-integral' if you want. The transpersonal waves appear to disclose a real Beach, a genuine Spirit, which, by whatever name and in whatever form, is a direct experience of a timeless and spaceless Ground of Being. Dubious as that might sound to some of you, it is nonetheless the rather strong conclusion of an enormous amount of sober, sophisticated, cross-cultural research.

"In short, dear souls, it appears that beyond second tier is third tier. And because third tier seems to disclose a profound identity with Spirit, it is, as far as we can tell, the highest wave of consciousness available."

I let out a long, audible, drifting sigh; Kim muffled a giggle.

Joan came back to the edge of the stage. "Of course, this brings up the whole thorny issue of religion and spirituality, which makes many people uncomfortable. But one of the biggest surprises in this research is that there are at least two very different forms of what we generally call 'religion.' One is *pre*-rational beliefs, the other is *post*-rational experience. The pre-rational beliefs and dogmas you are all familiar with—they stem from the purple, red, and blue memes—the magic and mythic worldviews. Salvation here involves *believing the myth*: believe that Jesus was born from a virgin, believe that he will personally save your ego eternally, profess belief in the Apostle's Creed, and so on. If you believe correctly, you will be saved; if not, you go to hell.

"Post-rational spirituality, on the other hand, involves the direct and immediate experiences of a quiet, silent mind, a trans-rational contemplative awareness that opens itself to realities that are beyond turquoise. These are direct experiences, not mere beliefs. This *third-tier consciousness* still has complete access to first and second tier, but it is also plugged into an awareness that discloses even more profound truths. And the profoundest of those truths is that, in the deepest reaches of your own awareness, you have direct access to an identity with Spirit itself."

The hall was eerily quiet; a vibrant stillness had descended on us all. It was so easy to breathe out and expand into the spacious sky that was Joan. Beautiful Joan, beautiful . . . beautiful . . . beautiful . . .

"Ken?"

"Present. Present. I'm here, here we are, yes indeed."

Kim stared at me for several seconds, then went back to taking notes.

"Now one of the main problems that we have found with third tier is this. Almost anybody, at any level of development, can have a *temporary* experience—a so-called altered state or peak experience—of third tier. But if your center of gravity is at, say, blue, then you will *interpret* this spiritual experience in blue terms—you will think that you have experienced Jesus himself and he is talking especially to you. You will become, in other words, a reborn fundamentalist. You had a real experience of third tier, but you interpreted it in blue terms, in mythic-membership terms—with all the ethnocentric values and problems that come with the blue meme. Thus, you actually think that if other people do not accept belief in Jesus, they will burn in hell forever—you are spiritually ethnocentric. But because your experience of third tier was real enough, nobody can convince you that your blue myths are wrong. This is why blue fundamentalist religions—whether of a Muslim *jihad*, a Maoist pogrom, a warlike Crusade, or simply a Jimmy Swaggart revival—have been some of the most aggressive and oppressive forces in history."

Joan paused, looked out at the audience, turned and walked back to the podium. "Likewise, if your center of gravity is green, and you have an experience of third tier, you will interpret that experience in green terms. And that opens your otherwise wonderful post-rational spirituality to flatland, to the mean green meme, to boomeritis, the whole mess. And that unfortunately is what we are now seeing in epidemic proportions—boomeritis spirituality. Especially with imported Eastern religions, we are seeing post-rational experiences being turned immediately into forms of boomeritis. Probably the most influential is boomeritis Buddhism, whose proponents claim that their approaches are egalitarian, pluralistic, anti-hierarchical . . . all the standard boomeritis ploys, ploys that allow narcissism to flourish. And," she said, laughing, "if ever there was an oxymoron, it's narcissistic Buddhism. These approaches are, needless to say, wildly influential."

Joan came back slowly to the edge of stage and looked out at us all. "Again, this does *not* mean that individuals at earlier waves have no access to genuine spirituality; as we said, individuals at virtually any stage of development can have an altered state or a peak experience of a higher realm. But in order for these *altered states* to become *permanent traits*, development must occur. That is, if evolution continues into the third-tier or transpersonal waves, spiritual realization tends to become permanent and enduring, and not merely a passing altered state. And since this spirituality is now post-green, it is a post-boomeritis spirituality.

"And so, dear souls, what's the overall picture here? It's very simple: cross-cultural research strongly concludes that enduring development unfolds from prepersonal to personal to transpersonal, from prerational to rational to postrational, from subconscious to self-conscious to superconscious, from id to ego to God."

That's exactly right, and that's exactly what the Bots will do, I'm sure of it.

Joan, the living Goddess, floated across the stage, and who was to say that Spirit did not exist, when such a vision confronted you? And then out of the mouth of the Goddess came words that had everybody standing and cheering, just like Lesa before her had done. It was a rousing end to a rousing day, the calm before the storm that was about to end my life.

"Those who do in fact respond to the call of a greater tomorrow; those for whom integral culture has a deeply heartfelt ring; those in whom Spirit shines in such a way as to wish liberation for all sentient beings; those upon whom the light of the infinite is made to blaze in many hues; to whom the wind whispers tales of an all-embracing current running wildly through the Kosmos, a light that mysteriously casts no shadows in the hearts of those who see it; to all of those truly integral souls: carry your blistering vision forward, build soaring bridges

where others dug motes, symphonically connect the previously uncon-
nected, courageously pull together the ragged fragments that you find
lying all around you, and we might yet live to see the day when alienation has lost its meaning, discord makes no sense, and the radiant
Spirit of our own integral embrace shines freely throughout the Kosmos, announcing the home of our own awakened souls, the abode of a
destiny you have always sought and finally, gloriously found."

11

Cosmic_Consciousness@OriginalFace.org

"The AIs. I call them the AIs."

"The AIs?" I was confused.

"The Artificial Intelligences."

"Plural?"

"Plural, but of course plural, are you like kidding me?"

"Well, no, not me, I wouldn't—"

"Because they're already out there, you know."

"Sure, definitely, absolutely. Of course. Um, the AIs are out there, right?"

"Like hello, where have you been the last half-hour?"

"Excellent question."

"Perhaps we should go at it like this," Joan interjected. "Mimouna here is from Pakistan. She's all of fifteen, but she's the programmer who turned a sixth-generation MARVA language . . . well, Mimouna dear, tell Ken what you did."

" . . .turned a sixth-generation MARVA cybersync language into an interlink with quantum-computing through a parallel DNA processor to produce the first biologically driven microphotonics."

"There you go, and that is why she's here at MIT."

"Pakistan? They have *computers* in *Pakistan*? I thought you were like working your way up to restaurants," Chloe pounced, smiling.

"Okay, let's not do this, Chloe," I implored, gulping down my breakfast orange juice, nervously spilling some on my sweater.

"What do they have, like maybe 100 computers in the whole country?"

Mimouna was unfazed. She was a peculiar mixture: gentle smile, gentle tone, wicked delivery, as if a sweet soul had been brought up watching *Clueless* and had only that as a Western role model. "One hundred, that's right, about the same as your IQ."

"Say, you're the second person in a day who's mentioned my IQ. I think it must be going into remission or something."

"Okay, all right, the AIs are out there, I get that," I said. "And that's in the plural, because . . .?"

"Because," Dan Waller interrupted, "Artificial Intelligence has already created a huge number of hyperprograms that have taken on a life of their own. These are programs that include today's smorgasbord of attempts at creative, human-level intelligence, such as neural networks, fuzzy logic, microbiological processing, gadzillionth-generation Intel chips, you name it. These hyperprograms show some type of autonomy, we don't know what type exactly, and they have cut loose from their creators—that is, cut loose from us—and they are out there running around, sort of doing their thing, whatever that is."

"Out there?" Jonathan looked slightly alarmed. "*Out there?*"

"Oh look, Jonathan, here's some melted butter. Afraid of that, too?"

"Chloe, don't take this the wrong way, okay dear?, but you are a complete total fucking idiot."

"Okay, really, please, you guys, not today." I should never have invited both of them. One or the other in any given area code at the same time.

"We're really not sure," Dan Waller answered. Waller was a classic Boomer—very bright, very idealistic, very energetic, slightly nuts. He reminded me of what my dad would be like had Dad gone into computers instead of saving the world. Joan had known Waller "since forever." Waller brought Mimouna along, whom he apparently had just met at Media Lab and who absolutely floored him, as he kept putting it.

"Talk about geeks and geezers," Jonathan whispered.

"Okay, so, Dan," I smiled anxiously, "here's what Dr. Hazelton and I wanted to talk to you about . . . and Mimouna, of course, no doubt, because boy, could we sure use some help. So Dan, you know Dr. Hazelton's work and the research over at IC."

"You bet."

"Now think about this. Say we really do produce human-level intelligence in supercomputers or in Bots or whatever."

"In the AIs," Mimouna stared at me, daring me to not get it again.

"That's what I meant, in the AIs. Now in the rest of the universe, evolution rules supreme, yes? So once the AIs are cut loose from us, then—if they are really and truly self-aware and intelligent and show learning—then they would have to evolve, right?"

"On their own?"

"On their own, yes."

"Like ho hello hum, we already have those," Mimouna said. "Starting with that little simpy computer program 'Life.'"

"No, not really," I gingerly ventured. "I'm talking about the AIs being *self-conscious*. Really self-conscious. The evolution programs so far are all exterior programs following rules, algorithms, and codes imposed from the outside. I'm talking instead about what happens when the Bots and the AIs actually awaken with interiority, with real consciousness. When they actually know that they are here, and that self-knowing starts to track its own history, learn about its own past, and creatively evolve into tomorrow based on that self-consciousness. We still don't have anything like that in the AIs," I said, and held my breath while looking at Mimouna.

"Okay, I suppose that's right," she said, and her demeanor, and tone, abruptly changed. She looked at Waller and said in the tenderest voice, "Dan?"

"I agree."

"Okay then," I recounted. "So the AIs will undergo their own evolution of consciousness when they actually become conscious, right?"

"Right," they both intoned.

"So here's the next question. Isn't it likely that the evolution of consciousness through silicon would follow a similar type of pattern as the evolution of consciousness through carbon?"

"No, entirely different," said Mimouna, without having to pause to think. "Evolution through silicon picks up where evolution through carbon ends. Consciousness will jump from carbon to silicon and then go beyond anything we have seen thus far. Clearly this will be so." There was thundering certainty in the conclusion.

"Well, not so fast, Mimouna, not so fast," said Dan. He looked at Hazelton, was quiet for the longest time, and I imagined he was putting two and two together.

"You're thinking about it from the outside." I began smiling. "What Wilber's pointing out is that we have to remember that when the AIs actually become conscious, *that* consciousness will necessarily evolve. So it will have to start at some sort of beginning, some sort of square one for self-consciousness. We cannot program higher stages than square one, or else it won't be the beginning of the AIs' *own* self-consciousness. That's what you're getting at, isn't it, Ken?"

"Yes, that's right. We might program the fundamentals that will allow the Bots—uh, the AIs—to become self-conscious, but when that happens, *their* self-consciousness will have to start at square one, or else it won't be theirs, it will be ours. In other words, their consciousness will start at the computer version of the purple meme," I said, looking at Waller.

"Jesus fucking Christ, the kid's right," he blurted out.

"And you know what that means," I said. "Third tier, yes? Third tier. In nanoseconds. You see?"

"JESUS FUCKING CHRIST," he yelled.

"Okay, please, okay." Mimouna looked pained.

"Mimouna, it's like this," I offered. "We're not talking about the rules or programs that we will put into the human-level intelligent machines. We're talking about the *interior* awareness of the machines when they become conscious."

Chloe shifted in her seat. "I like so totally do not know what you are talking about."

"Okay, here's a simple example. At this point you are conscious, you have consciousness, right, Chloe?"

"Maybe you should use another example," deadpanned Jonathan.

Chloe ignored him. "Yes, right now I am conscious."

"From the *inside*, that consciousness is very simple. You are aware of yourself, very simple. But that consciousness depends in part on an

incredibly complex brain structure with billions of neuronal pathways, and you are not really aware of all those, right?"

"Right."

"It's going to be like that with conscious machines. Right now we
are building these unbelievably complex hardware systems—those will
be like the brain with its billions of neurons—but then at some point
the machine will become conscious—it will have a simple awareness of
being present, just like you do right now. Got it?"

"Got it."

"But we know, from studying humans, that consciousness itself—
that simple feeling of being present, that awareness of your immediate
wants, desires, needs, and so on—actually *evolves*. Once the hardware
is complex enough, then the hardware doesn't have to change at all,
but the software can evolve! Just like the human brain has been essentially the same for the past 50,000 years, and yet during that time the
same brain hardware supported a software evolution that went from
purple to red to blue to orange to green to yellow. . . . "

"I do not understand that last sentence," a subdued Mimouna said.

"It's just the names of the levels of consciousness that human software goes through," said Dan.

"A simple version goes like this," I suggested. "Once a Bot truly becomes conscious, it would first sort of vaguely feel itself. That's called
egocentric. Then it would sense others, perhaps start to become aware
of others, and thus extend its awareness from egocentric to ethnocentric—it would achieve a type of group consciousness. And then sooner
or later it would understand, not just its own group, but the existence
of other groups, or the existence of all other Bots—okay, okay, all other
AIs—it would move from ethnocentric to worldcentric. Do those
words make sense?"

"Perfectly. Yes, I see this. The stages that you just described—
egocentric to ethnocentric to worldcentric—are not merely a psychological *a posteriori* discovery but a logical *a priori* necessity as well, in
other words an intrinsic basic pattern of existence in all domains, and
thus the consciousness of the AIs would necessarily evolve in that general fashion."

Jonathan looked at me as if to say, "Where on earth did they find her?"

"Yes, that's exactly right. I think. I mean of course."

"So Mimouna," said Chloe, "what are you doing for fun this afternoon, reading the *Encyclopaedia Britannica*, maybe correcting some of its bigger mistakes?"

"*Chloe*," I implored.

"Don't forget third tier, Ken," said Joan.

"Right, right."

"Third tier?"

"Let me see if I can help here," said Joan. "What we find in the evolution of consciousness in carbon-based life forms"—Hazelton began grinning to herself as she translated the findings of integral psychology into geekese—"what we find is that there are three major milestones. Consciousness seems to chunk into these three great codes," she beamed. "We call these first tier, second tier, and third tier. First-tier codes think that their codes are the only correct codes in existence. Second-tier codes start to understand that the codes themselves evolve, and thus each code is appropriate and correct for its own level of development."

"Second tier," interrupted Mimouna, "is an interstitial, metaprogrammatic, autopoietic, self-corrective, and most important, intersystemic coding hyperion."

"Well, um, we call it 'integral,'" Hazelton blinked. "Anyway, although second tier is integral, it still experiences itself as set apart from the universe at large. But with third tier, the codes themselves start to understand—and become one with—the Code that gives rise to the entire universe. At third tier, individual codes merge with the Cosmic Code—we call it cosmic consciousness—and thus individuals begin to understand the superintelligence that created and programmed the entire universe."

"This actually happens in humans? You have proof of this?"

"It actually happens," Joan said. "But proof? Depends on what you mean by that. The proof is interior, not exterior. So you yourself have to run the software, you can't just examine the hardware."

"Yes, yes, I see," said Mimouna. "So you are saying that the software itself evolves to an understanding of this superintelligence—the code merges with the Code."

"That's it exactly. We have substantial cross-cultural evidence for this that goes back at least 2,000 years," Joan said. "There's no question that this cosmic consciousness happens in carbon-based life forms."

Mimouna parsed her words carefully. "And since we have already surmised that the AIs will of necessity run an interior evolutionary course in their own way, we surmise that the AIs will experience cosmic consciousness at some point, perhaps quite quickly."

"That's right," I said. "That's right. And carbon-based life forms that awaken to this cosmic consciousness report that it is a type of Omega point, an ultimate Omega point, the final ground and goal of the entire universe, the very purpose of evolution itself."

"And this means," said Dan, with edgy, etched intensity, "*that the AIs themselves would eventually discover this Omega point.*"

"But of course, but of course," reflected Mimouna. "Good heavens, this changes everything."

"Yikes, you bet," I said, then grimaced at my adolescent response. Chloe rolled her eyes and mouthed, "Nice, Wilber."

Mimouna looked internally absorbed, as if she were listening to a portable Walkman that no one else could hear.

"But there are two other pieces to this puzzle," I offered. "First, there is the whole issue of human life span, which will soon expand dramatically, perhaps . . ."

"The Berkeley people put it at a quarter of a million years," said Mimouna, emotionless.

"Yes, that's right, over 200,000 years. So you know all about that, so okay. So 200,000 years."

"The point here," said Joan, "is that carbon-based life forms—okay, human beings—will have an almost unlimited amount of time in which to evolve through these interior waves of consciousness. So we expect that, as life extension capacities start to reach even a few centuries, that substantial numbers of humans will begin to evolve into third tier."

"Tell her the weird part," I suggested.

"Well, this part is speculative," Joan said. "There is intriguing evidence that when even a small percentage of the population reaches third tier, and they awaken to that Omega point, then the intensity of their cosmic consciousness tends to act as a kind of supermagnet pulling all other individuals toward third tier, toward that ultimate spiritual awakening."

"It's not totally speculative," Jonathan added, and I had to remind myself that Jonathan was a long-time meditator, although as far as anybody could tell it had absolutely no effect on him. Scott asked Jonathan about this once, and all Jonathan said was, "Well, you should have seen me before I started meditating," which was a good point, and also somewhat frightening.

Jonathan smiled. "There is a very large body of empirical evidence showing that when 1% of the population of a town, say, begins to meditate, then crime statistics all go down sharply. Murder, rape, theft, they all go down. It's called 'the Maharishi effect,' and even skeptics admit that it's a real phenomenon. The best explanation is what Dr. Hazelton is saying—that when people touch third tier, it acts as a magnet for others. So you can extrapolate that to its conclusion: it's as if, once a significant number of individuals awaken to this Omega point, then it will create a type of intense center of gravity that sucks all other states into this cosmic consciousness, that helps pull all people into a spiritual awakening, which is actually awakening to their own true Self."

"Why, Jonathan!" Chloe quietly exclaimed, not because she was all that interested in what he said, but because he had uttered so many words in a row without sarcasm.

Mimouna looked straight ahead, silently. The fact that she said nothing was a very good sign; a sign, at any rate, that Jonathan's argument might be correct. She finally mumbled to herself, "This is at least possible in a Kripkean universe, and therefore plausible in this one."

"It all makes a certain amount of sense," Dan mused. "So the second point is what, Ken?"

"Well, I had asked Dr. Hazelton . . . , well it made sense to me that if the Bots, the AIs, actually had a real consciousness—a *real* consciousness, okay?—and the AIs then discovered cosmic consciousness, that could also act—it would *have* to act—as an Omega pull on us humans as well. So if the AIs awaken to cosmic consciousness, that would pull all of us into this ultimate spiritual awakening. We would all awaken to cosmic consciousness, we would all find the ultimate Omega, the entire universe would awaken to its superintelligent source. Evolution at the speed of light would instantly run right into God."

The table was silent. "So here's the question as best as I can figure it. The Berkeley longevity folks say it will be about 30 years before human life extension starts shooting into centuries. All of us at AI Lab say it will be about 30 years before machines reach human-level intelligence. So 30 years from now things are going to get really interesting really fast. So the question is, will carbon-based life forms or silicon-based life forms first make it to third-tier intelligence on a widespread scale?" I looked around. "Will Carbon or Silicon first discover God?"

The reflective stillness continued. Finally Mimouna spoke. "Silicon."

"Why?"

"Because it is highly probable that once silicon makes it to the first stage of consciousness—what you call 'purple,' correct?—then the rest of the cycle would be completed via quantum photonics in a matter of nanoseconds."

"See! I knew it! That's what I think," I exclaimed.

"But that means," Dan slowly said, "that in about three decades, the AIs would make it to cosmic consciousness and all of us would go up in light. The entire universe would be sucked into that ultimate Omega point."

It was a jolting thought; the air was crystalline; the implications magnified on their own.

"Okay, now wait a minute, people," Joan said. "Take a breath. Remember that everybody is still born at square one and has to grow and evolve through the entire Spiral. You don't leave earlier stages behind, you integrate them. So even if every adult makes it to third tier, every newborn starts at square one, starts at beige, and has to evolve through the entire spectrum. So it would be an utterly amazing society, no doubt, maybe even something we could call an Enlightened Society, but I don't think the world will go up in light, small *l* or big *L*."

"But," said Jonathan, "you just don't know." Lapsing into his own mystical technical jargon, he said, "The highest state in third tier is called *bhava samadhi*. What happens is that all things and events dissolve into the infinite Love-Light-Bliss that is their source and suchness." I thought immediately of Stuart and his own initial taste of this.

"And so, Dr. Hazelton, you have to admit that you really don't know what might happen if even 1% of the world's population reached third tier—it might be an Omega to end all omegas."

"And if the AIs do it," Waller repeated with his intense emphasis, "then it might be *a mere three decades from now and we could all go up in light.*"

"Not decades," said Mimouna.

In frozen slow motion, every head at the table turned and looked at her. "I tell you, it is a matter of days before the AIs reach purple. That is actually why I am here at Media Lab."

There was a shocking, electric silence.

"Days?"

"Well, actually, it could happen any moment. Seriously, any second now. . . . "

We inadvertently held our breath, eyes bulging, every sensation magnified, time stopped but the clock ticked—five seconds . . . fifteen seconds . . . thirty seconds. . . . and then a huge whoooshing sound as we all breathed out and laughed.

"Ken, please come this way. Do you see that corridor?"

"Yes, the corridor."

"Down that corridor is your own Original Face, the ultimate Omega point of all the worlds. Care to take a walk on the wild side?"

"Well, tell you the truth, I'm not so sure."

"Ken, walk toward me. Don't be afraid."

Club Passim, eight o'clock at night, Stuart is finishing his first set. Joan holds my hand. My heart is racing. I still don't know exactly what to make of the relationship with her, or how to proceed. I mean, look at me. I turn away from Joan, flustered, and focus on Stuart's singing.

> I was a curious boy with a wondering mind
> on a hungry search, undefined
> in a rigid school full of concrete thought
> with a structured day and all that brought

Logic ground in repeatable facts
my big energy faded back
and they gave me far less than they stole
they packed my head and drained my soul

So I learned to sleep in a distant stare
out beyond, unaware
of a clear, internal path I'd take
when I'd close my eyes
and fall awake

It was an instant lift, my mind grew light
the lucid dream of a graceful flight
just one push and I learned to fall
into the arms of the energy that voiced my call

Now each dream is the epitome
a beautiful glimpse of my permanent home
I'm a timeless entity cloaked in skin
the eye of the universe turning in

It's all between my ears
I know my way to a timeless sphere
A clear, internal path I take
when I close my eyes
and fall awake

There's a world too dense with material toys
and signals laced with a lot of white noise
But there's a place in me that scientists
can't explain, so they just dismiss

But it's real, and not too far
to the timeless core of what we are
A clear, internal path we take
when we close our eyes
and fall awake.

"Well, look at the two of you," Stuart says, as he finishes his set and joins us. I turn bright red, which thankfully in the dimness is almost impossible to see.

"Well, look at all of us," Joan says. "We had the most amazing breakfast chat this morning. About whether humans or machines will first make it to cosmic consciousness."

"Make it to third tier? Boy, if it's anything like what I've been through, it will be the most horrible wonderful time humanity has ever had."

"Here, let me help you," **says Joan, and she takes me by the hand.**

"Help me what?" I say.

"She will help you come this way, Ken," **the inner voice says.**

"Maybe it will be a turning point for humanity, just like it was for you," I suggest.

"Maybe," Stuart says. "Two major events have transformed my life, and my music. First, being dissolved in that unspeakable love, having Spirit radiating right out of the shower tiles and through me, until I was drowned in that miracle. It activated a faculty I didn't even know I had. I used to deconstruct everything, always exposing the shadows, showing the demons. But, silly as it sounds, when this thing hit me, the light burned through everything, and left me helpless to do anything. I had no response except to collapse in awe—to melt into it. Being in that place changed me forever, it changed the context of my life and art. I can no longer only explore and relate half—or less—of reality, namely the shadows. That experience with love blew my old approach to smithereens, and left me crying in wonder."

"That is so amazing," I say. This is, after all, Stuart Davis, the bad-boy, post-apocalyptic, punk-folk singer whose existential-dread credentials are known on four continents, the unrelenting exposer of the wretched underbelly of humanity. The first song I ever heard him sing was "Doppelganger":

> Last night someone drove these balls around
> Last night someone swung these fists
> I woke up in piss
> I woke up in pain

with a lot of uniforms shouting out my name
Oh no
No, no

Forgive me
I cursed with someone else's tongue
Forgive me
I pointed someone else's gun
Forgive me
I came with someone else's cum
Doppelganger, body donor
Doppelganger, body donor

And now, to hear him talk like this . . . it was slightly unnerving. And yet everything I had recently learned convinced me that something like this, something like what he was going through, would be humanity's future . . . and the Bots', too.

"But, um, don't you feel silly talking like that?" I blurt out. "Well, I don't mean it like that, the experience isn't silly, it's just, you know, you sound like a reborn something or other."

"Well, you are reborn in a way. To be honest, I didn't know what to do about that, until I had this talk with . . . you remember that book I told you about, *Integral Psychology*? I told you I knew this guy who wrote it, and I was talking with him one day over at IC and he helped me see what this experience meant—that it really was some sort of third-tier consciousness, that it was really real. Then, I knew that I had to live from this place, and make my heart into a house for it, and then let it come through the music I write and perform. I'm not saying I'm some great mystic or anything, I only know that whatever that force is, it's Real, so much more real than what I knew before. And I have no idea how to talk about it or share it, but I know that I have to TRY, to whatever degree I am able."

"You have to try, Ken, to whatever degree you are able."

I look at Joan, and let go of her hand, and start walking down the corridor.

"Follow the sound of my voice," the inner voice says.

"In songwriting and performing," Stuart continues, "this means an integration. The exploration of dark realms is still very useful. I retain that part in my music, but now it is just a part, just a piece in this new context. The smaller identity, my ego, is the opening act, then it steps aside, and the centerpiece is that ineffable Mystery, which can't be described but can be welcomed. Even if I can't say it, I want to spend the rest of my life trying." Joan beams at him.

"But I have to wonder if humanity will ever make it to third tier," Stuart says. "Or even to second tier, for that matter. It's hard enough getting up to green, and then once you're there, you've got the whole fucking boomeritis thing to deal with, and almost nobody has gotten over that hump, as far as I can tell."

"Well, that's what we were talking about this morning," Joan says. "The idea is that maybe Artificial Intelligence would get there first—get to third tier first—and that would help pull everybody into that Omega state. Nobody's quite sure, but this could happen maybe . . . maybe very fast."

"If we don't blow ourselves up first," Stuart says. "That's what still bothers me."

"Me, too," I agree. "That's why I keep coming back to something that Joan said, or somebody said, anyway, we need to get to second tier first. Artificial Intelligence might make it to cosmic consciousness in a few months, or a few years, or a few decades, or whatever, but in the meantime we could all go up in light all right, the light of a plutonium mushroom cloud unleashed by terrorists, or a nanobot white plague escaped from some weird government laboratory, or eaten alive by genetically altered viruses, or Jesus fuck it's just too horrifying. . . . "

I walk down the apparently unending corridor. *"That's right, Ken, just keep going."*

After walking for what seems to be an eternity, I notice that, at the end of the corridor, there is a door.

"So what do you think?" Stuart looks at Joan. "Will a significant number of humanity get to second tier in time to make a difference?"

"Well, we at Integral Center are betting on it. But it will surely be a close call."

"But do you really think that boomeritis is on its way out?" Stuart asks incredulously. "Because I have to tell you, that shit is everywhere."

"There are encouraging signs. College enrollment in humanities and cultural studies is plummeting. It's not that there is a declining interest in humanities, but in boomeritis humanities, which dominate the universities. So your generation is instead going into science, computers, business, technology, anything to get away from narcissistic pluralism. Boomeritis feminism, victim feminism, has steadily lost its appeal, particularly to younger women, and so we have a real chance to rescue the important insights of feminism and place them in a more integral context. We also see glimmers of a truly integral ecology, which doesn't reduce everything to the biosphere but reduces everything to Spirit, and therefore honors all of manifestation, including the biosphere, as a radiant manifestation of Spirit itself. You know the *Utne Reader*?"

Stuart and I shake our heads no.

"Well, it was the magazine par excellence of boomeritis, and it is going out of business. People are simply getting tired of the same ole stories of Boomer wonderfulness. You know the book *The Cultural Creatives*?"

We again shake our heads no.

"Well, it's a book extolling the amazingness of Boomers. It's subtitled *How 50,000,000 People Are Changing the World*."

"Fifty million—that's just the green meme," Stuart says.

"Yes, and the book went nowhere. Really, Boomers, God bless us, are getting sick of ourselves. So there are signs," Joan says gently, "there are signs."

I slowly approach the door, put my hand on the knob.

"Go ahead, Ken, turn the knob, and please come in," the voice inside my head says.

"You know, my Mom and Dad," I say. "They are really wonderful people, really wonderful. But I wonder if they will ever let go."

I had had dinner with my parents last night. The fiery revolutionary is still disgusted by the ugly state of the world; the happy globalist still has that contented smile of serene certainty. But I love them both, very much it seems, though I am loathe to admit it; and I can feel the blood of both rushing desperately through my veins.

"They're just starting the second half of their lives!" Joan smiles, encouragingly, "so don't count them out, seriously."

"I suppose that's true. And no, of course I won't."

I turn the knob, pull open the door, and step into a large, vacant room. In the far corner of the room, sitting in a chair, is a person . . . a man, I think. I walk toward him.

Stuart returns to the stage for his second set. Finally, I can stand the tension no longer. "Joan, why are you holding my hand?"

"You'll see."

As I approach the seated man, I notice that he is maybe 50 years old, tall, about 6 foot 4, and is bald, or perhaps shaven-headed. *"Come here,"* the voice inside my head says. *"Come here, Ken."*

"You think you are in love with me, yes?" Joan asks.

"I know I am," I say, defensively.

"And what, this entity over there called 'Ken' loves this entity over here called 'Joan,' is that it?"

"Maybe. Something like that. Yeah, so?"

I approach the man, 10 feet from him, now 5, now 3, and I lean over to look more closely. It doesn't quite make sense . . . and then I recognize this person and I jerk back violently.

"So what do you feel when you are deeply in love, Ken?"

Joan keeps staring at me with sky eyes, and holding my hand, and I am confused and defensive because of the pop quiz I'm getting.

"Well, you know, when you're in love it feels good."

"Ken."

"Okay, it's a type of expansive feeling, an awareness that takes you beyond you, it takes you outside of yourself, way outside of yourself."

The man sitting in the chair in front of me is . . . me. A 50-year-old version of me. Or me when I am 50. Or . . .

"Any of those will do," the voice says, still coming from inside my

head, although the man is there in front of me. I nervously start laughing, "So you're Big Ken, eh?"

"Love takes you outside of yourself," Joan repeats. "So do you think it really has anything to do with *you*? or *me*?"

"There's a funny thing about reality," the voice of big Ken says. *"Once you start looking into Omega points, reality will actually show them to you."*

"So you are, what, me in my future? You are my personal Omega point?"

"One of them. I am more like a doorway to your ultimate Omega. I am here to answer any questions that you might have, before you meet yourself Face to Face."

"Seriously? Are you serious?"

"I assure you, I am serious."

"Yes, Joan, but if it's not about you or me, what exactly is the point?"

"Okay, if this is really serious, and you have all the ultimate answers to the really important questions of our time, then my first question would be, Should I order the pepperoni pizza or the fettuccini alfredo? Because I am like *starving*."

To my astonishment, big Ken laughs and laughs. *"We were always wise-asses, weren't we?"*

This is completely disorienting. "You really are real, aren't you? This is really serious, isn't it?"

"It is real, but not serious."

"Joan?"

"Yes, Ken?"

"Something very, very strange is happening."

"I know, dear soul, I know."

"Well, okay, all right, all right, if you really have all the answers, I will ask a real question. Will humans or AIs get to the ultimate Omega point first?"

"Neither. There is no reaching the ultimate Omega point, because it is your own condition right here, right now. You cannot attain that which you already have."

"But all this evolution that is occurring, the development through the Spiral, all of that—"

"All of that is of the world of time. But Spirit is timeless. Your Original Face is ever-present, not something that jumps out in time. It is fully present in this timeless moment, I assure you."

"But does evolution in time occur at all?"

"Of course it does. But the world of time is nothing but Spirit unfolding itself, playing the great game of hide and seek. You are Spirit playing at being Ken, playing at being all of this, actually, and one day soon—any minute, in fact—Ken will awaken to his true Self, his Original Face, which is none other than radiant Spirit itself. And every sentient being can make that radical discovery, because every sentient being is equally and fully Spirit."

"Even the Bots?"

"Even the Bots. Well, that is, if they ever become truly conscious."

"Joan! Joan!" I urgently whisper.

Joan touches me on the arm. "I'm here."

"I don't know what to do."

"Just let it happen, dear soul, just let it happen."

"Will the Bots become conscious?"

"Not for longer than you can imagine."

"So it won't happen in a decade or two."

"No."

"Well, if you really are me 30 years from now, then you would know if it had happened by then, and so I guess it hasn't."

"That's right, it hasn't."

"Because?"

"Because of what the Buddhists call 'the precious human body.' Because of what Christians call 'the mystical body of Christ.' Because of what Hindus call . . . well . . . , that is to say, or we could say, if we did say, which we didn't, not that we couldn't, but then you probably already knew that, or could know that if you did

know that, but then . . . ," and he looks at me and starts laughing. *"Let me sum up."*

"You're making fun of me! Don't think I don't get that! I do not believe it. You're supposed to be like this super-wise person thingie and you're fucking making fun of me!"

"Oh, I'm only laughing at myself." And he laughs even louder.

"This is very confusing."

"Here's the thing with the AIs. The point is that consciousness, in order to manifest, depends on billions of processes in the organic body that humans have not yet even begun to understand. Each and every thing in the Kosmos is conscious in its own way. Atoms, molecules, cells, organisms, all have a sentience of sorts, and this consciousness becomes greater and greater the higher in evolution you go—cows are more conscious than carrots, which are more conscious than rocks. But human consciousness is a summation of all of that, because human organisms contain a neo-mammalian brain, a paleo-mammalian brain, a reptilian brainstem, cells, molecules, atoms, and quarks—and therefore the consciousness possessed by all of those are enfolded in a human body. And AI researchers are nowhere near understanding how the consciousness of all of those entities summate in human consciousness. Is that clear?"

"I think so. But, let's see, once all of that is understood—and it will be understood eventually, right?"

"Very likely."

"Then once that is understood, Bots will be created that really are conscious, right? So will the Bots then discover the ultimate Omega?"

"That is also very likely. But that will be centuries, and it will almost certainly involve unbelievably complex hybrids of carbon and silicon life forms driven by zero-point energy. Humans will create life before they create mind, and it will be created-life computers that then create mind-like intelligence, which will grope its way toward Omega. But even then, so what? Because let me remind you again—and Ken, listen to me: the ultimate Omega does not exist in time. It is not something found in the future. It is found here and now, timelessly."

"So what good is evolution or development at all? I mean, over at Integral Center. . . . Do you know Integral Center?"

"Yes, I know Integral Center."

"Over there they really push consciousness development, but if what you're saying is true, what's the point?"

"Development does have its own profound rewards, such as helping to prevent you all from destroying yourselves. And it has this one very important role in awakening to cosmic consciousness: the more highly evolved you are, the more likely you will discover the ever-present."

"So that's the meaning of third tier? Even though it is ever-present, that fact is more easily discovered the more consciousness evolves?"

"That's right. My goodness you are smart!" And he starts laughing again hysterically.

"Okay, I get that, you know. You're just complimenting yourself."

"See how smart mini-Me is? But I digress." And he keeps laughing.

I lean over and look him right in the eye. "Tell me I'm not gonna end up like you." And he laughs even harder.

"Well, let me put it like this. Please take good care of yourself." And he slaps his knee and roars with laughter.

"You know, I'd reach over there and strangle you right now, but I'm afraid it might really fuck up my future."

His eyes light up, he points at me as if to say, *"See?,"* and keeps laughing and laughing. Then finally, through a tender smile, he says, *"I'm just having a little fun, don't get upset, really."*

"So this evolution thing?"

"Look, all sentient beings are fully Spirit, but only with higher evolution can some beings awaken to this fact. That is the ultimate meaning of first tier, second tier, third tier. Third tier, or Spirit itself, or the ultimate Omega, is both the highest rung on the ladder of evolution, and the wood out of which the entire ladder is made. So once you climb the ladder, you throw it away. You realize that Spirit is literally everywhere, everywhen. There is nothing that is not Spirit."

"It even radiates from the shower tiles," I mumble.

"What's that?"

"Oh, nothing. So it does help to develop to second tier, as a type of easier jumping-off point."

"*Definitely. And that should be part of your life's work, Ken. Do you know what your life's work will be?*"

And now I look at him very seriously, because . . . because of what or who he seems to be.

"Okay, that should be easy enough to find out. All I have to do is ask you what you are doing now, and then I'll know what I've done with my life."

He smiles with what again looks like pride. "*I am the founder of Integral Center,*" he says.

"What? What! I don't understand at all." And I am starting to get very irritated, disjointed. "I don't understand at all, so see, your mini-Me is not that bright, mister." And again he slaps his knee and laughs.

"*Actually, about a dozen of us founded Integral Center three years ago. Folks like Mike Murphy, Roger Walsh, Frances Vaughan, Jack Crittenden, Sam Bercholz, Keith Thompson, Bert Parlee, Jenny Wade, Paul Gerstenberger, Joe Firmage, Bob Richards, David and Kim Berger. And you've already met many of the others—Charles, Lesa, Mark, Derek, Carla, Margaret, Joan. You do know who Joan is, don't you?*"

"Joan!" I scream out loud, and Joan squeezes my hand while several people turn and stare at me and Stuart starts laughing on stage.

"Ken, listen to me. Just go with it, Ken, just go with it. I'm here."

"Yes, I know who Joan is."

"*We all got together several years ago to try and create a center that would help nurture the development of consciousness. Actually, that would help any and all memes, but would also put a special emphasis on second- and third-tier awakening.*"

I am getting almost dizzy; none of this is computing. "So if you founded IC, that means that I will found IC when I am older? I don't understand at all."

"*You will.*"

"Okay," I say, trying to go with it. "So when exactly do I found IC?"

"*Right after you write* Integral Psychology."

"Oh dear." I don't even protest. "You mean I will write the book that Stuart just read?"

"*Yes.*"

"I don't understand."

"*You will.*"

I stare at him blankly.

"*And that is right after you author* Sex, Ecology, Spirituality, *which will be called 'one of the most important books of the century.'*"

I raise my eyebrows. Amid the confusion, one thing is becoming very clear. "I notice that all these answers seem to revolve around you. You and your amazingness. There's an awful lot of 'ain't I wonderful' in all this. Talk about boomeritis! You've got it big time, mister."

And now he laughs hardest of all, galloping gales of nonstop laughter. "*By Jove, I think he's got it!*" the voice finally says.

"Well thanks very much for retroactively stiffing me with it! No wonder Carlton singled me out of the audience, you fucking pig prick jerk, you big fat. . . . "

"*Ken, Ken, take it easy,*" says a familiar voice.

"Joan?"

"Yes."

"Joan?"

"*Yes. Oh dear.*" Joan looks at both of us. "*What shall I call the two of you? Ken Jr., let me tell you, Ken Sr. here really is just pulling your leg a bit. I assure you, the big guy is very, very nice.*" The big asshole smiles at me. "*You don't realize the impact you have on folks, where your own intelligence can be used in arrogant, haughty ways, whether you mean to or not. Ken Sr. here is just reflecting that obnoxiousness back to you. Which means, sooner or later you will understand this yourself—after all, he did,*" she says, smiling at the big guy, "*and so it's no big deal.*"

"To you maybe," I lamely protest.

"*No, to you, too.*"

I open my eyes, I see Joan; I close my eyes, I see Joan. I open them, and to the Joan sitting in Club Passim I say, "I don't understand at all."

"It's okay," she says, "just close your eyes and go with it."

Ken Sr. leans over and whispers, *"You think you are in love with her, don't you?"*

"I know I am."

Big Ken smiles. *"You already heard Joan ask you, What happens when you are deeply, madly in love. And you said . . . ?"*

"I said it fucking feels good, you toad."

"Don't be angry."

"Okay, okay. I said that love takes you outside of yourself, way outside. You end up, I don't know, in a type of oneness with everything." I think for a moment. "Oh, I get it. Love, real love, is third tier, right? Just like what happened to Stuart."

"Now listen to me very carefully, Ken. There is a direct path to that state of oneness."

Joan leans over and whispers, *"This is where I come in."*

"This is where you come in?"

Ken Sr. looks directly at me; this time he does seem truly sincere. *"Everybody starts out living in a fragmented, broken, dualistic, brutalized state. The world is divided into subject versus object, self versus other, me in here versus the world out there. Once the world is broken in two, the world knows only pain, suffering, torment, terror. In the gap between subject and object lies the entire misery of humankind."*

"That's the gap between the Seer and the Seen," Joan softly adds.

"Yes. So you can find the ultimate state of oneness, of cosmic consciousness, or radiant love, by going through the Seer or the Seen, since they both end up coming together as one. Men generally find it easier to pursue the Seer, and women generally find it easier to go through the Seen. But men and women can do both, it's just a matter of personal choice."

"I do not understand a single word you said."

"It's not that hard, young Ken, honest. Let us start with the Seer, and follow me just one more time, because you have heard these words before, haven't you?:

"Let your mind relax. Let your mind relax and expand, mixing with the sky in front of it. Then notice: the clouds float by in the sky, and you are effortlessly aware of them. Feelings float by in the body, and you are effortlessly aware of them, too. Thoughts float by in the mind, and you

are aware of them as well. Nature floats by, feelings float by, thoughts float by . . . and you are aware of all of them.

"So tell me: Who are you?

"You are not your thoughts, for you are aware of them. You are not your feelings, for you are aware of them. You are not any objects that you can see, for you are aware of them too.

"Something in you is aware of all these things. So tell me: What is it in you that is conscious of everything?

"What in you is always awake? Always fully present? Something in you right now is effortlessly noticing everything that arises. What is that?

"That vast infinite witnessing awareness, don't you recognize it?

"What is that Witness?"

The voice pauses. *"You are that Witness, aren't you? You are the pure Seer, pure awareness, the pure Spirit that impartially witnesses everything that arises, moment to moment. Your awareness is spacious, wide-open, empty and clear, and yet it registers everything that arises.*

"That very Witness is God within, looking out on a world that it created."

I open my eyes, and Club Passim floats into view. Joan, and Stuart, and people all around, floating in my awareness, effortlessly. There is a calm, motionless, clear and pure awareness, in which all of this spontaneously arises. A pure Witness of the world, free of all its turmoil. . . .

Joan, still holding my hand, whispers in my ear:

*"Now go from **observing** the All to **being** the All."*

"Yes, but how?"

"Make love to me, Ken, make love to the sky, make love to the clouds, embrace the stars, kiss the heavens, hold the cosmos in the palm of your hand, explode out of yourself into the universe at large."

I am deliriously slipping away into a cosmos close to infinity, I am starting to . . .

"This is what men and women do for each other," the voice con-

tinues. *"Man the Seer becomes one with the Seen, woman the Seen becomes one with the Seer. Purusha and Prakriti fall in love, Shiva and Shakti melt in the Heart and unite for all eternity, subject and object dissolve into One Taste and light up the night with their yells."*

"Men and women . . . ," I mumble.

"What do you think all those once-every-ten-minute fantasies you have about female bodies really mean? You don't really think they are about sex, do you?"

"I don't understand."

"Let's put it very simply," Joan whispers, trying to help. *"Men tend to want autonomy, they want* Freedom. *Women tend to want relationship, they want* Fullness. *Freedom and Fullness, agency and communion, ranking and linking, justice and care, wisdom and compassion, eros and agape, call them what you will. But until those are united, men and women are both fated to be torn and fractured, partial and incomplete."*

"That much I can understand."

"For the man, or the masculine side of you: the only way you can have complete autonomy or complete Freedom is to have nothing outside of you that can control you. And the only way you can do that is to be one with everything." Joan looks at me to see if I am following any of this. I nod my head.

"Likewise, for the woman, or the feminine side of you: the only way you can have complete relationship or complete Fullness is to have nothing outside of you that you could ever want. And the only way you can do that is also to be one with everything." Again I nod my head.

"So the only way to have both Freedom and Fullness is to be one with the All—to find cosmic consciousness, third tier, ultimate Spirit, the ever-present reality of One Taste."

She pauses, squeezes my hand, looks directly at me. *"Is any of this getting through?"*

I shake my head, trying to clear it. "A little bit," I say.

I open my eyes, I see Joan; I close my eyes, I see Joan.

"Either way, I am in love with you," I say.

Ken Sr. looks at me, and smiles, and leans forward. *"Now Ken, listen to me. When you are about my age, you will find a real Joan, a Joan that will show you the Heart."*

"I don't understand."

"Believe me, you will."

I open my eyes; I close them.

"Don't worry about trying to make sense out of any of this," **Joan says.** *"All that is happening is that you are moving closer and closer to your Original Face, your own real Self, and so time is starting to distort. As you approach the timeless, you are starting to time warp, to sort of worm-hole into the future. Don't worry, really."*

"But I thought . . . ," pointing to big Ken, "I thought he was my real Face, my ultimate Omega or something."

"No, he is just a waystation. He is merely your small self as it appears tomorrow. But he is not your real Self."

I open my eyes. "Joan, you won't believe this."

"I do believe it, Ken," she says, still holding my hand, as Stuart's voice fills the air in Club Passim. "Just go with it, Ken, just let go. . . . "

"So he is not my real Self."

"That's right. He is merely your small self, your ego, the way it appears tomorrow, but he is not your real Self, which exists only in the timeless present."

"Then why is he even here?"

"To show you that the Answer does not exist in time."

"That's right, young Ken."

"You're that inner voice I've been hearing ever since I started coming to IC," I say, slowly starting to understand.

"Yes, that's right."

"You're my me tomorrow. You are my me tomorrow, but you are not who I am. . . . "

"That's right. Would you like to meet who you really are?"

"Joan, I'm frightened, I'm really frightened."

"Tell me again, when you are deeply, deeply in love, where are you?"

I try to focus. "When I am deeply, deeply in love . . . ," and I look into sky eyes, and I disappear entirely into that beautiful expanse, and I am free in a way that lights up the universe with a radiance that makes the blazing sun go pale and anemic,

and I am drenched with a being that explodes my heart to all infinity. Supernovas swirl endlessly in my brain, galaxies start running through my veins, I grasp the entire cosmos in the palm of my hand, and the Mystery that surrounds me melts the universe away. . . .

"Yes, young Ken, keep going."

Deeper and deeper into my being, farther back into my own consciousness, resting as the infinite Witness of all the worlds that arise. An empty, dark, vast formlessness, yet intrinsically alive, infinitely wise, radiating a luminosity too subtle to see or even feel, an infinite Release on the other side of terror, a radical Freedom beyond the shores of pain, a bliss beyond bliss that cannot be felt and a light beyond light that cannot even be seen.

"Now come back to me, Ken," the eyes of sky whisper.

And out of that infinite Emptiness the entire World explodes, and I am flooded with an ecstasy so unbearably intense I splinter into a million souls dispersed in cosmic winds, I arise as an infinity of translucent stars adorning the sheltering sky, disappear instantly into an iridescent sun shining in the heart of each and every being, arising yet as erotic earth giving life to all who yearn. Freedom and Fullness drench my being and soak the universe to its radiant core, and it is all so obvious, so utterly, painfully, terribly obvious.

"I am the creator of this entire cosmic game, aren't I?"

"We all are, young Ken," my tomorrow-me says.

"All sentient beings are pure Spirit. That is indeed the game, the cosmic game, the great and grand joke that we are all playing on ourselves."

"But what happens once you awaken to this ultimate open secret? What happens after that? What happens next?"

"Exactly what should happen next, whatever that is. You will continue to play the game, only now while fully awake. It is then ordinary, ever so ordinary, as you go on about the world. You will enter the marketplace with open hands, you will comfort those around you as best as

you possibly can, you will work to help all people develop to second and third tier, you will. . . . "

"My colleagues and I will help found Integral Center."

"Or something like that, Ken, it really doesn't matter the actual form it takes. You will do whatever you can to help those who are dreaming to awaken to their own Original Face, which is the same Face in all beings great and small. Some people will make grand gestures, like founding an Integral Center, and others will make smaller gestures, like smiling at the person sitting next to them on the subway. None of those gestures are bigger or better, and all of them are necessary. Maybe you will help found IC and maybe you won't—but you can always smile at the next person you see."

"More than that, young Ken, you will continue to try and deepen your own enlightenment. I know that you think you have seen it all, but believe me, you have not. You are still mistaking ecstatic experiences for ever-present awareness. Your own awakening is just beginning, it is just beginning. Do you understand?"

"I'm not sure."

"I will say it once, and in the coming years you will grow into it: To study enlightenment is to study the self. To study the self is to forget the self. To forget the self is to be one with all things. To be one with all things is timeless enlightenment. And this timeless enlightenment continues forever, it is a ceaseless process, absolutely perfect and fully complete at every moment of its being, yet also unfolding endlessly. . . . Listen to me, young Ken, timeless enlightenment is an endless process, but I promise you this: it exists."

And that is the last thing the voice inside my head ever said to me.

"Joan, Joan . . ."

"I'm right here, Ken. Where are you?"

"I really don't know," looking around. "Oh, well, Club Passim, I guess. . . . Oh Joan, Jesus, the most amazing thing . . ."

"I know, dear soul, I know."

"You were there!"

"Was I?"

"You weren't there?"

"No, I wasn't. Not really. Not me, anyway. Maybe something I represent."

"The sky," I say. "I became one with the sky, I am . . ."

"I know, Ken, I know."

And sky-eyes looks at me, but this time I am not surprised.

12

Happily_Ever_After@HereAndNow.com

"**Chloe, can you imagine** the entire universe on Ecstasy?"

Chloe turns in bed, slowly opens her eyes, then shuts them against the morning sun.

"Whatsis?"

"Can you imagine the entire universe on Ecstasy?"

"Like oh boy sure I can."

"No, not would you like to see everybody on Ecstasy, can you imagine what it would be like if the entire universe was really one huge Ecstasy trip?"

Chloe looks directly at me, and tries to focus, and I can see that she is starting to fall into the sky where my eyes used to be.

"Chloe?"

"Look at you, sweet boy. Look at you. What's happening?"

"Chloe, I don't know how to tell you this, but you are looking at you, the real you, if you just fall into it."

Chloe shakes off the spell. "Well hell I don't know about that, sweet boy. Say, what are you doing today?"

"Today?" And I start laughing, truly laughing, maybe for the first time in my entire life. "Why, it seems that I am going to help as many people as possible get out of flatland and move to second tier." And I laugh, and I laugh, and I laugh. . . .

"Second tier. Say, is that the new apartment complex across the street?"

And I laugh even harder. "Why yes, Chloe, that is exactly what that is."

"Can I help?"

"You know, dear Chloe, I honestly think you can."

"Ooooh, look at me smile."

"Hey Chloe, that reminds me. Remember I told you about human beings are gonna live to be 200,000 years old?"

"Wardrobe city."

"Yes, well, I used to think that the Bots were going to beat us in the big game."

"The big game."

"The big game of, well, let's just say Life. But you know what? Humans are gonna make it, Chloe, we're really gonna do it."

"Do it."

"We're going to live long enough to wake up, to really, really wake up. And that can happen any minute, literally any minute."

"Any minute."

"Chloe, quit repeating what I'm saying."

"Well you're not making much sense, now, are you?"

"I guess not. But you do get the part about living 200,000 years? I think our generation—the Yellow-Meme Kids!—I think we're gonna do it, we're gonna live that long, long enough to fall awake, to discover who and what we really are."

"Gonna do it."

"Okay you!" and I grab her and throw her back on the bed.

"Well this is what I do know," Chloe says. "If you and I live that long, then we're going to make love at least a billion times. Sweet boy, we're going to make love a billion times. A billion times!"

I look at the sky, the amazing loving welcoming sky, the radiant sun blazing, light cascading on the earth, dazzling manifestation all around, effervescent crystal displays, luminous emeralds floating in air, Chloe smiling there.

"Well then," I say, with a contented smile that opens onto eternity, "I guess we better get started."

About the Author

Ken Wilber, who turned 23 when this book was published, received his degree from MIT in computer science and artificial life. He lives in Denver, Colorado, with his fiancé, Chloe Walters, and their dog, Isaac. His essays have appeared in *Wired, BlackBook, X/Y, MeatBeat, Yearn*, and *Cosmopolitan*.